STAY
with me

STAY
with me

J. LYNN

AVON

An Imprint of HarperCollinsPublishers

STAY WITH ME. Copyright © 2014 by Jennifer L. Armentrout. Excerpt from WAIT FOR YOU © 2013 by Jennifer L. Armentrout. All rights reserved. Printed in the United States of America. No part of this book may be used or reproduced in any manner whatsoever without written permission except in the case of brief quotations embodied in critical articles and reviews. For information address HarperCollins Publishers, 195 Broadway, New York, NY 10007.

HarperCollins books may be purchased for educational, business, or sales promotional use. For information please e-mail the Special Markets Department at SPsales@ harpercollins.com

FIRST WILLIAM MORROW PAPERBACK EDITION PUBLISHED 2014.
FIRST AVON PAPERBACK EDITION PUBLISHED 2022.

Library of Congress Cataloging-in-Publication Data has been applied for.

ISBN 978-0-06-229480-7

22 23 24 25 26 LSC 10 9 8 7 6 5 4 3 2 1

Always for the readers. Without all of you, this story wouldn't be in your hands now.

STAY

with me

One

The Hot Guy Brigade surrounded me.

A lot of people believed that the Hot Guy Brigade was a myth. Nothing more than a campus urban legend, kind of like the story about the homecoming queen who'd pitched herself out of one of the dorm windows because she was tripping balls on LSD or crack, or she had fallen in the shower and busted her head open or something. Who knew? The story changed every time I heard it, but unlike the supposed dead chick who haunted Gardiner Hall, the Hot Guy Brigade was a real living and breathing thing—several things to be exact.

Several *hot* things.

It was rare that they were all together nowadays, which is why they'd become sort of campus lore, but wow-wee, when they got together, it was a whole lot of eye candy.

And it was probably the closest to perfection I'd ever get in my lifetime—that and the miracle makeup called Dermablend, because it almost covered the scar on my face.

We were all piled into Avery Morgansten's apartment. Based on the rock on her ring finger, she was well on her way to getting a last-name change, and although I didn't know her well, really didn't know anyone except Teresa, I was happy for her. Anytime I'd been

around her, she was always sweet. She could be a little quiet sometimes and seemed to disappear into her own head, but anyone could
tell she and her fiancé, Cameron Hamilton, were deeply in love by
the way they watched each other.

Like the way he was watching her now, as if there were no other
woman in the world but her. Even though they were sitting together,
Cam on the couch and Avery in his lap, those bright blue eyes were
fixed on her as she laughed at something his sister Teresa said.

If I had to rank the Hot Guy Brigade, I'd say that Cam was the
president. It wasn't just his looks, but also his personality. No one
felt odd or left out around him. He had this . . . *warmth* that was
absolutely contagious.

Secretly, and I'd totally take it to my grave, I envied Avery. I
barely even knew her, but I coveted what she had—the gorgeous hot
guy, who was also genuinely a good guy, who still could make you
feel comfortable around him. That was rare.

"Want another drink?"

I dipped my head to the left and then back, toward the voice of
Jase Winstead, and my breath caught a little. Here was the opposite
of Cam—extremely good-looking, but totally did not make me feel
comfy when my eyes locked with his deep gray ones. With his swar-
thy skin, longish brown hair, and almost unreal, model good looks,
he'd be the lieutenant of the Hot Guy Brigade. He was by far the
sexiest out of all of them, and he could be supersweet, like now, but
he wasn't as easygoing or charming as Cam, which was why Cam
held top position.

"Nah, I'm good." I raised my half-full bottle of beer I'd been sip-
ping since I'd gotten there. "But thanks."

He smiled and then moved off, circling his arms around Teresa's
waist. She cocked her head back against his chest as she placed her
hands on his arms. His face softened.

Yeah, I was a wee bit envious of Teresa, too.

I'd never been in a serious relationship. There hadn't been any dates in high school. The scar on my face had been a hell of a lot more vibrant then, something no miracle makeup could camouflage . . . and high school kids, yeah, they could be unforgiving when it came to very visible flaws. And even if someone could look past that, with the way my life had been back then, there hadn't been room or time for a date let alone a relationship.

Then there had been Jonathan King. He was in my history class freshman year, really cute guy and we'd hit it off. For obvious reasons, I'd been reluctant to go out with him when he asked, but damn, he'd been persistent and I'd finally said yes. We'd gone out a few times, but as the relationship progressed and he, being a totally normal guy, had made a move on me one night, when we'd been alone in my dorm, I'd been stupidly convinced that since he could see past the scar on my face, he'd been able to see past everything else.

I'd been wrong.

We didn't even kiss and we sure as hell didn't go out again after that, and I hadn't told anyone about him and that disastrous night. I didn't think about him. Ever.

Well, except for right now, damnit.

As I watched the Hot Guy Brigade being all hot, I was totally aware of the fact I was boy crazy due to my lack of . . . well, of boys in my life.

"Got it!"

My chin jerked up as Ollie rounded the couch, his girlfriend, Brittany, trailing behind him, her eyes rolling back so far in her head I thought she might pass out as she shook her head.

Ollie approached the coffee table and leaned down, holding some kind of box tortoise in his hands. My brows rose as the little guy's legs wheeled. What the . . . ?

"It's not a party until Ollie breaks out the turtle," said Jase, and my lips curved up in a grin.

Cam sighed as he leaned around Avery. "What in the hell are you doing with Raphael?"

"Correction." Ollie placed him on the table. With one hand, he brushed his shoulder-length blond hair back behind one ear. "This is Michelangelo, and I think it's pretty fucked-up you don't even know which one is yours anymore. You've probably sent Raphael into a depression."

"I tried to stop him," Brit said, folding her arms. The two of them looked like they finaled in the Perfect Blond Couple Award. "But you know how he is . . ."

Everyone knew how he was.

Ollie was in grad school now, to become a doctor—surprisingly—but his antics were as big a legend as the Hot Guy Brigade. Ollie would be second to the lieutenant. He got a lot of bonus points for coming down to Shepherdstown every other weekend to see his girl-friend and for being a shameless goofball.

"As you can see, I have fashioned a new leash." He gestured at what looked like a miniature belt secured around the tortoise's shell.

Cam stared up at him. "Are you serious?"

"You can walk them now." And then he proceeded to demon-strate this by leading Michelangelo across the table, and I had to wonder if Avery and Cam ate off it. "It's better than yarn."

Walking a turtle? That . . . that had to be worse than walking a cat. I started giggling. "It looks like a Barbie belt."

"It's a *designer* leash," he corrected, his lips twitching. "But I did get the idea while we were in Wal-Mart, checking out the toy section."

Teresa frowned. "Why were you in the toy section?"

"Yeah," Jase drew the word out. "Is there something you two aren't telling us?"

Brit's eyes widened.

Ollie just shrugged. "I like to check out the toys. They are so much cooler now than when we were kids."

This statement led to an all-out discussion about how our generation had been sorely cheated when it came to the sophistication and cool factor of today's toys, and I had to think really hard about the kind of toys I'd played with. There'd been Barbies—of course, there'd been Barbies, but instead of Big Wheels and board games, I had satiny sashes and sparkly crowns.

And then I had nothing.

As the group started talking about summer plans, I tried to pay attention to where each of them was planning to go. Cam and Avery were going to spend their summer in D.C., since Cam had made it onto the United team. I'd never been to D.C., even though Shepherd wasn't too far from the capital. Brit and Ollie were doing something amazingly crazy. They were leaving a week after school let out and heading to Paris, and they were planning to road-trip across Europe. I'd never been on a plane, let alone overseas. Hell, I hadn't even been to New York City. Teresa and Jase were in the midst of planning an awesome beach trip to the Carolinas with his parents and little brother. They were getting a condo on the beach, and all Teresa could talk about was soaking her toes in ocean water. I'd also never been to the beach, so I had no idea what sand felt like under my feet.

I really needed to get out more and have a life. Seriously.

But that was okay, because those things, including gallivanting across the continent with a Hot Guy, weren't part of my goals—the three F's.

Finish college.

Find a career in the nursing field.

Finally reap the benefits of following through on something.

Goals were good. Boring. But good.

"You're awful quiet tonight, Calla."

I tensed up, unable to help myself, and then I felt heat seep across my face at the sound of Brandon Shiver's voice. Lowering the bottle between my knees, I forced the muscles along my shoulders to relax. It wasn't like I'd forgotten that Brandon was sitting next to me, to my *left*. How could I forget that? I was just currently pretending he wasn't there.

I wetted my lips as I shifted my head so a sheet of my own blond hair fell over my left shoulder, shielding my cheek. "I'm just taking it all in."

Brandon chuckled. He had a nice laugh. And a nice face. And a nice body. And a really nice ass.

And then there was Brandon. Sigh. Like an extended sigh felt around the world. He would also be a close second to the lieutenant of the Hot Guy Brigade with his brown hair and broad shoulders.

"With Ollie here, it's always a lot to take in," he commented, eyeing me over the rim of his bottle. "Wait until he starts talking about the turtle roller skates idea he has."

I laughed, relaxing a little more. Brandon was hot, but he was also a nice guy, somewhere in between Cam and Jase. "I can't even imagine turtles on roller skates."

"Ollie's either bat-shit crazy or a pure genius." Brandon shifted on the ottoman. "Jury's still out on the verdict."

"I think he's a genius." I watched Ollie scoop up the turtle and head back around the couch to the pretty extravagant habitat the little green man lived in. "The way Brit talks, he's acing all of his courses. Med school can't be easy."

"Yeah, but most really smart people are totally insane." He grinned when I laughed under my breath. "So, has the epic battle for next-semester classes ended?"

I nodded as I grinned again, settling back in the moon chair. With only a semester and a half left before I graduated with my BSN in nursing, getting into classes was like arm-wrestling Hulk Hogan. Everyone who knew my name, or was within earshot, knew I'd been battling my schedule for what felt like an eternity. We were currently a week away from the end of the semester and almost a month since academic advisement for next semester had closed up.

"Yeah, finally. I think I had to give up my right leg to get my classes, but I got all I needed. I have to meet with someone in financial aid on Monday, but I should be good."

His brows knitted as I glanced at him. "Is everything okay with that?"

"I think so." I couldn't think of any reason why it wouldn't be. "Any plans for this summer?"

One broad shoulder rose. "Haven't really thought much of it since I'm taking summer classes."

"Sounds like fun."

He snorted.

I started to say something else ridiculously *not* clever since I was doing pretty good with this one-on-one convo with Brandon, but I lost track of what I was about to say when there was a knock. My gaze tracked Ollie to the door. He answered like he'd lived here.

"What up, pretty lady?" he said, and I sat up, my fingers tightening around the neck of the beer bottle.

A pretty, little brunette cruised on into the apartment, a red Sheetz bag dangling from her fingertips. She smiled at Ollie and gave Brit a little wave.

I didn't know her name.

I sort of refused to learn it, because after the last two semesters of knowing Brandon, I didn't put the effort into knowing any of the girls he "hung out" with because there were many and they never stuck around long.

But this girl—with her tiny brown pixie cut and ballerina body— was different. They had a class together this semester and they'd started hanging out in March, but this was the first I'd seen her with Brandon outside of campus.

Actually, I'd never really met her. I'd never really met any of his frequent flyers, just seen them around school and sometimes at parties, but Brandon hadn't been on the party scene since . . . well, since March.

"There she is." His green eyes lit up.

Oh shit.

I was a slow learner.

I inhaled through my nose and smiled as she made her way around the couples, coming to Brandon as he straightened from the ottoman and opened his arms. She went right into them, easing onto his knees and looping her arms around his neck. The Sheetz bag bounced over his back, and her mouth was like a Brandon-heat-seeking-missile, and I couldn't blame her for that.

They kissed.

A big, wet, and deep kiss—a real kiss. Not the "we're getting to know each other" kind of kiss or "we're just hooking up" kiss, but a "we've already swapped lots of body fluids" kind of kiss.

And God, I watched them kiss like they were trying to eat each other's faces up until the moment I knew I was upping my creeper status to a whole new level. I forced myself to look away, and my gaze collided with Teresa.

A sympathetic look crossed her pretty face as she turned in Jase's arms, because she knew . . . oh lawd, she knew I'd been harboring a big gushy crush on Brandon.

"I brought you a cheesy pretzel," the girl announced when they came up for air.

Brandon loved cheese-stuffed pretzels like I loved double fudge brownies.

"She brought you a pretzel?" Ollie asked. "Man, you put a ring on that."

Brit rolled her eyes as she looped her arms around Ollie's waist. "Does not take much to impress you."

Twisting in her arms, Ollie dipped his head to hers. "You know what it takes to impress me, baby."

I kept waiting for Brandon to fly out of the chair and run away from the idea of putting a ring on the finger of a girl he'd known for only a couple of months, but since I didn't get the lovely view of his ass heading for the door, I glanced at him when I knew I shouldn't. But I was a glutton for punishment.

Brandon was staring at the girl, grinning in a way that said . . . that said he was absolutely happy.

I swallowed my sigh.

And then he looked over at me, and before I could freak over the fact that he caught me staring at him like a stalker, his smile went up a blinding notch. "You haven't gotten a chance to meet Tatiana yet."

Damnit. I didn't want to learn her name, but Tatiana was such a cool freaking name.

Tatiana shook her head as she turned brown eyes toward me. "No, we haven't."

"This is my friend, Calla Fritz," he said, smoothing a hand up her back. "We had music class together last semester."

That was who I was—Calla Fritz, always and forever the friend of the Hot Guy Brigade. Nothing more. Nothing less.

I blinked back the stupid sudden rush of tears as I wiggled my fingers in Tatiana's direction. "It's nice to meet you."

That wasn't a lie. Not really.

On Monday, I left my dorm early enough to head down to Ikenberry Hall, which was all the way down a huge hill my ass so did not appreciate. It was early May, but the temps were already cracking into the eighties, and even with my hair pulled up into a hasty knot, I could feel the humidity cloaking my skin and threading its annoying fingers through my hair.

Soon, before the end of my finals today, I'd look like a frizz ball.

I cut down the side path outside of Ikenberry and winced when I had to open the door and dip inside before a spiderweb of epic proportion dropped from the little roof over the door and onto my head.

Cold air was cranking in the building as I pushed my sunglasses onto my head and walked down the hall, entering the financial aid offices. After giving my name, the overworked and frazzled looking middle-aged woman motioned me to take a seat.

I only had to wait five minutes before a tall and slender older woman with silvery hair cut in a fashionable way came out to get me. We didn't go into one of the cubicles where aid advisers worked. Oh no, she led back into one of the closed offices farther down the hall.

Then she closed the door behind us and walked behind her desk. "Please have a seat, Miss Fritz."

Knots formed low in my belly as I sat.

This had never happened before. Usually, when I got called down here, it was due to information being missing from the file or a paper needing to be signed. After all, it couldn't be a big deal. I only used financial aid for living expenses that weren't covered by the crappy waitressing job I had, and it came in really handy when I quit at the beginning of the semester to focus more fully on my studies.

The nursing program was no joke.

I slowly placed my book bag on the floor beside my legs as I scanned her desk. Elaine Booth was on her nameplate, so unless she was pretending to be someone else, that's who I was sitting in front of. There were also a lot of photos on her desk. Family photos—black-and-whites, colored, photos ranging from toddlers all the way up to my age, maybe even older.

I looked away quickly as an old pang hit me in the chest. "So . . . what's going on?"

Mrs. Booth folded her hands over a file. "We received word from admissions last week that your check for next semester's tuition has bounced."

I blinked once, and then twice. "What?"

"The check didn't clear," she explained, glancing up from the file. Her gaze drifted over my face and then quickly averted away from my eyes. "Due to insufficient funds."

She had to be wrong. There was no way that check bounced because that check was attached to a savings account that I *only* used for tuition, an account that held all of my money for school. "There has to be something wrong. There should be enough money in there for the next semester and a half."

Not only that, there should've been enough money in that account just in case of some crazy emergency, and to carry me through at least a couple of months after graduation while I did the job hunting thing and decided where I wanted to live, if I stayed here or . . .

"We verified with the bank, Calla." She'd dropped my last name and somehow that seemed worse. "Sometimes we have problems with checks due to the amount or a typo in entering the account number, but the bank confirmed there was insufficient funds."

I couldn't believe it. "How much did they say was in the account?"

She shook her head. "That's proprietary information we're not privy to, so you'd need to talk to the bank about that. Now, the good news is that you've always paid your tuition early, which means we've got time to work something out. We'll get this fixed, Calla." Pausing, she opened my file as I stared at her like my butt was suddenly frozen in my seat. "You're already in the system for financial aid, and what we can do is adjust the requests for next semester, ensuring that your classes are covered. . . ."

My stomach had dropped to my knees at some point and was quickly plummeting to the floor as she continued on about increasing loan amounts, applying for Pell grants, and even a crap ton of scholarships.

At this moment, I didn't give two craps about any of that.

This couldn't be happening.

There was no way there wasn't money in that account. I was meticulous when it came to which account I used for which bill or need, and I never used that account unless it was for tuition. I hadn't even activated the debit card attached to it.

Then it hit me as I watched Mrs. Booth pull form after form out from racks next to her desk, stacking them neatly and calmly as if my entire life hadn't just slammed on the brakes.

Ice drenched my veins as I tried to drag in my next breath, but it got stuck in my throat. This might not be a giant fuckup by the bank and the college. This could very well be seriously happening.

Oh my God.

Because there was someone other than me who had the means to get access to that account—one person who was virtually dead to me, so virtually that I behaved as if she were dead—but I couldn't believe she'd do *this*. There was no way.

The rest of the meeting with Mrs. Booth was fuzzy to me. Numbly, I took the FAFSA applications and I walked out of the chilly offices, out into the bright sunlight of an early May morning, loaded up with forms.

There was still time before my final, and I found the nearest bench, sat down, and shoved the papers into my bag. I pulled out my cell phone with shaky fingers, looked up the number to the bank back home, and hit call.

Five minutes later, I sat on the bench, seeing nothing beyond the shades of my sunglasses, and feeling nothing, which was good—the blank and empty feeling in the pit of my stomach was all right because I knew it would turn to red-hot, blinding and murderous, cut-a-bitch rage in no time. I couldn't do that. I had to stay calm. Keep my emotions in check, because . . .

All my money was gone.

And I knew—every cell of my body knew—this was just the beginning, the tip of the iceberg.

Two

*H*ow my life went from mostly being okay, with the exception of being a little lonely sometimes, to one giant hot mess in a span of a week was beyond my ability to comprehend.

I was so screwed, and not in the fun and sweaty way.

It wasn't just my savings account that had literally been cleared out two weeks before I'd written my check for tuition. Oh God, if *only* that was it. I could've bounced back from that. I could've even let that go, because what else could I have done?

After all, I knew it had been my own flesh and blood that had cleared me out, my own *mother*—my hocked up on pills, and most likely drunk off her ass, mother who my closest friends believed was dead. In a way, that hadn't been too far from the truth. A terrible lie, but I hadn't talked to her in ages and the alcohol and the pills and God knows what else had over the years killed the caring and fun mother I remembered from when I was little.

But she was still *my* mom. Therefore, the last thing I wanted to do was involve the police, because seriously, her life was already shitty as it was, and inexplicably, after all the drama and the heartache, a whirl of pity always surfaced when I thought of her.

That woman had to experience things no mother ever should.

But it hadn't only been my savings account. Over the course of last week, during my finals, which I somehow managed to still complete without losing my ever-loving mind, the tip of the iceberg sunk the *Titanic*.

I pulled my credit just because . . . well, I had this horrible feeling it was worse. And it had been.

Credits cards I'd never seen in my life had been taken out in my name and they'd been maxed out. A student loan with a major bank I hadn't even known existed had also been taken out, and that alone cost more than four semesters at Shepherd did.

I was in debt, to the tune of over a hundred thousand dollars when it was all said and done, and that wasn't even including the debt I racked up on my own with the small student loans I'd taken out and the car loan I now wasn't sure I could afford.

My stomach dipped and my chest seized every time I thought about how badly I was screwed, and it took everything in me to talk myself down from losing my shit. Credit and debt made or broke you in this world. I wouldn't be able to get a loan if I needed one. Worse yet, even if I managed to scrape together the money to finish out college, any job I applied for could pull my credit and base their decision to hire me on what it showed.

On Thursday, after my last final, I'd suffered a minor breakdown, which involved a lot of tears, even more double fudge brownies, and maybe a little bit of rocking in the corner. I would've stayed in that corner for at least a month, but I refused, absolutely flat-out *refused,* to allow my life to get sucked away from me again.

Obviously, none of my friends knew what was going on or knew anything about me. Hell, they thought my mom was dead and Teresa thought I was from around the Shepherdstown area.

All lies.

And how could I tell Teresa, or worse yet, Brandon? *Oh hey, I got to go home, and you know, commit an act of homicide and strangle my mother—yeah, the one you thought was dead, because I'm also a horrible liar—to death for dicking me over. Can we hang out at your place and have drinks when I get back?* That convo was way too humiliating to even think about, because then I'd have to tell them about the drugs, the alcohol, the absolute fail at life, and then the weird separation between Mom and Dad, which really was just Dad freaking disappearing, and then that convo would ultimately lead to the grief and the fire that had destroyed my entire family and almost destroyed *me*.

I wasn't going there.

So I told them I was spending the summer with extended family, and hopefully, they didn't end up reading about me in the news after I murdered someone.

No one questioned those plans, because just last year I had pretended to go home over break when in reality I had checked into a hotel in Martinsburg, had splurged on room service . . . like a loser.

A total loser.

Anyway . . .

I was putting the Three F's on hold and I was going home. And hopefully, praying to every god out there, Mom still had some of the money that had been awarded to *her,* and that money had been *substantial*. There was no way she could've blown through all of her money and mine. I just needed to get her to—I don't know—get her to fix this somehow.

That was Plan A.

Plan B consisted only of the realization that if she didn't have a dime to her name, then at least—again hopefully—I had free housing for the summer, a summer where I'd be praying that my financial aid would go through. I was also praying that I managed to make it through the summer in a nowhere town and not murder my mother, so I could put use to the financial aid if I got it.

My hands had shaken as I clenched the steering wheel and hit the exit that led to Plymouth Meeting, a town just a few miles out of Philadelphia. I'd thought I might vomit all over myself as the thick oaks and walnut trees crowding the two-lane highway had thinned out and the hills stopped climbing. The trip hadn't been long, a little under four hours from Shepherdstown, but it had felt like forever.

Now I was stopped at the red light across the street from a dollar store, in a town I never ever—*ever*—wanted to go back to, and I rested my forehead against the steering wheel.

I'd gone home first. No cars. No lights on.

Lifting my head an inch or two, I dropped it back onto the steering wheel.

I'd pulled out a house key I'd never ever—*ever*—wanted to use again, and had let myself in. The house had been virtually empty. A couch and an old flat screen in the living room. The small dining room had been vacant with the exception of a few unopened boxes. Barely anything in the fridge. The bedroom downstairs had a bed in it, but no sheets. Mom's clothes had been piled on the floor and it had been a mess, scattered with papers and stuff I hadn't wanted to take too close a look at. Upstairs, the loft bedroom that had been mine for a few years was completely changed. The bed was gone, as were the dresser and the little desk my grandmother had bought me before she passed away. There was a futon that looked a little clean, and I didn't even want to know who was sleeping up there. The house hadn't looked lived in. Like someone, namely my mother, had dropped off the face of the earth.

This had not boded well.

There also hadn't been a single photo in the house. No picture frames on the walls. No memories. That hadn't surprised me.

I lifted my head and dropped it on the steering wheel again. "Ugh."

At least the electricity had still been turned on in the house. That was one good thing, right? That meant Mom had some kind of money.

I winced on my third steering wheel head bang.

A horn blew behind me, and I immediately straightened and peered out the windshield. Green light. Whoops. My hands tightened on the steering wheel as I blew out a determined breath and continued on. There was only one other place she could be.

Ugh.

Yet another place I never ever—*ever*—wanted to see again. Forcing myself to take several long and deep breaths, I coasted along the main road, probably driving under the speed limit and annoying every car behind me, but I couldn't help it.

My heart banged around in my chest as I hung a right and hit what was considered the main drag in town, only because it was where all the fast-food joints and chain restaurants surrounded the mall and shopping centers. About ten miles down the road was where Mona's sat, across from what looked like a pretty dicey strip club that was lined with rough-and-ready-looking motorcycles.

Oh boy.

The streets were congested, but as I cut across the lane and pulled into the all too familiar parking lot littered with potholes and God knows what else, there weren't a lot of vehicles there.

Then again, it was Monday night.

Parking the car under the flickering neon sign at the back of the parking lot that was currently missing an *a* in the name Mona's, I took several more deep breaths and repeated, "I will not kill her. I will not kill her."

Once I was sure I wouldn't break down and go all redneck on her ass when I saw her, I climbed out of my Ford Focus and tugged on the hem of my denim cutoffs, then readjusted the soft and flowing cream long-sleeve blouse that would've been longer than my shorts if I hadn't tucked the front of it into them.

My flip-flops echoed off the pavement as I crossed the parking lot, clutching the strap of my bag in a way that meant I could wing this thing around like a deadly weapon.

As I neared the entrance, I shored up my shoulders and let out a low breath. The square window in the door was clean, but cracked. The white and red paint that used to be so vibrant and eye-catching was peeling off like someone had splashed acid across the walls. The big window, tinted black and with a flashy OPEN sign, was also cracked in the corner, forming tiny spiderweb fissures across the center of the glass.

If the outside looked like this . . .

"Oh God." I so did not want to do this.

My gaze drifted back to the dark square window in the door, and my blue eyes looked way too wide and my face too pale in the reflection, which also made the superhot scar cutting down my left cheek, starting just below the corner of my eye to the corner of my lip, more visible.

I'd been lucky. That's what the doctors and the firemen and everyone in the world who had an opinion had declared. Less than an inch higher, I would've lost my left eye.

But standing where I was now, I didn't feel so lucky. Actually, I was pretty sure Lady Luck was a coldhearted bitch who needed to die.

Telling myself I could do this, I grabbed the rough handle and yanked the door open. And I immediately stumbled to an awkward stop just inside the bar, losing one of my flip-flops as the familiar scent of beer, cheap perfume, and fried food washed over me.

Home.

No.

My free hand closed into a fist. This bar was not home to me. Or *should* not be home to me. It didn't matter that I'd spent almost every day after high school holed up in one of the back rooms here or that I snuck out to the main floor to watch Mom because this was the only place where she smiled. Probably because she was usually drunk when she was here, but whatever.

Things looked the same. Kind of.

Square and high round tables with rough and worn tops. Bar stools with backs and tall chairs. The clang of billiard balls snapping off one another drew my attention to the back of the bar, beyond an empty raised dance floor, to the pool tables.

A jukebox in the corner played some kind of tear-in-my-beer country music as a middle-aged woman I'd never seen before barreled out of the Dutch doors across from the dance floor. Her bright blond hair, obviously not natural, was piled atop her head. A pen was shoved behind one ear. Dressed in blue jeans and a white T-shirt, she looked like a customer, but then again, Mona's had never been a uniform-wearing kind of bar. She carried two red baskets stacked high with fried chicken wings as she sashayed over to one of the booths lining the wall near the jukebox.

Balled-up napkins were under tables and there were patches of the floor that looked sticky. Other sections looked like they simply needed to be replaced. With the dim bar lighting, I knew I wasn't even seeing half of it.

Mona's looked like a woman who'd been ridden hard and left out to dry. It wasn't dirty, but more like almost clean. As if someone desperately tried to stay on top of the losing battle and was doing the best they could.

Which could not be Mom. She had never been into cleaning, but she used to be better. There were distant, blurry memories of her being better.

Since I was standing at the door long enough to look like an idiot, and as I scanned the floor, I didn't see Mom, I decided it would be a good idea to, I don't know, move. I took a step forward, then realized I'd left one of my flip-flops by the door.

"Damnit." I turned, dipping my chin as I wiggled my toes back into the shoe.

"You look like you could use a drink."

I twisted toward the sound of a surprisingly deep male voice, a voice so deep and smooth, it rolled over my skin like I'd been draped in satin. I started to point out that, duh, since I was standing in a bar, I probably did look like I needed a drink, but the snappy words died on my tongue as I faced the horseshoe-shaped bar.

At first, the guy behind the bar seemed to have straightened, as if he was drawing back. It was a strange reaction. In this low lighting and the way I was standing, there was no way he saw the scar, but then I got a real good look at him, and I wasn't paying attention to that anymore.

Oh my, my, my . . .

There was a man behind the bar, the kind of guy I would not ever in the history of ever expect to see behind Mona's bar.

Whoa, hot-bartender alert to the max.

Goodness, he was gorgeous, stunning in the way Jase Winstead was, maybe even more so, because I couldn't quite remember seeing someone who looked as good as he did in real life, and I was only seeing Hot Bartender Dude from the waist up.

He had brown hair that looked like a rich, warm color under the brighter lights of the bar area. It was cut close to the skull on the sides and a little longer on the top. Wavy, it was styled back off his forehead in an artfully messy look, showing off his broad and high cheekbones. His skin was tan, hinting at some kind of foreign and exotic ancestry. With a strong and sculpted jaw that could cut rock, he could be the poster boy for shaving ads. Under a straight nose that had a slight hook in it were the fullest, most downright sinful, pair of lips I'd ever seen on a guy.

Good lawd, I could stare at those lips for hours, like way beyond the acceptable time limit and right into creeperville, population Calla. I forced my gaze back up.

His brows appeared to be naturally arched over the corners of his eyes, which drew the attention right to his eyes.

Brown eyes.

Brown eyes that were currently slowly and casually drifting over me in a way that felt like a warm caress. My lips parted on an inhale.

He was wearing a worn gray shirt that clung to broad shoulders and an unbelievably defined chest. I mean, I could actually see the cut of his chest through the shirt. Holy crap, who knew that was even possible? From what I could see down to where the bar top cut him off was an equally hard, and probably equally dazzling, stomach.

If this dude went to Shepherd, he would've dethroned Jase for lieutenant of the Hot Guy Brigade. And the sigh associated with Hot Bartender Dude would most definitely be felt around the world and in the lady parts.

Probably in some boy parts, too.

Those delicious lips curved up on one side. Yep, he even had a panty-dropping hot smile. "You okay, honey?"

He used the term *honey* like it was natural to him. Not cheesy or slimy, but a sexy endearment that had my belly warming.

And I was staring at him like an idiot.

"Yeah." I found my voice to say one word, and it had croaked out of me. God, I wanted to body-slam myself through the floor as heat zinged across my cheeks.

That sexy half grin tipped up a notch as he extended an arm, curling his fingers back toward him. "Why don't you come over here and have a seat?"

Okay.

My feet moved forward without any brain involvement because, seriously, who didn't respond when Hot Bartender Dude wiggled long fingers at you like that? I found my butt planted in a bar stool with a ripped and slightly uncomfortable cushion.

Dear God in Heaven, up close like this, he was truly a masculine masterpiece of mouthwatering hotness.

That half grin didn't fade as he placed his palms on the edge of the bar top. "What's your poison?"

I blinked at him, real slow like, and all I could think about was why in the hell was he working in this dump? He could be in magazines, or on the TV, or at least working at the steak house down the street.

Hot Bartender Dude tilted his head to the side as his grin spread to the other corner of that freaking mouth. "Honey . . . ?"

I resisted the urge to plop my elbows on the bar top and stare up at him, even though I was already halfway to doing that. "Yes?"

He chuckled softly as he leaned in, and I mean, *waaay* in. Within a second, he was all up in my personal space, his mouth mere inches from mine, and his biceps flexed, stretching the worn material of his shirt.

Oh my golly gee, I hoped his shirt just ripped up the sides and fell right off.

"What would you like to drink?" he asked.

What I would like was to watch his mouth move some more. "Um . . ." My brain emptied.

He arched a brow as his gaze tracked from my mouth to my eyes. "Do I need to card you?"

That snapped me out of my hot-inducing stupor. "No. Not at all. I'm twenty-one."

"You sure?"

Heat infused my face again. "I swear."

"Pinky swear?"

My gaze dipped to his now-extended hand and to his pinky. "Seriously?"

A dimple started to form in his right cheek as his grin turned into a smile. Holy crapola, if he had a set of dimples, I was so in trouble. "Do I look like I'm not serious?"

He looked like he was up to absolutely no good as I stared at him. There was a downright mischievous glimmer to his warm, cocoa eyes. My lips started to twitch, and then I reached up and wrapped my pinky around his much larger one.

"Pinky swear," I said, thinking that was one hell of a way to verify age.

That grin of his was downright delicious. "Ah, a girl who'll pinky swear is after my own heart."

Yeah, I had no clue how to respond to that.

Instead of letting go as I pulled my hand away, he slipped his fingers around my wrist in a gentle, but firm, hold. As my eyes started to pop out of my head, he somehow got closer, and he smelled . . . *good.* A mixture of spice and soap that went straight to my before-mentioned lady parts.

My phone went off in my purse, blaring "Brown Eyed Girl." As I dug around for it, Hot Bartender Dude laughed.

"Van Morrison?" he asked.

I nodded absently as my fingers wrapped around the slim phone. The call was from Teresa. I hit silent.

"Nice music taste."

My lashes lifted as I dropped the phone back in my purse. "I . . . um, I like the old-school stuff better than what's big today. I mean, they actually sang and played music then. Now they just prance around half naked, scream, or talk through songs. It isn't even about the music anymore."

Appreciation lit up his eyes. "You pinky swear and listen to old-school music? I like you."

"You aren't very hard to impress then."

He tipped his head back, exposing his neck as he laughed, and good golly Miss Molly, it was a damn nice laugh. Deep. Rich. Playful. The sound turned my tummy to mush. "Pinky swearing and music are very important," he said.

"Is that so?"

"Yep." Amusement danced over his face. "So is swearing on Boy Scout honor."

The twitch at the corners of my lips spread into a grin. "Well, I was never a Boy Scout, so . . ."

"Want to know a secret?"

"Sure," I breathed.

He tipped his chin down. "I wasn't a Boy Scout, either."

For some reason, I wasn't very surprised by that. Especially when he was still holding on to my wrist.

"You're not from around here," he announced.

Not anymore. "What makes you think that?"

"Well, this is a small town, and Mona's usually sees regulars, and not hot little pieces of distraction like you, so I'm pretty sure you're not from around here."

"I used . . ." Wait. What? *Hot little pieces of distraction like you?* My train of thought was totally derailed.

He let go of my wrist, and not all at once, and he didn't break eye contact, either. Oh no, it was a slow slide of his fingers along the inside of my wrist and then across my palm to the tips of my fingers, sending a wave of shivers dancing up my arm and then doing a jazz routine down my back.

God, it made me feel crazy, but it felt like there was a spark there. Something tangible that snapped between him and me. Totally insane, but I was finding it hard to breathe and to make sense of my thoughts.

Without taking his eyes off me, he reached down into the ice cooler and pulled out a bottle of beer, twisted off the lid, and sat it on the counter. A second later, I realized there was someone standing next to us.

I glanced to my side, spying a young and good-looking guy with something close to a buzz cut. He nodded at Hot Bartender Dude as he grasped the neck of the bottle. "Thanks, bud."

And then he was off and we were alone again.

"Anyway," Hot Bartender Dude said. "How about I make you my special drink?"

Usually when a guy offers to make me their "special drink," I'd run for the hills screaming bloody murder and mayhem, but I found myself nodding again, which totally cemented the fact I was shallow and maybe a little dumb.

And totally not in control of the situation, which was a . . . unique experience for me.

I watched him pivot around, and the muscles of his back rippled under his shirt as he reached for the pricey liquor on display behind the bar. I didn't see which bottle he grabbed, but he moved with a fluid grace, grabbing one of the rock glasses, used for smaller mixed drinks and shots over ice.

The fact that I remembered the kind of glass made me want to bang my head off the bar top. I also resisted that urge—thank God. As I watched him make the drink, I tried to figure out his age. He had to be at least a year or two older than me. Within a few seconds, he placed an impressive mixed drink in front of me.

It was red on the top, then graduating into the color of a sunset, with a cherry to garnish. I picked up the drink and took a sip. My taste buds about had a mouth-gasm at the fruity flavor. "You can't even taste the liquor."

"I know." He looked smug. "It's smooth, but proceed with caution. Drink too fast and too much, it'll knock you flat on your pretty ass."

Chalking the "pretty ass" comment up to typical bartender charm, I took another tiny drink. I didn't have to worry about being careful. I never overindulged when it came to liquor anyway. "What's it called?"

"Jax."

My brows rose. "Interesting."

"Oh, it is." He folded his arms on the bar top and leaned in, giving me what I was quickly learning was a distracting and devastatingly sexy half grin. "So, you got any plans for tonight?"

I stared at him. That was all I was capable of doing. Besides the fact that after a handful of minutes of being in his presence, I'd almost forgotten why I was here, which was not to socialize, he seriously couldn't be doing what I thought he was doing.

Flirting with me.

Asking me out.

These things simply did not happen in Calla land. I couldn't even believe they happened to really hot chicks like Teresa or Brit or Avery, but I definitely knew they did not happen to me.

Hot Bartender Dude shifted his weight forward, and that did amazing things with the muscles in his arms, and then those gorgeous eyes locked on mine, and I forgot how to breathe for a second. The way his lips curved in that moment told me he was fully aware of his effect. "In case I need to clarify what I just said, I'm wanting to know if you're free to do something with me."

Three

*H*oly poo.

It was a good thing that I'd placed the drink down because I probably would've dropped it. "You don't even know my name," I blurted out.

His gaze lowered, giving me a view of ridiculously long lashes. "What's your name, honey?"

I gaped at him in what was probably a very unattractive manner. He couldn't be serious.

Hot Bartender Dude waited as he lifted those lashes.

Oh my God, was he really serious?

"Do you ask every girl out who walks into this bar?" If so, after taking one long look around the bar, he had some real slim pickings. With the exception of the guy who'd gotten the beer and was sitting with a couple other guys, most of the people in the bar were a few years shy of retiring.

His half grin spread. "Only the good-looking ones."

I went back to gaping at him.

Part of me wasn't surprised by his response. I *had* a face. Always *had* a face, ever since I was knee-high to a grasshopper and was wearing onesies. Mom *used* to praise how symmetrical my face was, how

perfect it *was.* When I was younger, I looked like one of those porce-
lain baby dolls and I'd been paraded around as such. And as I grew
up, my features had stayed symmetrical—full lips, high cheekbones,
small nose, and blue eyes to match the blond hair—real, blond hair.

But the key words here were *had* and *was,* and while I was a lot
of things, stupid wasn't one of them.

Well, on most days.

Right now, staring at this guy, I was feeling about three kinds
of stupid.

"Correction," Hot Bartender Dude continued, grinning until that
dimple appeared in his right cheek. "Hot girls with sexy legs."

This guy was so full of it. "I'm sitting down! How can you see
my legs?"

He chuckled deeply, and damn if that wasn't a nice sound, too.
"Honey, I saw you walk into the bar, and the first thing I noticed was
those legs of yours."

Okay. I did have really nice legs. Three days a week, I pretended
to be into my fitness and ran. I was lucky when it came to my legs.
Fat never deposited on my thighs or calves. It ended up in my ass
and hips. And okay, there was also a pleasant hum trilling through
my veins in response to his words, but I . . .

I sucked in a sharp breath, going cold on the inside.

Hot Bartender Dude and I were face-to-face, full frontal face-to-
face, and we had been this entire time. There was no way he hadn't
seen the scar on my face, and not once since laying eyes on Hot
Bartender Dude had I thought about the scar. So caught off guard by
him, it hadn't even crossed my mind.

But now that I was thinking about it, I immediately dipped my
chin down and to the left as I wrapped my suddenly boneless fingers
around the glass. Now I knew he couldn't be serious, because he was
totally a part of the Hot Guy Brigade, and I was Calla, the friend of
the Hot Guy Brigade. Not Calla, the girl they blatantly flirted with.

Maybe he was on crack.

I decided to ignore what he'd said as I studiously forced myself to remember why I was here. "It is a really good drink." Keeping my right cheek to him, I started checking out the bar again. Still no sign of Mom. "Pretty and tasty."

"Thanks, but we aren't talking about the drink. Unless talking about a drink involves you and me getting a drink when I get off," he said, and my gaze swung back to his sharply. He arched one brow when he had my attention. "Then I'm all about having a drink."

My eyes narrowed as I squirmed in my seat. This . . . this I wasn't accustomed to. "Are you for real?"

Both brows rose, but instead of backing off, he did that thing with his eyes again, slowly tracking over my face, lingering on my lips, before locking with my own blue peepers. "Yeah, honey, I'm real."

"You don't even know me."

"Isn't that what getting drinks together usually takes care of? The getting to know each other part."

I was floored. "We literally *just* met a handful of minutes ago."

"Already explained that, but I'll explain something else to you. When I want something, I go for it. Life is way too damn short to live any other way. And I want to get to know you better." Those lashes lowered one more time, his gaze tracking to my lips like they were some kind of mecca. "Yeah, I definitely want to get to know you better."

Holy cowbells.

I opened my mouth, but I had no idea how to respond to that, and before I could even come up with a coherent and worthy response, I jumped at the sound of my name.

"Calla?" boomed a deep, gravelly voice. "Calla, is that you?"

My attention swung toward the Dutch doors, and my mouth dropped as I put the familiar voice to the big, bulky, bald guy.

Uncle Clyde, who wasn't my uncle, but had been around since, well, forever, barreled his way toward us. A big, toothy smile broke out across his ruddy face. "Holy shit for Saturday dinner, it is you!"

I wiggled my fingers in his direction, and my lips split in a smile. Uncle Clyde hadn't changed one bit in the three years I'd been gone.

Hot Bartender Dude was quiet as he drew back, but I knew what he had to be thinking if he realized I was Mona's daughter.

Then Uncle Clyde was on me. The big old bear got his massive arms around me and lifted me clear out of the bar stool. My feet dangled in the air as he hugged me, forcing me to squeeze my toes around the thin strap of my flip-flops.

But I didn't mind if I lost my shoes or was currently having a hard time breathing. Uncle Clyde . . . God, had been there since the beginning, cooking in the kitchen when Dad and Mom first opened Mona's, and he'd hung around long after everything had gone to crap and then some. And he was still here.

Tears pricked my eyes as I managed to get my arms around his huge shoulders, inhaling the faint scent of fried food and his Old Spice cologne. I'd missed Clyde. He was the only thing I missed about this town.

"Good God, girl, it is so good to see you." He squeezed me until I let out a little squeal like a squeak toy. "So damn good."

"I think she can tell," Hot Bartender Dude said dryly. "Because you're suffocating her by squeezing her to death."

"Shut your trap, boy." Clyde lowered me to my feet, but kept one arm around my shoulders. His height and width dwarfed me, always had. "You do realize who this is, Jax?"

"I'm going to go with a yes," came another dry, low response, laced with an edge of humor.

"Wait." I wiggled to the side, turning to Hot Bartender Dude. "Your name is Jax?"

"Jackson James is actually my name, but everyone calls me Jax."

I mentally repeated his name. Admittedly, Jax was one sexy as hell nickname and made me think of a certain fictional biker babe. "You sound like you belong in a boy band."

A low laugh rumbled out from under his breath. "I guess I missed my calling then."

"Hell." Clyde's arm tightened on my shoulder. "Jax can actually sing, even strum a few chords on the guitar, if you get enough whiskey in him."

"Really?" My interest was piqued, mainly because there was nothing hotter than a guy with a guitar.

Jax leaned against the sink behind the bar, folding his arms across his chest. "I've been known to play a time or two."

"So, what brings you back here, baby girl?" Clyde asked, and there was no missing the heavy meaning in his words. As in, what in the hell are you doing back in this dump?

I turned toward him slowly. When I'd left for college, Clyde had been sad to see me go, but he'd been the driving force behind getting me out of this town and away from . . . well, everything. He probably would've been happier if I'd picked a school clear across the country, but I'd chosen one that was still sort of close by just in case . . . just in case something like this happened.

"I'm looking for Mom." And that was all I said. Right now, I didn't want to get into what was going on in front of Jax. The fact that he was now looking at me like he was truly seeing me as more than just some chick who had roamed into the bar was bad enough.

Some people believed the apple never fell too far from the tree.

And sometimes I wondered that myself.

I didn't miss the way Clyde tensed, or how his gaze darted to Jax quickly, and then back to me. Unease cut deeper, then twisted and spread like a weed across a flower bed.

Focusing fully on Clyde, I prepared myself for whatever was about to come winging my way. "What?"

His big smile lessened and turned nervous as he dropped his arm. "Nothing, baby girl, it's just that . . ."

I took a deep breath and waited as Jax grabbed another beer from the cooler of ice, handing it over to an older man in a red, torn flannel who didn't even get a chance to ask for what he wanted, but shuffled off with a happy, if slightly drunk, smile.

"Is my mom here?"

Clyde shook his head.

I folded my arms around my waist. "Where is she?"

"Well, you see, baby girl, I really don't know," Clyde said, shifting his gaze to the scuffed-up, and badly in need of a thorough cleaning, floor.

"You don't know where she is?" How was that possible?

"Yeah, well, Mona hasn't been around for like . . ." He trailed off, dipping his chin against his heavy chest as he scrubbed a hand over his bald head.

Those knots were back, tightening until I pressed the heel of my palm against my stomach. "How long has she been gone?"

Jax's gaze dipped to my hand and then flickered up to my eyes. "Your mom's been gone for at least two weeks. No one has heard from her, or even caught sight of her. She's skipped town."

The floor felt like it had dropped out from underneath me. "She's been missing for two weeks?"

Clyde didn't answer, but Jax shifted closer to the bar top and lowered his voice. "She came in one night, upset and tearing around the office like a maniac, which, by the way, wasn't really different from any other night."

That sounded familiar. "And?"

"She reeked of alcohol," he added gently, watching me intently from behind thick lashes.

Which was another common occurrence. "And?"

"And she smelled like she'd been in a sealed-off room, smoking pot and cigarettes for several hours."

Well, the pot was something new. Mom used to be into pills, lots of pills—a smorgasbord of pills.

"And that wasn't too uncommon, either, in the last year or so," Jax said, still watching me, and I now learned he'd been around for some time. "So no one really paid her much attention. You see, your mom kind of . . ."

"Did nothing while she was here?" I supplied when his jaw tensed. "Yeah, that's nothing new, either."

Jax held my gaze for a moment, and then his chest rose with a deep breath. "She left that night around eight or so, and we haven't heard from her since. Like Clyde said, that was about two weeks ago."

Oh my God.

I plopped down on the bar stool.

"I didn't call you, baby girl, because . . . well, this isn't the first time your mom has just up and disappeared." Clyde propped his hip against the bar as he placed a hand on my shoulder. "Every couple of months, she hits the road with Rooster and—"

"Rooster?" My brows flew up. Did Mom have a pet rooster? As bizarre as that would be, it wouldn't surprise me. She'd grown up on a farm, and when I was little, she had a thing for oddball pets. We had a goat once named Billy.

Clyde winced. "He's your mom's . . . um, he's your mom's man."

"His name is *Rooster*?" Oh dear lawd.

"That's what he goes by," Jax said, drawing my gaze again.

God, this was humiliating in so many ways. Mom was a drunk stoner who abused pills, never did anything with the bar she owned, and had run off with some dude, who was no doubt really classy, and went by the name Rooster.

Ugh.

Next, I was going to find out she was working part-time across the street at the strip club. I needed to find a comfy dark corner to rock in.

"A few months back, she was gone for about a month before she popped back up," Clyde said. "So, it's really nothing to worry about.

Your mom, well, she's out there, and she'll be back. She always comes back."

I closed my eyes. She didn't need to be out there. She needed to be here, where I could talk to her, where I could find out if she had any of the money left that she shouldn't have, and where I could scream and rage at her, and do something about the fact my entire life had spun out of control because of her.

Clyde squeezed my shoulder. "I can give you a call when she gets back."

That surprised me enough that my eyes popped open just in time to see Jax exchange a hard and long look with Clyde.

"You don't need to hang around here, baby girl. I think it's great that you've come by to visit, and I'm sure she'll be—"

"You want me to leave?" My eyes narrowed as my ears perked. Oh, there were most definitely more shenanigans than I was aware of.

"No," Clyde assured quickly.

And at the same time Jax said, "Yes."

I stared at him, skin prickling. "Uh, I don't think you have a say in this, *bartender* guy."

Those brown eyes seemed to turn black as coldness crept into him. A muscle popped in his jaw as I held his stare, daring him to disagree. When he didn't say anything, I turned back to Clyde, who was watching Jax. Something was going on, and with my mom, anything was possible. But I wasn't leaving—I couldn't leave because I had nowhere to go. Literally. Unlike the last couple of semesters, I wasn't taking summer courses, because this year I couldn't afford it. Which meant I also couldn't stay in the dorms, so when I packed up to come here, I had to seriously pack up everything. The small amount of funds I did have in my personal account had to get me through until I found Mom or got another job. Either way, I couldn't afford an apartment or a hotel, and I sure as hell wasn't going to intrude on Teresa for a place to stay until things got sorted out.

My gaze flickered over the worn-out bar, dancing over the old street signs and black-and-white photos framed on the wall, and, for some reason, I didn't see it before. Probably because I was too busy focusing on the eye candy that was in front of me, but I saw it now.

Behind the bar, under the red sign that had Mona's name in elegant cursive, was a framed photo.

Air lodged in my throat.

It was a photo, bright and colorful, of a family—a real family. Two smiling parents, attractive and happy. The mother held a baby boy, no older than one year and three months. Another little boy in a blue sweater, aged ten years and five months, stood next to a little girl, who had just turned eight, and she was dressed in a poofy blue princess-style dress, and she was beautiful, like a little doll, beaming at the camera.

My stomach roiled.

I had to get out of here.

Sliding off the stool, I grabbed my purse off the top of the bar. "I'll be back."

Jax frowned as he watched me back up, but he also . . . he looked relieved. The muscle had stopped spasming in his jaw, his shoulders had relaxed, and it was obvious he was happy to see me go whereas a handful of minutes earlier he was trying to get me to share drinks with him.

Yep. Like I'd thought, the guy wasn't for real.

Clyde reached for me, but I easily stepped out of his space. "Baby girl, why don't you come back to the office and sit—?"

"No. It's okay." I pivoted around and hurried out of the bar, into the warm night air before Clyde could continue.

Pressure clamped down on my chest as the door swung shut behind me and my feet hit the pavement. There were a few more cars in the parking lot, so I cut between them as I headed for the back.

Focus, I told myself. *Focus on fixing the problem at hand.*

I'd go back to Mom's house, sort through the crap in her bedroom, and maybe I'd find some clue to where her ass had disappeared. It was the only thing I could do.

Pushing the image of the family photo out of my head, I rounded an older-model truck that had been in the parking lot when I'd arrived and walked toward my parked car.

It was dark in the parking lot and the overhead lighting wasn't working, so my poor car was cloaked in creepy shadows. I ignored the cold chill snaking down my spine. I reached for the handle on my door when I saw something that didn't look right.

My fingers curled around empty air as I backed off the door and twisted toward the front. A strangled, surprised cry escaped me.

The windshield was gone.

Gone except for jagged chunks clinging to the frame, and even though it was dark, I could see a brick lying on the dashboard.

Someone had thrown a brick through my windshield.

Four

"*You* drive a Ford Fuckus?"

Squeezing my eyes shut, I blew out a deep, frustrated breath. After I'd discovered that my windshield had done a meet-and-greet with a brick, I'd walked my butt back into the bar. In a daze, I found myself standing before Jax and telling him what had happened.

Even though I'd been in a state of shock, I had recognized that he hadn't looked surprised. Anger had flashed across his striking face, deepening his eyes, yes, but surprised? No. Almost like he'd expected this.

And that was weird, but not really important right now. I had a windshield I couldn't afford to fix.

Opening my eyes, I turned to him. I hadn't noticed how tall he was while he'd been behind the bar, but standing next to him now, he was a good foot or so taller than me, pushing six feet and some odd inches. His waist was trim and it was obvious the guy took care of himself. "It's a Focus."

"Also known as a Fuckus," he replied, eyes narrowing as he leaned over the hood. "Damn."

He reached in through the glass, causing me to tense up. "Be careful!" I all but shouted, and maybe a wee bit dramatically, because he cut me a look over his shoulder, his brows raised. I stepped back. "Glass is sharp," I added dumbly.

One side of his lips kicked up. "Yeah, I know. I'll be careful." He picked up the brick and turned it over in his large hand. "Shit."

I couldn't even let myself think about how expensive fixing my windshield would be, because if I did, I probably wouldn't even wait to find a corner to start rocking in.

Jax tossed the brick to the ground and spun. Taking my hand in his large, warm one, he started hauling me toward the bar. My stomach ended up somewhere in my throat at the contact. A step or two behind now, I got a good eyeful of his rump.

Damn. He even had a nice ass.

I so needed to prioritize.

"I'll get someone out here to take a look at your car," he said, and I had to walk fast to keep up with his long-legged pace.

I blinked rapidly. "You don't—"

"Got a friend at a body garage a few miles back toward the mall. He owes me a favor," he went on as if I hadn't spoken. Ripping the door so open and so fast I thought it would fly off the hinges, he stormed inside, tugging me along,

"Stay right here," he said, sending me a look of warning.

"But—"

Letting go of my hand, he turned to me fully and got right up in my personal space. His boots to my toes, his scent surrounded me, and then he dipped his chin. Out of habit, I turned my cheek to the left, and then gasped when I felt his fingers curl around my chin, coaxing my face back to his.

"Stay right here," he said again, his gaze locking with mine. "I'll only be a minute. Tops."

Minute for what?

"Promise."

Knocked off kilter again, I found myself whispering, "Okay."

His gaze held mine for an instant longer, and then he wheeled around, and all I could think about was what he said. *I definitely want to get to know you better.* With long, graceful steps, he disappeared back by the pool tables, heading into the kitchen area.

I stood there.

No less than a minute later, he reappeared with car keys dangling from his fingers. Stopping near the waitress I'd seen carrying baskets earlier, he caught her gently by the elbow. "Can you handle the bar until Roxy gets in?"

The woman glanced at me and then back at Jax. "Sure, but is everything okay?"

Jax guided her over to where I stood rooted to the floor. Up close, she was really pretty, and while I thought she was maybe in her thirties, I didn't see a wrinkle on her face. "This is Pearl Sanders." Then he extended a hand toward me. "And this is Calla—Mona's daughter."

Pearl's jaw dropped.

Ugh.

And then the woman snapped forward. With one arm, she gave me a quick and tight hug that left me being the one standing there with my mouth hanging open.

"It's real good to finally meet you, Calla." She turned to Jax, pulling the pen out from behind her ear. "You take care of her, okay?"

"Of course," muttered Jax, like it was the last thing he wanted to do, which was stupid, because I didn't need to be taken care of, and I sure as hell didn't ask him to do it. And what the hell happened to him wanting to get to know me better?

"I think I need—"

"Come on." Jax got a hold of my hand again. The next thing I knew, I was being spun around and ushered out the door, back into the night, and then we were next to the truck that was in front of my poor car. He was opening the passenger door. "Up you go."

I halted. "What?"

He tugged on my hand. "Up you go."

Pulling my hand free, I pressed back against the car door. "I'm not going anywhere. I need to take care—"

"Of your car," he finished for me, cocking his head to the side. The silvery moonlight seemed to find his high cheekbones, caressing over the angles of his face. "I got that, and like I said, I got a friend who'll take care of that for you. Clyde's already getting in touch with him, which is a good thing."

My brain was shorting out. "Why?"

"Because it's going to rain."

I stared at him. Was he a weatherman also?

"You can smell it—late spring, early summer rain." He leaned in, and my head immediately tilted to the left. "Take a deep breath, honey, and you can smell the rain."

For some damn reason, I took a deep breath, and yeah, I smelled it, the musky damp scent. I groaned. No windshield meant rain damage.

"So we'll get your car taken care of so it's not out here when it starts raining," he finished.

"But—"

"And I don't think you want to drive around with your pretty ass sitting on glass and wind blowing in your face."

"Um, okay. Good point, but—"

"But I'm getting you out of here." He sighed, thrusting a hand through his messy hair. "Look, we can stand out here and argue about it for the next ten minutes, but you're getting in this truck."

My eyes narrowed. "Let me remind you of something. I don't know you. Like at all."

"And I'm not asking you to get naked and give me a private show." Pausing, his gaze seemed to drift down my body again. "Although, that is way interesting. A bad idea, but way interesting."

A second passed before those words sank in and my jaw dropped.

Muttering under his breath, he stepped around me. A moment later, he had his hands under my armpits, and I was shocked by the contact. His hands were incredibly large and that meant they were super close to my chest. The tips of his fingers brushed the under-swell of my breasts. A sharp wave of shivers, tight and unexpected, radiated from my ribs.

Then he hefted me up. Literally. Feet off the ground and all. "Dip your head, honey," he ordered.

I obeyed because, seriously, I had no idea what the hell was going on here. I found myself sitting in his truck and the door shutting on my other side. Christ. I smoothed my palms down my face, lowering my hands just in time to see him jog around the front. He was up in the truck in no time, closing the door behind him.

Once I was buckled in, I shot him a look and said the first thing that popped into my head. "You drive a Chevy?"

He smirked. "You know what they say about Chevys."

"Yeah, you'd rather be pushing one than driving a Ford?" I rolled my eyes. "Because that makes sense."

Jax chuckled as he shifted out of park. I didn't say anything as he pulled out of the parking lot and hit the road. Wondering about him flirting with me earlier and worrying about a MIA mom weren't at the forefront of my thoughts as I started nibbling on my lower lip.

"How much do you think it'll cost to repair the windshield?" I asked.

He slid me a look as he hit the stoplight near the mall. "At least a hundred-fifty, and with the whole thing being gone, probably more."

My chest constricted as I mentally deducted that from what I knew was in my checking account and groaned. "That's just great."

Jax was quiet as the light turned green and he coasted out into the intersection. "You staying at one of the hotels."

I snorted. Yep. Like a piglet. "Uh, no. Way too much money."

"You're staying at your mom's house?" Incredulity rang from his tone.

"Yeah."

He fixed his gaze back onto the road. "But she's not there."

"So? I used to live there." I shrugged a shoulder as I lowered my hand to my lap. "Besides, I'm really not going to spend the money on a hotel when I can stay some place free." Even if it was truly the last place I wanted to stay.

Jax didn't say anything for a long moment and then, "Have you had anything to eat?"

Shaking my head, I pressed my lips together. I hadn't eaten since that morning, and even then it was only a Rice Krispies Treat. I'd been too nervous to eat anything else. My stomach grumbled, apparently pissed-off that I was just now paying attention to it.

"Me neither," he commented.

We made a pit stop at a fast-food joint, and because I was hungry, I ordered a hamburger and a sweet tea, but when I dug around in my purse for the limited cash I had on me, Jax had already handed over money at the drive-through.

"I have money." I grabbed my wallet.

He slid me a bland look as he rested one arm on his window. "You ordered a hamburger and a sweet tea. I think I got it covered."

"But I have money," I insisted.

He arched a brow. "But I don't need it."

I shook my head as I started to open my wallet. "How much does it—hey!" I snapped as he took my wallet and my purse from my hands. "What the hell?"

"Like I said, honey, I got it covered." Closing up my wallet, he dropped it in my purse and then shoved it behind his seat.

My eyes narrowed on him. "That's *so* not cool."

"A thank-you would be cool, though."

"I didn't ask you to pay for it."

"So?"

I blinked at him.

Jax winked.

I drew back a little. He winked, and my lady parts were like *whoa,* way on board with that, which was probably a good indication I needed to pay more attention to said parts, because they were getting desperate.

And I was feeling a wee bit boy crazy, but who'd blame me?

A minute later we were back on the road and I had a huge bag of food in my lap and two sweet teas jostling around in a holder. I hadn't really paid attention to what he'd ordered, but by the weight of the warm and wonderful-smelling bag, it was half the menu.

"You look nothing like your mother," he said unexpectedly.

That much was true. Mom dyed her hair a sunny blond, or at least she used to. I wasn't sure since I hadn't seen her in a while, but the last time I'd been around her, the day I'd left Plymouth Meeting to attend Shepherd, she'd been looking . . . rough.

"Her life . . . it's been hard. She used to be really pretty," I heard myself saying as I stared out the window, watching the strip mall of fast-food joints disappear.

"I imagine so, if she looked anything like you."

My gaze swung to him sharply, but he wasn't looking at me. He wasn't grinning or smiling. Nothing about him would've led me to believe that hadn't been a genuine statement, but I wasn't pretty, and that belief had nothing to do with a low self-esteem. I had a scar cutting across my left cheek. That tended to universally ruin features.

I didn't know what Jax was up to and I didn't want to find out. I had bigger and more important things to focus on and worry over.

But when I saw that Jax was turning off the main roadway, hitting a back road—a shortcut—I was staring at him again. "You know where the house is?"

He grunted out what I assumed was a yes.

"You've been there before?"

His hand tightened on the steering wheel. "A few times."

A horrible thought formed in my head. "Why have you been to her house?"

"Don't you mean *our* house since you used to live there?"

"Uh, no. I might've lived there while I was in high school, but it was never my home."

He glanced at me, and then fixed his gaze on the road. A moment passed. "The first time I had to come out to your mom's house was with Clyde. Mona . . . she went on a bender. Got so shitfaced that we thought we were going to have to take her to the hospital."

I winced.

"Then a couple of times when she didn't show up for a few days and we were worried about her." His hand had loosened on the steering wheel and now he was tapping his fingers on it. "Every other day, Clyde or Pearl would check on her just to make sure she was doing okay."

"And you? You would check on her, too?"

He nodded.

Biting down on my lip, I ignored the wave of muddy guilt that threatened to rise up my throat. These people, with the exception of Clyde, were virtual strangers, and here I was, family, and I wasn't making daily, or even yearly, trips to make sure if she was alive or to find out if she'd finally overdosed. After all, I knew that was what "checking in" on her meant.

I tried to check the guilt and failed. "I'm not close with Mom. We have—"

"Calla, I figured you two weren't close. I get it," he cut in, tossing a reckless grin my way. And it was reckless because he had to know how powerful that half curve of his lips was and he just threw it out there, all willy-nilly. "You don't need to explain anything to me."

"Thanks," I whispered before I thought about it, and then I felt stupid. All he did was nod in response.

The rest of the ride out to Mom's house was silent, and I was surprised when he parked his truck in the driveway and followed me to the door, carrying the two sweet teas.

As I unlocked the door, I glanced up at him. "You don't have to come in."

"I know." He grinned. "But I'd prefer not to eat in my truck while driving. You cool with that?"

It was on the tip of my tongue to say no, but my head had a mind of its own. I nodded as I pushed the door open.

"Great." Jax dipped past me and entered the house before me.

"Make yourself at home," I murmured.

He didn't hear me because he was moving through the house stealthily, finding the switches on the wall to the lights and flipping them on. He scanned the house with an intense, wary eye, like he expected a troll to jump out from underneath the shabby couch. When he headed for the kitchen, I followed, and when he told me he needed to use the bathroom, I placed the bag on the counter and started unloading the items.

Damn, he really had been here before because he didn't use the bathroom downstairs. I heard his feet hit the stairs, and I wondered why he'd chosen the one upstairs, but my brain was too overworked to really give it too much thought. By the time he returned, I'd found my one hamburger among the array of food he'd gotten.

Jax pulled out a chair next to me and dropped down in it with grace. He was sitting to my right. "So." He drew the word out as he unwrapped a chicken sandwich. "How long are you planning on being here?"

I shrugged a shoulder as I plucked the pickles off my sandwich. "Don't know yet."

"Probably not long, right? There isn't shit to do around here, and with your mom out doing her thing, there aren't many reasons to hang around." There was a pause. "You going to eat those pickles?" When I shook my head, he helped himself to them.

I didn't respond and I got two bites in before he spoke again.

"You in college? Shepherd?"

My hands stopped halfway to my mouth. "How did you know?"

He'd moved on to his hamburger, placing the borrowed pickles under the bun. "Clyde talks about you every once in a while. So does Mona."

Every muscle locked up and my stomach soured. Anything that my mother had to say about me could not be good.

Silence fell between us while he removed one of the buns and folded his sandwich into a one-bun burrito. "So, what you studying?"

I dropped my half-eaten burger on its wrapper. "Nursing."

His brows rose as he let out a low whistle. "Well, my fantasies involving nurses in little white skirts just got a whole lot richer."

My eyes narrowed at him.

He grinned. "What made you pick nursing?"

Focusing on rolling up my discarded burger in its wrapper, I shrugged again. I knew exactly why, but the answer wasn't easy to admit, so I changed the subject. "What about you?"

"You mean, what do I do besides bartending?" He finished off the hamburger and grabbed for the fries.

"Yeah." I watched him. "Besides that and eating a lot."

Jax laughed that deep, sexy laugh again. "Right now, I'm just bartending. Got my fingers in a few other things."

He didn't elaborate, like me, and so I didn't push it, but that also left very little to talk about.

"Fry?"

I shook my head.

"Come on. It's the best part of eating fast food. You can't turn down a fry." Those eyes of his warmed even more. "It's pure grease, carbs, and salt. Heaven."

My lips twitched. "You don't look like you eat a lot of carbs."

One broad shoulder rose. "I run every day. Hit the gym before I hit the bar. Means I eat what I want, when I want. Otherwise, life would suck if you spent half your time begrudging yourself of shit you want."

God, did I know how super-true that was.

So I took a fry. And then two. Okay, maybe five fries before I got up to throw away our trash in a little bin that surprisingly had a fresh trash bag in it. As I washed off my hands, Jax stood and made his way over to the fridge, letting out another low whistle as he opened it up. I had no idea what he was doing. The fridge was empty with the exception of condiments.

He shut the door and propped his hip against the countertop. Taking in the buttercup-colored walls—walls that Clyde had painted before we moved in—and the scratched surface of the small round table we ate at, he drew in a deep breath and his striking face got all serious. Jaw set. Full lips thinned. Eyes deepened to a dark brown, almost mahogany.

"You're not staying here," he announced.

I blinked as I shifted so my right side was visible to him. "Thought we already had this conversation."

"There's no food in the fridge."

"Yeah, I kind of noticed that." I paused, crossing my arms. "There also wouldn't be food at a hotel—a hotel I'd have to pay for."

Jax angled his body toward mine, and my gaze dropped. Narrow waist and hips. Definitely a runner. "Hotels aren't that expensive around here."

Irritation pricked along my skin. I knew I was going to have to go to the grocery store at some point, because I did plan on staying, which meant I needed food. I also needed my car to be functional, so that was God knows how much money I'd have to spend. I knew that the longer I stayed here, the quicker I'd blow through my funds, but it was seriously my only option. I had no other place to go, at least not until school started back up in late August.

That was if I got approved for higher financial aid.

And if I didn't?

Maybe I could get a corner in a padded room to rock in.

These were things Jax really didn't need to know. "Thanks for taking me here and getting food. I really appreciate it, and if you could let me know who I need to contact about my windshield, that would be great. But I'm kind of tired and—"

Suddenly Jax was directly in front of me. Like one second he was by the fridge, and then the next he was right *there*. I sucked in a startled breath as I pressed back against the counter.

"I don't think you're getting what I'm saying, honey."

Obviously not.

"Your mom is cracked. You know that."

Okay. It was one thing for me to say my mom was screwed up. Totally another thing coming from his mouth. "Look, my mom is—"

"Not going to win any mother of the year awards? Yeah, I know that," he said, and my fingers curled against my palms. "She's also not going to win any boss of the year awards, either. But you probably know that already."

"What does any of that have to do with me staying here or not?" I snapped.

"You actually don't need to be in this town, let alone at *this* house."

My mouth dropped since I wasn't expecting that statement. "What?"

"You need to go stay in a hotel for tonight, and then as soon as your car is ready, you need to get your sweet ass on the road, which will hopefully be tomorrow afternoon, and you really don't need to come back."

Okay. That did it. I'd had it up to *here* with everything, and I didn't care that Hot Bartender Dude was probably the sexiest guy I'd ever seen or that he was nice enough to drive me here and buy me food. Or that he thought my ass was sweet and liked my legs.

I squared off with him, forgetting everything else. "Answer me one question."

His brown eyes locked with mine. "Done."

My voice dripped sugary sweetness when I spoke. "Who in the *fuck* do you think you are to tell me what to do?"

He blinked once, and then he tipped his head back and laughed. "You got attitude. You really do. I kind of like that."

That pissed me off even more, and besides, that was also kind of twisted. "You can leave now."

"Not until you get what's going on here." Jax planted two hands on the counter, one on either side of my hips, and then he leaned in, caging me. "I need you to listen to me."

I locked up and was unable to remember the last time a guy got this close to me.

"Calla," he said, and I shivered at how deep and soft his voice was as it wrapped around my name. "I don't think you realize just how far gone Mona is and what that means for everyone who knows her."

Air halted in my lungs. "How far?"

"It's not pretty."

"I didn't think it was."

His eyes continued to hold mine. "This house has been party central for the last couple of years. Not the cool kind of parties anyone with two working brain cells would want to go to. Police are here on the regular. This house has basically become a drug house, and I wouldn't be surprised if you find crack pipes stashed in some of these kitchen drawers."

Oh my God.

"The kind of people she hangs with? They are the bottom of the fucking barrel. Can't get any lower than them. And you can't get any shadier than them. And that's not even the worst part."

"It isn't?" How could it be worse than my mom owning a crack house? I guessed a meth lab could be worse.

"She's pissed off a lot of those shady people," he said, and my stomach dropped to my toes. "Owes them a lot of money from what I hear, too. So does her man Rooster."

Owes more people money? Oh God, that was bad news.

"Now I know Clyde probably doesn't want you to know this, but I don't think shielding you from the shit that's going down here is the right thing to do. Mona's got a lot of the wrong kind of folks gunning for her. The kind of people your mom is messed up with are bad news. The windshield?"

"What does any of this have to do with the windshield?"

"You came here first, right? Someone probably has an eye on this house, saw you, and decided to give you a good old-fashioned redneck warning. They may not realize yet that you're her blood, but they know you obviously know her since you're here. And hey, the whole windshield thing could be a fucked-up coincidence, but I doubt it. Let's hope they don't realize you're blood."

Oh, holy crap on a cracker, this was not good. My chest rose sharply as my pulse kicked up. This had veered off from crap, straight into shitville.

"Yeah, I see it's starting to make sense," he said softly, almost gently. "It'll get worse from here, especially if she doesn't come out of hiding."

Turning my head to the left, I heard his words. They sunk in, causing a shudder to snake its way down my spine. God, a meth lab would probably be better than this.

Oh Mom, what have you gotten yourself into?

Her life, what had become of it, hurt like a real physical burst of pain, and something that I long since believed was dead sprang alive deep inside me. A need I'd suffered with for so many years, an urge and drive to fix her—to fix Mom.

Two fingers landed on my chin, gently forcing my head center. My eyes widened as they once again connected with his. "They could use you to get to her."

My brain immediately shut down on that. The whole thing was just too much. Mom stole money from me and some crazy windshield-breaking rednecks that were hell-bent on revenge. It sounded like a plot from a movie featuring a washed-up action star.

"Honey, the best thing you could do is to turn around and leave town," he said again, his brown eyes holding mine in a steely gaze. "There's nothing here for you." Jax almost sounded disappointed by that, and when my breath caught again, his gaze finally left mine, flicking down to my parted lips. His voice was deeper, rougher when he spoke again. "Nothing but trouble."

Five

$\mathcal{I}$ didn't go home the next day like Jax had ordered me to do. Not because I currently wasn't in possession of my own car or because he had absolutely no business telling me what to do. I seriously had no choice but to stick around and . . . and do what? Track Mom down and find out just what kind of crap she'd gotten herself in, and hopefully get my money back?

The idea that there was no money left at all was something I couldn't allow myself to think about, but at this point, it was either staying here for the summer or living in my car. Whenever I got my car back.

But it was more than that. Yeah, the money was huge, it was linked to my life, but it was also about Mom. It was always about Mom.

When Jax had left last night, he'd wanted me to leave with him, so that he could drop my "sweet ass" off at a hotel that he actually offered to pay for, but I refused, figuring the last thing I needed was to owe someone money. He'd warned that he was sending a cab.

He'd actually had the nerve to say to me, "I know you're smarter than this, honey, so I'm going to give you forty minutes to get over yourself, and when a cab pulls up in front of your house, you're going to get your sweet ass in it."

What in the hell?

So when the cab pulled up and honked for a straight minute, I'd ignored it, and it had eventually driven away.

Yeah, it was kind of nice of him to offer to pay for a hotel and to send a cab, nice in a really weird and overbearing kind of way. But it was something, his domineering niceness, that I couldn't allow myself to give a lot of thought.

I had a restless night on the couch and spent a good part of the morning going through Mom's mess of a bedroom—and finding absolutely nothing of any use, not even a crack pipe. However, the closet did hold a few items I wished I hadn't seen.

One was a framed photo of me when I was around eight or nine years old. The other was a trophy—about two feet tall, still shimmery and glittery. They were mementos of a past I could no longer claim.

After placing those items in the back of the closet, covering them up with old jeans, I got ready to head to the bar. I didn't really care about how I dressed, but I took my time with the makeup, carefully blending it until the scar sloping down my cheek was less red, more pink, and almost invisible if someone was far enough away. I could leave the house wearing ratty sweats and a T-shirt full of holes, but I never left home without having the thick makeup smacked across my face. Once I was done, I called up Clyde, knowing there was only one other place where there could be any info like bank accounts or evidence of where she could've run off to.

He showed a little after noon, and I'd been waiting for him on the stoop. I hopped into his truck, a Ford that was a lot older than Jax's, and buckled myself in before he could get his massive size out of the vehicle.

"Baby girl—"

"Like I said on the phone, I need to go to the bar. I wouldn't have called you if I had my car."

"Jax is taking care of your car."

I wrinkled my nose as I plopped my purse in my lap. "That's reassuring," I muttered, which was bitchy, because even though he was a wee bit bossy, he had been helpful.

Shifting his girth around in the seat, he twisted toward me. "Baby girl," he began again. "Are you really staying in this place?"

I sighed as I slid my sunglasses on. They were nice. Total knock-offs, but I thought I looked good in them. "In the reputed crack house? Yes. I'm not getting a hotel room.

"Calla—"

"Jax already tried to take me to one. He even called a cab!" Even though I waved my hand around, I didn't miss the way Clyde's lips twitched. "Mom . . . she really screwed me over. Like bad. And I'm figuring that what she's going through is pretty bad, too."

Clyde pressed his lips together as he threw the truck into reverse. "It is bad."

A breath shuddered through me. "Is it as bad as Jax told me?" There was a little part of me that was hoping that Clyde would tell me that Jax tended to exaggerate.

No such luck.

Even though I didn't elaborate, he grunted out an affirmative. "I don't know exactly what he said, but I'm imagining that he didn't tell you all of it."

I closed my eyes, just listening to the tires eat away at the road. God, what was I doing? Maybe I should've just gone to the hotel and headed back to school, called up Teresa—*No*. I stopped myself there. She and Jase had a lot of plans this summer. Traveling. Beaches. Sun and sand. I wasn't going to mess that up by dumping my problems on her—on them. Plus there was something completely out of control about crashing on friends' couches that I couldn't deal with.

Minutes passed before Clyde spoke again. "This is the last thing I wanted you to do."

I didn't open my eyes.

"Coming back here? Well, I've always been real with you, baby girl, and I'm gonna keep being real with you."

My heart lurched into my throat, and all I could think about was what Jax had said to me. That there was nothing but trouble here.

"This is the last place I wanted you to be and, well, there are things you don't need to know about. You don't ever need to know about, but one thing ain't changed, and that's you, baby girl."

My eyes popped open.

"You're good to the core. Always have been, no matter what shit Mona put you through, even before the fire."

A pang lit up my chest, licking through my body, and it spread across the scar on my cheek, and washed over the other scars—the worse ones. It was like it had just been yesterday. The *fire*.

"But you know there ain't no helping your mother."

"I know that," I whispered around a sudden knot in my throat. "That's not why I'm here. She did me wrong, Clyde. I'm not lying."

He spared me a quick, knowing glance. "I know that and I believe that, but I also know that you're here, and now that you know your mom has got herself in a mess, you're going to want to help her somehow."

I sucked in a sharp breath.

"But it's worth repeating," he continued. "There ain't no helping Mona. Not this time. The best you can do is get back to that school and don't look back."

A bowl of corn nuts sat on a scuffed-up oak table in the office situated at the end of the hall leading to the restrooms. There were two file cabinets behind the desk, and butted up against the wall was a couch that was made of leather and looked surprisingly new—a lot newer than the one I'd slept on last night.

I hadn't been able to bring myself to sleep in the loft upstairs.

I'd never run a bar before and I wasn't perfect when it came to numbers, but after poring over the statements, receipts, and bills I'd found neatly organized, I knew two things.

First up, there was no way Mom had been keeping track of any of this during the last year. If you looked up the opposite of organized, there'd be a picture of Mom smiling happily. Someone else was keeping track of the books, and I seriously doubted it was Clyde. God love him, he was good at keeping things real, great at being practically the only positive role model around, and awesome in the kitchen, but running the financial side of a bar? Uh. No.

Second thing I learned was that the bar *wasn't* bleeding money like it had been stabbed repeatedly with a wicked hunter's knife. This piece of news confounded me. If Mom had blown through my money and potentially hers, I'd imagined the bar would be next on her list. Plus, it wasn't in the greatest condition.

Well, on second thought . . .

I'd checked out the bar since I was alone when Clyde had headed into the kitchen to do some cleaning after explaining that my car, which was no longer in the parking lot, was down the street at a garage getting the windshield replaced.

No way did I even want to think about that bill.

Back in the day, before I'd left for college, Mona's had been a mess. Bar top always sticky and so was the floor, but the origin of *that* stickiness was always questionable. Taps were broken. Kegs should've been eighty-sixed ages ago. Days-old lemons being used, fruit juice beyond the expiration dates, and a whole slew of other grossness went on. Mom had always hired her friends to bartend. Her friends basically being middle-aged men and women who hadn't grown up and thought working behind a bar meant they got free booze. So cleaning was never high on the priority list.

Although the bar wasn't looking like it was in its prime any longer; more like it was in its geriatric stage, it was cleaner than I gave it credit for yesterday. Behind the bar, the ice had recently been dumped and the ice well flushed out with hot water, preventing a slew of gunky bacteria growth to grow. I hadn't seen fruit flies or small critter droppings, which were unfortunately commonplace in bars. The bar tops were freshly wiped down and the floor was also clean behind the bar; the bottles were stacked and organized.

Even the tables out on the floor had been cleaned, as were the ashtrays. So, while the bar might need a renovation, someone definitely cared about it, and I knew that wasn't Mom.

My gaze flicked to the printed-out spreadsheet for last month—the spreadsheet stapled to a gazillion receipts—and I scanned the lines. Like the dozen spreadsheets before it that I'd found, all the way up to March of last year, everything was tracked—monthly bills, like electricity and other utilities, income coming in, food and beverage costs and breakdowns, and, most surprising, payroll.

Freaking *payroll*.

The reason why Mom always had friends working for her who were interested only in free drinks was that she could never make payroll. The idea of Mona's making enough money to pay its employees on a regular basis had been laughable. Not funny laughable, but maniacal, slightly crazed laughable.

But Mona's had been making payroll for about a year now and had employee names I didn't recognize with the exception of Jax and Clyde. There was even some dude who worked in the kitchen on weekend nights, helping Clyde out.

Mona's was turning a profit for the last four months. Nothing major, or to get overly excited about, but a profit was a profit.

Leaning back in the chair, I slowly shook my head. How was this possible? If Mona's was making money, why was she stealing—

"What in the hell are you doing in here?"

Emitting a low shriek, I jumped in the chair as my chin jerked out. All the air whooshed out of my lungs. Jax stood in the doorway, and he must've been part ghost and part ninja, because I hadn't even heard him approach. The floors creaked about every other step when I'd walked down the hall to the office.

It had only been a handful of hours since I'd last seen Jax, and it wasn't like I'd forgotten how hot he was in those hours, but geez, all I could do was stare at him for a moment.

Freshly showered, his hair was slightly darker as it curled against his forehead. The black shirt he wore appeared tighter than the one he wore last night, which I'm pretty sure the female population was thankful for.

But he didn't look happy at all to see me.

Jaw set and lips pressed together, he glared at me as I stupidly gazed back at him like a fawn. "What are you doing in here, Calla?"

At the sound of my name, I snapped out of it. Placing the spreadsheet and receipts on the desk, I narrowed my eyes at him. "Well, considering this bar is my *mom's,* I have every right to be in the office."

"That's some dumb rationale considering I've been at this bar for about two years and last night was the first time I'd seen your sweet ass."

Heat flashed across my cheeks as I tilted my chair to the left. "Can you stop referring to my ass as sweet?"

His eyes deepened to dark chocolate. "Would you prefer I refer to it as hot?"

"No."

"Sexy?"

I inhaled through my nose. "No."

"How about heart shaped and thick?"

My hands curled into fists. "How about not at all?"

His lips twitched and then the humor fled from him as his gaze dipped to the stack of papers. He stalked over to the desk. "You were going through the files?"

I shrugged forced casualness. "Wanted to see how the bar was doing."

"I'm sure that's really not your business."

What the hell? "I'm pretty sure that it is."

He planted one hand on the desk, right on top of the spreadsheets. "Do tell."

Swiveling the chair, I angled the right side of my body toward his. "Well, considering that this bar is the only thing my mom will leave me one day, I have every right to look at those papers."

Something flashed over his face as he tilted his head to the side. "Leave you this bar?"

"Mom has a will. Has had one for *years*. So unless she's changed it recently, which I doubt has been high on her to-do list, if something happened to her, God forbid, the bar is mine."

Again, there was a strange tightening to the skin around his eyes I didn't understand. A moment passed. "Is that what you want? The bar?"

Hell to the no. I didn't say that.

"What would you do with this bar if you did unexpectedly end up with it?" he demanded.

I said the first thing that popped in my head. "I'd probably sell it."

Jax drew back from the desk, straightening to his full height. His eyes were like shards of glass as he stared down at me. Gone was the teasing, flirting bartender. "If you don't care about this bar—"

"I never said that." Not exactly.

He ignored that. "Then why are you here? For your mom? That's a lost cause and you damn well know that. And you didn't stay at a hotel last night, did you?"

His rapid change of subject left my head wheeling. There were days when I thought she was a lost cause and then others where I couldn't allow myself to think that. "Thanks for sending the cab, but—"

"God, you're going to be a pain in my ass." He moved away from the desk, scrubbing his fingers through his damp hair. The muscles in his back tensed under his shirt.

I drew in a sharp breath, feeling my cheeks redden once more. "I'm not a pain in any part of your body, buddy."

He barked out a laugh as he faced me. "You're not? I told you what kind of crap your mom is messed up in, and the fact that a lot of nasty folks want a piece of her, and you're still here. On top of your window being busted out—"

"Look, I get that my mom is in trouble and all that. Newsbreak, but that's nothing that new to me." Well, she did seem to be in a lot more trouble than normal, but at this point, whatever. "And the stuff with my car? I was in that house for a handful of minutes. There is no way someone saw me that quickly. Not to mention, my car was parked in a bar parking lot with a strip club across the street. These things happen."

"Do they?" He folded his arms across his chest again. "Are you frequently around stripper bars."

"No," I hissed.

A muscle fluttered along his jaw. We were engaged in an epic stare-down for what felt like an eternity before he spoke again. "Why are you here, Calla? Seriously? There's nothing here for you. Your mom's not. You don't have family here. And from what I know of you, you've spent the last couple of years at college, not even making brief visits. Not judging, but you haven't really cared this entire time. So, why now?"

Whoa. His words slipped through me like a sheet of ice.

Jax started backing up toward the door, his eyes never leaving my face. "Just go home, Calla. You're not—"

"My entire life is on hold!" The moment those words left my mouth . . . holy crap, I realized how true they were. And that sucked like I'd swallowed a vial of acid. I didn't even know what made me say it. Maybe it was the softness in his voice that reminded me of pity. I don't know.

Swallowing hard, I watched him stop and stare at me. "My entire life is on hold," I said again, much lower, and then everything just came out in the worst case of diarrhea of the mouth. "Mom cleaned me out. She took my entire savings account, which held all my money—my tuition money and what I planned on using for emergencies and for when I searched for a job. Not only that, she took out a loan and credit cards in my name and didn't make a single payment. She tanked my credit, and I'm not even sure I'll qualify for any student loan now."

His eyes widened slightly as he lifted an arm, running his palm over his chest, above his heart.

"I don't have any place else to go to," I continued, feeling an odd lump in my throat and a stinging in my eyes. "I can't stay in the dorms because I couldn't enroll in summer classes. She left me with nothing except the little money I have in my checking account and a house that apparently is a crack house. On top of that, she's run off doing God knows what with a dude named Rooster. And my only hope—my only prayer at this point, is that she has some kind of money, something to pay me back with. So, yeah, I get that there's nothing really here for me and that I'm a giant pain in your ass, but I seriously don't have any other place to go."

"Shit." He looked away, jaw tight.

Then it hit me. Humiliating. I squeezed my eyes shut. Where were the staples? I needed them for my mouth.

"Shit," he said again. "Calla, I don't know what to tell you."

I forced my eyes open and found him staring at me. There wasn't pity in his gaze, but his eyes were lighter again. "There's nothing you can say."

"There is no money here, honey. Nothing that she can give you." His eyes searched mine. "I'm not bullshitting you. It sucks. Fucking really sucks, but there's nothing. Not a drop outside of what this bar is just starting to make and that isn't much."

I sat back as I let out a shaky breath. *No. No. No.* That one word was on repeat.

"If she took your money, she doesn't have it. And if she had any money herself, it's also long gone, too. Trust me." His voice dropped lower. "A week doesn't go by that there isn't someone sniffing around this bar looking for her because she owes them money."

Shifting my gaze away, I drew in another deep breath. "Okay. I need to accept that there is no money and I won't get a red penny back." He didn't respond to that, which was okay, because I was mostly talking to myself. "That's it. I'm broke. All I can do is pray that financial aid comes through."

Bile rose in my throat as what I was saying really sank in. I was seriously broke. My life was seriously on hold. I also might seriously be sick.

"I'm sorry," he said softly.

I flinched.

Jax had moved around the desk and he was closer. I didn't want him closer. Nervous, I smoothed my hands over my denim-clad thighs. "Plan B," I whispered.

"What?"

My voice shook as I spoke. "Plan B. I need to get a job and make as much money as I can this summer." I glanced around the office and I suddenly knew what I needed to do, to get the control back. There was a knot in my chest, and I wanted to cut it out, but there would be no cutting it out. "I can work here."

He started, and then he frowned. "Work here? Honey, this is not your kind of place."

I spared him a look. "It doesn't look like it's your kind of place, either."

"Why is that?" he fired back.

"Look at you." I gestured in a wide circle in front of him. "You don't look like you should be working in a dive bar."

An eyebrow rose. "I like to think it's one step up from a dive bar."

"A little step," I muttered.

One side of his lips kicked up. "Where do you think I should be working at?"

"I don't know." Sitting back, I brushed my hair off my forehead and sighed. "Maybe at Hot Guys R Us."

His brows flew up. "So, you think I'm hot."

I rolled my eyes. "I can see quite fine, Jax."

"If you think I'm hot, then why were you so resistant to going out with me when you first came into the bar?"

I stared at him, wondering how the conversation veered off to this. "Does that really matter?"

"Yes."

"No, it doesn't."

His eyes glimmered with amusement. "We'll agree to disagree."

"We aren't agreeing on anything." I pushed up and stopped. He hadn't moved, and the space was cramped. I couldn't walk around him. "I can work here."

"A rough crowd comes in on the weekends. Maybe you should try the Outback down the street or something."

"I'm not afraid of any rednecks," I grumbled.

Jax narrowed his eyes at me.

"What?" I threw up my hands. "Not like the bar can't use my help. And I *need* money. Obviously. And maybe by working here I can make some tips and maybe get back some of the money, even if it's a small percentage."

"Making tips?" He took another step forward, and I was stuck between him and the chair. "What do you think you'd be doing here?"

I shrugged a shoulder. "I can bartend."

"Have you ever done that before?" When I shrugged again, he laughed outright. Now my eyes were narrowing on him. "Honey, it's not that easy."

"Can't be that hard."

Jax stared at me for a long moment, and then probably one of the most fascinating things to watch happened. Each tensed muscle relaxed, and a slow, knowing grin appeared on his lips.

My tummy did a cartwheel.

"Well, we can't have this, now can we?"

"Have what?" My tumbling tummy? There was no way he knew about that.

"You not having any place to go." When I didn't answer, he cocked his head to the side. "Okay, honey, you want this . . . you got it."

For some inane reason, it felt like he was talking about something else, and tiny, tight coils formed in my belly. "Good."

His grin spread until a flash of straight white teeth appeared. "Great."

Six

The bar opened at one in the afternoon, and since no one had moseyed on in, Jax set me up behind the bar slicing fresh lemons and limes, with one warning.

"Please don't cut your fingers off. That would suck."

I'd rolled my eyes and hadn't bothered to respond, working quietly until I had all of them cut and ready to roll. For the most part, I was comfortable behind the bar as long as I didn't pay attention to the framed photo I wanted to rip down and toss across it.

But I did have better things to look at.

Every so often, I stole a quick glance at Jax. He was leaning against the far corner of the bar, ankles crossed and arms folded across his chest, and his head was tilted toward the TV screen hanging from the ceiling.

When we'd left the office, he explained that I'd be on his schedule, which apparently started at four in the afternoon and ran to closing. Why he'd been in the bar this early today, I had no idea. He worked the busiest nights—Wednesday through Saturday night, ten-hour shifts.

Way past my normal, boring bedtime of like, eleven, but I could do it. I *had* to do it. I didn't have time to waste trying to get a job at Outback like he suggested.

As I kept stealing quick peeks, I tried once again to figure out his age. I could've just asked him, but I wasn't sure if that was my business. He couldn't be much older than me, but there was something about him that screamed maturity. Most twenty-one or so year-olds I knew could barely make it out of bed in the morning, including myself, but he had this air of confidence and know-how that I thought would come with someone older—someone with a lot of responsibilities.

I glanced around the bar, seeing that it was still empty, and it struck me then, something that was right in my face. My gaze flickered back to Jax, his hair now dried and not styled, and the deep-bronzed brown waves fell this way and that all around the crown of his head.

He was running the bar.

It had to be him.

Granted, I hadn't met anyone else besides Pearl. I had seen the schedule in the office and there were two more bartenders, a Roxy and a guy named Nick. Another server who worked only Friday and Saturday nights named Gloria, and then there was a Sherwood who worked in the kitchen with Clyde.

Maybe I was wrong and it was one of them, but I had a feeling I wasn't, and I had no idea what to think about it. But I was curious. Why would he invest so much into Mona's?

Out of my control, my gaze drifted from where his hair was trimmed neatly above the back collar of his shirt, down the length of his back, and then lingered on the well-worn, faded jeans.

God, he had a nice ass. A freaking work of art. Even though his jeans were nowhere near tight, but the general form—

Jax unexpectedly twisted his neck, glancing over his shoulder at me, and I was staring at him. Like totally staring at him.

One side of his lips curled up.

He'd caught me.

Heat swept over my face as I hastily looked away, stringing to-gether a buttload of curse words. I wasn't checking him out. I *didn't* need to be checking him out. I mean, I spent a lot of time checking out guys, because checking them out never led to anything.

It never could.

"What's next?" I asked, clearing my throat as I washed my hands before I ended up with lemon-juice-covered fingers all up in my eyeballs.

"We don't have a bar back, so every day we've got to make sure the bar's stocked. We also need to do a stock count. That's already been taken care of today, but I can show you where it's at. I'm sure it's changed since you've been around."

A lot of things here had changed since I'd been around. As I dried my hands off, I wondered if Mom had ever done a real stock count. "Who's been running the bar?"

The line of his back stiffened, and then he turned fully toward me. "I need to show you where we keep everything. Beer is kept chilled, off the kitchen. Liquor is back in the stockroom." He pushed off the bar top and headed out, leaving me no choice but to follow him down the hall.

As he stopped in front of the door near the office, I flipped the heavy length of hair over my left shoulder. "I know it's not Clyde."

He fished out a key ring. "Not sure what you're talking about, hon."

I frowned as he unlocked the door. "Who's been running the bar? Keeping track of everything?"

The door swung open. "See this clipboard?" He jerked his chin at where it hung next to the stocked shelves. "Anything that gets taken out of here, gets marked. Anything. This is also the same sheet we do inventory on."

I quickly glanced over it. Seemed pretty self-explanatory.

"The same with the walk-in. Everything is in good order in here, so it'll be easy to find." He turned then, ushering me out of the room, but when he started past me, I got in his way.

"Who is running the bar, Jax?" I asked again, and when his gaze shifted behind me, eyes narrowing slightly, my suspicions were confirmed. "It's you, isn't it?"

He didn't say anything.

"You've been running the bar and that's why it's not a complete crap hole."

"Complete?" Brown eyes landed on mine.

I ducked my chin to the left. "It's nothing like it used to be. Things are organized and clean. Mona's is making money."

"Not a lot of money."

"But it's doing a hell of a lot better in just a year than it had for years," I pointed out. "That's because of—" My words got stuck in my throat as his hands landed on my shoulders. I swallowed.

He dipped his head, his gaze following mine as he spoke quietly. "It's not just because of me. We have a staff that gives a shit, and Clyde has always given a shit. That's why we're doing better. It's been a group effort. Still is a group effort."

Our gazes were locked head-on, and like last night in my mother's kitchen, I was stunned into silence at his proximity. I didn't like anyone getting this close, enabling them to see beyond the makeup.

"We've got better crowds coming in now," he continued, and his stare alone refused to allow me to look away or hide. And damn, that was majorly uncomfortable considering I was the bomb diggity when it came to hiding. His voice dropped even lower. "Off-duty cops. Some students from the local community college. Even the bikers who do come in don't cause problems. Without the shitty people Mona had in here, even though the crowd can get a little sketchy at times, it has gotten better."

"Obviously," I murmured.

His impossibly thick lashes lowered, and then so did my gaze—lowered right about to his full lips. God, how did he get a mouth like that? That half grin appeared, causing my entire face to warm. "Interesting," he said.

I blinked. "What's interesting?"

"You."

"Me?" I tried to step back, but the hands on my shoulders tightened. "I'm not interesting at all."

His head tilted to the side. "I know that's untrue."

Why did it feel like the weight of his hands on my shoulders was possibly the most pleasant thing I'd ever felt? Although he was only touching me there, I felt the exquisite heaviness all the way through my body.

Oh whoa, this was bad.

"It's not," I whispered finally, and then the verbal diarrhea was back like Montezuma's revenge. "I'm the most boring person to ever live. I haven't even been to a beach or to New York City. Never taken a plane ride or even been to an amusement park. I don't do anything when I'm at school and I . . ." I trailed off, blowing out a breath. "Anyway, I'm boring."

One brow arched up. "Okay."

God, I needed to find a needle and some thread for my mouth.

"But we're going to have to agree to disagree on that, too." Humor shone through his warm eyes, and as close as we were, I noticed the darker flecks of brown near his pupils.

I tried to step away again, but didn't get anywhere. My chest rose sharply on a deep inhale. "Why do you care so much about this bar?"

It was his turn to blink. "What do you mean?"

"Why have you put so much effort into it? You could be working at a better place, probably dealing with less stress than running a bar you don't own."

Jax stared at me a moment, and then his hands slid off my shoulders, down my upper arms, leaving a trail of shivers in their wake before he dropped them completely. "You know, if you knew me better, you wouldn't have to ask the question."

"I don't know you."

"Exactly." He stepped around me and headed back out to the bar, leaving me standing in the hall, more than a little confused.

Of course I didn't know him. I'd *just* met him yesterday, so what the hell? It was just a question. I turned, flipping my hair back over my left shoulder. I breathed in. Then I breathed out.

I had a problem.

Well, I had *lots* of problems, but I also had a new one.

I wanted to get to know Jackson—Jax—James better and I shouldn't. That should be the last thing I wanted, but it wasn't.

Bartending was *hard*.

Because of basically growing up in bars, I'd avoided them once I'd left home and it had been years since I'd really been inside one. Back in the day, I knew how to make most mixed drinks just from seeing them done so many times, but now? I officially sucked at it. Like sucked hard-core. On almost every mixed drink, my eyes were glued to the cocktail menu taped near the serving well.

Luckily, Jax wasn't a dick about it. When someone came in, which they started to do around three, one after another, and they ordered a drink that sounded like a different language to me, he didn't make it hard for me. Instead, he stepped back, giving soft corrections if I reached for the wrong mixer or poured too little or too much of a liquor.

Having worked as a waitress, I knew I could smile my way through about every mess-up. With old and rheumy-eyed men, it worked even better.

"Take your time, sweetie," one older man said when I had to toss his drink since I wasn't good at free pouring and probably poured enough liquor to kill the dude. "All I got is time."

"Thank you." I smiled as I redid the drink, which was a simple gin and tonic. "Better?"

The man took a sip and winked. "Perfect."

As he stepped away, heading to a table near one of the pool tables, Jax moved in from behind me. "Here. Let me show you how to free pour." Reaching around me, he grabbed one of the shorter glasses and then picked up the gin. "Paying attention?"

Uh.

He was standing so close to my side I could feel his freaking body heat. He could be talking about how many times Mars circled the sun for all I knew. "Sure," I murmured.

"We don't really use jiggers, but it's pretty simple. Basically, for every count, you're pouring a quarter ounce. So if you're pouring one and a half ounces, you're going to count to six. For a half ounce, you're going to count to two."

Sounded easy, but after pouring a couple of them, I still wasn't pouring the same amount with each count, and all I was doing was wasting liquor.

"It only gets better with practice," he said, propping his hip against the bar top. "Luckily, most of the people are beer folk, straight-up shots, and a few of the simpler mixed drinks."

"Yeah, but someone's going to come in here asking for a Jax special, and I'm going to look like an idiot," I said as I wiped up the liquor I'd gotten on the bar.

Jax chuckled. "Only I make that, so you don't have to worry about it."

I pictured him offering that drink to girls he wanted to lay, and then was immediately disturbed by how much I didn't like that image. "Well, that's good to know."

"You're doing fine." Pushing off the bar, he placed his hand on the small of my back as he leaned in, his lips dangerously close to my ear, causing me to stiffen as he spoke, and warm air danced over my skin. "Just keep smiling like you are, and any guy will forgive you."

My eyes popped wide as he sauntered off to the other end of the bar, leaning down on his folded arms as one of the guys at the bar said something to him.

I think I forgot how to breathe while I stood there, staring at the back of a fuzzy white and balding head of some guy.

There was no doubt in my mind that Jax knew how to bring the flirt. As I pushed away from the bar top, clearing my face of what I hoped wasn't a stupid grin, I chanced a look down the bar.

Jax was laughing. He had this deep, unfettered laugh, where he'd raise his chin and let loose the deep, rumbling sound like he didn't have a care in the world. The sound pulled at the corners of my lips. Whoever he was talking to looked about his age, which was a mystery age currently. The guy was also attractive—dark brown hair, a little longer than I'd like, but not as long as Jase's. From what I could see, he was also broad in the shoulders.

Hot guys always flocked together, and there had to be some kind of scientific evidence supporting this fact.

Roxy arrived at the start of the evening shift, and she was yet another surprise. I wasn't the tallest girl around, coming in around five and seven inches, but she was a tiny thing. Barely crossing over five feet, she had what looked like a mass of chestnut hair streaked with deep red piled into a bun atop her head. She was rocking Buddy Holly black frames that added to the impish cuteness of her face, and was dressed much like I was, in jeans and a shirt. I decided that I immediately liked her, mainly because she was wearing a *Supernatural* T-shirt with Dean and Sam on it.

Her wide eyes flickered over me as she crossed the bar, and Jax quickly tagged her, motioning her over to where he was still leaning against the bar. Whatever he said to Roxy caused her to glance in my direction.

I hated being the new person.

When he was finally done with her, he went back to his conversation with the other hot guy. I forced myself to take a deep, calming breath. Meeting people for the first time was . . . hard. Teresa probably never saw that side of me because we quickly bonded over our mutual disinterest in music appreciation, but typically, I wasn't good at meeting people. As pathetic as it sounded, I always worried if they were busy wondering about the scar on my face, and I knew they would, because *I* would. It was human nature.

As she came around the bar grinning, I wondered if people could actually *see* her behind the bar. "Hi," she said, shoving out a dainty hand. "I'm Roxanne, but everyone calls me Roxy. *Please* call me Roxy."

"Calla." I shook her hand, laughing. "Nice to meet you, *Roxy.*"

She slid her purse off her shoulder. "Jax says you go to college at Shepherd, studying nursing?"

My gaze flickered over to where he stood. Damn, he worked and talked fast. "Yeah. You're at the community college?"

"Yeppers peppers." Reaching up, she adjusted her glasses. "Nothing as cool as nursing. Working toward a computer graphics degree."

"That's pretty damn cool. You can draw, too?"

She nodded. "Yep. Drawing and painting kind of runs in the family. Not the most lucrative career choice, but it's something that I love to do. Figured taking it into the graphic design world would be better than choosing the life of a starving artist."

"I'm jealous," I admitted, brushing my hair over my left shoulder. "I've always wanted to be able to draw, but I can't even draw a stick figure without it looking half stupid. Two things I generally lack—art and talent."

A laugh burst from her. "I'm sure you're talented at something else."

I wrinkled my nose. "Does talking and not knowing when to shut up count?"

Roxy laughed again, and I saw Jax glance at us. "That is a true talent. I'm going to drop off my purse. I'll be right back."

When she came back, we worked the bar together and, like Jax, she was supercool and patient. The customers loved her kooky sense of humor, which included doodling on the napkins she gave out, and apparently had to do with her T-shirt choices. It seemed like a lot of people rolling in checked out what her shirt said before they even placed an order.

The bar wasn't too busy, but as Thursday evening rolled on by, the seating area filled up, and because I was slow, I moved out from behind the bar.

Jax caught my arm. "You're forgetting something."

"What?"

The half grin appeared as he turned his hand around my arm, tugging me toward him. I bit down on my lip as I stumbled forward, having no idea what he was about. I got close to him, close enough that when he reached down to a cubbyhole, his arm brushed my thigh.

"Got to wear an apron when you're out there."

My brows rose as I stared at the half apron. "Seriously?"

He jerked his chin at Pearl.

I sighed when I saw she had one tied around her waist, and then snatched it from him. "Whatever."

"It goes great with your shirt."

I rolled my eyes.

Jax laughed. "Let me help."

"The last time I checked, I can tie an apron without—" I gaped at him. Somehow the apron was back in his hand and his other hand landed on my hip, startling me. "What are you doing?"

"Helping you out." He bent his head toward my left ear, and I immediately turned my cheek. "Jumpy?" he asked.

I shook my head, finding that I had no idea how to form syllables, and that was embarrassing.

Without saying a word, he turned me around so my back was to his front, and then he slipped an arm between his waist and mine. I didn't dare move.

"You can breathe, you know." His arm trailed across my lower stomach, setting off a chain of flutters, as he spread the apron.

"I'm breathing," I forced out.

Amusement colored his tone. "You sure about that, honey?"

"Yeah."

Pearl entered the bar just then, carrying a tray of clean glasses. She arched her brows in our direction. "Getting hands-on, Jackie boy?"

"Jackie boy?" I mumbled.

Jax chuckled not too far from my ear. "Tying knots is hard."

"Uh-huh," replied Pearl.

"And I like getting hands-on with her," he added.

My face felt like I'd been baking in the sun by the time he finished, which was an absurdly long time if you thought about it. When I felt the final tug of the knot being secured, he gripped both sides of my hips.

Holy sparks in a room of flammable material.

"All good." His hands slid off my hips, and then he was giving me a gentle shove toward the exit to the bar floor. "Have fun."

Shooting him a look over my shoulder, my lips pursed as he let loose that damn laugh that I decided that I did not, under any circumstances, find sexy. Nope. Not at all.

It was totally sexy.

Seven

Helping work the floor with Pearl, taking bar orders, and running food from the kitchen wasn't bad. Wasn't sure what it meant when it came to tips, and since I wasn't really employed, there was no hourly wage, so I hoped it didn't mean suck.

Mindless work, but I didn't think about much of anything as I zoomed back and forth, and I could almost pretend that I had chosen this job out of want and not need. The only thing I couldn't help wonder about was Mom, where she was and if she was okay. It was a familiar worry I'd spent many years obsessing over until I could practically feel the ulcers forming in my belly. I wasn't going to do that again. At least that's what I told myself, but if I was being honest with myself, and who wanted to do that on the regular, I knew better.

I dropped off a plate of wings at a table I was guessing was full of off-duty cops or army guys, based on their nearly identical buzz haircuts. And holy billy goats, there were a lot of yummy-looking guys sitting there. The hot guy Jax had been chatting with earlier had joined them, and I was a little nervous approaching their table since I was busy picturing each of the guys in different uniforms and liking what I saw in my head.

"Thanks," one of the guys said as I placed a truckload of napkins on the table. Up close, he had the most amazing blue eyes.

I smiled as I clasped my hands together. "Need any refills or anything?"

"We're good," another one spoke up, grinning.

Nodding, I quickly skedaddled back to the bar to relieve Roxy for her break. I had no idea how Jax looked like he just arrived, full of smiles and energy, even though he'd been here as long as I had. Working a kink out of my neck, I headed to where a guy who couldn't be much older than me was waiting. The day had been long and flip-flops were so not appropriate for bar work, causing my feet to ache, but I didn't want to complain.

The cash in the pocket of my apron helped keep my lips in a smile formation.

"What can I get you?"

He rubbed a hand across the front of his oversized white shirt as his gaze quickly shifted away from me. "Uh, how about a Bud?"

"Tap or bottle?"

"Bottle." His gaze swung back to me as he hitched up his baggy jeans.

"Coming right up." Turning, I stepped around Jax and grabbed a bottle. When Mona's got busy, it had to be crazy behind here, and I was kind of, surprisingly, excited about the prospect. There had to be a sort of Zen in being that busy. Heading back to the customer, I popped the lid, smiling as a little cool air rolled up from the open neck. "Tab or pay as you go?"

"Pay as I go." He took the beer as he leaned back from the bar and muttered, "Shame."

My brow arched up. "Shame?" Seriously doubted that was his name or something. "I'm sorry?"

The guy took a long swig of his beer and his brows knitted. "It's a shame."

I glanced around, not sure what he was talking about and wondering if he was already drunk. I hadn't had to cut anyone off yet, and I really wasn't looking forward to that moment. Out of the corner of my eyes, I saw Jax stop and angle his body toward us. "I'm sorry," I said. "I'm not really following."

With the hand holding his beer, he made a circle in the air around about where my head was. "Your face," he clarified, and I sucked in a sharp breath. "It's a shame."

Every muscle in my body locked up as I stared at the guy. Somehow, maybe because I'd been so busy running back and forth, I'd done the impossible. Forgotten about the scar. That wasn't an easy thing to do. Not only had the scar cut into my skin, it had sliced deep, becoming a very tangible part of me. I knew it was visible, even with the Dermablend, just faded into a thin cut, but I had forgotten.

Taking another deep swig of his beer, he continued. "I bet you were really hot one time."

That statement stung. Oh yeah, it was like stepping on a pissed-off hornet. It shouldn't bother me, some random asshole's opinion, but the sting coursed through me. I didn't know what to do or how to respond. It had been so long since anyone even commented on it. Probably because people who knew me, who weren't shocked by the scar, always surrounded me when the makeup faded after a long day.

"Get the fuck out."

I jumped at the sound of the deep voice growling behind me and turned. Jax stood there, his eyes flashing and jaw tight, set in a hard line. Dumbly, I wondered why he wanted me to leave. I hadn't done anything, and it wasn't like he didn't realize my face was slightly on the disfigured side.

But he wasn't talking to me.

Of course not.

Duh.

Jax was staring down the guy on the other side of the bar, and then he was moving forward. Slamming one hand down on the bar top, he launched up over the bar, landing nimbly on the other side, inches from the guy.

"Holy crap," I whispered, eyes wide.

I'd never seen anyone do something like that. Didn't even know it was possible. Jax hadn't even hit a bar stool. It was like he propelled himself over the bar all the time. Maybe that's what he did during downtime, winging himself back and forth over the bar.

Pearl stopped in the middle of the bar floor, staring at Jax, and she didn't look too surprised, which I found odd. His buddy at the table stood. The rest of the guys at the table were twisted in their seats, faces set, but not with curiosity. More like they were ready to jump to their feet any second.

Jax snatched the bottle out of the guy's grasp as he slammed a hand in the middle of the guy's chest, knocking him back several feet.

"Whoa, man, what the hell's your problem?" White Shirt asked, catching himself.

"I said, get the fuck out of here." Jax got right up in his face, and him being a good head taller than the other guy, it was pretty impressive. "Right this fucking second, you wannabe fucking gangster."

"What the fuck? I didn't do anything wrong." White Shirt shot back. "Just trying to get a drink."

"I don't give two fucks what you were trying to do." The muscles in his back rippled under his shirt. "All I care about right now is you getting the fuck out of the bar."

"Man, that's messed up." White Shirt Guy cocked his head like he was about to throw down, which by the sound and look of Jax, I was going to say would be a very bad idea. "You can't just kick me out for that shit."

And White Shirt Guy pointed right at me.

My stomach tumbled again, and before I realized what I was doing, I'd reached up, pressing my fingers against the slightly raised line on my cheek. I jerked my hand away.

He wasn't done. "What did you expect, man? Not my fault she's Mona's daughter. Ain't like you can't notice her face—"

"Finish that sentence and I'll fuck *your* face up so badly you'll be seeing double for the rest of your life, ass hat."

Oh God, this was getting out of hand. I stepped against the bar top. "Jax, just drop it. Not a big deal."

The White Shirt Guy's face flushed a deep pink. "Aw, bro, you're really starting to piss me off."

Thank God his friend was up and standing beside them now because Jax didn't seem to hear me. "Come on, Mack," Jax's friend said, catching him by the arm and not too gently leading him to the door. "Get the hell out of here before Jax lays into you."

"What the fuck?" Mack exploded, causing me to jump again, and the muscles to tighten in my neck and back. "You're not on duty, Reece, so you can—"

"On duty or off, you might want to rethink that sentence."

Ah, so Reece, his friend, was a cop. Hands shaking, I smoothed them down my thighs, hoping this whole scene would be over soon. Everyone in the bar was listening over the music, watching the confrontation go down. That made everything so much worse.

Jax stalked them toward the door, his hands clenched into big fists at his sides.

"You fucked up," Mack said, stopping at the door, having to get one last word in. "You think you got trouble now? You ain't seen shit, you mother—"

"God, you guys never fucking learn," Reece muttered, shoving Mack out the door, and as he disappeared into the night, Reece glanced back at Jax. "I'll make sure the piece of shit gets out of here."

"Thanks," Jax muttered, wheeling back around. His gaze landed on me.

"Was it because of Mona?" Pearl asked in a low voice, and that answered why she wasn't surprised when Jax had vaulted over the bar. "Did she—"

"No," he growled, heading around the bar. "Watch the bar until Roxy gets off break."

Confusion pulled at Pearl's lips, but she nodded as she smoothed a hand back over her blond hair. "Got it."

I didn't move as I watched Jax stalk around the bar, stopping at the entrance. He motioned at me. "Come here."

My heart was pounding, and I didn't want to move forward, because he sounded and looked pissed, and I wasn't sure if he was mad at me. After all, he'd relented quickly on the whole idea of me working here, but that didn't mean he was pro Calla. Considering a fight had almost broken out the *first* night I was working probably wasn't good.

"Come here," Jax demanded again, voice hard as slate. "Now."

Breath lodging somewhere in my throat, my feet moved toward him. As I passed Pearl on the way out, she sent me a concerned look. I knew I hadn't done anything wrong, but still, none of this was good.

"Jax—"

He clasped my hand, pulling me the rest of the way out from behind the bar. "Not right now."

It took a lot in me, but I clamped my mouth shut as he led me back down the hall, toward the office. Opening the door, he hauled me inside, and my stomach was somewhere around my toes as he slammed the door shut. I tried again, but when he wheeled on me, his hand still around mine, all the words died on the tip of my tongue.

Our gazes collided for a fraction of a second, and then I dipped my chin to the left and drew in a deep breath. "I'm sorry about what happened out there. I—"

"Are you fucking apologizing?"

My gaze rose to his. "Yeah, I guess. I mean, the guy was a dick, but he—"

"You're fucking serious?" His eyes were so dark I wondered how they changed color like that. "You have no reason to apologize for that fucking asshole."

"It's my first night and you had to kick someone out."

"I don't care if it was your first night or your tenth night, someone acts like that, then they're out. No second chances." He was staring down at me, and the look in his eyes was so intense it was like he could see right through me.

"You're not mad at me?"

"What?" His eyes widened as his hand slipped up to my elbow. "Why in the hell would I be mad at you, Calla?"

I shook my head. Thinking about it, it did sound like a stupid question.

His eyes narrowed. "You can't be serious."

Suddenly, desperation to be out of this room, or at least change the subject, washed over me with the force of a tidal wave. "He said something about trouble—Mack did. Was he talking about Mom?"

"That doesn't matter right now."

I thought it did. "Then why am I back here?"

"I wanted to make sure you were okay."

The words repeated themselves through my head. He wanted to make sure I was okay and that . . . that was sweet.

"You did nothing wrong out there," Jax went on as he squeezed my arm gently, reassuringly. "I'm pissed because that was utter bullshit."

"Yeah, well, it was, but . . ."

He cocked his head to the side. "But what?"

Warmth crept into my face, and I took a step back, going as far as I could with his hand around my elbow.

"What, Calla?" He reclaimed the space, the tips of his boots brushing my toes.

I took another step back, and I was against the wall, back flush with it, and he was still right in front of me. The entire length of my body shimmered with awareness. I started to look away, to turn my head.

Like the night before, two fingers curled around my chin, forcing my face straight on with his, and it was with his head lowered near mine. And his mouth . . . it was inches from mine.

"You don't believe what he said, do you?" His voice was deceptively low, soft.

My throat dried.

He let go of my arm and pressed his hand against the wall, beside my head, keeping the other one at my chin. "I can't believe this shit."

I blinked. "It's not like I have a low self-esteem. I just believe in reality—like I'm Realistic Rachel."

"Realistic Rachel?" His brows knitted as he mouthed the words again silently.

"Yeah," I breathed. What I was about to say was true. "I know what people see when they look at me. Most people don't say anything because they're not jerks, but I know what they see. It's been that way since I was ten years old. And there's no changing that."

Jax stared at me, his full lips slightly parted. "What do they see, Calla?"

"Do I really need to spell that out?" I shot back, irritated and frustrated and about a thousand other things. "I think it's pretty obvious."

His eyes searched mine. "Yeah, it is obvious."

Even though that's what I'd been saying this whole time, hearing him agree still felt like a punch to the boob. I wanted to look away, but he wasn't allowing it. "I think I need to get back out—"

His mouth landed on mine.

Oh my lawd . . .

There was no warning, nothing that would've given away what he'd been about to do. One second I was talking, and then the next, his warm mouth was on mine.

Jax kissed me.

Eight

$\mathcal{M}$y brain short-circuited the moment it fully recognized that Jax was kissing me—that, in fact, his lips really were on mine.

And it wasn't just a peck on the lips.

No, it wasn't deep and there weren't tongues involved, nothing like the kisses I read about in romance novels, the wet kind that seemed a little gross to me, but I imagined, if done right, would have me dropping my shorts like no tomorrow, but this kiss . . . it was real.

His lips were melded to mine, and I was awed by the way they felt. They were soft, but firm, and I didn't know one thing could be both. They followed the curve of my lips, as if he were just mapping them out.

My arms were frozen at my sides, but I could feel my body start to lean forward, off the wall and toward his. Our bodies didn't connect, though, which was probably a good thing.

I was already only seconds away from combusting.

Jax lifted his head from mine, and I realized then that my eyes were closed. Even so, I could feel his gaze on my warm cheeks, on the tip of my nose . . . my lips.

"You kissed me," I whispered, and yeah, it was a stupid statement, but I was feeling pretty stupid.

"Yeah." His voice sounded deeper, gruffer. Sexier. "I did."

I forced my eyes open and was staring at an unofficial member of the Hot Guy Brigade.

He leaned in, his arm against the wall taking his weight as he dropped his hand from my chin. "I don't kiss girls that I don't find hot as hell or beautiful. So, you get my point?"

There were fuzz balls in my brain. "You kissed me to prove a point?"

A ghost of a smile appeared. "Felt like it was the quickest way to prove the point."

That it was. I didn't know if I should feel offended that he kissed me to prove a point and that most likely meant there was nothing else driving the kiss, or if I should be flattered that by kissing me he thought I was hot as hell and beautiful.

I didn't know what to think or say, so I just slumped back against the wall as he pushed off it. Half grin in place, he reached over and opened the door.

"Nothing like that will ever happen again in this bar," Jax said, and then he was out the door.

He'd said that like it was a promise—a promise there was no way he could keep, but it was another . . . sweet thing to do.

I closed my eyes again, letting out a breath as I ducked my chin to my chest. Three weeks ago, I was living in Shepherdstown with my Three F's, close to graduating, and this bar wasn't even a forethought in my head. My life had been focused around goals—graduating, finding a job in nursing, and reaping the benefits of following through with said goal.

That was all.

Weeks later, everything had changed. Here I was, standing in Mona's with an MIA mom, no money, my future completely up in the air, and an unofficial member of the Hot Guy Brigade had kissed me.

Nothing planned about that and none of those things fell into my carefully crafted Three F's plan.

But that kiss . . . to prove a point or not, it had been important. Really important. After all, it had been my first real kiss.

For about a billion reasons, I was grateful when Pearl appeared in the hall, telling me she was taking me home. Although I hated being shuffled around like I had no say in what I was doing, after what had gone down with Mack and then Jax, I wasn't against getting out of the bar and clearing my head of the nasty and the not so nasty.

I'd grabbed my purse and said my good-byes to Clyde. On the way out, I told myself not to look for Jax, and I managed to listen to that demand for about two seconds. At the door, I glanced at the busy bar. Jax was there with Roxy. Both were smiling and laughing as they were working the customers.

Roxy looked up, giving me a quick, distracted wave, which I returned.

Jax didn't even look up.

A twinge of unease, and something far more annoying and ridiculous, lit up my chest. I stomped the feeling down as I followed Pearl outside and focused on getting my car back ASAP the next day.

Pearl chatted idly as she drove me to the house, once again without me having to give her directions. I liked her, and being that she was probably the same age as my mom, I kind of imagined that this was what my mom would look like if she hadn't decided to go traipsing through trashville.

When Pearl arrived at the house, she stopped me before I climbed out. "Oh, I almost forget." Stretching back against the seat of her older-model Honda, she pulled out a wad of cash. "The boys who ordered the wings left you a tip."

Ah, the cop table. Smiling, I took the money, already knowing that it was way too much for a normal tip. "Thank you."

"No problem. Now get your butt inside and get some rest." She flashed a big smile.

I opened the door. "Drive safe."

Pearl nodded and she waited until I'd unlocked the door and stepped inside. Flipping on the hallway light, I tried to ignore the nostalgic feeling washing over me. My eyes closed and I was transported back to when I was sixteen, coming home late from spending the evening with Clyde at the bar. I didn't have to imagine the sound of Mom's laugh. She always had a good laugh—boisterous and throaty, the kind of laugh that drew people to her, but the downside of her laugh was she didn't do it often. And when she did, it usually meant she was flying so high she could lick the clouds.

That night had been bad.

The house had been packed with her friends, other overgrown children who probably had real kids at home and were more interested in partying than being responsible.

I walked down the hallway, seeing what had been there five years ago. Some stranger dude passed out on the living room floor. Mom on the couch, bottle in her hand; another guy I'd never seen before had his face buried in her neck and a hand between her legs.

The guy on the floor hadn't moved.

Mom had barely been aware that I was home. It had been the guy all up on her that had noticed and they had called me to join in, to *party.* I'd gone upstairs and had wanted to pretend that they weren't there.

Except that guy on the floor still hadn't moved for an hour, and finally someone in the house had grown concerned.

He'd been dead for God knows how long.

I stared at the spot near the couch, shuddering, because I could see the guy there still. Shirtless. Dirtied jeans. He lay facedown and his arms were awkward at his sides. People had bailed out of the house faster than I could blink, leaving Mom and me alone with a dead guy on the living room floor. Police had shown. It hadn't been pretty. Paperwork had been filed, but no one from child services showed. No one came around. Not a real big surprise there.

Mom had gotten cleaned up after that . . . well, for a few months. That had been a good couple of months.

Shaking my head, I dropped my purse on the couch and pushed those thoughts away. I reached into my pocket, grabbing a hair tie, and pulled my hair up into a quick twist.

Not wanting to spend another night on the couch and not up to staying upstairs, I finally caved and stripped the sheets off the bed downstairs and threw them in the washer with the blanket I'd found in the upstairs linen closet, resisting the urge to Lysol the hell out of the mattress. The only thing stopping me was that the mattress seemed relatively new, and there were no suspicious stains or smells radiating from it.

Feeling antsy and full of energy instead of tired, I cleaned up Mom's bedroom, throwing everything that looked like trash in the black garbage bags I'd found in the pantry, and then placed the bags on the back porch. There hadn't been any clothes in the tall dresser and the vanity, something I hadn't checked before, and there were just a few jeans and sweaters in the closet. What I found on the floor didn't add up to a full wardrobe.

Further proof that Mom really had hit the road.

I didn't know what to think about that or how to feel. She stole from me, throwing a major wrench into my life. She'd stolen from others. And she was out there, either freaking out or so messed up she didn't even know what she'd done.

Digging the money out of my pocket, I counted out thirty bucks and added that to the twenty dollars the cops had left. That amount seemed excessive, and probably had more to do with pity than my service, but fifty in tips my first night wasn't bad. I stashed the cash in my wallet after moving my purse into the downstairs bedroom.

Sighing wearily, I made up the bed and put away the clothes I'd brought with me. I took a quick shower and dried off in what Mom used to call her "cozy" bathroom. Cozy, because if you spread your legs and stretched out your arms, you could pretty much touch the sink, bathtub, and toilet.

As I turned to head out into the bedroom, the fogged-over mirror caught my attention. I don't know why I did what I did next. It had been years since I even briefly entertained the idea, but I leaned forward, swiping my hand across the mirror, clearing it.

Maybe it was the stress of everything going on. Maybe it was what the guy—Mack—had said at the bar. Maybe it was Jax and his kiss. Probably the kiss, but it didn't matter, because I was doing what I was doing.

I'd always avoided looking at myself, especially immediately afterward, and then through the many skin grafts that came afterward. Like I said—years since I looked at my body in the mirror. It was just something that I didn't allow myself to do.

I bit down on my lower lip as I forced myself to really look. Not a glimpse, and my next breath lodged somewhere between my sternum and my throat.

My collarbone was okay, a peachy cream complexion. I had a great skin tone, perfect for piling on makeup and showing it off. My upper chest was smooth. Then my gaze dipped.

Everything looked like a fucked-up Picasso painting from there.

The same kind of scar that screwed up my face had gotten a hold of my left breast, slicing right over the top of the swell, across the areola, narrowly missing my nipple. I was lucky. Having only one nipple would suck. Not that anyone saw either of my nipples, but still, I didn't want to think of myself as One Nipple Calla. My other breast was fine. Both were decent sized, I thought, but the skin between them was discolored, a lighter color. Second-degree burns. Scarring was just pigment changes, but then there was my stomach.

I looked like an old couch that someone had used different flesh tone fabrics to piece together. Seriously. Third-degree burns were no joke. None whatsoever.

Patches of the skin were a deep pink, other parts faded to a rose color, and otherwise smooth, but the edges of the scars along my side were raised. I could see that in the mirror. Kind of looked like a birthmark, but when I twisted around and craned my neck, I saw my back. From just above my rump and all the way across my shoulder blades, it matched my front, except the scars were worse, rugged and puckered skin, almost wrinkled in some areas, and a much deeper color, almost brown.

There had been no skin grafts there.

Dad had left by that point, disappearing into the drama- and grief-free great unknown. When I graduated from high school, with the help from Clyde, I'd managed to track down my father.

He'd remarried.

He was living in Florida.

He didn't have any kids.

And after one phone call with him, I knew he didn't want to rekindle any father/daughter bond.

So he'd been gone when it came time to do the skin grafts on my back, and Mom . . . well, I guessed she'd forgotten about the doctor appointments or stopped caring or something.

The back of my eyes stung as I forced the air to become unstuck. The pain from the burns had been the worst thing I'd ever experienced in my life, at least physically. Many times, even as young as I had been, I had wanted death in those hours and days afterward. The scars didn't hurt now. They just looked like crap.

I closed my eyes as I turned back around, but I could still see myself. That hadn't been pretty. Could've been worse. When I'd been on the burn floor, I'd seen worse. Little kids that played with fire. Adults in fiery car accidents. Skin literally melted. And then there were the people—*the kids*—who didn't survive fires, be it the heat or the smoke. So I knew it could've been worse, but no matter what I did, no matter how far I traveled or how long I stayed away, the night of the fire had left its mark on me, physically and emotionally.

And it had done a number on Mom.

Kissing.

I bit down on my lip until I tasted blood.

Kissing was stupid. Crushing on Brandon had been dumb. Kissing Jax Johnson was even dumber. Everything was dumb.

Hurrying away from the mirror, I changed into a pair of cotton sleep shorts with a long-sleeve thin shirt. For some reason, no matter the time of year, this house always stayed cool and could get downright chilly at night, so I pulled on a pair of long socks to keep my toesies warm.

I headed into the kitchen, tummy grumbling, but the trip was pretty pointless because all there was in the pantry was saltine crackers. Grabbing the box, I promised myself that no matter what condition my car was in, I was going to the grocery store and spending some of that fifty dollars on oodles and noodles.

Taking a packet of what I hoped wasn't stale crackers and the leftover tea I'd had last night into the living room, I came to a startled stop when I heard a knock on the front door.

I dropped the packet of crackers on the couch cushion and turned to look at the clock on the wall. If the time was accurate, it was almost one in the morning, so what the hell?

Standing still, I winced when I heard the knock come again. Nervous, I spun and hurried quietly to the narrow and short hallway. Stretching up, I peered through the peephole.

I frowned.

From what I could see, no one was there. Pressing my hands against the door, I stared through the peephole. The porch was empty.

"What the hell?" I muttered.

Thinking I might be going crazy, I rocked back and unlocked the door. Opening it up about a foot, I immediately recognized my mistake. The porch hadn't been empty. The guy had been sitting down and he rose suddenly, causing my heart to throw itself against my ribs painfully.

What I could see of the guy in the dim light wasn't good. Tall and really skinny, he had shoulder-length blond hair that was stringy and greasy. His face was gaunt and lips chapped. Yuck. I didn't want to see anything else. I inched back, clutching the doorknob, about to shut it when he slammed a large hand into the door.

"I need to see Mona," he rasped in a scratchy, dry voice.

"She's n-not here. Sorry." I started to shut the door again, but he got one leg in and then pushed—pushed harder than I thought he could, flinging me back. I bounced into the wall, cracking the back of my head. There was a flare of pain that quickly spiked when the door flew at me, smacking into my forehead.

"Holy crap," I gasped.

The greasy guy stepped inside, glancing at where I was smashed like a gross bug. "Sorry," he grunted, hauling the door off me and kicking it closed with a scuffed-up biker boot. "I need to see Mona."

I blinked a couple of times as I pressed my palm against the side of my head. For a moment, I think I saw birdies.

"Mona!" the man shouted, moving down the hall.

Wincing, I dropped my hand and straightened just as the guy walked into the living room, still shouting my mom's name like she was going to magically appear out of thin air.

I hurried down the hall, still somewhat in a daze. "She's not here."

Greasy Guy stood in front of the couch, his shoulders hunched. In the brighter light, I really didn't want to see what I saw. The man was dirty—his shirt and his jeans. His arms were bare, the insides of them covered in red, puckered marks.

Shit.

Track marks.

Greasy Guy was strung-out.

Shit galore.

"Mona isn't here," I tried again, my heart kicking into high gear, which caused the ache in my temple to feel like a miniature jackhammer.

He turned to me, his jaw working. "She owes me."

Shit galore everywhere and on my shoes.

Greasy Guy turned to me, and his eyes were a pale blue, unfocused. I wasn't sure he even saw me. "She's got shit here. I know she does."

My eyes widened. There had so better be no shit here.

Without saying another word, he brushed past me, heading for the bedroom. My heart lurched in my chest. "What are you doing?" I demanded.

He didn't respond as he went straight for the bed, ripping off the clean sheets and blankets.

"Hey!" I shouted.

Still, he ignored me as he slipped his hands under the mattress and then flipped it over. When he found nothing, he let out a string of curses.

Oh, this was so not good and quickly spiraling out of control.

I started toward him, but he threw out a jacked-up arm and growled, "Stay the fuck back."

My stomach tumbled, and I stayed the fuck back as he went to the dresser, pulled out my folded clothes, and then went over to the closet. Out of some small miracle, he didn't go for my purse after demolishing the room I'd straightened.

Then he stopped at the entrance to the bathroom, his back straightening. A strange look crossed his face. "Damnit." Greasy Guy turned and jogged out of the bedroom, aiming for the stairs.

Oh no. Where in the hell did he think he was going? Hands shaking, I whirled around and got in front of him, blocking the stairs. "I'm sorry, but she's not here. I don't know where she is or what you're looking for, but you need to—"

He planted a hand in the center of my chest, pushing me back, and then he got right up in my face. His teeth were yellow, some completely rotten out, and his breath smelled like days-old garbage. Bile rose in my throat.

"Look, I don't know who you are and I don't give a fuck. But I don't have a problem with you," he said. "So, don't make me have a problem with you. Okay?"

I forced a jerky nod. I did not want to have a problem with him. "Got it."

He stared at me a moment, and then his gaze narrowed over my left cheek. "You're Mona's kid, aren't you?"

I didn't answer because I wasn't sure if that would mean I'd have a problem with him if I did.

"Shit sucks for you," he said, and then dropped his hand. Greasy Guy climbed the stairs.

Against common sense, I followed him up the stairs and into the loft bedroom—my old bedroom. Greasy Guy knew what he was looking for. He went straight to the closet and ripped the door open so hard I was surprised it didn't come off the hinges. Then he dropped to his knees and leaned into the tight space. Holding my breath, I crept behind him, debating if I should go for the lamp on the nightstand and knock him out.

Greasy Guy reached in, brushing shoe boxes out of the way, and then I couldn't see what he was doing when he grunted and jerked back. He tossed a piece of the wall aside—a piece that had been cut out, which probably hid a cubbyhole.

Oh no.

"Fuck yeah," Greasy Man breathed as he scuttled back out of the closet, stumbling to his feet. "Jackpot. Motherfucking jackpot."

I didn't want to look, but I had to. Greasy Guy was holding, not one, but at least eight Ziploc bags in his hands—bags full of something off brown that reminded me of clumpy brown sugar.

"Oh my God," I whispered.

Greasy Guy didn't hear me. He was staring at the bags in his hands like he was seconds away from ripping one open and shoving his face into the crap.

My knees felt weak. There had been drugs in the house, drugs hidden in a secret spot in the closet of *my* old bedroom. Not pot or something else relatively harmless, but something I bet was real bad and real costly.

Greasy Guy seemed to forget that I existed, which was okey-dokey fine with me. He headed down the stairs, and then a few seconds later, I heard the front door slam shut, causing me to jump.

I don't know how long I stood in the bedroom, staring at the open closet door before I forced my feet to move. I went downstairs and into the bedroom, dragging my cell phone out of my purse. My hand shook as I called Clyde.

He answered on the third ring. "You okay, baby girl?"

It was late, and he was probably still at the bar. "Some guy was here."

There was a pause, and then his voice got real low and real serious. "What happened?"

I told him everything in a rush, and then he told me to make sure the door was locked—good point—and to hold still. He was coming over. There wasn't anything he could do now, but I appreciated it. Admittedly, I was freaked-out. Way freaked-out.

I made sure the closet door in Mom's bedroom was closed, reapplied my makeup even though it was only Clyde, and then the next twenty minutes or so, I sat on the couch, clutching the phone to my chest until there was a quick, loud knock on the front door.

I checked the peephole again, and this time I saw someone out there—someone that sent my already overworked heart into cardiac arrest territory.

Jax was standing on the other side of the door.

Nine

"*W*hat the hell were you thinking?" was the first thing out of Jax's mouth when I opened the front door.

I had a better question. "What are you doing here? I called Clyde."

"And Clyde told me, so I'm here." He pushed inside, pulled the door from my grasp, and pushed it shut, locking it. "You didn't answer my question."

Having not come to terms with the fact that it was Jax that was suddenly standing in the foyer, I blinked slowly. "What question?"

"Why in the hell did you answer the door in the middle of the night?"

"Oh. I checked the peephole first, you know."

Jax stared at me.

"And I didn't see anyone," I added in my defense.

He folded well-defined arms across his chest. "So, let me get this correct. You heard knocking on your front door, went and actually used the peephole, but when you didn't see anyone, you thought, *Oh, what the hell, I'll just open the door*? Did it ever occur to you that someone could've been hiding?"

Oh wow, he looked and sounded pissed, but he could kiss my rosy red behind. "The guy wasn't hiding. He was sitting down."

His dark brows flew up. "Did you know that when you opened the door?"

"Well, no, but—"

"So, why in the hell did you answer the door?" he demanded again, eyes turning dark.

"Look, I get that answering the door was stupid." My hand tightened around my cell phone, and I sort of wanted to slam my other fist into his chest. "I wasn't thinking."

"No shit," he growled.

My eyes narrowed. "I get it. I don't need you to keep pointing it out."

"Jesus Christ, Calla, I've told you about the kind of shit your mom was messed up in, and I told you not to stay here. The least you could do is not answer the door in the middle of the night."

I drew in a deep breath as I reached up and brushed the still damp hair back behind my right ear. "Got it. Thanks for hand-delivering your message. Now you can . . ." I trailed off, eyes widening.

A scary look entered his eyes, and then he was right in front of me, moving like he had in the office earlier in the night. I backed up, hitting the wall, and there was no other place to go. The tips of two of his fingers pressed lightly under my right temple. His gaze, troubled and stormy, was fixed to that area.

My heart was pounding as fast as it had when Greasy Guy had busted up into the house. "Jax . . . ?"

His gaze swept over to mine. "Did he hit you?"

"No," I whispered.

"Then what happened to your temple? It's red and swollen." His voice was icy and hard.

"It was the door. When he pushed it open, I was kind of standing in the way." Anger flashed in those eyes, and his jaw tightened. "He actually didn't try to hurt me, Jax. He just wanted to get to what was in this house."

The tension in his jaw didn't ease and a long moment passed where I didn't think I took one single breath. "Are you okay?"

Our gazes were locked. "Yeah. It just . . . it shook me up. I didn't expect that." It sounded stupid considering what he'd warned me about. "I didn't know that stuff was in the house."

"I know." His voice dropped, softened, and the longer he stared at me, the more tiny flutters grew in my chest, which caused a dozen or so warnings to fire off. "Clyde said you told him that the guy found stuff?"

I nodded. "Yeah. Upstairs in my old bedroom. The closet."

"Shit," he muttered, clearly disgusted. His fingers slowly trailed off the side of my head, and then he pivoted around, moving deeper into the house.

A moment passed where I just stood there, the hand holding the phone pressed close between my breasts. Then I forced myself away from the wall. Still having no idea why it was Jax who had come instead of Clyde, I followed him. He was halfway up the stairs, and neither of us spoke until he was crouched down in front of the closet, holding the piece of drywall.

"Did you see exactly what he got?" he asked.

"It was several bags of something that looked like brown sugar. I'm guessing that wasn't it."

"Fuck," he muttered, sounding distracted. "Sounds like heroin. Little bags or big?"

Heroin. God, was Mom doing that shit now? "What do you mean by little? Like sandwich-bag size?"

"No." He coughed out a laugh as he rose, facing me. "A sandwich bag of heroin would not be little. Talking this small?" He held up his finger and thumb, changing the space between them to a couple of inches. "What about that?"

"It was several Ziploc-sized bags, Jax. There were about eight of them, and they were full." My heart skipped a beat when his face went blank. "That's . . . that's bad, right?"

"Fuck yeah." He thrust his hands through his hair. "Sounds like there could've been a kilo or more in those bags. And, by the way you describe it, sounds like black tar heroin."

I knew what a kilo was due to the kind of classes I took, but I had no idea what that translated into in the drug world. "Black tar?"

"More expensive shit from what I hear."

The walls shifted suddenly. "How expensive?"

"Shit. Anywhere from seventy thousand to over a hundred thousand per kilo," he explained, drawing in a deep breath. "Really depends on how pure it is—if it was high-end shit or not. Could even be worth a couple of million."

"Oh my God." My knees suddenly felt weak. "How do you know this stuff?"

His gaze landed on me. "Been around the block a few times."

"You did heroin?"

"Hell no." He didn't elaborate. "Tell me what this guy looked like." After I finished describing Greasy Guy, Jax looked even tenser. "Doubt that it was his shit he was retrieving. And I don't think it was Mona's, either."

My stomach flopped. "You think she was . . . holding it for someone?"

He nodded. "Let's fucking pray that this guy was who she was holding it for. If not . . ."

Oh God, I didn't need to be a drug kingpin to figure out what he meant. If Mom was holding drugs of that kind of value, the owner would eventually come looking for it, and with the drugs being gone, she was beyond being in hot water. She was drowning. All I could hope, like Jax had said, was that the crap belonged to Greasy Guy. He seemed to know exactly where it was.

As we headed downstairs, my phone rang in my hand. Lifting it, I saw that it was Clyde calling. "Hello?"

"You doing okay, baby girl?" came his deep, gravelly voice.

"Yeah."

"Jax there?"

"Yeah."

He expelled a long breath. "He's a good boy. He'll protect you."

I frowned, not just because of Clyde's words, but because Jax was in the bedroom, picking up the stuff Greasy Guy had thrown around, which included a couple of pairs of undies. "Uh, Uncle Clyde . . . I got to go."

"I mean it, baby girl, he'll do good by you," Clyde went on, and his words caused the flutter to return to my chest, more powerful than before. "You hear me?"

"Yeah," I whispered. "I hear you."

"Good. Call me in the morning. Okay?"

"Will do." I hung up and slowly entered the bedroom, my heart skipping around in my chest. I stopped just inside the door. "Jax, what are you doing?"

"What does it look like?" He righted the mattress. "I doubt this was your idea of rearranging a room."

"No, but I can take care of it. You don't—"

"I am helping, so don't argue with me about it." He bent down and grabbed a sheet, tossing it toward me. "And I'm staying the night."

The sheet hit the floor. "What?"

"I'm staying with you." He went about fitting the other sheet to the mattress. "I can take the couch." His thick lashes lifted, and his eyes were back to the warm brown. "Or I can stay in here . . ."

I had no words.

He took the other sheet from where it lay in a pile, and I just stood there as he finished the bed and went back to picking up the strewn-about clothes. As he grabbed a handful of colorful, silky items, I snapped out of it.

I stormed over, snatching my undies out of his hand. "You're not staying here."

"Then you're coming to stay with me."

A minute went by before I could even process that. "I am not staying with you."

"And then I'm staying with you." He started grabbing what was left of my clothes on the floor as I shoved my undies in a drawer. "This house isn't safe, obviously, especially when you're opening the door to random thugs—"

"I'm not going to open the door again!" I shouted.

Pausing while closing a dresser drawer, he straightened, and as he did so, his lips tipped up at one corner. "What are you wearing?"

"What?" I glanced down at myself. The shirt was black, with a built-in bra, thank God, because I didn't want to be all boobalicious, and the sleep shorts were a soft pink. "What's wrong with what I'm wearing?"

"Nothing." Grinning, he closed the drawer. "Like the socks. It's cute. You're cute."

The socks were a blue and pink plaid, and they were cute. "Thanks," I muttered, distracted by the pleasant buzz invading my thoughts. Which was bad. Very bad. Like very, very bad, because there didn't need to be any buzzing of anything. I bitch-smacked the buzz into next week. "You're not staying—"

"Then you're coming to my place? Awesome."

My temples began to pound. "I'm not going to your place."

Jax moved to the foot of the bed, near the mountain of pillows. That was one thing about Mom that never changed. She always had at least five pillows on a bed, and the pillows were never more than a month old. "Are you always so argumentative?"

I squinted at him. "Are you always so bossy?"

He cast a grin in my direction. "Honey, you haven't seen bossy yet."

"Yay . . ." I blessed him with some unenthused jazz fingers.

Smirking, he grabbed two pillows, and then rounded the bed. His long-legged pace carried him right to me, and he stopped only a few inches from my face. "You can tell me not to stay here all you want. Yell. Wiggle your fingers at me. Whatever. It's not going to change anything because I seriously doubt you can make me leave this house. You get what I'm saying?"

I felt my eyes widen. Yeah, I got what he was saying, and I didn't like it, so I wondered if I kicked him in the balls, if that would help him get what *I* was saying.

Jax tipped his chin down, and by doing so, his lips were within the same breathing space as mine. In spite of the irritation marching across my skin like an army of fire ants, my heart jumped in my chest. "I know deep down, you get why I'm here and why Clyde isn't."

Uh. Actually, I didn't. I started to tell him that, but then he went on.

"I want to make sure you're safe since you're staying for . . . however long." He shifted slightly, tilting his head to the side as he did. A heartbeat passed, and his eyes locked with mine. "And being here by yourself isn't safe, so I'm going to make it safe for you."

A breath pushed out between my now-parted lips. An urge rose out of nowhere. My body wanted to lean into his. Damn. That was the strangest thing ever. Never before had I wanted to lean into a guy. I'd read about the need, but never really believed in it. But it would feel safe to lean on him and to be close. The desire rode me hard, and worse yet, I knew his body would be warm, and it would be hard in all the right and interesting places.

Oh man, my thoughts were going down the wrong road—the pervy road—but I couldn't stop it. Jax . . . he was beautiful in a way that seemed impossible, untouchable, and he also had great eyebrows. Seriously. Darker than his wavy hair. Naturally slanted. Striking. They were just eyebrows, but they were hot.

But it was more than that.

God Almighty, I might've just committed a cardinal sin just by thinking it, but he was like Cam 2.0.

Because from what I knew about Jax, he was nice, really nice, which made him oh so very dangerous to my mental well-being, but I imagined going crazy for him would be a fun adventure.

I just knew I probably wouldn't recover from something like that.

But I could almost feel his lips on mine. When he'd kissed me earlier, it had been brief and to prove a point, but I could feel them now.

Something deep and warm stirred in his eyes, and I wondered if he knew what I was thinking. Oh God, I prayed to a chubby baby Jesus that he didn't. His lashes lowered, and my lips tingled from the weight of his gaze.

"Yeah, I think you're starting to get me." Then he swaggered past me into the living room.

"I need an adult," I muttered, slowly turning around to see him by the couch in the living room.

"Oh, before I forget—"

"Don't change the subject!" I stomped my foot and was damn proud of it, too.

He looked over his shoulder at me, brows raised. "Did you just stomp your foot?"

Heat crept across my cheeks as I grumbled, "Maybe."

Jax's lips twitched. "Cute."

"It's not cute! And you're not staying here. And I'm—"

"And you're going to give me a ride home tomorrow morning when you head to the bar," he finished, stopping in front of the couch.

"I'm not going . . ." My shriek faded off as his words sunk in. "What?"

"I'm going to need a ride tomorrow," he repeated, dropping the pillows against one arm of the couch. "I drove your car here. The windshield's been fixed."

I stared at him for so long he probably thought something was wrong with me, and then I hurried past him to the window near the TV. I yanked the curtains and there it was, my Focus sitting in the driveway.

"Let me guess. No cable?" asked Jax.

"What?" I gazed out the window, my heart racing.

"The TV? Mona probably didn't keep up on the cable bill." What sounded like the remote dropped onto the coffee table. "I have cable at my place. HBO. Starz. Just saying."

There was a knot in my throat as I faced him. "How . . . how much do I owe you for the windshield."

"Nothing."

"I need to pay you for that. It's not the same thing as you getting me fast food. I'm not *that* broke. I can pay—"

"I didn't pay for it." He ran his fingers through his hair as he eyed me. "Like I said, the guy—his name's Brent—owed me a favor. He took care of the windshield. No charge."

"He owed you a favor?" I repeated dumbly. "Are you, like, in the mob?"

He tipped his head back and let out a deep, rumbling laugh that caused my tummy to twist. "No."

I liked his laugh.

Inching away from the window, I suddenly felt . . . I didn't know how I felt. Relieved? Tense? Stunned? I felt all those things at once, but I knew not to look a gift horse in the mouth. "Thank you."

One broad shoulder rose. "It's no big deal."

"It is."

A moment passed. "You tired?"

No. I was wired, so antsy I felt like my bones and muscles were going to come out of my skin, but I lied and said yes, because I didn't think I could be in the same room with him any longer. There was a burning behind my eyes I needed to get under control.

His eyes met mine for a second, and then he dropped down on the couch. He didn't say anything else as I walked over to the small linen closet and pulled out the other blanket I'd seen earlier. I walked over, placing it on the arm of the couch farthest from him.

"By the way . . ." Jax gave me that half grin that caused my toes to curl inside my socks when I twisted toward him. "Those shorts and those legs? Fucking perfection."

Flipping onto my back, I stared with wide eyes. Several of the thin panels in the blinds covering the window in the bedroom were broken, so slim slices of moonlight spread like fingers playing peek-aboo across the ceiling.

I tossed and turned for what felt like hours, unable to shut my brain down. Each time I moved, the bed creaked a little. Or maybe a lot. It sounded superloud to me, but so did my heart as it pounded blood through my ears.

Jax was lying on the couch, mere feet away from the bedroom. And he'd kissed me earlier. And he'd gotten my windshield fixed. And he'd said my legs and my shorts were *fucking perfection.*

What was up with his fascination with my legs?

Flopping onto my stomach, I groaned into the pillow. My legs shouldn't matter. It obviously wasn't important, but I was fixated on how it was my legs he kept focusing on. There were other things about me, more noticeable things like my face that got attention. Not my legs.

But he *kissed* me and he was in the next room, right there, and my lips were tingling again. My first kiss—at age twenty-one, I'd experienced my first kiss. Finally. And I wasn't even sure if it was a real kiss.

"God," I moaned into the pillow.

I twisted onto my side, deciding I wouldn't think about Jax anymore, because that was seriously pointless. So the next thing I thought about was heroin. Lots of heroin. Like maybe hundreds of thousands' worth of it. How much heroin was that really? Like on the street? How many lives would it infect and ruin? Hundreds? Thousands?

And it had been in this house—Mom's house.

I squeezed my eyes shut as unease curled in my stomach, spreading like noxious smoke. Was she doing that stuff now?

Okay. This wasn't good to think about, either. My mind was empty for a few blissful moments, and then I started thinking about school. The initial panic surrounding how I'd pay my tuition had faded somewhat, and I knew I'd get federal aid. They didn't use credit, but that didn't fix everything. I'd need to get a waitressing job when I got back because I needed money to pay bills. That sucked because the last few semesters of nursing school were going to be ridiculously hard. And finishing school didn't fix the rest of the crap—the debt, the bad credit, and everything else.

I didn't know what I was going to do, and I didn't want to think about it anymore because I was doing the best I could do. I made fifty bucks today and that was better than making nothing.

Fifty bucks.

God.

I rolled onto my back and that position lasted all of five minutes. This sucked, and I moved again, this time freezing as I settled on my other side, facing the bathroom.

The old hinges on the bedroom door squeaked as it was slowly pushed open. I held my breath. My back was to the door, but I knew it was Jax. His presence practically sucked the oxygen out of the room.

What was he doing? Did my tossing wake him up? Probably, since the bedroom door wouldn't close all the way, leaving a half-foot gap between the door and the threshold. Something was wrong with the hinges. I didn't know what and it didn't matter.

The floorboard creaked under his footsteps.

Oh my God.

"Calla?" His voice wasn't loud, but it was still like a crack of thunder.

Should I pretend to be asleep? I squeezed my eyes shut, thinking that was stupid, but I was willing to give that a shot.

"I know you're not asleep."

Damnit.

I still didn't say anything because I was pretty sure I was beyond speaking. A wave of tiny goose bumps spread across my skin as I slowly opened my eyes. Sad, but true, I'd never been in bed before with a guy in the same room. Well, not entirely true. Jacob, a classmate at college, had been in my dorm once, but that wasn't the same thing as right now.

The floor didn't creak again, but the bed suddenly dipped under his weight. Forget pretending to be asleep. My body wouldn't allow it. I rose onto my elbow, twisting my neck back, my eyes peeling wide. In the silvery moonlight, I could see the tips of his high cheekbones and the form of his body. That was more than enough.

"What are you doing?" My voice was pitched embarrassingly high.

Jax was leaning on his hip, his hand planted into the bed near mine. "You weren't sleeping."

"Yes, I was." I was a terrible liar.

"I think I've listened to you moving around in this bed for the last hour."

I didn't know what to say to that, but my heart had turned into a steel drum.

"And I'll admit, it's pretty distracting." In the shadowy room, he shifted closer, and I tensed.

"I'm sorry," I blurted out.

His chuckle was deep and low. "You don't need to apologize. It was distracting in a good way."

After I mentally repeated that, I still had no idea what that meant.

"Do you normally have this much trouble sleeping?"

"Huh?"

"Sleeping," he repeated, and I could hear the amusement in his voice. "Do you normally have a hard time at it?"

Did I normally have this much trouble handling a conversation? I bit down on the inside of my lip and shook my head. "Not until I came back here."

Jax didn't respond for a moment, and then he said, "I feel ya."

"You do?" Surprise shuttled through me.

"Yeah, when I first came home—not here, but home, I had a hell of a time falling asleep and staying asleep through the night. Too much going on up here." He raised a hand toward where his head was.

Common sense told me I needed to tell him to get the hell out of my bed, or I needed to hightail out of it and put some space between us, but curiosity got the best of me. "Home from where?"

There was another pause, and then he shifted again—rolled onto his back, his head on the pillows next to mine. Onto his back, beside me, in a bed that I was in! What in the holy hell? My tongue was stuck to the roof of my mouth as my heart bounced around, and then the flutter in my stomach got all kinds of excited.

"I was overseas," he said, and it took me a moment to remember what he was talking about.

My brain sorted that out and I only came up with a one-word response. "Overseas?"

"Why don't you lie down and I'll tell you?"

Lie down? In bed? With him? No way. No way, Jose. I was frozen in this position. Nope. Nope. Nope.

"Come on," he said in a soft voice, the kind of tone that did funny things to my brain cells, melting them together like putting butter in a microwave. "Lie down, Calla. Relax."

I don't know what it was about the way he said it, but my left arm caved under me, and the next thing I knew, my right cheek was plastered to the pillow.

His voice was freaking magic.

"I enlisted when I was eighteen, as soon as I graduated," he explained. "It was either that or work in a coal mine like my dad and my older brother."

Coal mines? Holy crap. "Where are you from?"

The bed dipped again, and I imagined that he'd rolled onto his side, facing me. "Oceana, West Virginia."

"Oceana . . ." I whispered, staring at the bare wall across from the bed. "Why does that name sound familiar?"

Jax chuckled. "Probably because it's been nicknamed Oxyana and there was a documentary about the town. It has a little problem with the painkiller OxyContin, as in, half the damn town is on that shit."

Yeah, now that did sound familiar.

"Working in the mines, it's hard work, and some think it pays well, but I didn't want that. There isn't much else around, and I wanted out of that damn town." A sudden hardness to his voice caused a shiver to roll down my spine. "Enlisting seemed like the only other option."

"What . . . what branch did you enlist in?"

"Marines."

Wow, marines were badass. They were like the ass kickers of the military. My dad's brother had been a marine, and I remember the stories he used to tell about training and how hard-core it was. Not everyone was cut out to be a marine, but apparently Jax was, and seeing how he vaulted over the bar earlier and got right up in Mack's face, I could see the marine in him.

Kind of hot.

An image of Jax in a dress uniform, the kind I'd seen in my uncle's closet when I was little, formed in my head.

Okay. Lots of hot.

"I enlisted for five years, hit active war duty two years in, spent almost three over in the desert," he explained, and I swallowed hard. Active war duty was no joke. "When my term was up, I wasn't sure I wanted to reenlist. And when I got back home, I couldn't sleep. Didn't know what I was going to do with myself. There wasn't shit back home and being over there wasn't actually the best thing in the world, you know? It's a different life over there, and it changes you. The things you have to do. The things you end up seeing. Some nights I could only sleep for a few hours. Some nights I didn't sleep at all. My head wouldn't shut down, so I had a lot of restless nights."

I wanted to roll over and look at him, but I couldn't move. "Do you . . . regret enlisting?"

"Hell no." His reply was quick and firm. "Felt good doing something for the country and all that shit."

Something warm invaded my chest, and I really wanted to see him, but that required effort and courage. So, I went with words because that was all I had to offer, and I wanted to give him something. "I think that's amazing."

"What?"

Heat crept across my face. "Enlisting in the marines and fighting. It's brave and honorable and amazing." Three things I wasn't, and three things I honestly couldn't say about a lot of people I knew, including the Hot Guy Brigade. Well, with the exception of Brandon. He'd been overseas, too.

Jax didn't respond to that, and silence stretched out between us, and I squeezed my fingers together. "How long . . . have you been out?" I asked.

"Hmm, it'll be two years next spring." His voice sounded closer.

I quickly did a bang-up math job in my head, finally finding an answer to one of my questions. "So you're . . . twenty-four?"

"Yep, and you're really twenty-one, even though you look like seventeen."

My lips twitched. "I don't look seventeen."

"Whatever," he murmured. "When's your birthday?"

"It's in April—the fifteenth."

"No shit?" A deep laugh came from him, causing the twitch in my lips to spread. "My birthday is April the seventeenth."

I grinned. "April's a cool month."

"That it is."

As I grew accustomed to his closeness, my body relaxed. "How did you end up here?"

"You met Anders, right? At the bar?"

"Anders?" I frowned.

"You probably know him as Reece."

Oh. "The young cop guy?"

"He's actually a deputy in Philadelphia County. Met him when I was enlisted. He got out a year before me, but we kept in touch," he explained. "He knew I hated being back home. Offered a place for me to crash. Took him up on the offer and headed up here. At first, I was kind of all over the place."

Nibbling on my lip, I stared into the dark. "How so?"

"Just all over," he responded without really answering. "Went to Mona's one night, ended up with a job, finally got my own place, and here I am, lying in bed with Mona's pretty daughter. Life is fucking strange like that."

I sucked in a soft breath. *Pretty daughter?* "You're . . . you say nice things." It was a stupid thing to say, but now I was tired and my brain wasn't functioning properly.

"I speak the truth."

A moment passed. "Do you still have problems with sleeping?"

There was no response to that, and as more silence drifted out, I dropped it and whispered a concern. "Do you think someone will come looking for those drugs?"

He drew in a deep breath. "I don't know, Calla."

I didn't believe him. Probably had to do with the doubt he expressed earlier about Greasy Guy being the owner of the crap ton of heroin, and honestly, the guy didn't look like he had the means to have that amount of drugs. "Mom . . . she's in a lot of trouble, isn't she?"

"Yeah, she is."

My heart turned over heavily.

"It's not the kind of trouble you need to get involved in," Jax added quietly, firmly. "And this is the kind of trouble you're not going to be able to fix this time."

God, that sucked, because I knew that was true, but I didn't know how he realized that over the years, I'd spent a lot of time fixing Mom's problems. It was like an after-school job.

"Okay," I whispered, because I didn't know what else to say.

As I lay there, trying to swallow a loud, obnoxious yawn, I remembered something he'd said when we first met, about life being too short. I imagined he had firsthand experience with shortened lives while he was serving. That mentality came from experience. I got that now. Could even understand it, but there was something I didn't understand.

"Why?" I asked.

There was a beat. "Why what?"

Jax sounded tired, and I should shut up or point out that I was now tired and could sleep, so he could leave. But I didn't. "Why are you here? You don't know me and . . ." I trailed off, because there really wasn't anything left to say.

A minute went by, and he hadn't answered my question, and then I think another minute ticked on, and I was okay with him not answering because maybe he didn't even know. Or maybe he was just bored and that was why he was here.

But then he moved.

Jax pressed against my back, and the next breath I took got stuck in my throat. My eyes shot open. The sheet and blanket were between us, but they felt like nothing.

"What are you doing?" I asked.

"Getting comfortable." He dropped an arm over my waist, and my entire body jerked against his. "It's time to sleep I think."

"But—"

"You can't sleep when you talk," he remarked.

"You don't need to be all up on me," I pointed out.

His answering chuckle stirred the hair along the back of my neck. "Honey, I'm not all up on you."

I freaking begged to differ on that point. I started to wiggle away, but the arm around my waist tightened, holding me in place.

"You're not going anywhere," he announced casually, as if he wasn't holding me prisoner in the bed.

Okay. The whole prisoner thing might be melodramatic, but he wasn't letting me up. Not when he was getting all kinds of comfy behind me.

Oh my God, this was spooning. Total spooning. I was spooning with an honorary member of the Hot Guy Brigade. Did I wake up in a parallel universe?

"Sleep," he demanded, as if the one word carried that much power. "Go to sleep, Calla." This time his voice was softer, quieter.

"Yeah, it doesn't work that way, Jax. You have a nice voice, but it doesn't hold the power to make me sleep on your command."

He chuckled.

I rolled my eyes, but the most ridiculous thing ever was the fact that after a couple of minutes, my eyes stayed shut. I . . . I actually settled in against him. With his front pressed to my back, his long legs cradling mine, and his arm snug around my waist, I actually did feel safe. More than that, I felt something else—something I hadn't felt in years.

I felt cared for . . . *cherished.*

Which was the epitome of dumb, because I barely knew him, but feeling that, recognizing what the warm, buzzing feeling was, I fell right asleep.

Ten

$\mathcal{I}$t was warm and oh so very toasty when I woke up, and I didn't want to leave the bed. I was in this snug cocoon of awesomeness and I wanted to snuggle down, cozy up against—

My eyes peeled wide open. All drowsiness disappeared and I came wide awake.

I wasn't alone.

Oh hell no, I *so* wasn't alone in the bed and I knew I hadn't gone to bed alone, but if I remembered correctly, I hadn't fallen asleep with my cheek on a hard male chest. Which was really strange, because I was one of those sleepers who never moved around once they fell asleep. I stayed in that position all night, so this . . . this was weird and I took no responsibility for my current position.

Oh my golly God, every muscle in my body locked up as I fully became aware of how I'd been sleeping.

My cheek wasn't the only thing all up on Jax. My shoulder and my breasts were smushed to his side, as in there was not even a centimeter of space between us. My left arm was thrown across his stomach, and with every breath he took, I could feel the hardness of his abs, tightly rolled. He still had a shirt on, thank God, because I'd probably combust in flames if he hadn't. One of his legs was thrust between mine, pressing against an area that pretty much had had nothing that didn't belong to me pressed against it. Our legs were literally curled together.

Jax shifted slightly, causing his leg to move between mine. I bit down on my lip as my lower stomach tightened and a wave of sharp tingles shimmied up my spine. His breathing hadn't changed, it was still deep and steady, but the hand curved along my hip started to slide.

A shiver chased after his hand, and my chest rose sharply against the side of his body. His hand slipped lower.

Jax cupped my butt cheek.

Totally hands-on, cupped my butt cheek.

Holy shit balls raining from the sky.

I should've been ticked off that he was copping a feel in his sleep, but that wasn't what I was feeling at all. A languid heat invaded my body, sinking beyond the skin and muscles, spreading through every cell. A slight throbbing picked up in certain areas of my body. My breath came in short inhales as my hips jerked against his thigh. The feelings intensified, rushing through me like molten lava. The throbbing between my legs increased.

This was bad, because it wasn't fair. There was no reason to allow myself to get so worked up when nothing would ever come from it, so I needed to get out of this bed. Panic swirled around in me like a dust storm, mixing with the acute and rapidly swelling arousal.

Jerking back, I started to rise, but I didn't get very far. The hand on my rump moved to flatten across my stomach as his arm tightened along my back.

"Where you going?" His voice was raspy with sleep.

My gaze shifted down to him. His eyes were heavily hooded, lips parted. Dark stubble spread across his jaw, adding to the ridiculously sexy, bed-messy look.

He turned his head to the side, looking at the clock on the nightstand. A groan rumbled through him. "It's too early. Go back to sleep."

Too early? It was almost nine o'clock! Granted, being a bartender meant one's idea of early and late were two different things.

When I didn't move, Jax tugged me back down so that I was half sprawled across him once more.

"Jax—"

"Sleep," he grumbled.

"I'm not—"

"Sleepy time."

What the hell? I managed to wiggle back enough to get my hand between us. I pushed back as I rose. "I'm not going back to sleep and I don't think this is really appropriate. I need . . ." I trailed off as I stared down at him.

Oh wow.

Jax's head was tilted back against the pillow, exposing his long, tan neck, and the tips of straight white teeth bit down on his full lower lip. The look on his face, like he was stopping himself from doing something very naughty and very fun, confused me.

And then I realized why.

I'd planted my hand on his lower stomach, like way lower stomach, and my thigh was now pressing in between *his* legs. "Oh God," I whispered, feeling my face heat as I jerked back my hand.

Jax moved lightning quick, capturing my wrist in his hand. "You probably should've just gone back to sleep."

My heart flounced in my chest. Yes, literally *flounced*.

He rolled suddenly, and before I could take my next breath, I was flat on my back and he was hovering above me, one hand still curled around my wrist and the other planted in the bed beside my head, his lower arm curved into the mattress.

"What are you doing?"

Not immediately clueing me in, his warm brown gaze traveled

over my face—*my face*—before fixing on my mouth. "You know what they say about guys in the morning?"

"What?"

One side of his lips kicked up, and then I got it and then my face really was burning. A deep, husky chuckle shook him. "I'm kind of glad you didn't go back to sleep. This is by far more interesting."

My brain emptied.

The hand around my wrist slid down my arm, stopping at my elbow, where it was jabbing into the side of my stomach. "You know what else I find really interesting?"

"What?" Why was I asking? Why did I care?

His head lowered until I felt his nose brush mine, and I tensed. "It's interesting how much I liked waking up with my hand on your ass and my leg between yours."

"You were awake!"

He grinned. "Maybe."

Using my other arm, I pushed my hand against his chest. "Get off."

"Would love to."

My eyes narrowed with irritation. "Yeah, that's not what I'm talking about, jackass."

Totally unfazed, he moved his thumb in a slow circle over the inside of my elbow. That tiny, almost unconscious touch sent a shock wave of sensation through my system. One second I was ready to knee him in the nuts and the next I was thinking of other more pleasant things involving said nuts.

"What are you doing?" I asked again, my pulse racing and even pounding.

His chest expanded, brushing mine, and my toes curled in response. "Doing something better than sleeping."

That really wasn't an answer.

Jax dipped his head and the tip of his nose grazed my right cheek. "I like you."

My heart stopped flouncing and did a twirl on one toe. "What?"

"I like you," he repeated, voicing dropping to a whisper that glided over my skin.

"You don't know me," I pointed out for what felt like the hundredth time in the short time I had known him.

"What I know of you I like."

Perfect answer. It really was. I swallowed hard. "But—"

"Don't overthink it, honey. Life's too short for that shit," he said, his lips grazing my skin. Every muscle tightened in the most delicious way, and his thumb, it was still swirling, still dragging out an array of sensations. "I like you. That's all."

"But you can't." The words sort of popped out of me.

His lips stilled against my cheek and then he lifted his head. Our gazes collided, and I wanted to look away, but couldn't. "I can."

Then Jax lowered himself, and all the air in the world was sucked out of that room. His weight . . . I'd never felt anything like it before. He was heavy, but it was good, and his hips were cradled between my legs, and . . .

Holy mother lode, there was no mistaking what I felt pressed against me.

"Get it?" he asked in a voice that probably caught a hundred panties on fire.

I didn't get it.

Jax *liked* me and he'd known me only a handful of days. That made no sense. If I looked like Avery or Teresa, I could get it. They were gorgeous in their own unique, practically fucking flawless ways. They had members of the Hot Guy Brigade, rightfully so. And I was Calla—Calla whose makeup, my Dermablend, most likely had sloughed off my face, leaving the scar a hell of a lot more visible. It wasn't like I was Miss Shiny and Wonderful Personality, either. Hell, for all Jax knew, a piece of rock could be smarter than me.

So I didn't get it and I told him.

"I like you, Calla. Yeah, I've only known you a couple of days. But you've made me laugh," he said, his gaze never leaving mine. "I can also tell you're nice and sweet when you wanna be. I think you're cute as hell and you make me hard."

Whoa. Did he seriously just say that?

"You've made me hard a couple of times in the last seventy-some-odd hours and I gotta say that's not a bad thing," he went on. "I want to fuck you, and all I need to want to do that with you is to like you. It's really not that hard to get from point A to point C on that, honey."

Double whoa.

He'd laid it out to me, right to the point and taking no prisoners, and I found something refreshingly . . . hot about that, which probably meant something was wrong with me. Or it was just lack of experience when it came to guys saying they wanted to get bow-chick-a-bow-wow with me.

Either way? Daaaaammmn.

Taking my dumbstruck silence as acceptance, he dipped his head again, and I didn't freak out this time. He wanted me, and I honestly didn't know what that felt like until . . . until now, and I was awed by the blossoming heat rippling through me. I forgot about the fact that most of my makeup had to have wiped off during the night. My eyes drifted shut and my toes did the curling thing once more. He was going to kiss me, and I wasn't going to stop him. Maybe this time there'd be tongue. I was really interested in exploring that.

Jax didn't kiss me.

Not my lips at least. His mouth veered off to the left at the last second, skating over my lips to my left cheek. He kissed the scar.

He fucking kissed the *scar*.

Emotion—violent and energetic—warred inside me. A mixture of a thousand screwed-up thoughts and feelings. Beauty. Fear. Panic. Lust. Ice. Heat. Revulsion. Confusion. I felt it all and it was too much.

I slammed my hands into his chest. "Get off."

He froze. "What?"

"Please."

Jax got off. It had to be something in my voice, because he rolled right off me, and I rolled right off the bed, coming to my feet. I backed up until I hit the corner of the dresser, sending a burst of pain across my hip.

He sat up and moved over the bed, both hands on the mattress. "Calla, baby, are you scared of me?"

"No. Yes. I mean, no. I'm not scared of you." I squeezed my eyes shut briefly. "It's not like that."

"It's like what then?"

We would never fuck.

There. I couldn't say it out loud, but there it was. I would never get naked with him. I would never get that close.

God, that shouldn't be as disappointing as it was, but this with Jax—being in bed, tangled together and wanting each other—was normal. And I wouldn't get any kind of normal, not with a guy like Jax. Not when he might've gotten over my jacked-up scar on my face, but hadn't seen or felt the rest of me.

This wasn't about having a low self-esteem, being inexperienced or weak or being too nervous to get naked because I needed to drop twenty pounds. My body was *wrecked*. There was nothing attractive about it.

Drawing in several deep breaths, I forced the sting out of my eyes and the back of my throat. "This is what I'm about. Okay? So this isn't going to happen."

His dark brows rose.

Damn, he gave good brows.

I was distracted again. "I mean, you're really hot. Don't get me wrong. And I'm sure you know that, because there is no way you don't know that."

The corners of his lips started to tip up.

God, I needed to shut up. "And I'm flattered that you . . . um, that you like me, but that . . . it *can't* happen. Okay? There's no way. I'm not your type of girl."

"How do you know my type of girl?" he asked, sounding genuinely curious.

I almost rolled my eyes. "I know. Trust me. And that's okay. You're nice and I appreciate everything you've done for me and are doing, but this . . . this isn't going to happen. All right? You got that?"

He stared at me a moment, seeming to want to push the issue, but then he nodded slowly.

"Got it," Jax said.

And then he grinned.

I didn't think he got it at all.

Jax lived closer to the bar, in a neat and well-kept row of townhomes not even a mile outside of town. I hadn't gone in when I'd dropped him off and I hadn't hung around after he'd climbed out of my car. Having woken up the way we had and my subsequent freak-out had sent me clamoring for alone time.

Time where I could make sense of what Jax wanted and how he could want it. It shouldn't matter. It would never be, but Jax was stunningly gorgeous. He couldn't be hurting when it came to females willing to jump in bed with him. There was a crap ton of obvious reasons why I shouldn't be anywhere near the top of his I Want to Hit It list.

God, there wasn't enough time in the world for me to figure that out.

I actually hadn't gone to the bar, either, when I'd dropped Jax off. That day I moved onto the shift that he worked and I didn't have to go in until that afternoon. So I'd picked up just a handful of groceries that made me feel like I was going on a diet and then headed back to the house. During the day, I wasn't too worried about junkies or crazy heroin drug lords, which was probably stupid, because it wasn't like they were vampires and only came out at night.

Things were just scarier at night, and after my shift on Friday night—and after I made pretty decent tips, I would've dreaded going back to the house if I hadn't been so damn tired. I'd stayed while Jax showed me how to shut down the bar, including how to close out the registers and cash out.

That entire shift he'd acted like nothing had happened between us that morning, like things were normal. Or at least what I thought was normal with him. He charmed and he flirted. For the second night in a row, he made a point of tying my apron when I worked the floor and his hands lingered on my hips, causing me to blush, but that was all.

I'd only made it to my car when I heard my name being called out. I turned, feeling my heart do a quick jump when I saw Jax.

"I'll be right behind you," he said, stopping at the side of his truck.

My brows furrowed. "For what?"

He fished his truck keys out of his pocket. "Heading to your house, babe."

I stared at him, thinking my ears had taken a drive into crazy town. "You're not coming to the house."

And that started an argument over whether he was or wasn't coming that lasted a good thirty minutes, and I ended up giving up, because I was yawning more than I was speaking.

So Jax followed me to the house.

He'd actually brought a change of clothing with him, for crying out loud—a change of freaking clothing.

When we'd gotten to the house, I tried ignoring him as I made myself a cup of hot tea, but it had seemed rude not to at least offer him one since he'd planted himself on the couch and had become my personal security system.

"Thanks," he'd said as I'd placed the cup on the coffee table.

Tired and nervous, I'd found it hard to look at him as I'd cradled the cup between my hands. "I didn't know if you liked sugar or honey in it, so I didn't add a lot of either." Out of the corner of my eyes, I'd seen him reach for the mug and take a sip. "If you want those things, they're in the kitchen."

"It's perfect." There'd been a quick pause. "You went to the store."

"Yeah." I'd shifted my weight restlessly.

"Why don't you sit with me for a little while?"

A flutter had taken up residency in my tummy. "I'm really tired."

"Not used to those shifts, huh?"

My gaze had slowly tracked over to him, and that was when I'd seen a book tucked in his lap. He read? Oh my God, guys that read were like unicorns. They only existed in fairy tales. I wanted to ask him what he was reading, but I didn't. All I had done was nod.

Part of me had expected him to put up a fight, to kick up the charm, but all he'd kicked back was his feet when he stretched out on the couch. "See you in the morning, babe."

And I'd stood there for a second, weirdly disappointed until I'd forced myself into the bedroom, where the door didn't shut all the way. After I'd cleaned up and changed, too tired to shower, I'd fallen asleep within minutes and wakened to Jax making the eggs and bacon I'd picked up at the store.

Saturday night had been a repeat of Friday, with the exception of meeting Nick for the first time. Since my earlier theory about hot guys flocking together, I hadn't been surprised when I saw that the tall, dark hair, and green-eyed bartender could be featured in the Hottie Bartenders Calendar I so needed to create. The kind of cash I could bring in featuring just Jax and him . . .

Nick was different than Jax, much quieter, more reserved. When we first met, he stared at me for a long moment, until I felt my cheeks heat. There'd been a strange pull to his face, a recognition in his gaze I didn't understand, and I wondered if he was from this area. But then he said hello and moved on. We might've exchanged a couple of words that shift. It wasn't that he'd come across rude. More like the kind of guy who didn't talk unless he had something he wanted to say. He was kind of broody.

Like the night before, I closed down the bar and Jax followed me to the house. It was a little creepy thinking that he or someone felt the need to be there because of what could happen, so I tried not to really focus on it.

That night when I made tea, I didn't bolt straight into the bedroom. I'd lingered in the living room and finally I'd sat on the arm of the recliner. The book was in his lap again.

"What are you reading?" I'd asked when I hadn't the night before.

"Lone Survivor."

My brows had rose. "Uh . . . ?"

He'd given me a half grin. "It's a true story about the Navy SEAL, Marcus Luttrell and his failed mission. Not happy bedtime reading, but it's good stuff."

"So you only read nonfiction?" Curiosity was going to kill Calla, but I hadn't been able to help myself.

"Nah. I like David Baldacci, John Grisham, and even some Dean Koontz and Stephen King." He'd looked away as he'd rested his head on the back of the couch as I'd started to see a theme there. "I didn't do a lot of reading in high school, but being overseas, there were periods of time when there wasn't much to do. Picked up reading and it stopped me from going bat-shit crazy from boredom and . . ."

"And?" I'd asked when he didn't finish.

Jax hadn't responded, and I hadn't needed my imagination to figure what reading had helped him with besides boredom. I thought about his background—a military man. That explained why he was so protective, but there had to be better things he could be doing on a Saturday night, because he wasn't going to be doing me.

I want to fuck you.

A near-suffocating warmth infused my skin as the words had re-played through my thoughts. My gaze bounced around the scarcely decorated living room before landing on Jax. He'd been watching me with a look on his face I couldn't decipher. There was an imme-diate bubbling of fear that he was finally going to address what had happened between us that morning.

I hadn't hesitated. I'd stood. "You know, you don't have to stay—"

"Don't start," he'd replied, opening his book. He was done with me.

I'd gone to bed not too long after that, resting my head on the pillow, my eyes trained to the bedroom door. I'd fallen asleep quickly and in the morning, Jax hadn't made breakfast and had left pretty early on.

Being off Sunday, I got to chat with Teresa and that felt great. I missed her and Jase, and the way they were with each other. They were days away from leaving for the beach, and I knew Teresa was as excited as she was nervous. It was their first trip together as a couple. I'd never experienced that, but I could get why that would be nerve-racking.

"So, you're really staying up there all summer?" Teresa asked, surprise causing her voice to pitch.

I nodded, like an idiot, since she couldn't see me. "Yeah."

"You've never talked about your family . . ." Teresa's voice trailed off, but what was left unsaid was obvious.

I'd never talked about my family for lots of reasons, so she had to be confused by my sudden willingness to spend time with said family, which in reality was nonexistent. "Thought I'd do something different this summer."

"But you normally take classes," she remarked, and I heard a door shut on her end, followed by a deep, male voice. Jase. Hottie-mc-hottie-Jase.

"Yeah, I know, but I've been bartending and making money—"

"Bartending? I didn't know you knew how to bartend."

I winced. "Well . . ."

There was a scuffling over the phone and then "Hold on, Jase. Goodness, my lips will still be here in five seconds, as will the rest of my body."

Oh dear. "Uh, I can let you go."

"No." Her response was immediate. "Jase can wait." There was a husky chuckle, and my lips turned up at the corners. Then Teresa said, "I feel like my entire life has been a lie."

"What?" I blinked as I'd peeked out the front window.

"You. Us. Our life together. There's so much I don't know about you."

I laughed. "There's not a lot to know."

"You're a bartender. I didn't know that." There was a pause. "When Jase and I get back from the beach, maybe we can come up and visit."

My eyes widened. That hadn't been a question, more like a statement, and I was sure that would be a bad idea, but it wasn't like I could say no. That would've been rude, so I mumbled an okay and then we got off the phone since Jase apparently needed access to her mouth or other parts of her body.

I want to fuck you.

Oh man, I really needed to stop thinking about that.

I had five minutes to panic over the maybe visit from my friends at an undecided time in the future, before Uncle Clyde showed up randomly. I met him at the door.

"What's on the list today, baby girl?" he asked, ambling into the house, wearing a Philadelphia Eagles jersey that even on his big frame seemed two sizes too big.

"Um . . ." I'd looked around. Hadn't known there was a list.

Clyde gave me a toothy grin. "First things first, baby girl. We got to check this house out, top to bottom, and make sure there ain't any more junk in here."

Oh.

That was an incredibly good idea. Clyde and I moseyed around the house most of Sunday. Moseying as in searching for more cubbyholes filled with drugs. It was a weird thing to do, but I loved having Clyde around and it was kind of a bonding moment. Like we were repeating history, in this together when it came to dealing with Mom. And Clyde and I had been the ones to deal with her most of my life. It was kind of sad, but it was *familiar,* and right now, *familiar* felt good.

We hadn't found any more drugs, thank the Good Lord for that, and he'd ended up running to the store before it got dark and coming back with the goods to make tacos.

Tacos.

As Clyde had put the hamburger meat on the counter and found a frying pan in the cabinets, I stared at him from the doorway to the kitchen, my lips trembling and my hands pressed together against my chest.

Clyde had been married once. I barely remembered Nettie, his wife, because she had passed away unexpectedly from a brain aneurism when I was six years old and that had been many years ago. At least fifteen years and Clyde had never remarried. I wasn't even sure if he dated. He'd loved Nettie and some nights, when I'd lived here before, he'd talk about her.

I didn't think he'd ever gotten over her loss.

But one of the things I remembered him talking about was his and Nettie's Sunday night ritual—making tacos from scratch. Good tacos. Red and green peppers, sautéed with onions, and smothered in melted cheese and shredded lettuce.

It had also become a Sunday night ritual for Clyde and me, and sometimes when Mom was around and had her head on straight, she'd take part.

I smiled as I watched him unload the bags. This was so *familiar,* and I had missed this. Missed having someone who felt like family even though they weren't blood.

In that moment, something came unhinged in my chest. I didn't get it, but suddenly I was uncomfortable. Not with what was happening now, but what had been happening the last couple of years.

Tears burned the back of my eyes. I didn't know why. It was dumb. I was back to everything being dumb.

Clyde pulled out a head of lettuce. "You know what to do, baby girl, so get your ass over here and start chopping."

I dragged myself over to the counter, swallowing back tears. *I will not cry. I will not lose control.* My cheeks were damp.

"I didn't pick up that Mexican cheese blend. We are gonna do this from . . . Aw, baby girl." Clyde put down the block of cheese and twisted his big body toward me. "What are those tears for?" he asked.

Lifting my shoulder, I wiped at my cheeks as I whispered, "I don't know."

"Is it your mother?" Those large hands were gentle against my face, his fingers calloused from years of work as they chased after the tears. "Or is it the boys? Kevin and Tommy?"

I sucked in a rattled breath. I never thought about them or that night when the entire world burned in bright oranges and red. Not to be cold or uncaring, but it was too hard to think about them, because I could barely remember what they looked like, but I remembered their coffins, especially Tommy's. So I refused to even think their names, but their names were cycling over and over again.

"Or is it everything?" he prodded gently.

God, Clyde knew me. Squeezing my eyes shut, I nodded. "Everything."

"Baby girl," he'd murmured against the top of my head after he pulled me to him, enveloping me in one of his big bear hugs. "Everything might seem like it's too big, but it ain't. You've seen and been through worse, baby girl."

"I know," I agreed. My breath hiccupped as I struggled to rein my emotions back in. "It's just that . . . this is so familiar. We did this for years, and I never thought we'd do it again. Or that I'd be standing here and working at Mona's. I was going to be a nurse. I had it all figured out." And none of it included a guy like Jax or making tacos with Uncle Clyde, but I didn't share that. "I don't have it all figured out anymore."

Clyde patted my back like a baby that needed to be burped, but I loved it. "Calla-girl, you're a lot of things, a lot of beautiful things rolled up into one. You're strong. You got a good head on your shoulders. You're still gonna be a nurse. This ain't going to be your life. You still got it figured out."

I nodded, but he'd gotten it wrong. The hysteria wasn't because I was disappointed at the way my life had veered waaay off course or because of that nightmarish night. Not that I wouldn't prefer some aspects, namely the heroin and Mom being in trouble, to be different, but I wasn't crying because of that.

That wasn't the reason for the tears. I was crying because all of this was *familiar* and the familiarity had made me happy.

Eleven

$\mathcal{I}$t had been a week since the night Greasy Guy had shown up at my mom's house and left with a fortune's worth of heroin. There hadn't been any more visits like that and that could be because there was always some random dude at my house. Okay. The guys weren't random. It was either Clyde or Jax.

On my days off, it was Clyde duty and when I went back to work on Wednesday, it was Jax who followed me home, which had surprised me a little. During my time off, I hadn't heard from him. Not once. I knew he had access to my cell number, because I had to list mine in the office, next to everyone's phone numbers in case of emergencies.

Granted, I hadn't tried to get in touch with him, either, because I told myself that would've been pointless and dumb. And I was trying to avoid all things dumb, but I'd actually looked forward to returning to Mona's on Wednesday, and that was kind of dumb.

So I failed like a giant whale at avoiding dumb.

On my days off, Jax didn't exist, but on Wednesday when I'd come in and he'd already been there, inspecting receipts at the desk when I entered the office to stow my purse, he'd looked up, grinned, and called me honey.

And then he'd acted like he had Saturday when we last worked together, flirty and charming . . . and touchy. But he still acted like he hadn't told me he wanted to get to know me in the inappropriate biblical sense.

Maybe he'd changed his mind since then, had woken up that day with a good old-fashioned case of morning wood and wanted to get laid.

And I was okay with him changing his mind.

Totally.

That wasn't why I'd put effort into my hair and makeup and clothing again today. It was for the tips.

Jax was here now, but he was back in the office doing God knows what, and I felt like I should be back there because this *was* my mom's bar, but before I could act on that, Reece approached the bar. Sometimes when I saw Reece, I thought about my brother Kevin. He'd been fascinated with firemen and police officers. There'd been a good chance that if he'd been allowed to grow up, if heaven hadn't needed angels, he would've been a cop or a fireman.

No more than a second after Reece reached the bar, Roxy spun on her heel and pretended to be dusting bottles or some crap. This wasn't the first time she'd done that.

Every time Reece was in the bar, which seemed to be whenever he wasn't working, which also seemed often, Roxy bounced like a rubber ball. And it was obvious.

"Hey," Reece said to me, but his eyes were on Roxy's back. "Can I get two Buds?"

"Yeppers." I tilted my head to the left as I grabbed the chilled bottles. Popping off the caps, I handed them over. "On a tab?"

"Works for me." His gaze finally shifted back to me. He had pretty blue eyes—vibrant and almost startling in depth. "So, you're really sticking around?"

Since Reece didn't look at me like he looked at Roxy, who still had her back to him, I wasn't self-conscious. Well, not really. It was like talking to Cam, Jase, or Ollie. In other words, hot guys who had eyes for only one female and didn't care if I looked like the cousin of the Joker.

Worked for me.

"Yeah, at least until the end of the summer." The words sounded weird to my ears, and I wasn't sure why.

"Cool." He leaned against the bar, head cocked to the side. He had a wonderful jaw and bone structure. And I was easily distracted. "This bar has really changed since Jax stepped in."

I had to agree with that. "When I lived here, Mom had some . . . um, real winners working the bar."

Reece laughed, and it was a nice laugh. "I'm pretty sure we have files at the sheriff's office on the fuckers she had working in here."

My lips twitched. "Probably true."

He grinned, and a dimple appeared in his left cheek. "See you in a little bit."

Roxy waited to make her way over to me until Reece was back at the table near where a pretty serious-looking game of pool was going down. I glanced at her as I tossed the caps into the trash. "Can I ask you a question?"

"Sure."

"Why do you walk away every time Reece comes up to the bar?"

She pulled off her huge glasses for what had to be the first time since I'd met her and wiped the lenses off with the hem of her tank top. Without the glasses, I got a good look at her face. The girl was literally as cute as a pile of kittens sleeping together. Tiny, pert nose and baby-doll-looking lips, paired with big brown eyes. Those bow-shaped lips pursed.

"I don't serve him," she said as she placed her glasses back on.

Before I could further explore that statement, the words "Calla-freaking-Fritz?" were shouted from the door of the bar. "You really are working here!"

What the?

I spun to where the sound traveled from, and at first I had no idea what I was seeing standing there.

It was a life-sized Barbie.

Kind of.

If Barbie had smaller boobs and dressed like a stripper.

The female prancing toward the bar was wearing some kind of skintight Lycra dress that covered her from her butt cheeks to her boobs, and nothing else. It looked like someone had taken a bedazzler to the dress. She was as sparkly as a disco ball on New Year's Eve.

Her blond hair was blown out and large and as she hurried toward me on sky-high shoes that had see-through heels in them; her hair flowed like she was strutting down the runway.

As she got closer and her big smile spread, I started to see past the glitter on her cheekbones and eyelids. I recognized her.

"Katie?" I placed my hands on the bar, stunned.

"You recognized me!" She stopped and then did something in those heels that I'd break my neck doing. She jumped, bouncing as she clapped excitedly. "No one recognizes me!"

I could see how. Katie Barbara had been a quiet girl in high school. Some would've called her *different*. She'd always brought her lunch in a Hello Kitty lunchbox, straight through senior year. She always had her nose in a book and always wore floppy hats that at some point during the day a teacher always made her take off. I vaguely remembered her giving a speech in English class in the third person. Throughout school, her hair had been a multitude of colors—blond, brown, black, purple, and fire engine red. Pink had been a favorite, though, and still was, because now I could see that the ends of her hair were dipped pink, matching her dress.

"You do look . . . different," I said, at a loss for what to say.

"Of course I do. I got one with my body." She slid her hands down the sides of said body as she did a little shimmy. "Did a little makeover."

Roxy giggled from somewhere behind me.

"You look great." Disco ball dresses weren't my thing, but Katie did look hot. Hot in a way that probably had guys doing stupid things just to get close to her. Very different from high school, and I wondered what our classmates thought of her now.

"You look the same. The scar has faded a lot. You can barely see it with makeup on," Katie said, and Roxy sucked in a breath as Katie popped down on the empty seat in front of me.

I realized she hadn't changed completely. She was still painfully blunt. Not rude. Just had no filter whatsoever. I smiled instead of letting the comment get to me, because I knew it wasn't coming from a bad place. "Yeah."

She popped her tan elbows on the bar and rested her chin in her palm. "I can't believe you're back in town, working at your mom's bar. I thought you were off doing bigger and better things."

Well, this was awkward. It was like the kid who partied so hard they failed at college coming home with their tail between their legs. "I'm here for the summer."

"Visiting Mom of the Year?"

Roxy sucked in another sharp breath and whispered, "*Daaammmn.*"

Again, Katie was as blunt as my fingernail. "I was planning on it, but she hasn't been around."

"That's probably a blessing in disguise, girl." Her blue eyes rolled. "I think it's cool you're back."

"Thanks." I bit down on my lip as I glanced at Roxy. She was grinning at Katie. "So what have you been doing?"

Katie leaned back on the stool as she waved her hands around her body. "Um, what does it look like? Not working in an office."

I thought she looked like she was a stripper, but if that wasn't the case, then I really didn't want to throw that out there.

"She works across the street," Roxy explained, leaning against the counter. "At the club."

Oh. Double oh. So she *was* a stripper.

Katie giggled as she batted thick and long lashes at me. "I absolutely love it."

Triple oh.

"Let me tell you, most girls do. This whole you only strip because you have daddy issues?" She flicked her wrist dismissively. "I strip because dumbass guys pay me to flash some skin when they can get that shit for free at home, and I make damn good money doing it."

Well, if she was happy doing it, then whatever. I smiled. "Sounds good."

"But you?" Those lashes batted again. "Working at a bar? I didn't think you drank at all," she stated, her glossy pink lips turning down at the corners in confusion. "Have you ever been drunk?"

I didn't get drunk. Well, because of Mom. I could feel Roxy's eyes on me. "I will drink a beer or two, but I've never been drunk."

"What?" Roxy all but shouted.

Reece and the boys looked up from their tables. I lowered my voice as I felt my cheeks burn. "Well, it's probably good that I don't really drink since I'm working at a bar."

Roxy gaped at me. "You've never known the wonders of being shitfaced?"

"Getting tipsy is fun . . . ." Katie trailed off as a good-looking man, maybe in his late twenties, saddled up to the bar.

"Whiskey. Straight up," he ordered, his gaze flickering over me and then to Roxy, who reached for the short glass.

Katie's gaze started at the tips of the man's dark-colored boots, up his jeans, white shirt, and traveled straight up to his wavy ash-blond hair. "Damn, I'd like to get tipsy with that."

The guy gave her a long, lingering look—a purely male look I'd seen tossed around a lot during my short time at the bar, that said he was all about seeing her naked. He then grinned before turning back, heading for the table Reece was sitting at.

"Anyway, your whole life is about to change," Katie announced randomly. She plopped her chin back in her palm. "For real."

I blinked once and then twice, and managed to ignore Roxy's elbow that she shoved discreetly in my side. "Come again?"

"I'm telling you. Your whole life is going to change," Katie continued, and Roxy bumped her hip into mine. "This summer is going to be epic."

I had no idea where this conversation was going. "Well, my life has already kind of changed."

"Oh, no. I'm not talking about what has already happened. It's what's about to happen." Katie leaned onto the bar, and I thought her boobs were going to spill right out of the top of her sequined dress and wipe down the bar for me. It would be like a nipple wipe-down. "You see, I got the gift."

The gift of stripping? "Um. What kind of gift?"

"Oh boy," muttered Roxy.

Katie tapped a long, French manicured finger off her temple. "The gift. Sight. Psychic. Whatever they're calling it nowadays. I get *feelings* about things and I just *know* things."

Um . . .

I had no idea how to respond to that, and I wasn't sure if she was serious, but Katie had always been odd, so I was going to go with yes, and Roxy was absolutely no help. From behind her glasses, she was squinting at the ceiling, her lips twitching as she pressed them into a firm line.

"So, um . . . did you have this gift in high school?" I asked.

Katie laughed. "No. I had an accident. Woke up the next day with the gift."

"What . . . what kind of accident?" I asked, wondering if I should know or not.

"Oh Lordy Lord," muttered Roxy.

"Fell off the damn pole."

Oh my God. "The pole?"

She nodded as she ran a fingertip along the bottom of her lip. "Yep. Those damn bitches oil themselves up like they're going to take a skinny-dip in a deep fryer, so sometimes the pole gets slippery if it doesn't get wiped down. And trust me, after *some* of the girls, you want to wipe that pole down."

My eyes widened, and all I could picture was a slicked-up stripper pole.

A short giggle escaped Roxy and ended in a forced, fake cough as she grabbed a bottle and then three shot glasses.

Oh no.

"Anyway, I got on the pole for a show. Busy night, too. On a Saturday, and I was doing this thing where I hang upside down." Katie leaned back and raised her arms, and for a second I thought she was going to reenact the whole thing, and I had a feeling it was about to become a boob apocalypse. "And I was all like this." Twisting her arms together, a rather convincing sexed-over look crossed her pretty face. "Just upside down, right?"

"Right," I mumbled as Roxy poured brown liquid into the three shot glasses.

"Next thing I know, my legs are slipping down the pole, and I'm all like 'Man down!' or at least 'Stripper down!'"

Another funny-sounding cough escaped Roxy as she slammed the bottle on the bar, and I forced myself to take several deep breaths as I murmured, "Oh noes."

"Yep," she said. "Cracked my head right off the stage. I was out like a belly button."

Out like a belly button? What the what?

"And the rest is *Long Island Medium* history, but without seeing the dead people or the cool, poofy blond hair."

"Really?" I gasped out.

She nodded. "So your life's going to change. Ain't going to be easy, but it's going to change."

I turned slowly and looked at Roxy.

"Shots anyone?" she offered.

"Shots! Shots! S-S-S-hots!" Katie shrieked, snatching one of the glasses as she bounced her shoulders back and forth. A freaking second later, her shot was gone.

"Impressive," I said.

Katie grinned.

After Roxy took her shot, both of the girls looked at me, and I shook my head. "I don't think so."

"Told you," Katie said.

Roxy frowned at me. "I want to see you taste liquor for the first time, and I poured you the good shit."

My stomach coiled tight. The idea of seriously drinking, of not having control and . . . I couldn't even think about it.

Sighing, Katie reached over and grabbed my shot. "Snooze, you lose." She downed it and then cracked the glass off the bar top. "Yeah, I just said that. And yeah, I got to go and make some mon-nay! See you later, bitches!"

I watched Katie spin like a ballerina on her heels and head for the door just as it opened and two other girls walked in. One of them, a busty redhead, curled her lip in Katie's direction and then whispered something to her friend, causing the other lady to giggle.

Eyes narrowing, I realized I didn't like that.

Katie stopped, looked the redhead straight in the eyes, and said, "I'll cut a bitch."

Roxy's mouth dropped open.

I snorted. Yep. Like a pig in a cozy blanket.

The redhead paled and the other woman flushed.

"And those bitches back there won't serve you, so you can go hang out at Apple-Back down the street." Katie glanced over her shoulder at us. "Right?"

Since I figured I had some ownership over the bar, I nodded. "Right."

"Be gone, bitches." Katie all but ushered them back out the door, pausing to throw us what looked like a gang sign. "Peace out, home skillets!"

Roxy and I were quiet for a good minute and then I looked at her. "Katie's always been a wee bit different, but I've always liked her."

She nodded as she grabbed up our shot glasses, grinning. "Oddly enough, she has been right with some of her predictions. She told me something once . . ." Her tiny button nose wrinkled. "Something I really should've listened to."

I gaped. "You're kidding me, right?"

"Nope," she remarked. "But I love that girl. Crazy shit always happens when she's in here. And I like her *feelings*."

"Feelings . . ."

"Feeee-lings," Roxy crooned loud enough that Reece's table turned in our direction again.

Namely Reece.

His lips were hitched at the corners as he watched Roxy spin around like a drunk go-go dancer and place the shot glasses in the tray to be cleaned. She twisted back to me and pointed. "Nothing more than—"

"Feeee-lings," I sang, just as badly and loudly. Probably more badly. "Trying to forget my feeee-lings . . ."

"Oooof loooove," Roxy belted out as she spread her arms and bowed dramatically.

A round of applause went up from Reece's table, and we broke into a fit of giggles just as Jax rounded the bar. He stopped a few feet from us, grinning as he eyed me. "What in the holy hell is going on out here?"

"Nothing," Roxy sung, and I stared at him a moment too long, but he looked good in his jeans, like always, and in his worn shirt, but then she twirled back to me. "So you've never been drunk?"

"Back to this again?" I crossed my arms. I'd rather be singing.

Jax's grin slipped into a look of incredulous disbelief. "What?"

I rolled my eyes. "Is it really that big of a deal?"

"She's never been drunk," Roxy pointed out to Jax, who was still staring at me like I had whipped off my top and was shaking my ta-tas at him. "Like ever."

"Do you drink at all?" he asked, strolling forward, and somehow he managed to get in the minuscule space between Roxy and me, which meant the entire left side of his body was pressed against mine.

I tried to suppress the shiver of response and lost. "I drink a beer or two every once in a while." Truth was, I never finished a whole beer in my life.

Placing a hand on the bar top, he angled his body toward mine, which lined our hips up and put me at eye level with the tight black shirt that stretched over his chest. Oh my. I could see his pecs. The boy had actual pecs. "Have you ever drunk liquor before?"

I shook my head as I stared at his chest.

"Not once?"

"Nope," I whispered. Staring at a guy's chest like it was a choco-late mousse cake was dumb, but it was the kind of dumb I liked.

"Before that drink I tried, I'd never tasted liquor," sighed Roxy. "Never been drunk. Missing out on a lot of stupid."

"We're going to have to change that." Out of the corner of my eyes, I could see Jax move his other hand. My chin jerked up as he tucked a strand of my hair back behind my left cheek. "Soon."

When he exposed my left cheek, I jerked back, banging my butt into the ice well. I could see Roxy watching us, brows raised and grinning. God, this bar needed to be busier on Thursday nights so it would leave Jax less time to torture me.

And Jax was really in the mood to torture me with his charm and flirt. He dipped his head, and I knew it wasn't just Roxy watching us. "What else haven't you done? I think you said something about this before."

My breath caught in my throat and then was released. Him being so close threw me. "I haven't been to the beach."

Roxy shook her head.

"And . . . and I haven't been to New York City or been on a plane. I've never been to an amusement park," I rambled on, stomach tumbling. "I haven't done a lot of things."

Jax held my gaze for a few moments and then he backed off, heading toward the other side of the bar. I stood where I was, finding myself staring at Roxy.

She arched a brow and mouthed, *What?*

I shook my head, feeling warmth in my face as she turned back to Jax, her grin spreading. I had no idea what she was thinking, but I was sure it involved something dumb. Turning to the stack of dirty glasses, I figured it was a good time to hit the kitchen.

The door opened, and I felt the change in the atmosphere before I saw who walked in. Tension poured into the air, crackling with strain and anger. Biting down on my lip, I caught the way Jax stiffened as I turned.

Oh no.

Mack Attack was back, and he wasn't alone this time. A buddy was with him, just as big and just as shady looking. They looked across the bar at Reece's table, and then Mack's gaze swung back to mine.

He grinned a shit-eating grin.

My stomach tumbled some more.

"You're not welcome here."

That came from Jax, and as my gaze swung toward him, I saw that his jaw was so hard it could cut ice.

"Oh boy," murmured Roxy.

Mack's buddy chuckled darkly, sending a shiver up my spine.

"I ain't planning to stay," Mack responded, eyes never leaving mine. "I just got a message to deliver—a message I'm fucking thrilled to deliver."

Jax got in between the bar and me. "I don't give two shits, Mack. Get the fuck out of here before I make you get the fuck out of here."

Whoa.

Mack's dark eyes turned into flints of obsidian. "I told you once and I'll tell you twice, you don't know who you're fucking with."

"I know exactly who I'm fucking with." Jax leaned against the bar top, his voice low and dangerously calm, like an eye of a hurricane. "Nobody."

Mack looked like he wanted to say something, but his buddy shifted and he moved, too, so that he could see around Jax's tense frame. "Isaiah needs to talk to your mom. Like last week."

Who the hell was Isaiah?

"That's not her problem," Jax replied.

"She's her mom's bitch, and since her mom ain't around, it's her job to make sure her mom talks to Isaiah," Mack fired back.

Mom's bitch? What the—

The cop table was starting to pay attention, and I doubted that if this Isaiah dude was looking for Mom, he was on the up-and-up. So that had to make Mack and his buddy pretty stupid to do this in front of a bunch of off-duty cops.

"She's got a week," Mack said, backing toward the door. "Before Isaiah gets impatient."

Mack and his buddy were out the door before I could say a word. My heart was pounding as Jax turned to me, a muscle throbbing along his jaw. "Who's Isaiah? Like some kind of Amish mafioso?"

Some of the tension eased in his face as his lips twitched. The look in his brown eyes softened a bit. "Not quite. But close."

Oh no. I didn't like the close part.

"What's going on?" Reece was at the bar, his gaze steady on Jax.

"Isaiah is looking for Mona," Jax replied.

I glanced at Roxy, kind of surprised that she hadn't hurried off to pretend to be doing something. "I don't know who Isaiah is and I don't know where my mom is," I said, feeling like I needed to throw that out there.

"I know." Jax's voice was level. "Reece knows that, too."

His cop buddy looked over at me. "You sure you want to hang out here for a while?"

I started to open my mouth.

"It's a done deal," Jax answered for me. "She's staying."

My gaze swung toward him; I was surprised that he'd done that. On the plus side, I was glad I didn't have to stumble through a non-embarrassing explanation for why. On the negative side . . . well, I wasn't sure there was a negative side.

Reece blew out a breath as he focused on me again. "If you have any problem with that shithead or any of those shitheads, you let me know."

I nodded.

"She'll let me know first," Jax said to me, and again, I all but gaped at him. "Then we'll let you know."

Reece arched a brow. "Man, I don't know what you got going on *here*," he said, and my spine stiffened. "But you need to stay out of any shit with Isaiah."

"I'm already in shit with Isaiah, because of this place, and you know this." Jax tilted his chin up. "And it's not my shit I'm worried about."

Oh wow.

"Okay. Who is Isaiah?" I asked, determining that was the most important thing. "And why is the word *shit* included with his name a lot?"

Reece's lips formed a half smile. "He's a bit of a problem around here. Usually runs in circles in Philly, but his stink has traveled far and wide."

"Drugs," Jax added, voice low.

I thought about the heroin. Oh shit.

"I'll have some boys pay him a visit," Reece said, turning his gaze to Jax. "Make sure he understands that Mona is not Calla's problem."

"I'd appreciate that," he replied, relaxing a fraction of an inch.

So did I. "Thanks . . . I think."

Reece chuckled.

Raising an arm, Jax rubbed his fingers through his messy hair. "Roxy, you good closing the bar down tonight?"

She nodded. "Sure."

"I'm going to be here," I tossed at him, but Jax shook his head. "What? I've got *hours* left on my shift."

"Not anymore." He took my hand and started walking, leaving me no option but to follow. On the way across the bar, he grabbed a bottle of brown liquor. "We're going to scratch out one of those 'never done before' things tonight."

"What?" I shrieked.

Roxy's grin spread into a full smile. "Right on."

Twelve

One would think that Isaiah, who may or may not be a drug kingpin, sending his minions to the bar would be the most pressing problem at hand, but because I specialized in dumb, it wasn't.

Standing in the kitchen of the house, my gaze shifted from the bottle of José and the two shot glasses Jax had also taken from the bar, to the current huge pain in my ass.

Half of his full lips were tilted up in a lazy grin that matched the lazy look to his brown eyes. He was leaning against the counter, well-defined arms folded across his chest.

An attractive pain in my ass, but still, a pain in my ass.

"No." I said again, for probably the tenth time. We'd been back at the house for about forty minutes, and every minute had been spent with him telling me to take a shot and me telling him various reasons as to why I couldn't.

Not once did he lose his patience.

Not once did he get angry.

Not once did he make fun of me for not wanting to drink.

Not once did I not have to stop myself from telling him the truth to why I didn't drink.

I was running out of excuses, and my gaze shifted back to the full shot glasses. I swallowed, frustrated and . . . just really *frustrated*. It wasn't like I never wanted to drink. I wanted to. I wanted to experience what everyone and their mother apparently liked to indulge in. Being drunk was a great unknown to me.

A lot of things were the great unknown to me.

I wanted to throw myself on the floor and roll around like a toddler, like my brother used—I cut that thought off, shaking my head.

"Hon, you've got to try it. Just one shot."

My gaze flickered to his. I liked it when he called me hon or honey, which was the stupid icing on the dumb tier cake. Our eyes collided, and those thick lashes, those eyes, those eyebrows, and that face.

Fuck.

If being distracted by a hot guy with a beautiful face made me one-dimensional, then at least I recognized that about myself.

"Is it because of Mona?" he asked.

Whoa. The force of him hitting it right on the nail caused me to take a step back. I hit the chair at the table, and its legs rattled against the floor. "What?" I whispered.

He pushed off the counter, arms going to his side. "Is it because of your mom? Because of how she is?"

Holy holes in the moon, my feet were rooted to the floor as I stared up at Jax. I hadn't known him for more than a week and some-odd days, and he seriously got it. Just like that. Might have something to do with the fact that he knew my mom when no one—not Teresa or Avery—had ever laid eyes on her or had a chance to experience the wonder of Mona.

It was because of my mom. That wasn't a surprise to me, but to hear him hit it like that floored me.

I'd seen my mom *do* terrible, stupid things when she was drunk or high. I'd seen horrific and humiliating things *done* to her when she was drunk or high. She never had any control when she was like that. Hell, she never had any control before then, but it was worse when she was drinking or popping pills. She was the reason I didn't do a lot of things and I wanted complete control, because I . . .

I never wanted to be her.

I wasn't her.

I would never be her.

My feet moved before my brain caught up to what I was doing. Walking toward the counter, I brushed past Jax and I felt him turn as I reached for the shot. My fingers trembled as they closed around the cool glass.

I turned to where Jax stood, my hand steadying. "I'm not my mom."

And then I tipped the glass to my lips.

Just one shot. Ha! Famous last words.

Four shots later, I was lying on the floor, on my side, cuddling the half-empty bottle of liquor to my chest. My eyes were closed. There was a warm, electric blanket coiled up in my belly and a pleasant buzz trilled through my veins. I'd long since kicked off my shoes and was currently deciding on if I wanted to take my shirt off or not. I had a tank top on underneath, but sitting up, raising my arms, seemed like it required too much effort.

A soft caress, a feather-light touch, traveled over my forehead, causing the electric blanket in my belly to heat and the trilling in my blood to hum louder. "Tequila . . . Jax, tequila is . . ." I ran out of words, because . . . well, words were so hard to think up and string together.

"Awesome?" he drawled, pulling his hand back.

I opened my eyes and grinned. He was sitting next to me, his long legs stretched out in front of him with his back pressed to the couch. We were only a couple of inches apart, and I didn't remember how I ended up lying on the floor, but I do know that he'd gotten down there with me immediately.

"Calla?"

"Hmm?" My eyes had closed on their own, so I opened them again. He reached over, tapping my knee with his fingers, and I giggled. "I'm a lightweight, aren't I?"

His smile spread. "Since this is the first time you've ever been drunk, I'm gonna say four shots is pretty damn good."

"Tequila is like a long-lost, not so annoying friend." I squeezed the bottle in my arms, pressing it against my chest. "I really like tequila."

"We'll see how you feel in the morning. Why don't you hand over the bottle?"

A frown pulled at my mouth. "But I like it. You can't take that from me."

Jax leaned forward, chuckling. "I'm not going to hurt the bottle, Calla."

"Maybe I want another shot."

"I don't think that's a good idea."

I tried to pull off a pissy look, but I think all I ended up doing was crossing my eyes. Sighing loudly, I eased up on my bottle death hold.

He gently pried the bottle out of my grasp and placed it on the coffee table, just out of my reach. I immediately missed the golden bottle of happiness, and I thought I should sit up and retrieve it, but again, *effort*. When his gaze settled back on me, his grin made me feel funny in my chest and in my tummy.

And in lots of other places that made me giggle.

"So back to the things you haven't done." He leaned back against the couch, obviously not feeling as good as I was. We'd gone over most of what I hadn't done in my twenty-one years of life, a staggering list of embarrassing material, but I didn't care. I liked how he grinned each time I'd told him what I hadn't done and how this look would creep into his striking face, like he was coming up with something clever. "Never felt sand on your toes?" he added.

I shook my head. I thought I did. "I have plans. My plans don't involve those things."

"What are your plans?"

"They're the Three F's."

His brows rose. "Three F's?"

"Yep!" I shouted and then I said much lower and in a much more serious voice. "Finish college. Find a career in the nursing field. Aaannnd finally reap the benefits of following through on something." I paused, curling my upper lip. "Though I'm not sure on the following through part. I kind of follow through on most things, but there's not a lot of things that start with the letter *F* that would involve planning, so . . ."

He grinned. "So that's it? Your big plans are basically finish college and find a job?"

"Yeppers peppers and pandas!"

He shook his head at me. "Honey, that's not much."

I started to tell him that was *everything,* but then I thought about it, and it must've been the tequila, because I thought he was right.

And then I said, "You were my first kiss."

"We need to get—*wait.*" The easy, lazy grin slipped right off his face. "*What?*"

At first I didn't realize what I said to him, so I had no idea why he was staring at me like I'd said something crazy. Then I realized what I had admitted and . . . yeah, I didn't care that I'd blurted out that little humiliating factoid.

Tequila was awesome.

"I'd never been kissed before," I told him.

One dark brown eyebrow rose. "At all?"

I shook my head. Or I kind of wiggled on the floor.

His brown eyes widened. "You're twenty-one and you've never . . ." The look on his face got even better as his gaze flitted to the ceiling, as if he were praying to the heavens.

Feeling a little weird lying down now, I forced myself to sit up. The room spun for a second and my stomach dipped precariously. I did not like that feeling—the spinning—but it settled quickly and then I was staring at Jax.

Gosh, he was so . . . so good-looking. The longer I stared at him I realized it wasn't so much a conventional hotness. Some might think his lips were too full or his brows too thick, but he did it for me. He made me wish I was . . .

I really needed to stop thinking about his hotness, because low in my belly, my muscles were tightening and my breasts felt heavy.

Jax tilted his head toward me, his expression odd. "Damn, honey, that wasn't even a real kiss."

"Oh," I whispered.

Oh.

Dipping my chin, I let that settle in, and though it didn't make it very far through the tequila haze, there was still a pinching deep in my chest, a feeling of things settling into place where they should be. Of course.

"What?" Jax asked.

I'd said that out loud. Lifting my gaze, I focused on his shoulder. I felt a little stupid for thinking that it had been a real kiss. I mean, he barely knew me now, but then, he'd only known me for a few days. And boys like him—guys who looked like him and talked like him and walked like him . . . and breathed like him, didn't kiss girls like me. Not girls who looked like me, and who grew up pulling the white in white trash.

"Calla? You feeling okay?"

The concern in his voice tugged at the pinch in my chest. "I . . . I still like tequila."

There was a pause and Jax burst into laughter. "Wait until you try vodka."

"Mmm. Russians."

Jax grinned. "And you can't forget about the whiskey."

"Whiskey?" I gasped, eyes going wide as I clasped my hands under my chin. I was beginning to realize I was a bit overdramatic when I drank or I was sobering up. "No. Not whiskey. Mom used to drink whiskey and things . . . yeah, she would be really happy or really sad." I rose to my knees, pushing my hair back over my shoulders. "Is it hot in here?"

"It's comfortable." He wrapped his hand around my wrist, steadying me. "Mona does like her whiskey."

Yeah, duh. Jax knew Mom. Our gazes collided, and I thought . . . I could tell him this. "I thought . . . I'd be like her if I drank, you know? Doing dumb stuff and . . . I saw things done to her when she was drinking."

An alertness seemed to bleed into Jax, and maybe later, when there wasn't so much tequila sloshing around inside me, I'd realize that he was nowhere in the near vicinity of being as trashed as I was. "What kind of things?"

Rocking back so my butt was pressed against my calves, I knew I shouldn't tell him the things I'd seen. No one wanted to hear that. It was messy. It was ugly. Not ugly like the scars on my body, but deeper and nasty.

But I had tequila tongue. "The first time—and it was the first because it happened more than once—she was having a party. She was always having parties, but this night it was late and I was thirsty. I had a cold or the flu. Something. I needed to get something to drink. I had to come downstairs. Mom had told me before not to come downstairs when she was having parties, but I had to."

"I get you," he said quietly. "How old were you?"

Shrugging, I struggled to flip through my memories. "Twelve, I think? I don't know. It wasn't too long after . . . well, anyway, I came downstairs and there were people passed out on the floor, and I heard Mom. She was making these weird noises—not good noises and her bedroom door was open. I looked in, and she was on the floor. Some guy was with her. He was . . ." I shook my head slowly, seeing the fuzzy, cloudy images in my head. "Mom saw me. So did the guy. She freaked, and I ran upstairs. She'd been so drunk that night."

His chest rose sharply. "Did any of those guys ever . . . mess with you?"

I stared at him a moment and then laughed. It wasn't funny. It was far from being funny, but back then . . . I looked worse than I did now. "No."

"That doesn't make it any better."

"No. I guess not."

"I've seen people get themselves in stupid situations while drinking and I've seen some in really precarious ones," he said, his brown eyes serious. "You don't have to worry about any of that here. You're safe to enjoy yourself."

"Thank you," I said, thinking that needed to be said.

"But God damn, Calla . . ." His fingers squeezed my wrist gently as a hard look entered his eyes. "You shouldn't have seen shit like that."

"I know, but I did and there aren't any take-backs in life." I trailed off as his gaze held mine. I wished he thought I was pretty and that his kiss had been real. "But it's not like that. Tequila is better than whiskey."

His expression softened. "We'll take whiskey off the list, honey."

I smiled. "Good. This . . . this hasn't been like those times with Mom. Why was I so afraid?" I didn't give him a chance to answer, because I jumped to my feet, my wrist slipping free from his loose grasp. The sudden movement caused me to stagger, and I threw out my arms to steady myself. "Whoa doggie . . ."

Jax rose easily and he didn't sway. "Calla, baby, maybe you should sit down."

Sitting down sounded smart. "What was I about to do?"

He was grinning again. "I'm not sure. You were talking about being afraid."

I wrinkled my nose, and then it hit me. "Oh! Stay right there." I took off before he could stop me.

"Calla—"

Heading into the bedroom, I went to the closet and grabbed my items. Holding them close to my chest, I stumbled back into the living room. Jax was standing by the couch, both brows raised.

I walked to where he stood and placed the trophy I'd won at the Miss Sunshine Pageant, or some stupid shit name like that, on the coffee table. "That's mine."

Jax sat on the edge of the couch, his gaze falling onto the trophy. The metal and plastic glittered under the living room ceiling light.

"I used to be in pageants." Part of me, the tiny slice that was stuck in the haze in my head, couldn't believe I was telling him this. I hadn't told *anyone.* "Since I was, like, a newborn. No joke. I couldn't even sit up and Mom had me in pageants. I could've been on the TV show—you know, *Toddlers & Tiaras*? That was *so* me, for like *years.*"

His gaze finally drifted back to me, to the photo I held close to my chest. Again, there was a strange look to the way he stared at me.

So I lifted the frame and turned it around, facing him. "This is what I used to look like. I mean, yeah, I was like eight or nine in this picture or whatever, but this is what I *used* to look like."

Jax's lashes lowered for maybe a fraction of a second.

I started blabbing again. "I won trophies and crowns and sashes and money. There were more—hundreds of crowns and trophies, but I got mad once. I was fourteen or fifteen—anyway, I was in high school and threw them out the window. They broke. Mom flipped out. Went on a bender for days. It was bad. There wasn't any food in the house or any detergent to clean my clothes."

His brows furrowed together as he stared at me *now,* not the picture of me back *then.* "Did she do that often?"

I glanced down at my photo, all blond ringlets and big smile, with big fake white teeth—flippers, they were called flippers, and I hated the way they felt and tasted. The fake teeth had hurt my mouth, but when I wore them Mom said I was *beautiful.* All the judges said I was *beautiful.* I won awards because of the stupid teeth. Dad . . . he would just shake his head. "What?"

"Leave you for days without food and basic shit to take care of yourself."

Shrugging, I shook my head. "Clyde would usually come over and stay with me. Or I'd stay with him. It wasn't a big deal."

"That's a big deal, honey," he said quietly.

My gaze lifted to his and there it was again, that *something* in his stare I didn't understand but wanted to. I lifted the photo again, practically shoving it in his face. "I used to be really pretty," I whispered, sharing the secret. "See? I used—"

"There is no 'used' to be." He snatched the frame out of my hand, and my mouth dropped open as he tossed it. The photo whizzed through the air, bouncing off a cushion and landing harmlessly on the couch. "You're really fucking pretty now."

I opened my mouth and I laughed real loud. Might've even snorted. "You're so . . ."

"What?" His lips turned down.

"You're so . . . fucking nice," I finished, raising my arms in a grand gesture. "You're nice. And you're a liar."

"What?" he repeated.

I plopped down on the couch, suddenly tired and maybe a little dizzy. "I'm not really pretty."

He stared down at me. "I just said you're really pretty now. So you are really pretty. Fucking end of discussion on that."

My mouth opened to point out all the reasons why that wasn't true, but then I shrugged. It was nice of him. I'd take it. "You're nice," I stated again. "This was nice. Thank you for doing this with me. I mean, I'm sure you could be doing like loads more interesting stuff than babysitting me while I got drunk for my first time."

He tilted his head to the side. "You don't need to thank me."

"Thank you," I murmured.

One side of his lips kicked up. "Anytime you want to drink, I'm here for you."

Well, that was nice, too. Out of nowhere, a knot formed in my chest. It felt wet and messy. "Really?"

He nodded. "Like I said, you're safe with me. Whenever. Seriously. Whatever you want to explore, you'll always be safe with me."

Those words . . . oh gosh, those words unhinged something in me. Not that I had felt unsafe. Well, things weren't warm and fuzzy when I lived with Mom, and shit had obviously gotten hairy a time or two.

"Actually, you know . . . I think I can help you knock off a few of those other things on your list," he continued, and that lopsided grin spread into a full smile that could stop hearts.

I wasn't really listening to him, because I was staring at him as that knot moved from my chest to my throat, and it was most definitely wet and messy. Jax was more than just a hottie to end all hotties. He was nice—nicer than Jase, probably even Cam and even Brandon.

He said I was safe with him.

And he said I was really fucking pretty.

I sprang up and toward him. Didn't even stop to think about what I was doing, but I was up on my feet, and less than a second later, I was throwing my arms around Jax's neck.

My sudden movement caught him off guard and he stumbled back a step before he steadied himself. A moment passed, and then his arms circled me, folding around my back.

"Thank you," I said, my voice muffled against his chest—his really hard chest. "I know you said not to thank you, but thank you."

He didn't respond right off. Instead, one arm loosened and his hand trailed up my spine, tangling in the ends of my hair. A rush of shivers followed that hand, and those shivers spread out through my arms, to the tips of my fingers and down to my toes, and everywhere in-between, especially the in-between part.

God, his chest was really hard.

I lifted my face off said chest and then raised my lashes. Jax was staring down at me, a soft smile curved on his lips. His other hand shifted off my lower back, and smoothed its way to my hip, and great googley moogley, that felt *good*. So good I didn't even take into consideration what he might've been able to feel through my shirt and tank top.

Tequila was fucking awesome.

His warm chocolate gaze drifted over my face as his hand tightened on my hip, which caused lots of my muscles to go squishy. "I'm glad you came home, Calla."

My heart stopped. The freaking world stopped. "Really?" I heard myself say.

"Really," he replied.

Okay. I didn't care if it was the tequila making me hear things, and I didn't care that my entire chest was turning to mush, and if that made me dumb or not, and I didn't care that I was about to do something I'd never done before, or that the room was spinning slowly like we were on a merry-go-round.

I stretched up on my toes as I lowered my hands to his shoulders and I went for his mouth. I was going to kiss him. I'd never tried to kiss a guy before, but I was going to do it now. I was going for a home run of my lips against his wonderful lips, because he said I was safe, and that he was glad I came home, and that I was really fucking—

Jax jerked his head back. Actually his entire body jerked back, and my mouth didn't land on his, but more or less skated off his chin and down his neck. Since my mouth was open, I got a good taste of his skin.

Wowzers, his skin tasted good.

Who knew?

He sidestepped the coffee table, putting space between us. Without him being there, I toppled forward. His hands curled around my upper arms, stopping my fall and . . . and keeping me an arm's length away.

Confused, I stared at him. His eyes were wide again, all laziness and warmth gone from them. Uh oh. This wasn't good.

"Calla," he began softly, too gently. Like way too gently.

Oh no. This was so bad.

"Honey, that's . . ."

My heart started pounding violently, drowning out whatever Jax was saying. This was like fucked-up bad. As in the kind of bad one did not live down. I tried to kiss Jax, beautiful and charming and so fucking nice Jax.

I actually tried to kiss him?

Oh my God . . . tequila sucked butt.

" . . . I said you were safe with me." His voice was deeper, lower when I tuned back in to whatever the hell he was talking about. "I wasn't lying."

What the hell did *that* have to do with the price of tea in China? Or the tequila that had suddenly turned on me like a crackhead with a rusty spork? I tried to kiss him and he had jerked back from me, physically *removed* himself from my mouth.

Holy shit balls.

The messy and wet ball was back, this time in my stomach and my chest, but it was mingling with something else that was vile, and quickly rising.

Oh no.

I lurched back, tearing myself from his grasp. "Oh my God," I gasped out. "I can't believe I tried . . ." I swallowed a hiccup, a bad hiccup. "Oh wow."

"It's okay. Why don't we sit down?" he offered, taking a step toward me.

Another hiccup. "Tequila is a dirty whore."

Jax frowned, brows coming down. "Calla—"

Spinning around, I darted for the bedroom. I could feel it. The mess was almost there. I stumbled around the bed, my feet slipping as I hit the bathroom door, slamming my hands into it. The door cracked off the wall, no doubt denting the plaster.

I hit the floor on my knees in front of the toilet—oh God, was this toilet even clean? Too late. I grasped the sides as my stomach heaved and rolled, bringing up everything and anything.

Tequila fucking sucked.

Thirteen

*T*equila was the wild juice of the devil and I'd never partake in it again.

The most messed-up thing was that people always claimed that they didn't remember what they did when they were drunk. I call bull poop on that, because I remembered—oh God, I could recall it all—in painstaking, humiliating detail.

I'd told Jax all the things I hadn't done, and some of that crap was just ridiculous. Like things that probably made him think I grew up in a bomb shelter or something.

Then I'd cuddled the bottle. *Cuddled* it. Like it was a puppy. Or a kitten. Whatever. Something furry that was not a fucking bottle of liquor.

I'd also shown him a trophy and a picture of me all gussied up like a baby doll and told him I *used* to be pretty. That alone made me want to shove my head in an oven, but oh, there'd been more.

I'd also told him about the Mom stuff, which was too horrifying to even repeat.

And I'd also tried to kiss him.

Aaand then I puked my guts up while Jax held my hair and rubbed my back. He'd actually rubbed—*wow*—my back, and I *think* he'd talked me through it. I don't know what he said, but I remembered his voice, low and soothing as my stomach cramped and heaved. But he had to have felt the scars. My skin wasn't exactly even on my back. It was rough and raised in some areas, and I knew it could be felt through my shirt.

Once I was done hurling up all the tequila and what was left of my pride, I'd lain on the bathroom floor, because it was cool, smooth, and perfect. He let me stay there while he snatched a damp towel and then—oh God, even more embarrassing—he wiped down my face. To top it all off, he'd picked me up once he'd been sure I wasn't going to vomit on him and carried me to bed, where he forced water and two ibuprofens down my throat.

I'd passed out on my side with Jax sitting next to me, his leg pressing into my hip, and when I woke up at some point during the morning, feeling like I'd been hit by a fire truck full of hot, muscular firemen, Jax was still there.

He'd been stretched out behind me, the front of his body pressed to the back of mine, and his arm had been a heavy weight on my hip. If I hadn't felt like my head was going to split open, I might've enjoyed waking up like that. Instead, I panicked like I'd just been busted in the wrong person's bed.

I'd jumped from the bed, literally, and nearly ate the floor. I had no idea how I grabbed fresh clothes and made it through the shower, washing away the grossness of the tequila yuck that seemed to have bled through my skin, without sitting down in the tub and crying over the pain behind my eyes and all the dumb, *dumb* things I'd done and said the night before.

Jax was awake when I shuffled out of the bathroom, all bright-eyed and bushy-tailed as he walked into the bathroom with his own toothbrush, which he'd stashed there after the second night of staying in this house.

When he'd come out, his hair damp from obviously splashing water over his face and head, I was sitting on the couch and quickly averted my gaze, staring at the spot on the floor where I'd cuddled the bottle of tequila.

The tequila bottle was mysteriously absent. I hope it crawled back into whatever hole it was birthed from.

I'd tried to kiss him and he'd jerked back from me.

God, someone shoot me now.

I couldn't look at him. Could not do it. Not even when he said my name.

"How are you feeling?" he asked when I didn't answer.

Lifting one shoulder, I studied my purple toenail polish. "Like crud."

"I have a cure for that."

What? A semiautomatic weapon?

"We're going to indulge in the official breakfast of champions for hangovers."

Brows knitting, I lifted my head. He was grinning at me like I hadn't gotten trashed the night before and tried to molest him. "What?"

"Waffle House."

I stared at him, blinking slowly, and then I looked away, feeling my cheeks heat under the makeup I wore. "I don't want to eat. I don't even want to think about food."

"You think that now, but trust me, the grease will do wonders for your stomach. I know. Have had a lot of practice at it."

Shaking my head, I stood, now staring at the window. "I really think I just need to go back and take an eight-hour nap before I head into the bar tonight. And I think you need to leave. Not to be rude—"

"Don't do this," he said, and he was right beside me. I hadn't even heard him move. "Don't, Calla."

My gaze shifted to his chest. How could he look good in the same damn shirt he'd slept in last night? I wanted to scream it wasn't fair. "Don't what?"

"Be embarrassed," he said softly.

I squeezed my eyes shut, wrinkling my nose. "Easy for you to say."

"Nothing's easy for me to say. You have no reason to be embarrassed. You drank last night. You had fun, or at least you did up until you got sick—"

"Thanks for reminding me of that," I groused.

"It's common. Hell, do you know how many times I've found myself curled around a toilet swearing I'd never drink again? You don't even want to know the horror stories I could share."

But I bet he'd never tried to kiss a girl and gotten rejected, either.

"Calla, look at me."

Hell to the no. "Like I said, I'm really tired and could really go for a nap." Or a lobotomy. "So, if I could do that, it would be great."

"Honey, don't." Two fingers curved around my chin, and there was no fighting when he lifted my gaze to his. I sucked in a breath, feeling a little dizzy again, and I wondered if there was still some tequila in my system. "You're not going to listen to me, so this calls for drastic measures."

I opened my mouth, but then Jax stepped back, dropping his fingers. Maybe a second passed and he dipped down. Before I could move or process what he was doing, he slipped one arm behind my knees and the other around my waist, and I was suddenly in the air, pressed against his chest.

"What the hell?" I shouted, grabbing on to his shoulders as he turned around. "What are you doing?"

Looking down at me, he took a deep breath. "When I was fourteen, I drank beer for the first time. Drank way too much at a buddy's house and spent the entire night circling the toilet."

I glanced around the bedroom. "Okay."

"Did that so many times when I was kid, you'd think I'd learned my lesson," he continued, watching me. "Then when I got back from overseas, some nights whiskey was all that got me to close my eyes for a few hours."

My body stiffened even more. Whiskey. God, I hated whiskey,

but I really wasn't thinking about my mom. I couldn't imagine the kind of things that kept him awake at night.

"Even when I came here, it was a whiskey and . . . well, anyway, the point is, I've spent many nights and days regretting what I did. But what you did last night and even though you feel like shit right now, you didn't do a damn thing you need to regret."

Deep in my chest, my heart clenched as our eyes locked. "What . . . what else did you do?"

Something flickered over his features, and he shook his head. "Let's get going."

I frowned at the abrupt change of topic. "Where?"

"Taking you to Waffle House."

"You don't have to carry me!"

He grinned down at me. "And you don't have to shout."

"Put me down!" I shouted again, making my own temples pound.

Ignoring me, he headed for the door and then stopped, back-tracking to the kitchen. "Grab your keys and sunglasses. You're going to need both."

I glared at him and he grinned at me. "Jax, come on."

He lowered his head, speaking in a low voice that caused my toes to curl. "Honey, you can argue and shout all you want, but I'm still going to carry your ass out to that truck, put you in it, and we're going to Waffle House, and you will eat fried eggs, bacon, and a goddamn waffle."

My eyes narrowed. God, he was freaking high-handed.

There was a sparkle to his deep brown eyes. "And maybe even a slice of apple pie, if you're a good girl and you stop arguing with me."

"I've never had apple pie," I blurted out.

Standing in the middle of the kitchen, cradling me in his arms like I weighed nothing—and I most definitely weighed something—his mouth dropped open. "You've never had apple pie?"

"No."

His brows rose. "Why?"

"I don't know. Just never tried it."

"That's so . . . so un-American," he said, and I rolled my eyes. "Are you a terrorist?"

"Dear God," I muttered and started to wiggle to get free.

Jax tightened his arms. "Honey, you kill me. Really, you do. Never been drunk. Never been to the beach. Never had an apple pie? We've already scratched one of those things off, and we're about to mark off another one."

I figured this was not a good moment to share the fact that I'd never been to a Waffle House, either.

His grin was back, and there was something utterly disarming about it. "Stick with me, babe, and I'll change your life."

Katie's words rushed over me. *Your life is going to change.* I stopped thinking, at least for a little while, and I stopped fighting. I reached over, grabbing my keys and my sunglasses. I slipped the latter on.

What Jax didn't know was that he'd changed my life already, even if it was just a little bit, but what he did knowingly do was carry me out of the house, put me in his truck, and drive my ass to Waffle House.

"So, Jax took your cherry?"

The margarita glass almost slipped out of my hand as I turned to where Roxy stood. Behind her, Nick was staring at us. It was probably the first time since we'd met that he'd actually shown any interest in Roxy or me. Then again, when you say things like 'taking cherries,' it tends to get people's undivided attention.

"Oh my God, this is such a perfect conversation."

My cheeks were warm as I glanced back to where Katie was sitting. "This is not the perfect conversation."

Her heavily lined eyes widened. "Were you a virgin? Like in past tense?"

The guy beside her turned and looked at me. I was seconds away from screaming. "Roxy is talking about being drunk. I'd never been drunk before. Last night was my first time. Jax took my—"

"I took what?" Jax appeared out of freaking nowhere.

Oh God.

Katie leaned forward and her boobs almost popped out of her halter and blinded me. "You took Calla's cherry?"

"I took . . . what?" He blinked and then looked at me, head tilted to the side. "Is there something about last night I don't remember? Because honey, I'm going to be seriously disappointed if that happened, and I don't recall it. Like really fucking—"

"No!" I shrieked, causing several heads at the bar to whip my way. "She's talking about never drinking. Not my . . . you know . . ."

"Cherry?" supplied Roxy as she straightened her glasses.

Oh God . . .

Jax stared at me a moment, jaw working, and then he turned to Nick, saying something in a low voice that I prayed had nothing to do with me.

It had been hard to sit through breakfast with him without feeling like a dumbass for last night, but he didn't bring anything up, and the slice of apple pie that I'd eaten was freaking delish.

"Oh." Katie looked disappointed. So did the guy. "Well, hell, never mind. Back to the pole for me."

I watched her jump off the stool as she winked at us and then sauntered through the crowd.

"But it wasn't her only cherry I took," Jax announced.

Oh double God . . .

Roxy's head whipped toward him, an eager look creeping onto her pretty face. "Do tell?"

Nick turned around again.

A sexy, lazy grin appeared on Jax's lips. "No. She never had apple pie. I changed that this morning."

"You've never had apple pie?" she exclaimed.

"Here we go again," I muttered.

Jax wasn't done. Nope. Not at all. His eyes met mine, and something in them caused a shiver to go low in my belly. "I also broke her into Waffle House."

My mouth dropped open. "How did you know I'd never been there before?"

"Honey, I know things." Our gazes held, and yep, that shiver increased, because he was saying something entirely different that had nothing to do with Waffle House, tequila, or apple pies.

But definitely had something to do with cherries.

"Last night was the first time you got drunk?" Nick spoke, surprising the hell out of me.

Roxy nodded as she headed for a girl who was waving her hand like she'd been standing there for ten minutes when it had only been like ten seconds.

"What did you drink?" he asked.

"Tequila," answered Jax, winking at me. "She was liking some tequila."

Nick's lips pressed together. "That's some strong shit."

"Well, I'm never, ever drinking again," I told him, heading for where my apron was stashed. With all the seasoned bartenders behind the bar, I needed to be out on the floor helping Pearl since Gloria was MIA.

Nick nodded. "Okay."

"Like *never*."

There was a tiny movement in his lips, like he was so close to smiling. "Gotcha."

I stared at him a moment, actually stopped in the middle of the floor behind the bar, and stared at Nick. "Tequila is a dirty whore," I told him.

A low, husky chuckle slipped out of him. "I've heard that before."

My lips split into a smile.

Jax's hand wrapped around mine. "You're coming with me."

My gaze went from Jax's face to where his hand closed around mine. "Going where?"

He didn't answer, but gently tugged me along, walking me past the apron and toward the exit of the bar. More curious than annoyed, I let him lead me down the hall to the office. He pulled me inside, shutting the door, and I remembered the last time he'd done this. He'd kissed me, but it hadn't been a real kiss.

Jax didn't let go of my hand as he leaned against the edge of the desk, and he didn't say anything.

I shifted my weight from one foot to the next and tried to pull my hand back, but he didn't let go. "What?"

"I want to take you out on a date Sunday."

"*What?*" I hadn't expected that. Nope.

A grin flashed across his face. "A date. You and me. Sunday night. Not at the Waffle House."

My ears were deceiving me. There was no way he was saying what I thought he was.

"There's this new steak house in town. Only been open a year or two, but everyone loves it," he continued as he watched me. "I can pick you up at six."

"You . . . you are seriously asking me out on a date?"

"I seriously am."

Two things were happening inside me. One was the rush of warmth that was whipping everywhere, lighting me up from the inside. The other was icy disbelief. I didn't understand why he was asking me out, unless it was some kind of weird, pity date.

My stomach tumbled.

Oh my God, it was a weird, pity date.

"No," I said, pulling my arm. He didn't let go, but I also wasn't going to be a part of this. "I'm not going on a date with you."

His hand slipped off mine and slid to my wrist. "I think you are."

"No. I'm not."

"You'll like their steaks," he continued as if I hadn't spoken. "They have a great filet."

"I don't like steaks," I lied. I loved red meat, all kinds of red meat. I was a meat girl, meat and more meat.

He arched a brow as his thumb smoothed over the inside of my wrist. "Please tell me you like steaks. I don't know if we can be friends if you say you don't."

I almost laughed, because that was ridiculous. "I like steaks, but—"

"Perfect," he murmured, tipping his head back. "Did you bring any dresses with you? I'd like to see you in a dress."

I did bring summer dresses and the appropriate shrugs with me to hide the scars, but that was beside the point. "Why do you even want to go out with me?"

"Because I like you."

My heart jumped in my chest, and if it had hands, it would have been clapping happily. "You can't like me."

"I've already told you that I want to fuck you. You can't forget that."

Holy crap. "I kind of blocked that out."

He laughed deeply, clearly amused. "You can't be surprised that I like you."

"Fucking and liking are two different things."

"Yes. And no." His eyes locked with mine. "Are you saying no because you don't think you're pretty?"

Holy crap on a Conquistador.

"I know."

I tried to pull back this time, digging in my feet, but his arm curled, keeping me in place. Panic dug acid-tipped claws into my skin. My chest rose with a deep breath and I forced my eyes to narrow, giving him the most bitchtastic look I could come up with, anything to take attention off how he'd hit my rejection right on the head.

"I know," he said again, tugging me forward as he spread his legs. I ended up between the V of his thighs. Close, too close to him.

I didn't understand that statement, so I continued staring at him with my bitchy glare. "Let me go."

One arm slid around my back and he kept moving his thumb up the inside of my arm. The touch, his closeness, all of it was doing strange things to my body. My knees were going weak while every muscle was tensing. "I already knew about the pageants," he said, keeping his gaze on mine. "Before you showed me the picture and the trophy last night, I already knew."

There were no words.

"Your mom used to talk about it a lot, tell us how pretty her baby *is*. Not used to be, but *is*."

I was going to kill my mom.

"Clyde would talk about it, too," he went on, having no idea that I just added Uncle Clyde to my murderous list, and then I'd have to off myself for last night, because I'd done the same thing. "He wasn't a fan of the pageants or the way your mom paraded you around. Neither was your dad, right?"

Clyde had hated the pageants, but my dad . . . "I don't know," I heard myself saying. "Dad never said anything to Mom."

"I think he talked to Clyde." Jax smiled a little. "You know what I said last night about the whole pretty thing? I wasn't fucking around. That's why I'm taking you out."

Then his arm curled even more, and I was chest to chest with him. The contact sent a shock wave of sensation swirling through me. His head dipped, his mouth inches from mine. My free hand ended up pressed against his chest.

I couldn't breathe.

I didn't care.

"You didn't kiss me last night," I said, and then I wanted to kick myself in the lady parts.

His eyes narrowed slightly. "Fuck no, I didn't."

A pang lit in my chest. "Then why do you want to take me out?"

Jax stared at me a moment, and then his features returned to the lazy, relaxed look that was somehow incredibly sexy and nerve-racking. "Honey, I'm not going to do anything with a girl who's drunk, especially you. No way in hell. When I said you were safe with me, I wasn't bullshitting around. I even told you that last night."

"You did?" All I remembered was Jax jerking back, but he had been talking while I was knee-deep in freak-out mode and about to hurl. "Oh."

"Oh," he murmured, and then he rocked my world. "And I remember you telling me I was your first kiss. That shit in the office earlier doesn't count, but I'm going to be your *real* first kiss. After I take you out on Sunday."

My mouth dropped open. I was back to freaking out, because he'd known about my years as a pageant queen, and needing to get away and being turned on. Yes, I was turned on. I might be very inexperienced for obvious reasons, but I recognized what my body was going through. Which wasn't good, because there was no way I could explore any of that with him and I didn't plan on being around long enough to give either of us time.

"Actually . . ." His head dipped again and his chin grazed my right cheek. "I want to kiss you now."

I shivered.

Jax felt it. "And I think you want me to kiss you. Correction. I know you want me to kiss you."

I shuddered this time, nearly overcome by the heaviness in my breasts and the sharp whirl of tingles down below. My hand fisted in his shirt. He couldn't kiss me. I couldn't go out with him. This wasn't why I was here.

Why was I here again? It didn't matter. The reason had to be dumb.

He made a deep sound in the back of his throat that really twisted me up in delicious little knots and now it was his lips sliding over my cheek, following the curve of the bone, heading straight for—

The office door burst open. "Jax, are you—whoa. Not expecting that."

I jerked at the sound of Uncle Clyde's voice and started to pull away. Jax let me get turned around, but he didn't let me go. His arm was still around my waist.

Clyde looked at me and his gaze moved over my shoulder. I could feel the heat of Jax behind me, and then Clyde looked at me again.

He smiled a big, toothy smile.

He smiled!

"Wasn't expecting that," he said, smoothing his hand over his apron. "Not at all."

I had to do damage control. Stat. "It's not what—"

"We're going out on Sunday," Jax announced to my disbelief. Then he pulled me back against his chest, into his heat, and I almost died right there. The way my heart sped up, I was sure that was going to happen. "I'm taking her to Apollo's."

Apollo's?

"Good choice, boy, very good choice." Clyde sealed the comment with a nod of approval.

Holy shit!

I had to get out of here. This time when I pulled free, Jax let me go. I stumbled forward, shooting him a look over my shoulder.

Jax winked.

He winked!

I stomped off, passing Clyde, or trying to pass him, but he looked down at me and he *also* winked. "Good choice, baby girl, very good choice."

There were simply no words.

Heading back out to the bar, I drew in several deep breaths. Hands shaking, I ignored the looks Roxy *and* Nick shot my way as I grabbed my apron. Tying it on, I hurried onto the semi-busy floor before Jax made his way out.

He wanted to kiss me.

He wanted to take me out to get steaks at Apollo's.

And Uncle Clyde approved.

Oh dear Lord in heaven, how in the world did I end up where I am? But I had done the right thing by getting out of that room, and I was going to do the right thing by not going out on a date with Jax. I needed a broken heart like I needed my mom being in a bigger mess than she was already in.

My step faltered at that thought, and I almost dropped the basket of fries I'd grabbed from the window on the head of the guy I was carrying it to.

Broken heart?

The older man looked up, the skin around his eyes crinkling. "You doing okay, girl?"

I nodded, recognizing the man. He was in his late fifties. A regular. In the bar every night I worked, even the busier nights when the crowd was younger, like tonight was getting. "Mind is all over the place, Melvin."

"Know the feeling."

Placing the basket on the table, I smiled. "Need anything else? Another beer?"

"No, sugar, that'll be all for now." When I started away, he stopped me by placing his hand on my arm. "It's good to see you here, doing what your momma should be doing."

My jaw opened, but I had no idea what to say to that or how to feel about everyone knowing who I was. Then again, it wasn't a secret. He patted my arm and then turned to his fries, which were smothered with Old Bay Seasoning.

Okay. Tonight was going to be weird. My life was weird. And dumb—couldn't forget dumb.

Pivoting around, I saw Jax swaggering behind the bar. He looked smug. Pleased. Wholly confident. His gaze cut in my direction.

I whirled, aiming for the front of the floor to check the tables that didn't need to be checked. The bar picked up, and I only went behind the bar to relieve Nick, and then I took my lunch, and it was weird taking a lunch late at night. I wasn't hungry, still full from the grease-capades, and I didn't want to hang out in the bar or in the kitchen, considering Clyde was already probably planning my wedding.

It had stormed earlier in the day, but it had eased off when I stepped outside. The air was still thick with humidity. Walking aimlessly around the building, I lifted my hair off my neck and wished I could wear ponytails on nights like this.

I like you.

I said I wanted to fuck you.

My knees wobbled a little, and I wondered how weird would it be if I just smacked myself in the head.

I'd taken two more steps when I saw the shadows clustered around the Dumpsters pull away and become thicker, solid. My heart stuttered as I backpedaled a step. The unexpected movement stirred tendrils of unease. Spinning on my heel, I headed back toward the front of the building. It was probably someone back by the Dumpsters relieving himself or doing something else nasty, but I picked up my step. A basket of fries would be good about right now.

I was almost to the corner of the building when, without any warning, the tiny hairs all over my body rose. The steady thump of footsteps behind me was close. My breath caught. Every instinct in my body fired off.

A second later I was grabbed from behind and shoved against the brick wall as a wet, warm hand folded around my throat.

Then Mack was right in my face.

Fourteen

"Say one word I don't want you to say and you'll regret it," he threatened, and in the dim light, something shiny and sharp flashed in the corner of my right eye. "I'll even out that face of yours."

Even as anger rose, ice built in the pit of my stomach as I stared into his dark eyes. The hard set to his face and the sneer to his lips told me he wasn't making idle threats. All I was able to get in was a shallow breath.

"You understand? Nod if you do."

I didn't want to nod, because I didn't want to lose an eyeball, but I did as he ordered. I nodded.

His sneer spread into a tight, cold smile. "Good girl. Now I tried to get a message to you the night before, but that fuckwad had to get involved, and I'm not telling Isaiah that he's fucked, you get me?"

I *so* did not get him on the last part, but I nodded again, because I really didn't want another scar. And I'd also thought that Reece, or one of his cop buddies, was going to pay Isaiah a visit and explain that I had nothing to do with my mom's shenanigans. Either that hadn't happened or it hadn't mattered to Mack or Isaiah.

"Mona's got a little under a week before Isaiah gets really impatient," he went on, and the knife he held shifted. Air caught in my throat. "If she doesn't show by next Thursday, it will be your problem. It'll be the fuckwad's problem, too."

I was assuming that fuckwad was Jax. "I . . . I don't know where she is."

"That's not my problem. And it ain't Isaiah's problem, either." Mack moved, and the front of his body was pressed against mine, and there was a good chance I was going to vomit again. "It's your problem. And don't even think about pulling any shit and leaving town. We know where to find you and you really don't want your friends back at that school to get pulled into this. You got that?"

My heart pounded in my chest as I nodded for the third time.

"You don't want to get on the bad side of Isaiah. Or me. We don't fuck around." When he moved against me this time, I held whatever little breath I had in my lungs. There was no space between us, and it felt nothing like when Jax was that close. This made my skin crawl. "If she doesn't show, we'll send her a message. You don't want to be a part of that message."

I so did not want to be a part of the message.

His beady eyes traveled over my face, lingering on my left cheek. "You know, you're not too fucked-up looking. I could do you doggy-style. Turn you around. Fuck you from behind."

My eyes widened, and now my skin felt like it wanted to jump off my bones and run far, far away. Acid churned in my stomach, fueled by panic and more than just a little bit of fury-tipped fear.

Mom brought this on, dragged this nasty piece of shit right to my doorstep.

His smirk turned even more vile. "Yeah, I think I have a good idea what message to send. Even better, it will send another message to the fuckwad inside."

Oh God, this wasn't good. I was pressing back against the wall, absolutely horrified by what he was implying in his threat. I knew what that message would entail.

My stomach hurled.

"And you better keep that mouth shut," he added, pulling back. The knife disappeared for a second, and then I felt the tip under my chin, causing my fingers to dig into the wall behind me. "Get me?"

"Yes," I whispered, not about to nod this time.

Mack laughed darkly, and then he was off me, walking across the parking lot all casual, like he hadn't just threatened me with nasty things or held a knife to my throat. He got into an SUV and drove off.

Then I moved.

Knees weak, I put one foot in front of the other and went back into the bar in a daze. I walked right past the bar, and I thought I heard someone call my name, but I kept walking. I went into the office and sat on the first available place to sit. The leather made a funny sound as I dropped down on the couch. Hands shaking, I placed them against my clammy forehead, and forced myself to take several deep breaths.

This was so not good.

"Calla?" Roxy called from the door. Like an idiot, I hadn't closed it. "Are you okay?"

I didn't lift my head or say a word, because I was pretty sure if I did either I would literally lose my shit. All I did was shake my head, and I wasn't sure if that was a good shake or a bad shake.

Roxy didn't speak again, and I squeezed my eyes shut. What in the hell was I going to do now? I had no idea where my mom was or where to even start looking for her, and I had this horrible sinking feeling a message was going to get delivered, because I'd never been able to find my mom in the past when she disappeared, so now wouldn't be any different.

Maybe I really should've left like Jax and Clyde had told me to do in the beginning.

"Calla?" This time it was Jax's voice and he was closer than

Roxy had been. I could tell he was right in front of me at head level with mine. He had to be kneeling, because the boy was Godzilla sized. "What's going on?"

When I didn't respond immediately, because I was trying to figure out what the hell I could say, I felt his hands circle my wrists and he gently pulled them back from my face. I was right. He was squatting in front of me, and his striking face was pinched with concern.

He moved onto his knees as he let go of one of my hands and cupped my right cheek. "Talk to me, honey. You're really starting to worry me."

That much was true. His eyes were darker than normal and his jaw was set in a hard line. Our eyes met, and I knew what I had to do.

I was so not keeping my mouth shut.

Screw that.

Keeping my mouth shut was absolutely the dumbest thing to do because I could not handle this mess on my own. I knew that. There was no way. "Mack was here. He was outside when I went out there. I guess he'd been waiting for me."

Jax took a deep breath as his gaze sharpened and his shoulders hunched. "He approached you."

"Yeah," I said in a dry laugh.

His features hardened, telling me he did not think the laugh was funny. It wasn't.

"He said that I needed to find my mom. That her being missing was my problem. And he said that if Mom didn't show up by Thursday, it really was going to be my problem." As I spoke, Jax's face literally locked down. No emotion. Nothing. His expression was bland, but it was as cold as an arctic blast. "He said that I would become a message that they would send to Mom."

There was a slight tremble in his hand and then Jax dropped it as he rose quickly. He took a step back. A muscle throbbed along his jaw.

"I don't want to be a message," I said, my voice small. "I really don't want to be the kind of message he was talking about."

He stared at me a moment and then understanding flickered across his face, and the whole atmosphere of the room changed. Tension poured like the rain had earlier. "I'm going to find that son of a bitch and fucking kill him."

Whoa.

I stood, raising my hands. "Okay. I don't think that would be the appropriate response."

"He threatened you?" he shot back.

"Well, yeah, but . . ."

"He threatened with what I fucking think he did?" Although I didn't confirm that, and it was a good thing I didn't share that Mack thought it would also be a perfect message to send Jax, he still got it. "And he threatened you on *my* fucking ground?"

I wasn't sure how this was his ground, but whatever. "Jax . . ."

"Did he touch you?" he asked, and I sucked in a breath.

I shook my head. "No. Not really."

"Not really?" His voice was low, hitting a pitch that was beyond calm.

Nick was suddenly in the doorway. "Is everything okay?"

"Not now," Jax spit those two words out in a way that would've sent me running in the opposite direction, but Nick stayed, his gaze bouncing between us, obviously reading that something was going down. "Calla."

Maybe telling Jax wasn't a good idea. I probably should've just gone straight to the police, because he was looking like he wanted to give some good old-fashioned redneck justice. I swallowed hard. "Mack had a knife."

"Shit," muttered Nick.

Jax stiffened, like his back went ramrod straight. "Did he hurt you?"

"No," I whispered. "All he did was threaten me. He said he was . . ."
I glanced at Nick, but he was like Jax, alert and ready. I lowered my
voice. "He said he would even out my face if I screamed."

There was a moment of silence and then Jax absolutely exploded.
Like a bottle rocket. "Son of a bitch!" he shouted, and I jumped a
good couple of inches off the floor. "I am gonna kill that mother-
fucker."

"Jax, jail time really isn't what you have in your four-year plan,"
Nick said, and dumbly I wondered if Jax really had a four-year plan,
and I'd also stupidly realized this was the most I'd ever heard Nick
speak at one time. "You knew this was bound to happen."

My gaze swung sharply to Nick, and they did know. Clyde had
warned me. Jax had warned me. They'd said that Mom had been
messed up in some bad shit, and they had said that shit would spread
to me. They hadn't been kidding around, but I hadn't really thought
it was *this* bad; even with the heroin, I hadn't realized it was like
this. I'd been more concerned with getting my own money back and
being pissed off at Mom and feeling bad for myself.

I should've gone back to Shepherd. I should've called Teresa and
asked if I could crash at her place. I should've gotten the hell out of
Dodge.

Should've. Could've. Would've.

Truth was, though, even if I had known from the beginning that
it was seriously this bad, I wasn't sure I would've left knowing what
Mom was messed up in. I probably would've tried to find her the
first day here if I'd realized it was *this* bad. Find her, steal money,
and send her on a one-way ticket to anywhere but here.

Jax twisted, thrusting a hand through his hair. "Knowing it was
going to happen and seeing it go down are two different fucking
things, Nick."

"I know," he replied quietly, way quietly.

I folded my arms around my stomach, shivering again. For the most part, I thought I was handling this pretty well. I wanted to clap myself on the back, but when I spoke, I heard the tremor in my own voice. "What am I going to do? I have no idea where Mom is and he said if I tried to leave, they knew where to find me. I'm going to end up as a real messed-up—"

Jax was suddenly right in front of me, cupping both sides of my face. His thumb touched my scar, but the look on his face was scarier than anything I'd ever seen in my whole twenty-one years of life, and I'd seen a lot of scary stuff.

"You're not going to be a message. You aren't going to be shit to any of them. You feel me? No one is touching you," he said, and he said it right in front of Nick. He touched me right in front of Nick, touched my scar. "We're going to take care of this and none of this shit is going to rub off on you. Okay?"

I believed him.

Wow. I really believed him.

"Okay," I whispered.

Jax dipped his head, brushing his lips across my forehead, and he did that right in front of Nick, too. And that pulled at something in my chest, really tugged at it. Then he turned to Nick, and as he did it, he slipped an arm around my shoulders, dragging me against him. I hesitated for a second, but then I went. I leaned into him, because at this moment, I thought I really needed to lean into someone.

"We need to call the police," Nick said. I opened my mouth, but he went on. "We're going to have to wait and not do it here."

"We need to do it where it's not public," Jax confirmed, his hand curving around my waist. "I'll call Reece, let him know what's going on. You got the bar for the night?"

Nick lifted his chin in universal boy-speak. "I've had it before you did."

There was a beat of silence and then Jax said, "True."

Fifteen

Clyde was beyond pissed, in a fit, when Jax filled him in on what had happened. I hadn't wanted to tell him, but then again, he shouldn't be left in the dark, either.

"I'm going to kill him," Clyde all but yelled.

A lot of people were going to kill Mack.

Clyde gave me one of his bear hugs that felt so good and promised that this would be taken care of. He did this with a spatula in one hand.

I loved the guy.

We waited an hour, and even though I felt out of it, I worked the bar during that time, keeping up appearances. Jax had warned, as did Clyde and Nick, that the bar could be watched—that there even could be people *inside* the bar watching. Not people who belonged to Mack, because everyone swore he was still a low-level wannabe gangsta, but Isaiah's people, and Isaiah was anything but low level, I would learn later that night.

It was closer to midnight when Jax and I left Mona's, and I hated leaving that early on a Friday, one of the best nights for tips, but money—unbelievably—was the least of my problems.

We drove to my house, and Jax followed me in, staying close. He wasn't really talkative as I quickly changed into a fresh pair of jeans and a shirt that didn't smell like a bar.

"We're going to meet up with Reece," was all he'd said before I headed into the bedroom.

I freshened up my makeup out of habit and then we were in Jax's truck, driving back toward town. My stomach was in knots by the time I recognized the road his townhouse was on.

"We're going to your house?" I asked.

He nodded, eyes on the road. "Reece will stop by here. If you're being watched, hopefully they'll think he's just coming by to see me. Everyone knows we're friends."

My hands curled inward. "Do you think I'm being watched?"

His hand tightened on the steering wheel. "It's possible."

"God," I breathed, shaking my head slowly. All of this . . . it seemed unreal.

We didn't speak as he pulled into a parking space, hopped out, and jogged around to my side by the time I had the door open. He took my hand, holding it firmly as he walked me toward the door that had 474 in silver numbers on it.

I wasn't sure what to expect when I walked into Jax's house. I hadn't been in a lot of guys' houses, at least not any that didn't have a girlfriend, so I was expecting the place to be a mess, full of pizza boxes and beer cans.

That's not what I saw.

Just inside the door were a couple of pairs of sneakers, neatly stacked against the wall. One of the pairs reminded me of basketball shoes, and an image of a young boy with blond hair racing through a house, holding a basketball against his chest, filled my thoughts.

Kevin.

Shaking those thoughts out of my head, I kicked off my flip-flops, but Jax left his shoes on. Straight ahead was a stairwell that led upstairs and downstairs, to what I assumed was the basement level.

I followed him into a very male living room—dark brown couch and recliner positioned around a TV the size of a small car. There were a couple of potted plants in front of the window. Blinds were drawn shut. The dining room had a small dark-colored wood table set, and it led right into a kitchen that looked like it was recently cleaned. With the open floor plan, it was nice and airy.

"I like your place," I said, and then flushed, because I was pretty sure I sounded like a dork.

He grinned over his shoulder at me as he dropped his keys. "It works for now, but eventually, I want a place with a yard and no neighbors right on top of me. Every once in a while, the couple next door gets into it. Hear everything. Sometimes it's entertaining. Sometimes not so much."

For some reason, I felt my stomach topple over. He was only a few years older than me and he already had what he wanted now and knew what he wanted in the future. I didn't know if I'd like living in an apartment, a townhouse, or a home. I never thought that far in advance and I didn't know why. It was something I seriously just realized right that moment.

My Three F's plan really wasn't much of a plan.

"You okay?"

I blinked slowly, finding Jax watching me curiously from the kitchen. "Yeah, just a lot on my mind."

"Understandable." Jax moved to where I stood just inside the dining area. Well, he didn't move. He stalked forward with the grace of a dancer. Stopping just short of being seriously on me, he placed both his hands on either side of my neck and tilted my head back with his thumbs under my chin. "Everything is going to be okay."

My heart did a little pitter-patter, and for the life of me, I couldn't prevent it. I wanted to ask why he was getting this far involved, but words like "I like you" and other stuff he'd said came to the forefront of my mind. And he'd kissed my forehead in front of Nick.

He dipped his head and brushed his lips across my forehead. "Want something to drink? I have soda. Water. Apple juice."

I didn't realize that my eyes were closed until I heard his deep chuckle and I opened my eyes. "Water," I said, clearing my throat. "That's good."

One side of his lips tipped up. "Yeah, I'm really looking forward to that date on Sunday."

What the what? If I recalled correctly, I hadn't agreed to the date. He let go, his hands sliding off my neck, leaving a trail of shivers in their wake.

Goodness, he'd just kissed my forehead again.

I didn't know what to do with this or how to respond. My hands were shaking again, but for very different reasons. I hurried into the living room and sat on the couch. I didn't feel twenty-one right then. Fourteen would've been pushing it.

"Actually," I called out, twisting around. I couldn't see where he had disappeared to in the kitchen. "Can I have apple juice?"

Another deep, sexy chuckle traveled to where I sat. "Sure thing."

I bit down on my lip and flipped around. Jax came out, holding a juice box with the straw poked through the top. My gaze shifted from his face to the box and back to his face. I couldn't help it. A laugh crawled up my throat and burst free. Here he was, this gorgeous guy who had this sexy, rough side to him, and he had juice boxes in his house.

Loved it.

My lips curved up as I took the juice box. "Thank you."

Jax stared down at me. There was no one-sided grin this time. He smiled, and boy, he gave a great smile. It reached his eyes, turning them into melted chocolate. "You have a great laugh," he said. "And a gorgeous smile. You should do it more often. Both things. Smile and laugh."

The juice box almost slipped from my fingers. Again, he struck me speechless. I had no idea what to say, and the only thing I could come up with was "Thank you."

Did I just thank him for that?

Yep.

My mouth was still blabbering on, because I zoomed right into deflection mode. "But *you* really do have a beautiful smile. I mean, it's actually kind of breathtaking, and your laugh? It's wow. I think it's your lips—you have great lips . . ."

Did I just say that out loud, seriously? Said he had great lips?

Jax's smile seemed to have widened, and hell, it was like the only star in the sky it was so bright.

Yep, I'd said that out loud.

Oh my God, I was an idiot.

Luckily, the doorbell rang, saving me from saying more stupid stuff. He reached out, swiping his thumb under my lower lip, absolutely stunning me. Then he turned and headed to the door.

I sucked a huge gulp of my apple juice and had barely recovered by the time Reece stepped inside the house and Jax closed the door.

Reece was in his uniform, and I was so used to seeing him in jeans, I gaped at him with the straw from my juice box resting against my lower lip. Somehow his shoulders looked broader in the dark blue uniform that had been tailored to the extreme, displaying the flat stomach, narrow hips, and strong legs.

"Hey, Calla," Reece said with a grin.

I snapped my mouth shut. "Hi," I murmured, taking another slurp.

Reece's grin went up a notch as he looked to Jax. "Sorry it took so long. I switched out the cruiser and drove my personal car here just in case there were eyes on the road."

I shuddered at the idea that there could be people watching the bar, the *roads,* and even Jax's house.

"Good plan," Jax said, sitting down beside me on the couch. And he really sat beside me. His entire thigh was pressed against mine.

"But what I want to know is how come one of Isaiah's fucking minions is out running around threatening Calla when you were supposed to warn the fuckers off."

Oh. Wow.

Reece narrowed his eyes on Jax, and he was no longer some random hot guy who hung out at the bar or just some hot cop dude. His whole stance changed. Shoulders squared, eyes sharpening, and legs spreading as he stood in front of the recliner. "We haven't been able to track the asshole down. It's not like he's easy to reach, but we will get to him."

"Make it easy," Jax said in a low voice.

"Jax," Reece warned.

Oh. Crap.

"Your job is to serve and protect, right?" Jax fired back, jaw hardening. "So fucking *serve* and *protect*."

For a tense moment, I thought they were going to throw down in the living room, but then Reece took a deep breath. "You're lucky you saved my ass in the desert or I'd be knocking you on yours."

Jax had saved his ass? I wanted to know more about that.

He smirked at his friend. "You'd try. Key word being try."

That comment was ignored as Reece sat on the arm of the recliner, his attention on me, and I knew I wasn't going to find out about saving asses. "I need you tell me everything, Calla."

I glanced at Jax for some unknown dumb reason, and when he nodded, I sucked up more apple juice, found the box empty, and sighed. So I told Reece everything—starting with the money Mom had stolen from me, the real reason I was here, and why I was working at the bar. While I'd told him that, Reece had sent Jax an odd look I couldn't figure out, but his attention centered on me when I told him about Greasy Guy, the heroin, and then what Mack had said to me outside the bar.

"Shit," Reece grunted when I was finished, and I figured that summed everything up quite nicely. "This is definitely some shit you've waded right into. It doesn't take a leap of logic to figure out that that heroin at the house wasn't your mom's. There's a good chance she was holding it for someone, and when you look at that kind of amount, then it was probably Isaiah's. And God only knows what kind of shit he has on your mom that she'd willingly hold that kind of dope. That's a huge fucking liability to be responsible for."

By the way my heart was beating, I didn't like how any of this sounded. "Who is this Isaiah?"

"He runs drugs, lots of drugs, among other illegal activity. The thing is, when you see Isaiah, which will be next to never, he doesn't look like a damn dealer. He comes across as a businessman." Jax's lip was curled in disgust. "I think the last time I saw him, he was wearing fucking Armani."

"He has legit business dealings and he's pretty damn powerful," Reece added, and I really didn't like what I was hearing. "He's got eyes and ears everywhere, and a shit ton of people in his pocket, even cops. He's the real deal when it comes to people you don't want to fuck with. Your mom and the shitheads she runs with aren't people he typically deals with. How she's involved with him is beyond me."

"Not like that matters now," Jax said. "Mona is messed up with Isaiah and owes him money or, knowing our luck, a ton of heroin." Jax leaned against the cushion, dropping his arm along the back of the couch. His hand landed on my opposite shoulder, causing me to jump. "And that has spread to Calla."

"Got it," Reece clipped.

As I sat there and listened to the boys, I thought about the last night I'd hung out with my friends back at Shepherd—Cam and Avery, Jase and Teresa, Brit and Ollie, and even Brandon and what's her name. We'd talked about school, going to the beach, and traveling the world. Not heroin and a drug lord who probably had a lot of experience giving people a cement swim.

"If you know he runs drugs, how is he not in jail?" I asked.

Both guys stared at me, and then Jax murmured, "Cute. She's cute."

I shot him a look that said go jump off a bridge.

"When I said Isaiah is powerful, I wasn't kidding around. The cops that aren't in his pocket have tried to take his ass down. Even the feds are on his ass, but evidence . . . well, it just doesn't seem to stick," Reece explained carefully, and I had this feeling there was a lot that he wasn't saying. "There's a world out there that doesn't operate by right and wrong and all we can do is try to minimalize collateral damage."

Collateral damage. Wow. It was then, in that moment as I stared at my fingers, I realized I was collateral damage. And the world out there, that little bit of it that I had a taste of growing up, was much bigger and much worse than I ever knew.

"We need to find my mom," I said, looking up. "I have no idea where she could be, but maybe Clyde knows. Or maybe I can try talking to Isaiah, explaining my—"

"You are not getting anywhere near Isaiah," Jax said, his hand tightening on my shoulder. "And there are some places where we can check for your mom, but they're shit holes you aren't getting near, either."

"Excuse me?" I twisted toward him as I jerked forward, but his hand remained. "The last I checked, you aren't the boss of me, buddy." Yeah, that wasn't a very clever response, but whatever. "This is my problem."

"It's my problem." His eyes locked with mine.

A shiver coursed down my spine. "It's not your problem."

"The hell it isn't."

My hand squeezed the juice box, crushing the cardboard. "Mona might be your boss, but she's my mom. It's my problem."

"Boss?" Reece muttered.

Jax leaned forward, his face getting right up in mine. "It's *my* problem, because it's *your* problem."

"That makes no sense!" Frustration pecked at my skin, mixing with confusion. "You barely know me, Jax. You have no reason to get involved in this."

"Oh, here we go again, with the 'barely know you' crap. I don't need to be your best friend forever, honey, to get involved," he shot back, eyes the darkest brown I'd ever seen. "The truth is, I have known you for a while now. You just didn't know me."

I blinked, sort of startled by that, but I recovered quickly. "Just because you know Clyde and my mom doesn't mean you know me or can tell me what I can or cannot do."

Reece sighed. "Kids . . ."

He was ignored. Again. "Oh, it's just not that. I've slept with you. That makes you my problem."

"Whoa," murmured Reece.

My mouth dropped open. "You have not slept with me!"

"Oh, we did sleep together." His lips kicked up on one side. "And I know damn well you haven't forgotten that."

Oh my God.

"Or waking up with me," he added, his eyes warming. "Yeah, *that.*"

Oh my good God. I whipped toward Reece. "He doesn't mean what you think he means."

Reece held up his hands as if he was saying don't bring me into this.

I whipped right back to Jax, who was grinning smugly, but before I could say a word, and I had no idea what to say after all that, he clapped his hand around the back of my neck, his fingers threading through my hair.

"It's *our* problem," he said, voice low. "Okay? You want to find your mom, I'll help and I'll be right beside you, but you aren't doing this alone."

I opened my mouth to argue that I didn't need his help. I'd spent most of my life not needing help, but Reece cut in before I could go further. "You did good, Calla, telling Jax what's going on. So many people out there think they can handle shit alone, when in reality, a first grader knows they need help. Continue being smart about this. While some of the people around here are mainly harmless, this whole situation is treading into dangerous territory. Be smart. Be safe."

Those words somehow made it through the haze of irritation. Be smart. Be safe. In other words, don't be dumb. And it was one thing being dumb when it came to Jax, but another when it came to getting myself hurt or worse.

So I nodded.

Jax gently squeezed the back of my neck and then dropped his hand. "That's a good girl."

I rolled my eyes.

"I'll get some of the boys looking for Mona, too, and we'll step up getting in contact with Isaiah. Meanwhile, I'd suggest staying close to Jax or Clyde." Reece took a breath. "And I want to talk to Mack."

I stiffened. "You can't do that."

"I didn't say I was going to talk to Mack about you. I don't like the fact that he's threatened you, but I'm also going to be smart about it."

"It can't bounce back on her," Jax said.

"It won't." Reece smiled tightly. "Trust me, Mack will do something within twenty-four hours that will warrant a visit from me. I can force his attention elsewhere, at least for the time being."

"Sounds like a plan," Jax stated.

None of this really sounded like a great plan to me, but what did I know? Reece got up to leave, saying he'd be in touch, and Jax walked outside with him. I slumped back against the couch and was in the middle of an obnoxious yawn when Jax returned.

"Is everything okay? I mean, when you went outside with Reece?"

"Yeah. He actually was talking about something unrelated to this. One of our buddies is getting married. I'm one of the groomsmen."

"Aw, that's nice. Is he one of the guys that come into the bar?"

He nodded. "It's Dennis. He was making sure I could do the bachelor party since it'll be on the weekday." He watched me for a moment. "Tired?"

I really was. The tequila from last night and the events of today had caught up with me. I wanted to close my eyes and forget for a little while. I nodded as I pushed myself onto my feet, figuring it was time for Jax to take me back to the house.

"So am I," he replied.

Instead of grabbing the keys he'd dropped off on the counter, he toed off his boots. I didn't understand what he was doing since I didn't think he'd drive barefoot. "Aren't you going to take me to the house?"

The socks came off next, and he dropped them near the boots. "I've been staying with you. So has Clyde. That's definitely not changing now."

I was sort of glad that one of them was staying with me now.

"It's late. There's no reason for us to drive back out," he continued. "You can stay here."

My heart did a backflip. I'd never stayed over at a guy's house before. "I don't think I should stay here."

"You can have another juice box."

I glanced at the front door as my insides knotted up and my hands started to get a wee bit clammy. "I don't want any more apple juice."

"I have fruit punch, too. Not the generic shit. Capri Sun."

He had a variety of juice boxes? I shook my head. That wasn't important. It was most definitely cute, but not important. "I don't have a change of clothing."

Jax grinned as he rounded the couch and neared me. Every muscle in my body tensed. "I'm sure I have something you can wear. And I also have unopened toothbrushes. You're covered."

Damnit.

"Calla, it's no different than me staying at your place."

But it was. My pulse kicked up as I searched for a logical reason that didn't involve me being dumb, but there really wasn't a valid one I could come up with. "Okay," I breathed.

That damn grin was back and now my stomach was doing cartwheels. "I'll . . . I'll sleep on the couch."

"Not happening."

"Then you're sleeping on the couch?" I asked, hopeful.

He laughed. "Hell no, that thing isn't comfortable. No one I even remotely like sleeps on that couch."

Oh dear. "Do you have another bed?"

"Only one, but it's big." He reached between us, taking my hand, and I cringed, because I seriously hoped my hand wasn't sweaty. "King-sized. There's room for both of us and a Saint Bernard."

"You have a Saint Bernard?"

He chuckled. "No."

That was a stupid question. "I don't think it's good that we sleep together. I mean, that's like really . . . I don't know, just not a good idea."

One eyebrow rose. "The best things in life are rarely good ideas."

My lips twitched, but I pressed them together. How did I respond to that? Jax then tugged on my hand as he turned, heading for the stairs, and I trailed after him silently, my heart racing in my chest. I didn't put up much of a protest as he led me up the stairs, because I was too busy freaking out.

There was a hallway bathroom and two bedrooms. Both doors were open. One room had been converted into an office/workout room. Dumbbells lined the wall, stacked neatly near a bench. But we didn't go in there. He led me straight into the other bedroom and flipped on a light.

I was having trouble breathing.

Jax didn't seem to notice as he walked around the huge bed and started to root around in a dark oak dresser. I stood perfectly still.

I was in Jax's bedroom.

In the middle of the night.

Muscles flexed and rolled under the shirt he wore as he straightened, and I wished I was normal. Not like that wish was the first time, and I'd wished for that for a ton of reasons, but if I was normal, I would be standing here excited instead of scared and full of hopelessness. I'd be eager and not tasting the bitter tang of dread. I'd be worrying about what kind of undies I'd put on that morning instead of thinking about the scars.

I'd just be a girl standing in the bedroom of a guy she liked. And dear God, I did like Jax. Yeah, I hadn't known him long, but what I did know about him, I liked.

"This shirt will probably double as a nightgown on you." He walked it over, handing it to me as I stared up at him. "That door over there leads to a bathroom. There's fresh toothbrushes in the drawer under the sink."

I still stared up at him.

"I'm going to make sure everything is locked up. Okay?"

Holding the borrowed clothing to my chest, I didn't say anything or move as Jax stepped around me. He stopped, placing a hand on the small of my back and leaned in, speaking into my ear. His warm breath there felt good. "Remember what I told you?"

He'd told me a lot of things.

"I figured you haven't spent the night at many guys' houses before."

My nose wrinkled. Was it that obvious? Ack.

"I like that about you," he continued, and I thought that was a weird thing to like. "It's cute."

He *was* weird.

But there was a mushiness in my chest.

"I told you that you were safe with me." His hand glided to my hip and squeezed tentatively. "That hasn't changed, Calla."

I exhaled slowly. He had said that and I did trust him. Time to pull the big girl panties on. I was staying here, sleeping in the same bed, but I wasn't having sex with him.

"You're staying," he said.

I sighed. "I'm staying."

"And you're not sleeping on the couch. Neither am I."

My heart did a handspring this time, and I sighed once more and nodded again.

Sixteen

*W*hen Jax left the bedroom, I all but ran into the bathroom and closed the door behind me. Like the rest of his townhome, it was clean and neat. Blue bath rugs on the floor matched a blue shower curtain. No other decorations. Not looking in the wide and long mirror, I quickly undressed. I had to take the bra off. I couldn't sleep in one, and I wasn't sure if it had to do with the scars or that it was just uncomfortable as hell. But Jax had been right, the shirt was so big and long that it went to my mid-thighs and wasn't tight. Plus I'd put the tank top back on under the borrowed shirt and it gave me extra layers.

My undies were cute—hot pink hipsters with a tiny bow in the center—but that didn't matter, because there was no way in hell he was seeing my undies, so thinking about them or the tiny bow was dumb.

I washed off my eye makeup and grabbed one of the toothbrushes, and tried not to think about why he had so many unopened toothbrushes in his bathroom.

Once I was back in the bedroom, I darted across the room, turned off the light, and then whipped back the covers on the side farthest from the door, and I climbed in. Rolling onto my side, I stared at the closed closet doors for a good twenty or so minutes, suddenly no longer tired.

The bed smelled nice. It smelled like him, actually, a mixture of his cologne and some kind of soap. I inhaled and then almost choked. Was I seriously sniffing his bed? That felt like an all-new low.

Then I heard him coming up the stairs.

It took everything in me not to roll around flailing and acting like a general idiot and to stay still. I ended up pressing my lips together and squeezing my hands tight as his footsteps hit the bedroom. I heard him walk to the dresser, and then the next sounds made me wish I'd taken a deeper breath before holding it.

A zipper was pulled down, the tinny sound stretching my nerves. Clothing rustled.

Pants hit the floor.

I dipped my chin, and even though the room was dark and all I could see was his shadowy form, I strained to see more. Might make me a perv, but oh well. He was pulling something on—bottoms, but he didn't appear to have a shirt on as he turned back to the bed.

I'd give an ovary to see those abs in the bright light.

The bed dipped under his weight and there was a slight tug when he pulled the covers up. He shifted around, and although he wasn't close to me, I could feel his warmth. He didn't say anything, and I thought of what he'd say earlier, about him knowing me longer than I knew him. That didn't make sense because he'd been surprised when he'd realized Mona was my mom.

I didn't want to think about that or anything, but my mind wondered and raced, refusing to shut down. And even though I was normally comfortable on my side, I suddenly wanted to lie on my back, but I didn't want to move, because I should just go to sleep. I wiggled my hips, hoping to get comfortable and hoping he'd fall right asleep. The first night he had slept in the other bed he'd fallen asleep pretty quickly.

"Calla?"

I squeezed my eyes shut and held my breath.

"I know you're awake."

Dang it. "I'm sleeping."

Jax chuckled deeply. "Amazing how you can respond while sleeping."

"I'm sleep-talking."

There was another toe-curling laugh. "You're not tired now, are you?"

"Yes," I lied. "I'm exhausted."

"Is that the reason why you've been squirming around since I got into bed?"

I pried my eyes open with a big, dramatic sigh. "You're not tired?"

"Not anymore," he replied, and oh wow, his voice did that deep thing that made my lips part. "You doing okay with everything?"

Aw damn, now the mushiness was back in my chest. That was sweet of him to ask. God, he was so nice, and I wasn't even drinking tequila, and I wanted to tell him. "Yes. And no. I mean, it could be worse."

"Yeah, I guess so." The bed did a little jiggle, and I could tell he was closer. I could feel his warmth under the covers. "I know of a couple of places where your mom might be. We can check them out tomorrow before we head to the bar."

I nodded. "That . . . that would be good."

"And Reece will make sure Mack isn't around in a week. You don't have to worry about him."

"But I have to worry about Isaiah?" I asked in a quiet voice.

The bed moved again as Jax rose onto his elbow. He was close, not touching me—shirtless—and I could feel his eyes on me, even in the dark. "We should find your mom."

I got my answer without the question even being answered. My lips were back to being pressed together, and there was this lump in the base of my throat. Mom . . . what had she gotten herself into? Needing to focus on something else, I thought back to when Reece was here. "You saved Reece's life?"

Several seconds passed, and then Jax settled behind me, closer yet again. I could almost feel his legs behind mine. "It's not really bedtime material."

I figured that. "I want to know."

"Do you really?"

Asking myself that same question, I realized that I really did want to know—to know more about him. "Yes."

There was one more pause. "We were in Afghanistan together, a part of a scouting group. There were at least twenty of us and we'd done it so many times it was like habit. All of us were on point, but we weren't worried, but that's the thing about habits. They can break you, too."

I bit down on my lower lip, unable to imagine the kind of world he'd seen.

"We were outside a small village—a village that looked like any number of them we scouted in the past, but it was different. Turned out to be heavily armed, and not all of them were a part of the cause. There was a roadside bomb."

I flinched. Oh my God, a bomb? You didn't live in America for the last decade or so and not be familiar with the destruction a roadside bomb, even the small ones, could wreak.

"It was an ambush," he added quietly, almost like an afterthought. "These things happen a lot. One minute everything is going smoothly, and then the next, the whole world is blowing up. Our group was scattered. Reece took a shot to the gut. I got him out of there."

The next breath I took felt funny. "You got him out of there?"

"Yeah."

And that was all he said about that, but I knew there had to be more. It wasn't as simple as getting someone out of there when bombs were going off and people were shooting at you. "Was . . . was that something that kept you awake at night?"

He didn't answer for a long moment. "Some nights . . . I dreamed that I didn't get to Reece in time. Then other nights, I saw the things that went down that day. Crazy how the brain holds on to those kinds of images."

My chest started to ache. "And whiskey helped with that?"

"Sometimes," he murmured. "It sort of dulled everything— dulled the detail."

I wanted to ask more, but then he asked a question that caught me off guard.

"Did you like doing the whole beauty queen thing?"

My eyes went wide. "I . . ." I didn't want to answer the question because I didn't like to even think about it, but I doubted Jax liked to talk about people shooting at him and bombs, so I owed him. "I liked it sometimes."

Okay. That wasn't a lot, but that was something.

"Sometimes?" he prodded gently.

I sucked my bottom lip between my teeth and then closed my eyes. "Sometimes it was fun. I was a little girl and I liked dressing up. I felt like a fairy princess." I coughed out a dry laugh. "So it was like playing dress-up every week and it made . . . it made my mom happy when I had my hair done and all the makeup on and I was onstage. And it made her really happy when I'd win, especially the big titles."

"What kind of titles?" he asked into darkness.

"Grand Supreme is one." I had to open my eyes, because I could see myself on the stage, turning and blowing kisses and folding my hands under my chin. "When Mom was happy it was like she loved me. I know she loved me, but it was like she really loved me then."

I wiggled my hips again, trying to find a spot without flopping onto my back. "But there were times when I wanted to be . . . I don't know, just be a kid. I wanted to play, but I had to practice walking, or I wanted to hang out with my dad, but he didn't like going to those things, and sometimes I wanted to spend time with . . ." I trailed off, closing my mouth.

"Spend what?"

Sometimes I wanted to be at home, spending time chasing after Kevin. He was older than me—the big brother—and when I was home, I was his shadow. And I also liked being with Tommy, because he was so small and so cute, like a real baby doll I'd played with.

But I didn't say that, because it had been years since I'd spoken their names out loud, and it had been years since someone else said their names, up until Clyde had over the weekend.

"It was okay," I said, hurrying on. "It's not something I think I'd ever do if I had a child."

"Me neither. I think it causes little girls to focus on the wrong thing—everything being about looks. So that's something we agree on."

"Yeah," I whispered, feeling my belly tighten. It was different lying in bed with Jax and talking about what we agreed on when it came to child rearing.

"What was something you liked doing as a kid that didn't involve the beauty queen shit?" he asked.

My heart squeezed because I couldn't answer truthfully. My favorite thing had been hanging with Kevin. I went with the next-best thing. "Playing basketball."

"Basketball?" The surprise was evident in his voice.

"Yeah, what about you?"

There was no hesitation. None whatsoever. "Pretending like my little sister got on my every damn nerve when in reality I loved when she followed me around, because with her, we were always getting into something."

My breath caught, and I didn't know what to be more affected by—the fact that he had a sister or the fact that his relationship with his sister sounded a lot like Kevin and my relationship or what it *could've* been. "You have a sister?" I asked after a few moments.

"Had."

A heaviness settled in my chest and not that good kind. "Had?"

"Had," he repeated.

Oh no. I squeezed my eyes. "She's not with . . . us anymore?"

"No."

I rolled onto my back. I didn't even stop to think about it, and when I turned my head, Jax's face was inches from mine. "What happened?"

His gaze was on mine. "When she was sixteen, she was in a car accident with her boyfriend. He was speeding and the truck he was driving rolled over. He was killed in the accident and my sis . . . well, she broke her leg and collarbone. So she was in a lot of pain after the accident and not just physical."

Oh, I had a bad feeling to where this was heading.

A small, sad smile appeared on his full lips. "Jena . . . she was such a cool kid, had bigger balls than most guys I knew. Would ski and BASE jump and skydive, and was constantly giving our parents heart attacks, but after the accident, she changed."

"How?" I whispered, but the bitter taste in the back of my mouth told me I wasn't sure I wanted to know.

Because I was staring at his face, I didn't see his hand move in the small, dark space between us, but I felt the sweep of his thumb across my lower lip, all the way to the tips of my fingers and toes. "She was given a lot of prescriptions for pain. It started off legit, but she got addicted. I think being high helped her not deal with her grief, you know?"

Oh God, did I ever know. I stared at him, unblinking and whispered, "Yes."

"The docs eventually cut her off, but she was hooked. She didn't want to deal, so she moved on to other things—heroin and Oxy-Contin." His thumb glided over my lower lip again, causing me to shiver. "My parents tried to get her help, but there was no stopping what was coming. I was in boot camp when our mom found her in her bedroom. She'd overdosed. Died sometime during the night." He drew in a deep breath. "For the longest time, I blamed myself."

My brows knitted. "Why?"

"I thought maybe if I'd been home, I could've stopped her," he replied. "Hell, a part of me still thinks that."

"You can't help people unless they want to be helped," I told him. "Trust me. I know."

"I know you do," came his quiet response. "But that's some guilt I'll probably carry with me for a while, if not forever. She was . . . she was my little sister. It was my job to keep her safe."

"Oh Jax," I whispered. The knot was bigger in my throat. "I'm so sorry," I said, and I knew it sounded lame, but I didn't know what else to say.

His thumb did another pass and then his hand moved away. "There's nothing you need to apologize for."

"I know." A moment passed as I dragged in a deep breath, and then I rolled back onto my other side, facing the closet door again. My heart ached for him and his family and a sister that never had a chance to become anything. We didn't have the same past. No way. But there was a similarity there. Mom was who she was today because she couldn't get past the grief and heartache, and I wondered, if Jax knew about the pageants, then did he know about the fire and about Kevin and Tommy? "I'm sorry you lost your sister and what you experienced overseas. You . . . you must be very brave."

"I think it was more of not wanting to die or to see my friends die than it was being brave."

That was a very modest thing to say. Since he shared so much with me, I felt like I needed to share something really unknown about me, but it was hard. It took a bit to get my tongue to form the words. "I'm a liar."

There was a pause and then, "What?"

Even though it was dark, my face filled with blood. "I'm a liar. My friends back home—Teresa and her boyfriend Jase, and Avery and Cam. Cam's Teresa's older brother, and him and Avery are like the cutest couple in the world," I rambled on, nervous. "Cam has a pet tortoise and he got Avery one."

His body shook with a quiet laugh. "Their turtles are in love?"

"Yep. You can't help but feel the love when you're around them; not even the turtles are immune to it." And I kept going. "Teresa and Jase are like the hottest couple in the world. Seriously. Then there's Brandon."

Another moment passed. "Brandon?"

Probably shouldn't have brought him up. "He's another friend. He has a girlfriend," I added quickly and then moved right along. "Anyway, they're great. They really are, and I love them, but I've lied to them. They know nothing about me and I've told them so many lies."

"Babe . . ."

"No. Seriously. I've told them that Mom was dead." When there was silence, I made a face at myself in the dark. "See? That's a horrible lie. But there was never any chance that they were going to meet her and in a way, she is kind of dead, you know? The drinking and the drugs killed my mom years ago."

"I see," he murmured.

I wasn't sure if he did. "And they think I'm visiting extended family right now."

"That's not a lie. Clyde is like family."

My mouth opened to correct him, but he was right. Huh. "Last semester, I told Teresa I was going home for break and you know what I did, Jax?"

"What?" was his soft reply.

"I stayed in a hotel and ate room service." When he didn't respond, I added, "The room service was really good, though."

"You're not a liar," he said after a few moments.

"Um, what part of this convo did you miss? I've lied to them. On purpose." And now that I really talked about it, I felt like a total tool for it.

"You had your reasons, Calla. You weren't lying to be a bitch or whatever. You didn't have a great childhood and your relationship with your mom is nonexistent at best. I'm sure your friends would understand if they knew the truth." He paused. "And everyone has secrets, babe. Not one person is always a hundred percent honest in every single situation. And that goes for your friends."

I closed my eyes as his words sank in and there was no denying that they helped make me feel a little better about all I'd kept from my friends. "Thank you."

He didn't say anything for a few and then he shifted again. His legs were most definitely touching mine. "Calla?"

My breath caught once more. "Yeah?"

After a beat of silence, he asked, "So you think I have great lips?"

"Oh my God," I groaned, forgetting I'd said that earlier. Jax's laugh danced over my skin, and just like that, everything felt okay. "I hate you."

He chuckled again. "No, you don't."

The room was dark, so I smiled, and I knew he didn't see it, but I had a feeling he knew I was smiling and he was right. I didn't hate him.

"Calla?"

"Jax?" I had no idea what he was going to say next.

He touched my hair, or I thought he had. It was so light and so brief, I wasn't sure, and then he said, "You have to be very brave, too."

I drew in a soft breath. "About what?"

Jax didn't answer, and I didn't push it, because I was afraid he would expand on that statement, and I wasn't even sure why I was afraid. After a while, I heard his breathing deepen and I knew he was asleep, and I lay beside him, feeling the knot in my chest now. It was a long time before my thoughts settled from what he'd told me, what he'd shared and said. And from everything else I hadn't told him.

Seventeen

*W*aking up the second time next to Jax James was like waking up the first time. He was most definitely a cuddler while he slept.

When I finally fell asleep, his thighs were against the back of mine, but it hadn't been like this. His entire front was flush with my back, and not only that, one of his legs was thrust between mine, and his arm was curled around my waist. Our heads had to be sharing the same pillow because his warm breath stirred the hair along my temple and danced across my cheek.

We were spooning again.

And it felt just as good and as dumb as the last time, but a good kind of dumb. A dumb I wanted to play around in, because his body heat had created this snuggly cocoon I didn't want to part with, but I remembered what happened last time.

Drawing in a deep breath, I started to basically throw myself away from Jax and off the bed, but that didn't happen. The moment I moved, the arm on my waist tightened, and suddenly I was rolled onto my back.

Jax tossed his leg over mine and he moved in—no, he *snuggled* in. When he spoke, his lips brushed the side of my neck, sending a wave of goose bumps across my flush. "Where do you think you're going?"

Oh wow. His voice, deep and rough with sleep, and mixed with the fact his lips brushed my skin as he spoke, was a wildly alluring combination. My heart skipped, kicking up my pulse.

"I . . . I was getting up."

"Mmm," he murmured, sliding his hand across my stomach and up, to where it rested just below my breasts. I bit down on my lip as a sharp sensation crowded my insides. His hand was way close and if he spread his fingers, his thumb would most definitely be getting some action. "You don't understand the concept of sleepy time."

My eyes were wide and fixed on the ceiling. I knew I should move his hand. I didn't think he could feel any difference in my skin through the borrowed shirt and tank top, but a nervous energy built in my stomach, mingling with a feeling I recognized.

I'd never been laid, sexed up, or whatever. Obviously. But I was as curious as any girl who'd gone through puberty and whatnot, so I'd gotten familiar with my body more than a few times, and I knew what that *edginess* was zinging through my veins.

"Do you?" he asked.

"I . . ." My tongue stopped moving because that was when his hand moved just the slightest and his fingers spread. His thumb brushed against the under swell of my left breast, and I jerked in reflex. I don't know if it had to do with the scarring or not, but my left breast was waaay sensitive.

His hand was still after that. Waiting. Instinct told me Jax knew exactly what his thumb had brushed against and now he was waiting to see how I responded. Or maybe he was copping a sleepy feel without realizing.

Jax's lips brushed a surprisingly hot spot just below my ear, and the air went right out of my lungs. *Wow.* Okay. He was probably not copping a sleepy feel and knew exactly what he was doing.

I needed to remove his hand.

I needed to get the hell out of this bed.

But I didn't move.

And whatever answer he was waiting for, he must've gotten it. His thumb drifted along the swell of my breast, and my throat dried. Holy hotness, what were we doing?

"Forget about sleepy time," he said, moving his lips against the skin of my throat again. "I think I like the fact you don't understand it."

"You do?"

That thumb went up about half an inch, and I bit down on my lower lip. "Yeah. I like you waking up."

I had no idea what to say to that, and my lashes were slowly, but surely, lowering, even as my heart was picking up its beat and warmth was invading my body, easing out the tautness in my muscles at the same time it was building a different type of tension.

"You know what's going on here." His statement caused my eyes to open wide once more. There was a beat. "Please tell me you understand what's going down here."

"Yes," I whispered, and then I said, "No."

"Yes and no?" His voice had gotten deeper, rougher. Tingles danced from the tips of my breasts down to my belly and lower, much lower. "Care to explain?"

"Why?" It was all I could say.

Those lips skated along the side of my throat. "Why what?"

I was having trouble forming thoughts. I'd never been touched like this before, and it was barely a touch, but he had my senses spinning. "Why is this going down?"

"Because I want to." His thumb glided again.

That wasn't an answer. "But why?"

"I've already told you." He pressed his lips against my pulse, causing me to gasp, and then he lifted his head, resting his weight on the arm next to my side. He stared down at me, his look intense. "It's the same reason behind why I'm taking you out to dinner tomorrow night."

My eyes were locked on his and my heart was pounding like it was stuck in a steel drum. That damn thumb of his was on the move again, evoking another wave of tingles.

"I like you, Calla," he said in a voice barely above a whisper.

I changed up my next question. "But *how*?"

Jax blinked.

The one word change sounded pathetic even to my own ears, but I seriously didn't get it. Half of my face was good. Half *wasn't*. He hadn't even seen the rest of me, and he was the kind of guy you wrote home about to your mom, your dad, and every single person you know. And I wasn't sure if he'd known me long enough to even judge what kind of personality I had or—God, I couldn't believe I was even going to think this—if I was rocking some inner beauty or not.

"What?" he said, eyes narrowing.

A different kind of heat crept into my cheeks. "I'm a realist, okay? I have been for a long time. I *need* to be, and you liking me—wanting to take me out on a date and do—"

"Really fun and interesting things to you," he supplied.

I flushed. "Yeah, that."

"Naughty things that are going to make you feel so good," Jax continued, and his words and the way he spoke them turned me on like I'd never been before. "That's what I want to do to you."

"Okay," I breathed. "I get that."

One side of his lips kicked up. "Good."

"But it doesn't make sense," I pushed on as I fisted handfuls of the blanket. "You're hot and—"

"Well, thank you."

I ignored that and tried desperately to ignore how his hand was almost entirely cupping my left breast. I didn't want to think about that, because it made me think that if I weren't covered up, he wouldn't be doing what he was doing now. I drew in a deep breath. "I'm not hot. I'm not—"

My words ended because he dipped his head and his lips brushed mine. "We've had this conversation before," he said, moving his mouth over mine. "And I've told you I wouldn't kiss a girl I didn't find attractive."

"But you said that wasn't a real kiss."

"It wasn't. This is."

And then Jax kissed me, like really kissed me. His lips pressed against mine, moving as if he was getting himself familiar with the layout of them. My fingers unclenched from the blanket and I placed them on his chest, just below his throat, to push him off. His skin was hot and hard and rough. It felt different, but before I could really investigate that, he caught my lower lip between his teeth and nipped. I gasped at the unexpected bite and the rush of sensations erupting. He took advantage of that and deepened the kiss, slipping inside me, and I was no longer thinking about pushing him off.

The kiss . . . it was wet and deep and it wasn't good or nice. It was great and everything the romance books claimed kisses were. Jax *tasted* me. There were no other words to describe that kind of kiss. Not when he slanted his head and touched his tongue to mine. Not when he flicked his tongue along the roof of my mouth, dragging up a throaty moan from deep within me.

Jax pulled back to say, "I like that sound. Fuck. I love that sound."

My eyes stayed closed as my lips tingled. "I . . . I didn't know you could be kissed like that."

"Hell," he groaned.

He kissed me again, and it was just as great as the one before, but this . . . this kiss turned into something more. The hand that had almost been cupping my breast was now seriously cupping my breast, and my body moved on its own. My back arched, and I made that sound again, and he seemed to really like it again, because there was a rich, decadent growl that rumbled through him. Then his fingers moved on my breast, and that damn, skilled thumb of his found the tip of my breast with unnerving accuracy. My head thrust back into the pillow, and his mouth followed me, nipping and kissing as his thumb smoothed over the hardened peak.

His lower body shifted under the covers, settling over mine. Using his thigh, he eased my legs apart and slipped in-between them. I gasped into his mouth as a sharp dart of pleasure pounded through me, centering into one spot.

My brain closed down. I wasn't thinking about *anything,* and I did it. I kissed him back. I slid one hand off his upper chest, around to the nape of his neck. My fingers tangled in his hair. I chased after him, wanting to taste *him,* and I did. He let me take as much as he took, and he let me learn the layout of his lips and mouth. My hips moved on their own accord, pressing against his thigh out of primal instinct.

"God, you're sweet." He shifted slightly, lifting himself to give enough room to do a slow slide of his hand down my stomach. "You know what I want? I want to see you get sweeter."

Sweeter? I was breathing heavy, panting really. My lips felt swollen; so did my breasts. The tension between my legs left me swimming.

"Have you come before?" he asked as his hand reached the hem of my shirt, which was twisted around my hips.

My eyes popped open. What was he doing? I couldn't let him get his hand under the top. Panic bit into the pleasure as I reached down with my other hand and grabbed his wrist.

His eyes were open, and they were the color of dark chocolate. They made me shiver and want whatever naughty things he was talking about. "Have you come before?" he asked again.

Heat bled into my face and I stuttered out an answer. "Y-Yes. Kinda."

"Kinda?" He tugged on his arm, and with him being so much stronger than me, I couldn't stop him. His fingers were below the hem, but not under it. "Meaning no one has ever made you come? No one but yourself?"

Oh my God, I could not believe he was asking me this—that this conversation was even happening. My heart was pounding too fast and I ached; my body literally *ached*.

His lashes lowered until his gaze turned hooded. "Yeah, I'm going to be the first to give you one."

Holy hot shivers, he did *not* just say that. "Jax—"

An instant later, his mouth was on mine again, and he got his hand farther down, way below the hem of my shirt. The back of his knuckles brushed the inside of my thigh, and my back almost came off the bed. His hand was moving up, the slight touch against my inner thigh shocking me. I tried to close my legs, but all I ended up doing was squeezing his legs with mine.

"I'm going to touch you," he said against my mouth, and my stomach coiled tight. Other parts of my body coiled tight, and I wondered if it was possible for a guy to make you come with just words. "That's all I'm going to do, okay?"

That's all? Before I could question that, he was kissing me again, and the back of his hand brushed over me—the *center* of me. This time my back did come off the bed, and he made a deep sound of approval. My fingers tightened in his hair and my other hand clenched his wrist. Then the tips of his fingers skated across my panties, and I thought I was going to have a heart attack.

"Calla, babe . . ." He kissed the corner of my lips. "Let me touch you."

I couldn't. There was no way. Letting him touch me was dumb.

"Let me," he said, and his voice was like silk over my skin.

My heart stuttered, and my hand around his wrist loosened and then slipped up his forearm, to his flexed bicep.

I was so dumb.

"That's my girl."

My girl? Parts of me trilled at the sound of that, and then my blood really was singing, because his fingers had made a couple more passes, an idle circle over my panties that got closer and closer until I moved my hips, and he was touching the bundle of nerves, pressing down with two fingers. Rolling. Pressing. Rolling.

"Oh God," I gasped against his mouth.

I felt his lips curve into a smile, and the kiss turned wilder as my hips moved against his hand. "That's it," he urged, working something like magic with his fingers. "Let me see you get sweeter."

My head thrust back and his mouth skated over my cheek as I cried out. I might've said his name. I wasn't sure. I was too focused on how the coil deep in the center of me unleashed, whipping out through my system in tight, intense shocks.

I could feel him watching me as the waves of pleasure eased off and my neck straightened. Part of me felt like I should be embarrassed. This was the first time I'd experienced anything like this with someone. As the pleasant haze of release turned my muscles to goo, I didn't know what to do other than just lie there. I did let go of his hair and my hand slipped to his neck.

"Sweeter than I imagined," he murmured, kissing the side of my neck. Then he rolled off, easing onto his side, and his hand slowly slid out from between my legs, stopping on my pelvis. "You still alive?"

"I'm not sure. I can't feel my legs."

He chuckled. "Just think. That's really nothing compared to what it'll be like when I'm in you."

My eyes popped open and I was staring at the ceiling. His words shocked me, and then I thought about the fact that I had most definitely gotten off, but he hadn't, and I looked toward him, about to point that out in what would probably be the most awkward thing ever, but all I could do was stare at him.

Jax was reclining on his side, resting his head in his palm. The cover was down by his hips and his bottoms were hanging low, showing off those sexy as hell indents on either side of his hips and the tightly rolled muscles of his abs. Yeah, he was rocking a six-pack, and yeah, as I slowly dragged my eyes to his pecs, I might've drooled a little. Or a lot. My mouth was definitely hanging open, but for different reasons.

His body was chiseled and cut and just wow, but his skin . . . it was another story. There were marks, dozens and dozens of them, all across his chest and over his abs, and I understood now why I'd thought his skin had felt rough.

Sitting up, I glanced at his face—at his lazy, half smile and raised brows—and then back to his body. The marks were like craters in some areas, where pieces of flesh had either been removed or sunken in. Other marks were puckered, healed over.

Without thinking, I reached out to him, and his free hand shot out like lightning, snatching my arm around the wrist. I swallowed hard as I lifted my lashes. "What happened?" I heard myself ask and then I swore under my breath, dipping my chin. Hair slipped over my shoulder, falling between us. "I'm sorry. That's a damn rude question. I should know."

"It's okay." He brought my hand forward, and the tips of my fingers brushed a scar. "Roadside bomb," he reminded me. "Shrapnel sucks ass."

Oh my . . .

I knew he hadn't been telling everything last night. I lifted my gaze. "So you got Reece out of there, but you had shrapnel in you?"

"Yeah," he said like it wasn't a big deal.

But it had to be, because so many of those marks were over his heart and a lot of other vital places. Some were deep. They had to have hurt and bled a lot. And he managed to get Reece out of there? God, he wasn't just brave. He was crazy brave. Our gazes locked, and I don't know what made my mouth move. "It was glass exploding that cut my face."

Jax didn't respond as he slid his hand down, pressing his fingers over mine, against his skin.

"It . . . it was a backdraft," I said. "There was a fire and pressure built up in the room . . ." My gaze broke free from his, shifting to his body, to the connect-the-dot map of scars. I'd never told anyone this. Ever. "When I opened the door, oxygen poured in or something like that and the window exploded."

"You're lucky." He rose into a sitting position and his knees knocked mine. He lowered his head and we were face-to-face. "You could've lost an eye."

Or a nipple, but I wasn't sharing that. "You were lucky, too."

"Damn straight."

Neither of us spoke for a long moment, and then he was up and off the bed in like a nanosecond. "Let's get breakfast. Maybe IHOP today," he announced while I stared at him. "Then we'll go looking for your mom. Plan?"

I blinked once, and then twice. "Okay."

That lopsided grin appeared. "You got to get off the bed."

Yeah, he made a good point, but . . .

"Wait." I hobbled off the bed, feeling my cheeks heat as the words rolled right off the tip of my tongue. "What about you?"

He'd stopped at the foot of the bed, head cocked to the side, bottoms hanging so low I could really see that happy trail of his. "What about me?"

"You know . . . I, well, I came and you . . ."

"Didn't?" The grin was spreading.

"Yeah. That."

He tipped his head back and laughed.

My lips slipped down at the corners. "What's so funny?"

"You are. You're funny. You're cute." He came forward and he was right in front of me. "And you're sweet as hell when you're coming."

Oh. Wow.

"I know I didn't come, but honey, you never had anyone but your own hands down between those pretty legs before." His gaze dropped to said legs, and I shivered. "That's the first time you've had that and it needed to be about you. Not me."

Oh. Double wow.

I gaped at him as he turned, starting for the bathroom. My insides started to melt, get a little gooey.

Then he stopped and twisted toward me, lips curved in a mischievous sort of way. "I'll take care of myself in the shower."

My jaw was on the floor.

Jax sucked his bottom lip in between straight, white teeth. "And I'll be thinking of you when I do it."

Eighteen

Things changed after a guy gave you an orgasm. Not something I'd ever considered before, since no guy had done that to me, but I was catching on pretty quickly.

I'd gotten back in bed while he showered since it turned out that we really were up early. It wasn't even eight in the morning. I tried not to imagine him in there touching himself, but my thoughts kept going back to that and what it must look like, and that was, well, it was turning me on, which was pretty shocking considering I still wasn't sure I had complete use of my legs yet. I really needed to stop thinking about all of that.

So I used that time to take stock of my life.

I finally had a non-Calla-induced orgasm, which was pretty epic. Part of me was proud that I'd finally jumped that hurdle, even though I was twenty-one when it happened. But I wasn't sure what to do with it. I mean, what did it mean for me? For Jax? For us?

Oh my God, was there an "us" now?

My heart rate kicked up a notch as I sat straight up in the bed, staring at the closed bathroom door as I held the blanket to my chin. I could hear the water running from the bathroom and then . . . I heard him. Not groaning or anything like that, but he was humming something or maybe singing, but it sounded like humming because of the water. Suddenly, all of this was so intimate I wanted to jump out of the bed and run screaming and flailing through the townhouse and out into the streets.

What was I doing here?

There couldn't be an "us" that involved orgasms and showers and songs being sung and breakfasts. I didn't plan on being here forever and I planned on going back to college in August once I got the approval for financial aid, and that's what I wanted, right? There was no future between us.

I blinked slowly.

And I needed to be focused on finding my mom so I didn't end up getting cut up by some low-level gangsta, or worse yet, meeting this Isaiah face-to-face.

More important, someone like Jax couldn't be in my life. The skin along my back had the consistency of—

So caught up in my own head, I hadn't heard the water shut off, so when the bathroom door opened and Jax stepped into the bedroom, I wasn't expecting it.

He had a towel knotted around his lean hips and his hair was soaked, brushed back off his forehead, and his entire body was on display.

Yummy eye candy for the win.

Damn, he looked good. Like good enough that I might've been drooling again.

"You want to shower before we head out?" he asked, strolling toward the bed like he wasn't wearing anything more than a towel.

"Huh?"

A half grin appeared. "A shower? Do you want to shower?"

I was an imbecile. "Yes," I squeaked, popping out of the bed. I grabbed my clothes off the dresser. "A shower is a great idea," I rambled on, trying not to look at him. "You're so smart."

Jax twisted sideways as I passed him and smacked my behind.

I jumped and emitted another squeal out of shock, and he chuckled. Looking over my shoulder to shoot him a glare, I then realized he hadn't smacked me with his hand.

It was the towel that *had* been around his hips.

And I was not only staring at his muscled back, which, wow, was a nice back, but also his muscled ass. "Oh my God!" I shrieked. "You're naked!"

That chuckle turned into a laugh, and I whipped around, almost throwing myself into the bathroom, but it was too late. Those firm globes were seared into my memory.

He'd been naked! Totally freaking naked, and didn't care. Complete lack of modesty there, and that further cemented there could never be an "us." I had more modesty than a church full of old nuns.

I took advantage of the soap that smelled like him and the two-in-one shampoo and conditioner. It wasn't until after I showered, had changed into my own clothing, and was twisting my wet, combed hair into a bun at the top of my head that I realized I had no makeup on.

Nothing.

What had been left on my face this morning had rubbed off a bit, letting the scar show more clearly. Dermablend was serious stuff, but it was most definitely off my face now.

"Oh God."

My wide eyes stared back at me in the reflection, the blue so bright in the early morning sun coasting in through the small square window. My face had that peaches-and-cream complexion without the Dermablend—a coloring that no makeup in the world could replicate. If I saw only the right side of my face, I knew I looked better without the makeup, but I didn't walk around with only half of a face.

Without makeup, the scar was still a deep shade of pink, standing out starkly against my complexion, slicing from the corner of my left eye almost to the corner of my lip. It was the only thing I could see.

"Calla?"

I stiffened at the sound of Jax's voice and then gripped the sink. I couldn't go out there. It was ridiculous, but I couldn't let him see me like this.

"Are you okay?" he called.

Holding my breath, I turned toward the door. Would it be obvious if I walked out with a towel over my head? I was being stupid. I *knew* this, but Jax had just been kissing me, he'd had his hands on me, and he'd touched me, making me feel something so beautiful and this—*this* was so ugly. I didn't want him to . . .

A whoosh of cold air swept through my body and I closed my eyes, drawing in several deep breaths. Jax knew the scar was on my face. He'd been all up close and personal with my face. He even kissed—

The bathroom door swung open, banging into the wall, and my eyes popped open as Jax barged in.

I hadn't locked the bathroom door.

Le sigh.

He did a body scan, as if he were checking to see if I was injured or something. "Jesus," he ground out. "I thought you fell in here and knocked yourself unconscious or something."

Well, that was kind of embarrassing, but not the most pressing issue. I angled my body to the left so he could see my right profile. "I can't go to breakfast."

"What?"

"I can't go to breakfast. I need to go back to the house." I knew it sounded irrational and stupid. "Can we go back to the house?"

Jax shifted and his denim-clad leg came into my view. His feet were bare, poking out from the frayed hem of his jeans. "Why?"

"I just need to go back to the house. If you want to go ahead to IHOP, I can get my car and meet you there. That would probably—"

"Hell no."

My chin jerked up and dipped to the left. "Excuse me?"

His eyes flashed with anger. "We're not taking separate cars when I just had my hand between your legs and you came while calling my name."

I opened my mouth, but really, what do you say in response to that?

"We're going to leave here together, eat some greasy goodness, and then we're going to go check out this place for your mom," he continued. "And when we're done, if we have time before our shifts start, we're going to indulge in a nap."

"A nap?" Really, out of all of that, that is what I focused on?

"Together."

"A nap together?"

"Yeah," and then his voice dropped, "and if we have time, I might make you come calling my name again."

Holy crap, he did not just say that.

Then he stepped farther into the bathroom, coming at me, and I backed up, hitting the sink. He crowded me, and as I tried to look to the left, his hand cupped my right cheek and the other circled the left side of my neck. He turned my face straight to his. This wasn't the first time he'd done that, I realized.

"I'm not stupid," he said, smoothing his thumb along the bones in my throat. "I'm also pretty damn observant when I need to be."

"Okay?" I whispered. "Um, thanks for the heads-up on that."

His lips twitched as he tilted my head back so our eyes locked. "I know why you're hiding in the bathroom."

Oh God. "Because I'm afraid you're going to make me try another pie I'd never eaten before?"

"Ha. No." His head lowered, and I swallowed hard. "I don't notice it."

My heart tumbled over and I went with pretending to be dumb. "Notice what?"

"Calla, babe, you know what I'm talking about. This." Then his head slanted and I felt his lips at the corner of my left eye, just below it.

I sucked in a sharp breath that hurt. He'd done this before, too, and it created the same maelstrom of emotion in me, but he did more this time. His lips followed that scar all the way down my cheek, right to the corner of my left lip, and then he kissed me. It was soft and sweet and it lingered. My hands went to his chest and I leaned into him.

When he lifted his mouth from mine and pressed his forehead against mine, tears had built in the back of my throat. "I don't care about it, Calla. I don't even think about it," he said. "I don't even see it."

I squeezed my eyes shut as my heart squeezed into goo. Immediately, I didn't believe him, because come the fuck on, but I stopped—I just *stopped*. Stopped telling myself I knew what was going on in Jax's head and that I knew what he wanted and didn't want. I *stopped*. Because I didn't know—no one ever knew, scarred or not. *Stopped* telling myself there was no point, because I planned on leaving. And all I had was what Jax was telling me, and what he was showing me. So I *stopped* all the other bullshit and I shook that crap off and it was like scrubbing Dermablend off my face at night, when I finally felt like *me*. All of this might be dumb. It might bite me in the ass later, but I was going to be dumb. I was going to be the best dumb I could be.

Whoa.

I wobbled a little and I exhaled through my nose and when I spoke, my voice was unsteady and the back of my eyes burned, but I pushed on. "Okay. Let's do this. And get this done, because I really want that nap."

Those lips curved against mine. "That's my girl."

When Jax walked out of the townhouse, he was tugging the back of his shirt down as he walked down the small set of stairs on the front stoop. He was rocking a pair of mirrored sunglasses, aviator style like Jase wore, and he'd looked just as good in them.

We didn't talk much as he drove to IHOP, which was good, because I was fixated on what might happen before or after the possible nap. More orgasms not self-induced? Count me in. I was so going to follow through with my newly desired dumbness and not worry about anything else while exploring the dumb.

Like any normal red-blooded female, I'd thought about sex a decent amount, but not as much as I had in the last hour or so. My brain was playing happily in the gutter, right up until the plate of bacon, biscuits, and something Jax had said were grits and that I needed to try.

It was hard not thinking about being out in public without makeup, but every time my mind wandered to it or I *thought* someone was checking it out, like when a small boy had peeked over the back of the booth or when the waitress smiled at me, I forced it out of my thoughts.

And then my thoughts went to this—this Jax and me *thing*. There was a *thing*. As he'd said earlier, he had his hand between my thighs and I'd called his name, so there was a *thing*. A *thing* I had little experience in, and I wasn't sure how far this *thing* really was going to go, because if my financial aid kicked in, I'd be heading three hours down the road. What kind of future was there for our *thing* when I'd be at college and he'd be all sexy working the bar?

Why was I even thinking about this? Because I was dumb and I'd already decided that I was going to go with this *thing,* whatever it was, and whatever going with this *thing* meant.

I poked at the white lumpy crap with my fork. "This is grits?"

"Try it."

"It looks like something out of a horror movie." I poked it again. "I'm afraid it's going to launch itself off the plate and cover my face."

Jax chuckled as he added some pancakes to the river of syrup.

"It's not funny. I'll end up birthing an alien grit baby or something," I muttered. "And then what are we going to do?"

He peered up through his lashes, a small, amused grin playing across his lips. "Just try it."

"What does it taste like?" I resisted.

"Grits."

I lowered my fork, looking at him blandly. "Details."

He laughed as he cut through what looked like ten pancakes stacked. "One cannot simply describe grits. One must simply enjoy them."

My eyes rolled, but I scooped up a small taste, made sure I had cheese in it, and gingerly tasted them. The whole time Jax watched and waited. I swallowed, unsure of what to think. I tried a little more.

"So?" he asked.

"I don't know." I shoved a mouthful in. "I haven't decided yet. I think they taste good, but they're called grits; therefore I'm not sure I can freely admit to liking something called grits. I have to really think about this."

Jax laughed. "Cute."

I grinned as I went for a slice of bacon. "So where are we going after this?"

"Inside Philly," he said in between mouthfuls. "There's a house she used to hang out at a lot. Maybe we'll get lucky and she'll be there or they've seen her recently."

"Sounds like—"

"Calla! And Jax!" shrieked a familiar voice. I twisted in the booth, spying Katie. She was trotting over to us. Literally trotting, and I blinked, wondering if we time-warped back to the eighties and I'd been unaware of it.

Katie was wearing hot pink spandex tights, slouchy purple socks, sneakers, and an off-the-shoulder black shirt. And a scarf—a polka-dotted red and blue scarf, and it was June.

"Hey," I said, waving a slice of bacon around.

"Gurl." Katie stopped at our booth, holding on to a carry-out box. "Look at you. Told you, your life was going to change."

Um.

Jax shoved a huge slice of pancake into his mouth, and I could tell he was trying not to smile.

"What are you doing up so early?" she asked, and then went on before I could answer. "I was doing yoga. Every morning. And I get IHOP, Waffle House, or Denny's every morning. It's like the universal counterbalance or some shit like that. But it's still kind of early for hot, busy bartenders to be eating breakfast. Together."

My gaze shifted to Jax.

"We woke up together," he said, and that was all he said.

Katie's eyes turned into spaceships, and I almost shouted that it wasn't what she was thinking, but then I realized that it *was* what she was thinking, so I forced myself not to say anything.

A big smile split across her pretty face. "Awesome sauce. Seriously. If you two stay together and end up getting married and having a kid, I think you should name your baby Katie."

Warmth crept into my cheeks. "Whaaat?"

"I mean, you could name a boy baby Katie, but they'd probably get made fun of in school, and I don't think you two would want that. Oh—is that grits?" She switched topics, not even taking a breath. "You need more cheese on them. One morning you need to come over to my house. I can make some mean-ass grits."

"That sounds good," Jax replied smoothly, his dark eyes twinkling in the lights. "And we'll take the name thing into consideration."

I turned my "what the fuck" stare on him.

Katie giggled. "Awesome. Well, I need to get home with my muffins and waffles. See you guys later."

Watching her spin on her heel and flounce out of the restaurant, I had nothing of any value to say, so I went with the next-best thing. "Did you know she fell off a pole, hit her head, and is now psychic?"

"That's what I hear."

I bit down on my lower lip. "Roxy says she's been pretty on point before."

"Katie," drawled Jax, and I looked over the table at him. He was smiling. "I wouldn't be opposed to naming a baby girl Katie."

"Oh my God," I said.

Jax tipped his head back and laughed that deep sexy laugh, and I couldn't help but smile.

I wasn't smiling when we entered the part of town one did not willing venture into forty minutes later. The street wasn't very active, as it wasn't even noon yet.

Jax found a parking spot in front of the worn-down brownstones across from a city park that looked like it belonged in a postapocalypse movie.

My gaze skipped over the boarded-up windows and doors on some of the units. "I'm not sure about this."

"This is the last shit hole I want to bring you to, but the last I checked, you served me with a dose of attitude about this being your problem and shit." He killed the engine and turned what was probably a very smug look on me. "So that's why we're here."

He had a good point, but it wasn't like I was going to admit to that. "Whatever."

His lips twitched. "Stick close to me. Okay? And let me do the talking—no, don't look at me like you just sucked on something sour. Let me do the talking. If you can't agree to that, then we're going to drive off, I'm going to lock you up with Clyde or Reece, and then I'll come back here on my own."

My eyes narrowed on him. "You don't have to be so damn bossy."

"Yes, I do." He leaned forward and kissed the tip of my nose. It was quick, but it still startled me. When he pulled back, he was grinning. "Do you agree?"

I hesitated and then sighed. Wasn't like I was Rambo and was going to run into the brownstones by myself, demanding to have them hand over my mother or else. "Oh, all right. Yes. I agree."

Jax nodded and then he climbed out. I sat there for a second, said a little prayer, and then got out. I did stick close to him as we walked down the block and then headed up the crumbling set of steps to a brownstone that had two windows boarded up on the second floor.

"Mom used to come here?" I asked, folding my arms around my waist.

He nodded as he glanced down at me. "Yeah."

Pressing my lips together, I knew I shouldn't be surprised. Wasn't like this was anything new, but seeing this and picturing my mom hanging out in a place like this just didn't set well, no matter how many trailers I'd pulled her out of when I was a teenager.

Jax rapped his knuckles on the door. A few moments passed and when no one answered, I figured this was going to be a no go, but then Jax pounded his fist on it.

"Whoa," I murmured, glancing around. "Do you think that's a good idea?"

He ignored me as he leaned in. "Open up the door, Ritchey. I know you're in there. Your piece-of-shit car is out front."

My eyes widened as my stomach dipped.

There was a beat of silence and then the front door opened to a crack. I couldn't see anyone, but I heard in a scratchy voice, "What the fuck do you want, Jackson?"

Um.

Jax placed his hand on the center of the faded red door. "We need to talk."

"Talk" was the response.

"Not on the front doorstep of your damn house, Ritchey. Let us in."

There was a pause. "Us?" Then the door opened to about a foot and a man's head appeared. I took an involuntary step back from the sight of the unshaven face, bloodshot eyes, and bulbous nose covered in broken blood vessels. "Who the fuck are you?"

I recognized the man even though he stared at me like he'd never seen me before. Holy shit, there was no way I'd forget those watery eyes and nose. He used to come over to the house and party with Mom.

"Really none of your business, Ritchey, and I'm not here to make introductions," Jax cut in, and his tone . . . wow, it was all kinds of badass. I was actually staring up at him, kind of shocked. "Open the door."

Ritchey didn't open the door.

There was a low curse and then Jax moved. Planting his foot into the door, he pushed with his boot and hand. The door opened and Ritchey went wheeling backward.

"Um . . ."

Jax took my hand, tugging me inside, and the smell—God, the smell was the first thing I noticed as he shut the door behind us. The room, which consisted of a blaring TV and two couches that had seen better days, smelled like a mixture of cat piss and booze.

Please do not let my mom be in here.

I know that I was wrong for thinking that. Finding her would ease my problems quickly, but I didn't want to think of her in a place like this.

"Not cool, man." Ritchey backed away, scratching at his throat with dirty nails. The skin of his neck was red. "Pushing the door open like you're a damn cop or something."

"You didn't open the door," Jax returned.

I had to wonder how much practice he had busting up into houses with um . . . questionable residents, because he was completely at ease doing so. I took a step to the side, because I realized there was a hole in the floorboard in front of me, and I could see over the back of a couch.

My chest squeezed.

There was a small child, maybe five or six, curled up on the couch, lying under a thin quilt. A cat was tucked in the little's boy lap. I stared at the kid, sickened.

"What's up?" Ritchey asked.

Jax kept his arms loose at his sides. "We're looking for Mona."

"Mona Fritz?"

"Like there's another Mona I'd come here looking for. And this isn't the first time I've come here looking for Mona," Jax said, surprising me. But then I remembered him saying he and Clyde had done this before. "Don't pull crap. You know how this works."

It worked a certain way?

Ritchey kept digging at the skin by his throat, but a certain gleam crept into his eyes. "I ain't got no part in Mona's shit."

Jax took a step forward, dipping his chin. "I'll only ask you once, Ritchey."

"Man, I ain't—"

"One time," Jax warned.

Ritchey didn't answer, and then Jax sprang forward, grasping the front of Ritchey's shirt and lifting him onto the tips of his bare feet.

Holy crap, this was going to get physical.

My mouth dropped and then I moved forward, keeping my voice low as I reached their side. "There's a kid on the couch sleeping, Jax."

"Shit," muttered Jax, but his hands didn't come off the guy. "You got Shia here, in this rat hole?"

"His damn mother skipped out. I'm doing the best I can."

His biceps flexed. "Let's take this into the kitchen and you're going to play nice. For Shia, okay?"

We took it into the kitchen, or what might have been the kitchen. It didn't have a sink, just a gaping hole where one should be. Out of the corner of my eyes, I thought I saw something brown and disgustingly large scurry over the wall near the fridge.

"Mona ain't here," Ritchey said finally.

"You mind if I check that out?"

"Have at it." Ritchey stepped to the side and leaned against the counter. "But I'm telling you. She ain't here and you ain't the first person to come looking for her."

I stilled. "We're not?"

"Who else has been looking for her?" Jax asked, not moving.

Ritchey's watery eyes narrowed on me. "There's something about—"

"Eyes on me, Ritchey." When he obeyed the demand, Jax didn't look any more relaxed. Unease formed in my belly. "Who came looking for Mona?"

"Some dudes. Some bad fucking dudes," he replied, folding his scrawny arms across his frail-looking chest. I thought this probably wasn't the best conversation to have in a room that a small child was sleeping in, but he went on. "Guys who work for Isaiah."

Oh. Bad news.

"We already know that," Jax replied calmly.

"There's some talk," he said after a few moments. "Mona's in deep."

"Another thing we already know."

Ritchey grimaced. "Yeah, but do you know she was the go-between to what was close to three million in heroin for Isaiah? And she was supposed to turn that stuff over a week ago?"

I almost groaned. My worst suspicions were confirmed. The drugs belonged to the uber drug lord and not Greasy Guy.

"Word on the street is that someone else has got the shit and Isaiah wants to hear it from the horse's mouth that she ain't got the shit no more." Ritchey hacked out a dry laugh. "Man, if I knew that stuff was at the house and she wasn't there, I'd have been all over that myself."

Nice.

And he kept going. "She's a dead bitch walking. You know that, Jax. Good thing she gave—"

"That's enough," he cut in harshly while my stomach ended up somewhere on the gross as hell floor. "Do you have any idea of where she is? Or Rooster?"

"Rooster?" Ritchey laughed again. "Man, he's holed up wherever Mona is, or if he's smart, he's gotten far away from where she is. Man, Jax, you know how Mona was. She'd get high, get to talking and acting like she was big shit because she was running mule for Isaiah and the shit got out. Mona ain't smart. She should've handed over that dope instead of sitting on it."

"Why didn't she?" I asked, and I could feel Jax's eyes on me. "Did you hear anything about that?"

He nodded. "Stupid-ass Rooster was talking about trying to run some game over Isaiah. Instead of taking the cut they got for going and picking the dope up, he wanted more before they handed it over. So they were sitting on it. And that put the asshole Mack in a bad position, because he was supposed to get that shit from them and hand it over. 'Cuz you know, Isaiah, he don't want to get his hands dirty."

Oh God, that was just worse in five hundred different ways. I didn't know what to say.

"And knowing Mona and Rooster, they probably got themselves a bit of it, got messed up, and then freaked, knowing they've pissed off Isaiah. Shit ain't looking good for them." He paused, spreading his arms. "And now, here we are, and all that shit rolls downhill, right through Mack, Rooster, and Mona."

A muscle thrummed along Jax's jaw. "Damn."

"Yep. You know who might have a clue to where they are?" Ritchey tilted his head to the side. Jax's chin went up a notch. "You know Ike?"

"Met him a time or two."

Ritchey nodded. "Track him down—he's been living north of

Plymouth, in the camp called Happy Trails. Can't miss him. Got one of those souped-up trucks." He glanced over at me again. "We've met, haven't we? Man, 'cuz you look familiar. I can't put it. Wait . . ." His pale eyes widened. "Holy shit, it's true."

"Ritchey," warned Jax in a low voice as he reached into his pocket. "Don't piss me off."

"Whoa, man, I'm not trying. I like you. Always have, being we both have seen battle." He raised his hands, and I saw it then, the vicious red track marks on his arms. "But you got to know, there's more word on the street, talking about how Mona's daughter is here. I just didn't believe it. You better hope Isaiah doesn't catch wind of that shit."

Well, a little late on hoping for that.

"Stop looking at her," Jax ordered, and Ritchey stopped looking at me as Jax pulled a wad of cash out of his pocket and dropped it on the counter. "Use that to get your boy some food. If I even fucking catch wind of you spending it on dope, I'm going to revisit and it isn't going to be pretty."

My breath caught as I stared at the money. It wasn't a whole ton of it, but it was a decent-size wad. Then I stared at Jax. He was giving money to Ritchey for his kid. I think in that moment, I definitely went from liking Jax straight into crush territory.

After Jax dropped the money on the counter, he said something to Ritchey about us not being there, and then he took my hand and led me out of the house. I wanted to grab the child and make a run for it, but considering how everything was going for me, I doubted he'd be better off with me.

"Should we have checked upstairs?" I asked as the door closed behind us.

Jax shook his head. "Ritchey isn't lying. Mona isn't there. We'll check out Ike and see if he has any idea."

I headed down the stairs, my mind caught up in everything. I'd come home thinking I could get my money back from Mom, or at least have it out with her; realized neither of those two things were going to happen; and tried to make some much-needed money, but in the end, found myself in the middle of a million-dollar drug dispute.

Mom.

Sigh.

"You okay?" he asked quietly, squeezing my hand as we hit the sidewalk.

Glancing up at him, I realized something else, something that was probably the most unexpected part in all of this. I'd found Jax. I nodded, and then I said, "No. I mean, it's been so long since I've been around any of this stuff. I forgot what it was like."

Jax tugged me closer until I was walking with my body pressed against his side and, letting go of my hand, he dropped his arm over my shoulders. This was nice. Brandon would do this sometimes, but it never felt like this.

"Not cool that you have to remember what this was like," he said. "That you couldn't just forget. I didn't want that—"

Tires squealed, shrieking, and the smell of burnt rubber filled the air. The sound raised the hairs all over my body as Jax's arm tightened on my shoulders. He spun around, keeping me tucked close, just in time to see a black SUV cut between two parked cars, smacking into one. Metal crunched and grinded, giving way as the SUV jumped the sidewalk.

My heart stopped and then sped up.

The SUV was coming straight for us.

Nineteen

*H*oly crap on a cracker, we were going to be run down in the middle of the crappiest part of Philly, looking for my jerk of a Mom.

The SUV was so close I could make out the damn emblem and smell the engine fumes. Air lodged in my throat as my heart threw itself against my ribs.

Jax sprang into action.

One second he had his arm around my shoulders and the next, he had an arm around my waist and my feet were off the ground. We were flying, or at least it felt that way, because I was up in the air and we were moving fast.

We crashed through a dried bush. Tiny, scratchy branches dragged over my arms and snagged in the hair tucked up in a bun at the back of my neck. Jax rolled at the last minute, and when we hit the ground, I landed on top of him. The impact was jarring and the air was knocked out of my lungs, pushing my eyes wide.

Jax rolled as he shoved me onto my back and reached behind him. He flipped up into a sitting position, his body shielding mine as he extended his right arm. Something black and slim was in his hand.

The SUV spun out over the sidewalk, bouncing back into the road and peeling off, sending puffs of white smoke into the air as the tires squealed again. Rising fluidly, Jax kept his arm trained on the quickly retreating SUV.

I lay there, half on the bush and half on a patch of yellow, burnt grass, absolutely stunned. Unless the driving ability of those who lived in Philadelphia had significantly gone down the pooper, someone had tried to run us over. And Jax was holding a gun. Not only was he holding a gun, but he had to have had the gun the entire time, and I remembered him coming out of the townhouse, tugging the back of his shirt down. And not only that, if that wasn't enough reason to be totally mind blown, he'd tucked and rolled like a pro and he handled that gun like he knew what he was doing.

Jax faced me and was suddenly kneeling beside me, placing his hands on my shoulders. They were shaking. "Are you okay?"

"Yes."

His face was pale, strained. "Are you sure?"

I nodded as my heart pounded for a different reason. There was panic in his face—a stark fear. "I'm really okay."

He squeezed his eyes shut for a moment. "When I saw that car coming, I thought . . ." He shook his head. "The roadside bomb—we never saw it."

"Oh God," I whispered.

His eyes were dark when they reopened. "Just fucked with my head for a second."

"Understandable. You okay now?"

He nodded, and the color was back in his face. Cursing under his breath, Jax jerked around as one of the doors down the street opened and someone shouted something. It sounded like Ritchey, and it also sounded like he was yelling something about bringing bad shit to his doorstep, but my attention was focused on Jax.

He looked down at me.

"Do I even know you?" I asked.

One eyebrow rose as he reached around to his back, and when

his hands returned to where I could see them, he wasn't holding the gun anymore. "You know me."

I blinked up at him as I sat up. "That . . . that was pretty impressive. You know, the whole thing."

"Had a lot of practice dodging shit in the past, honey."

That's right. Military training. Duh. "And the gun?"

"Working at Mona's, I've ended up face-to-face with people that make me feel a bit better chatting with knowing I'm holding a gun." He reached down, took my hands in his, and hauled me onto my feet. "Plus, holding and firing a gun aren't anything strange to me."

Double duh. Military training. "What . . . what do you think that was all about?"

A door—most likely Ritchey's—slammed shut. "Probably not something good." He gripped the sides of my face, tilting my head back. "You really okay?" he asked once more.

Breathing heavy, I nodded. Other than a little sore and scared out of my mind, I was okay. "Someone tried to run us over."

"They tried and they failed," he pointed out.

"But *they* tried." And then it really hit me. That someone did try to run us over and Jax carried a gun because of Mona's, or more likely because of *Mona,* and someone seriously tried to run us over.

My knees started to knock together. It made me feel weak, but in all my life, no matter how crazy or how crappy it got, I'd never had a knife held to my face and almost been run over in less than twenty-four hours. That was kind of scary.

"Shit," Jax said, and then he tugged me forward, against his chest, and I went, clutching the sides of his stomach. "Honey . . ."

I closed my eyes, soaking up his warmth and his strength, and I held on.

There were no naps or afternoon orgasms after almost being run over. Which sucked for various reasons. Besides orgasms just being a great thing to experience, I could really have used a nap after the morning and afternoon I had.

Jax had called Reece the moment we got in his truck and got the hell out of there. We ended up filing a police report with a cop I'd never seen before, an older gentleman with dark skin and tired eyes, but a warm smile. His name was Detective Dornell Jackson, and he seemed to know what was going on, because he asked a lot of questions that had to do with my mom and Mack and even Isaiah. Then we'd met up with Reece, and Jax had filled him in. Reece did not look happy, especially when we got to Jax's house and both guys noticed a few tiny—and by tiny, I mean harmless—scratches along my upper arm.

This discovery resulted in me being dragged into the half bath downstairs, peroxide being whipped out, and cotton balls being dabbed along my arm like there was a chance they'd get infected and my arm would fall off.

It was assumed that someone had been watching Ritchey's place, most likely for Mona, and that's how we ended up almost getting run down, but it didn't explain why. If I was potentially vital in handing over my mom or luring her out, why try to turn Jax or me into roadkill?

No one had an answer for that.

Before the start of my shift, Jax had taken me back to the house so I could get ready. Instead of leaving, he hung out until it was time. At some point, he'd made the universal decision that I was riding with him to and from work.

"I don't think that's necessary," I told him.

Jax dropped down on the couch, brows raised. "I want you safe, Calla. And obviously shit is going down. So you're going to stay safe. Besides that, we literally work the same damn shift. You can save gas money."

I really couldn't argue with that.

"Pack up some clothes, too, you're staying with me tonight," he went on, and my mouth opened. "Calla, it goes back to keeping you safe. My place is better. No offense, but I have more than oodles and noodles in the cabinet and I have cable TV."

Okay. Real food and cable TV were a bonus. "That's a lot, Jax. I mean, staying with you is—"

"Good," he cut in, grinning. "Fun. Better than staying in this house?"

I pressed my lips together as my eyes narrowed.

He leaned forward, resting his hands on his thighs as he sighed. "Calla, I just want to make sure you're safe while we deal with this crap, and, honey, you know this house isn't safe. No one is going to barge into my house, but this place? Anything goes."

Hesitating at the doorway to the bedroom, I had to acknowledge that he had a point and he was right. This house wasn't on the up-and-up. I would be safer at his place, but it was his place, and staying at his place meant something, and . . .

Damnit.

It did mean something. That was the third duh of the day. Jax wanted me at his place because it did mean something to him, to us—to our *thing*.

"I see it sinking in," Jax remarked smugly.

I whipped around. "Shut up."

He laughed as I all but pranced into the room. After changing into a pair of dark denim jeans that were on the tight side of things, I slipped on a pair of cute flats, a standard black tank top, and a loose thin shirt that had a tendency to slip off one shoulder, but didn't expose my back. When I took my hair down, it had dried in waves from being in the bun, and then I reached for my purple makeup case.

My gaze darted to the mirror. I'd washed my face before I changed and it was all kinds of fresh and clean. I felt light, like I always did without the makeup slathered on.

Pressing my lips together, I glanced down at the tube of foundation. I'd gone all morning and most of the afternoon without a lick of makeup on, and no one, not even small, easily frightened children, had run screaming for the hills. No one had really stared. And I honestly didn't really think about it. Meeting Ritchey and almost being run over might have something to do with that, but still.

My stomach jumped a little.

Most people wouldn't understand, but it was a big deal for me to put that tube back in the pouch without putting it on. The makeup was like a shield and it was literally a mask.

There was a knot in my throat and my fingers trembled slightly as I picked up the other foundation I wore—some kind of BB cream that gave the face a dewy complexion but really didn't do much for coverage. I put that on, smoothing it over the slightly raised scar. I had to blink a couple of times before I did my eyes, giving them a smoky, working the bar appropriate look. I put some lip gloss on and then I was done.

I backed away from the mirror slowly.

Taking a deep breath, I left the bathroom and grabbed my bag from the bed. When I entered the living room, Jax looked up, and then he sat forward, his head cocking to the side. His eyes hooded, his gaze turning lazy as it drifted over my face.

Jax smiled.

And my heart flipped, not a little, but a lot.

Word about killer SUVs on the warpath and Mack Attacks traveled at the speed of a rocket.

Clyde had grabbed me the moment I'd walked into the kitchen to say hi and had given me one of his giant bear hugs. "Baby girl, Jax told me you guys were going to go out and look for your momma, but I don't like this."

I didn't like it, either, but Thursday wasn't too far away and we needed to find Mom. "It could've been a coincidence," I said into his massive chest.

"There ain't no such thing as coincidences." He squeezed me again, and if I were a toy, I would've squeaked. "I don't want you in danger."

The thing was, I had a feeling I was in danger even if I wasn't out there looking for Mom, but I didn't say that. "I'll be okay. I promise."

Clyde pulled back and scrubbed a hand over his head. "Baby girl, I'm happy to see you around and to see you smiling again . . ."

I was smiling again? When had I stopped smiling? Well, when I'd lived here before there hadn't been a lot to smile about.

"But if being safer means heading back down to the school, then I'd rather see you safe."

"I can't go back now," I told him, and I smiled for him. "You know that." But I left out Mack's threat of them finding me if I left. "It's going to be okay."

Concern pinched his face and I knew he didn't believe that as he turned, picked up the spatula with one hand, and rubbed his chest with the other. I lingered at the double doors, wishing I could do something to ease his worry, but the only thing I could do was stay safe.

Back out on the floor, there was only a slight reprieve from random acts of concern. As soon as Nick came in for his shift, he offered to chauffeur me around, which surprised the hell out of me, but that offer was quickly pooh-poohed by one single look from Jax. But if Jax wasn't out on the floor while we worked, I noticed Nick was never too far.

I didn't know what to think about that. I barely knew Nick, but it was sweet and a bit disarming.

Roxy was concerned and offered up her apartment as a place to crash, but that was also shot down when Jax announced that I was "crashing" at his place, before he disappeared into the stockroom.

"You're staying with Jax?" she asked as we stood in the narrow hall. "Like staying at his place?"

"I guess so—for tonight." I paused, frowning. "And last night, too."

Her eyes got huge behind her glasses. "You stayed the night with him last night? And he took your drinking cherry the night before?"

"Well, yeah . . ."

A wide grin appeared. "Are you guys together?"

I didn't answer, because Jax had come out of the liquor room, carrying several bottles. His eyes narrowed on us as he strolled past, but there was a small grin on his full lips. He winked at me.

My tummy fluttered, because my tummy was dumb.

"You know, he really is a great guy," she said, not like I didn't already realize that. "Like the kind that really has your back. Last year, Reece . . ." She said his name with a pause that caused my eyebrow to rise. "He was in an officer-involved shooting. Totally legit, but you know, I think shooting someone kind of messes with your head. Jax was totally there for him."

Now both of my brows were in my hairline. Damn. I didn't know what to say to that.

She grabbed my hand and pulled me into the office. "So you two are together."

"No. I mean, I don't know." I squeezed my eyes shut and took a breath. "I guess we are. Kind of."

"Kind of?" Her brows shot up over her black rims. "Either you're together, like one-on-one with rules."

"Rules?"

"Yeah, like you're only seeing each other."

Oh. There was the fourth duh of the day. "We haven't discussed that."

"Then you're fuck buddies?" she asked, eyes narrowing.

My cheeks heated. "I don't think we're that, either." Or were we? I mean, it wasn't like anything was labeled or discussed or *anything*.

"Okay." Roxy patted my arm, and I blinked away thoughts of

fuck buddies. "I can so tell that being fuck buddies would not be cool with you. So that leaves, you guys are together, as in dating, as in seeing how it goes?"

"That sounds about right. We're going out tomorrow, to Apollo's."

She clapped. "Oh, that's a damn good place. Great steaks."

"That's what I hear," I murmured.

"Fuck buddies don't take each other to Apollo's." Her lips slipped down at the corners. "They take each other to places like Mona's. Trust me, I know."

I noticed that frown, but she went on. "Apollo's is for those dating who are serious. Like as in, the guy knows what kind of coffee you like in the morning and how you like it. Apollo's is impressive. And did I mention the steaks were great?"

Suddenly, I wanted to talk to Teresa. I wanted to tell her what was going on because I had a feeling I really didn't know what was going on. But it was late and Teresa was at the beach with Jase. I looked down at Roxy and bit my bottom lip. I didn't know . . . oh hell, fuck it. "I've never had a boyfriend."

Roxy blinked slowly and then took a step back. She raised a finger, walked over to the door and closed it, then turned to me. "Not a single boyfriend?"

I shook my head.

"Have you ever had a fuck buddy?"

I shook my head again.

She leaned against the door. "So I'm assuming that the cherry convo we had before hit close to home?"

"Uh. Yeah." I sat on the edge of the desk, crossing my ankles. "Cherry is intact."

"Wow," she murmured.

I frowned. "What?"

"I don't know. Virgin twenty-one-year-olds are kind of like Big Foot."

My shoulders slumped. "Gee. Thanks."

"You know what I mean." She slid her glasses up to the top of her head. "You hear about Big Foot, but no one has really seen Big Foot in person. Same with twenty-one-year-old virgins."

I was beginning to think sharing was a bad idea.

"Why?" she asked, and my brows rose. "Why no boyfriend?"

Cocking my head to the side, I stared at her. "Seriously?"

"Seriously."

I folded my arms across my chest. "You can see with the glasses, right?"

She squinted, scrunching her nose. "Yeah, I can see. And you're really pretty. And you're nice. You have to be smart to be in a nursing program, so what's the deal?"

"Pretty?" I murmured.

Then she blinked again as she pushed off the door, approaching me. "I get it. The scar on your face? It doesn't distract from your prettiness. You have to know that. And I kind of wanted to say something earlier, but thought it would be way uncool to bring it up," she went on. "But you look *nice* tonight. I can tell you're not wearing a lot of makeup, and you looked great before, but you look awesome without it."

Dermablend was no joke—a heavy makeup used for maximum coverage, and I always knew it was noticeable. I just thought I looked better with it.

"I'd kill to have your lips," Roxy continued, drawing my attention to hers. They were nice lips. Bow-shaped lips. "And I'd murder someone to have your boobs. You cover them up, but I know they are there, and they look nice."

"They're not," I blurted out before I stopped myself.

Confusion marked her face. "What do you mean? Do you have, like, the most awesome bra in the history of bras? If so, can you let me know where you got that?" She placed her hands over her small chest. "Because these babies could use some help."

I smiled softly. "No. It's not that. Sorry."

"Damn." She pouted. "Then what?"

I'd never talked to anyone about what I looked like in the buff and finding the right words was more than difficult. "The scar on my face is nothing compared to the rest of me. It's pretty bad. For real."

Roxy opened her mouth, but it was clear that she wasn't sure what to say, so I rushed on. "I don't have a lot of experience with guys, so I think we're dating, and I think I . . . I like that."

"You like him," she corrected softly.

Sighing, I nodded. "I do. I do like him. And I know it's dumb."

"It's not dumb."

I carried on as if I hadn't heard her. "I mean, he's hot, like so hot and so nice, he's the perfect combo, and with everything going on with my mom, now probably isn't the smartest time to get involved with anyone."

"Yeah, the stuff with your mom does suck." She shifted her slight weight from one foot to the next. "Sucks big-time, but also doesn't really have anything to do with Jax, you know? They are two separate things."

I could see that. "But I plan on heading back to school in August."

"So?" she said. "Shepherd is like three hours from here. Big whoop. You guys can still date. Not only can you drive, there are these neat things called trains."

I laughed. "I've heard of those things a time or two before."

"He likes you," Roxy said, and then nodded to drive the statement home. "Jax likes you, Calla. Trust me, I know."

"Do you?"

Her chin jerked up and down again, but before she could continue, the door opened and Nick stuck his head in. "If you two are done doing whatever you're doing in here, we really could use your help."

I glanced at Roxy, and she rolled her eyes. "Boys," she said, spinning around. "What would they do without us?"

I didn't answer, but I wanted to giggle at the look Nick shot her way. We headed back out and the bar was packed. Jax stopped me, tied on my apron, gave me a not so secretive tap on the behind, and sent me on the floor.

"Girl, I don't know what's going on tonight, but it's a madhouse," Pearl said as I picked up the notebook to write orders.

It was.

The crowd was a mixture of the young and old, and the moment Melvin caught sight of me, he motioned me over to the table with one crooked finger. He wasn't alone. Tonight he was joined by an equally old-looking dude.

"What's this I hear about you and Jackson almost getting run over by a car today?" Melvin asked, and I was reminded, once again, how fast news traveled.

I glanced at his buddy, and was unsure of what to say.

"That's Arthur." Melvin nodded at his friend. "This is Mona's daughter."

Arthur's heavily lined face crinkled as dark eyes centered on me. "Good to meet you, darlin'."

Giving him a short, somewhat awkward, wave, I admitted to being almost run over, but downplayed it to a run-in with a really bad driver since I didn't want to worry either of them. Melvin didn't look too convinced when he patted my arm and told me to be careful.

The crowd didn't thin as the night wore on, and when I replaced Nick for break, I was happy to be behind the bar and not out running the floor like a madwoman.

I was making two Jäger bombs when I looked up and saw them. Well, I saw him first and almost dropped the smaller glass in a way one was not supposed to drop it in a Jäger bomb.

The guy was huge—like bigger and broader than Jax, even taller. He wore a black shirt that stretched taut over a defined chest and arms. His brown hair was buzzed on the sides, a little longer on the top, and it stood straight up, a little longer than Jax's, which looked like it would be curly if it grew out. This guy had an angular face with definite Hispanic descent. Smooth brown skin covered high cheekbones and thick brown lashes framed dark eyes. There was a crescent-shaped scar under his left eye and another under the center of his lip, cutting into it.

He looked bad—like bad in a very good way.

The girl trailing behind him seriously could've been Britney Spears in the flesh—Catholic-schoolgirl Britney. Her blond hair was wavy and cut perfectly to frame a heart-shaped face. She had full lips and big brown eyes and a nice body. How did I know she had a nice body? Because most of it was on display.

She was wearing a strappy tank top that showed her trim midriff and a short jean skirt that revealed awesome tan legs. The chick had to-die-for boobs, and she was universally hot.

And she wasn't paying attention to the big, handsome guy next to her. She was staring straight at the bar. Not at me. Not at Roxy. Her brown gaze was fixed on the side of the bar farthest from Roxy and me.

On Jax.

Aaand she wasn't just looking at him.

"Do you know who that is?" Roxy asked, shoveling up a buttload of ice. "That hot as hell guy right over there?"

My gaze shifted from the girl to him. "How could I not notice?" I handed over the Jäger bombs with a smile and took the money. "Who is he?" I asked when I really wanted to know who was *she* and why was she staring at Jax like he was for dinner.

"Brock," Roxy answered, and started fanning herself. "The Brock."

"Um? Who?" I asked as I turned to a college-age guy. "What can I get you?"

"That's Brock 'the Beast' Mitchell," the guy said instead of answering, and I blinked. "You don't know who he is?"

I glanced over at "the Beast" and shook my head. "Should I?"

The guy snorted as he shook his head. "He does MMA—a pretty big deal. Or about to become a big deal." He looked over, an expression of awe creeping into his face. "Man, he is not a dude I'd want to piss off. Didn't know he was in town. Anyway, I'll take a Bud."

Grabbing the beer, I peeked over at Brock. I knew what MMA was—mixed martial arts, and I was guessing a pretty big deal meant he was fighting pro on one of those circuits that Cam and Jase were obsessed with. I knew for a fact that the guy wasn't local. I would've remembered a face like that even if he'd been a whole lot smaller in our high school days.

"Cool," I murmured, handing over the beer.

The guy forgot my existence as he took his drink and started toward Brock like he was drawn to the guy.

"Oh shit." Roxy straightened, and I saw she was staring at the girl now. She spun, and her gaze landed on Jax. "Oh *shit*."

"What?" My heart did a jump in my chest.

Roxy whirled toward me, her lips puckered like she tasted something bad. "That's Aimee—Aimee with two *e*'s and an *i*."

"Okay." It was official. I was confused.

"I have no idea what she's doing with Brock. Well, okay, I have a couple of ideas, but I have no idea why she is *here* with Brock."

And now I was starting to get a real bad feeling about this, especially because several guys crowded Brock, and Aimee with two *e*'s wasn't even paying attention to him. She was starting around the huddle.

Roxy looked like she'd just walked into a spiderweb and was about to start flailing, and there were people who needed to be served, but my gaze was tracking Aimee, and as she made it halfway across the length of the bar, I looked at Jax.

Leaning against the counter, he was handing over two mixed drinks to a group of giggling girls, and as he straightened and looked over, his gaze moved past Aimee with an *i* and then bounced back. He blinked, straightened as if someone had grabbed his ass, and my stomach sank a little.

Oh no.

"Oh no," echoed Roxy.

Aimee with two *e*'s squeezed in between the giggling girls and an older guy, planted her hands on the bar top, and stretched up, which made her boobalicious boobs strain against the tank top.

Then she spoke in a deep, throaty way. "Jax, baby, I've missed you."

Twenty

Jax baby stared at Aimee for a moment and then he gave her a half smile—not the half smile, but a lopsided grin that twisted up my insides. He said something and she tossed her head back and laughed huskily.

I turned away and focused on the people waiting for drinks. I wasn't sure how many minutes went by, and I didn't even try to stop myself from glancing over at them, but they were still chatting.

No big deal.

When I looked up for Brock, the guy she had walked in with, I didn't see him anywhere, but there was a huge group surrounding the pool tables, and I figured that was where he was.

Feeling weird and like I had swallowed a bunch of energy pills, I was overly smiley and happy while I helped out the customers until Nick returned. By then, I was ready to get out on the floor and I eased past Roxy, who was shooting me "we need to talk" looks and to which I shot back a "we don't need to talk" look.

I was hurrying out from behind the bar, eyes focused on Pearl, whose blond hair was escaping the twist, when I was snagged from around the waist and pulled to the side. Swallowing a squeal as I was spun around, I found myself between Jax and the end of the bar, facing Aimee.

Um.

Aimee looked as confused as I felt as she glanced between Jax and me, and then her gaze dropped to the arm around my waist.

"Aimee, I'm not sure if you've had a chance to meet Calla," Jax said, and his arm was like a brand around my waist. "She's from here, but has been gone at college. She's back for—"

"I know who she is," she replied, and her tone wasn't cold or snotty or anything really.

My brows rose. I had no idea who she was, and I had a feeling I would know her if I did.

Aimee smiled as she brushed her hair over one shoulder. "You obviously don't remember me. It was *ages* ago when we knew each other."

Jax shifted and his entire side pressed against mine. "How do you know her? You grew up like a county over."

I so did not care that he knew that Aimee with two *e*'s grew up a county away.

"It was a long time ago," she said, raising her voice as a loud cheer went off toward the pool tables. "We did some of the same pageants together."

Holy shit.

I stiffened as I stared at her. *Aimee . . . ? Aimee . . . ?* "Aimee Grant?"

Her smile spread, and damn she was breathtaking. Perfect freaking teeth, like she was still wearing flippers. "Yes! You do remember. Oh my God, Jax." Her eyes flipped to him as she reached over the bar, placing her hand on his other arm like she'd done it a million times. "Calla and I practically grew up together."

Uh, I wouldn't have gone that far. We'd probably run into each other every other month at the pageants and we weren't friends. If I remembered correctly, our mothers hated each other with the passion of all stage mothers. Mom was considered lowbrow for owning a bar, and Aimee's mom was stay-at-home, married to a doctor, or by the look of those perfect choppers, a dentist.

"Is that so?" Jax slid his hand to my lower back, and I pressed my lips together. He'd angled his body into mine, drawing back so her hand was no longer resting on his arm, and even though I hadn't done the relationship thing, I knew what he was saying with his body. I'd seen Jase do it. I'd seen Cam do it.

I got a happy feeling inside.

Aimee either was ignoring the message or wasn't getting it. "Yeah, it's such a small world. I haven't seen you in years." Her gaze was centered on me now. "Not since you stopped doing pageants."

A ball formed in the pit of my stomach, weighty like lead, and out of reflex, I tried to step back, but with Jax being so close, there was nowhere to go.

"She used to beat me," Aimee went on, and the ball in my stomach started to grow icicles. "Every single pageant. I'd get grand supreme and Calla would almost always take home ultimate grand supreme."

Jax's lips curved up into an easy grin as he watched me, but I was crawling out of my skin to get away from him, the bar, and from Aimee.

Her head cocked to the side as she leaned against the bar. "I haven't seen you since the fire."

Air lodged in my throat and the tiny hairs along my back rose.

"A lot of the organizations ran fund-raisers. I remember that," she continued blithely. "The girls who won money at the pageants for like six months turned over their winnings for you."

Oh my God.

I also remembered that—remembered Dad saying something about it while I'd been in the hospital, and Mom had been too out of it with grief to even come into my hospital room.

"So terrible," Aimee said, blinking large eyes. "Everything that happened to you, to your family. How long were you in the hospital?"

Who asked questions like that? But I knew the answer. Throughout my life, complete strangers shoved their noses in my business and asked questions one would think would be off the table or just not appropriate. People didn't think or they simply didn't care.

"Months," I heard myself say.

Jax's hand flattened against my back, and I felt the muscles tense in his body. The tiny hairs were prickling now.

"Excuse me." My voice was rough as I wiggled free from Jax and the bar. "I have to get back to work."

I slipped away, not hearing whatever Aimee said as I grabbed the round tray and headed out onto the floor to find empty glasses and bottles. My mind was spinning so many thoughts I couldn't pick up just one to focus on.

Aimee was an unexpected and unwanted blast from the past. She was a part of memories that, all these years later, I hadn't really reconciled with, and I wasn't sure I ever would. Not only that, but she represented everything I should've been.

The knot was in my throat again as I grabbed empty bottles, ignoring the faint smell of beer as I dropped them on my tray. Later, I'd probably not say Aimee represented shit, but right now, if I thought of her, I thought of everything before the fire. I thought about what life would've been like for my family—for Mom, for Kevin and Tommy, and for Dad and me, if the fire had never happened.

I'd probably be standing right here.

I stopped, breathing heavy as my fingers curled around the neck of another empty bottle. I stared straight ahead, at the backs of those clustered around the pool tables.

It hit me, right then and there, so strong that my fingers tingled along with my toes. If that fire never happened, I would probably be standing right where I was. I would've been groomed to take over the bar, because it had been successful, and it had been something my parents had built to hand over to us. Kevin would be running the place. Tommy would be here. So would Mom and Dad.

I would be right where I was, and I had no idea how to wrap my head around that epiphany. Not at all. My thoughts felt razor sharp, my skin brittle.

"Calla."

My chest squeezed as my spine stiffened. I didn't turn around. "I have tables to clear," I told him. "Lots of tables."

Jax's hand landed on my shoulder and he turned me around. Our eyes locked, and when he spoke, I knew—I just *knew*—what he meant and it shattered me.

He moved in close, lowering his mouth to my ear, and said, "I know."

I was quiet on the drive to Jax's townhouse, spending the ride staring out the window at the dark houses and storefronts. I was tired, mentally and physically, and all I wanted to do was crawl into a bed, tug a blanket up over my head, and say good night.

Aimee had stayed to closing, not once joining Brock, who ended up leaving well before her. Roxy said he'd left with a different girl, so I had no idea what was going on between him and Aimee, but she didn't seem fazed. And I knew why she'd hung around. She wanted to go home with Jax.

That didn't happen.

When last call was made and Aimee was staring up at Jax, Roxy told me, he kindly and gently asked if she had a ride home, but before she answered, he told her he could call her a cab.

Smooth move.

Roxy said Aimee had looked as if a ghost had just walked right past her, and while it would've been funny to see that go down, I wondered whether, if I wasn't here, Jax would've taken her home. That shouldn't matter, but it did, because I was a girl and I was feeling extra special dumb.

I know.

My breath caught as Jax turned onto the road leading to his

house. I knew he was talking about the fire. Since he worked with my mom and she had told him about the grand pageant days, it didn't take a leap of logic to figure she'd talk about the fire, but to what extent? How much did he know when his eyes landed on me for the first time when I walked back into Mona's?

At the townhome, I carried my bag upstairs while Jax headed into the kitchen, doing what he'd done previously, kicking off his shoes and dropping his keys on the counter.

I undressed, this time wearing a tank under my thin long-sleeve shirt and my sleep shorts, and after washing my face, I pulled my hair up in a loose ponytail. When I left the bedroom, I grabbed my cell phone out of my purse and turned on the nightstand lamp. A soft glow was cast into the long room.

There was a missed text Teresa had sent me, a picture of her and Jase on the beach. She was in his arms, throwing up devil horns with her fingers, and he was smiling broadly, his gorgeous and downright unique gray eyes hidden behind the same kind of sunglasses Jax wore.

Footsteps drew my attention as I placed the cell phone back in my bag and there Jax was, walking into the bedroom. He'd lost his shirt somewhere between being downstairs and here, and I wasn't complaining, because the rugged and flawed expanse of flesh was pretty darn nice to look upon, especially when his jeans hung low on his lean hips.

He was holding a beer in one hand and a juice box in the other.

My grin went up a notch. "For me?"

"Figured you could use a drink of the fruit punch kind."

"Thanks." I took the juice box and then sat Indian-style on the bed. The straw was already shoved in again. Perfect. Lifting my lashes, I saw him take a swig of beer and then he lowered the beer and shoved his other hand through his hair. I felt a shimmer of unease in my belly as I watched his chest rise and fall with a deep breath. "Is everything okay?"

Sounded like a dumb question.

His gaze slid sideways to mine as he tipped the bottle back to his lips again. He didn't say anything as his throat worked, and damn, he'd drained that bottle and I'd only taken a small sip out of my juice box.

The unease grew until it was like a weed flourishing in a garden. Had he changed his mind about me staying with him? He didn't look too happy. Maybe he was wishing he had taken Aimee with two *e*'s home. Given her perfect skin and smile, and a mom who currently wasn't MIA and messed up with drug dealers, I could totally get why he was probably rethinking a whole lot of things. After all, he'd almost gotten run over today and that hadn't been his fault.

I shouldn't even be in the house, let alone sitting in his bed, because I don't belong here.

All at once, I wanted to be back at Shepherd, sitting with Teresa and watching the Hot Guy Brigade from a safe distance. There I was safe, because no one knew anything about me, and I had my Three F's, and that was it, what I knew and what I forced myself to be okay with.

Clenching the juice box to the point it almost exploded like a volcano, I started to slide off the bed, my belly doing this terrible twisty motion. "I can sleep downstairs tonight and then tomorrow—"

"What?"

My toes were almost on the hardwood floor. "I said, I could sleep downstairs and tomorrow I can—"

"I heard you." He put the empty beer on the top of his dresser as he faced me.

I glanced around. "I'm confused. If you heard what I was saying then why did you say what?"

"Okay. Maybe I should've expanded on that statement," he corrected, and with wide eyes, I watched him bend over, and then I sucked in a short breath as he gripped my hips. An acute quiver radiated down my thighs, because wow-wee, this man knew how to grab hips. "Why in the fuck would you be sleeping downstairs?"

Slowly, I lifted my fruit punch and took a huge gulp. "I just thought that after . . . um, everything . . ." I trailed off as he lifted me back so that my feet weren't on the floor.

"You thought what? That I didn't want you up here with me?" He prowled onto the bed. There was no other word for what he was doing. One leg was on one side of mine, and the other on the other side. His hands were still on my hips. "That I didn't notice how great you looked today? And not once did you turn your cheek to the left to hide?"

Oh my God.

Fruit punch forgotten.

"You thought I didn't want to sleep beside you again? You guessed that wrong if that's the case." His fingers curled into my hips, sending a rush of warmth through my veins. "I really fucking enjoyed going to sleep next to you and waking up next to you. Which is new to me. I'm not usually a big fan of that, but you . . . yeah, you're different."

I never wanted to be more different in my life.

His hands dragged up my sides. "Or you thought I didn't notice that you were doing good all day, in spite of the shit we dealt with in the morning? We went to a shit hole and we almost got run over, but you still smiled afterward. You handled it, went to work. Then Aimee showed up."

Jax dipped his head and brushed his lips across mine. "Aimee and I never dated."

My muscles locked up as my brain called bull crap on that. "I don't think that's really any of my business."

He made a deep sound of disapproval. "You're in my bed right now, right?"

"Well, yeah."

"And my mouth was just on you, correct?"

I nodded.

"My hand has been between those pretty legs, too?"

Oh wow. That warmth turned to a molten heat that centered between said legs.

His forehead pressed against mine. "And I'm taking you out to dinner later. So tell me, how in the fuck does some chick showing up tonight, hanging all over me, and insinuating that we've got a past, have nothing to do with you?"

"Okay," I whispered. "When you put it that way, I guess it does."

"Guess?" He drew back, shaking his head. And then he sat back, his legs on either side of mine, his hands resting on my waist. "I get that you haven't done this before."

I raised my fruit punch and took another drink while there was a flutter in my stomach.

"But you need to understand where this is heading. I've already told you that I like you. I think I've made that pretty damn obvious. And when we get done with this conversation, I'm going to make it even more obvious for you."

Not going to lie. Big parts of me liked the sound of this.

"Aimee and I hooked up a couple of times," he went on, and an ugly feeling lit up my chest even though I'd already figured it out. "She normally stays in Philly and I guess she's still going to college up north. I don't know, and honestly, I don't care. Things were casual between us. She's been to my place. Never stayed the night here. Not once. And she sure as hell never got to drink fruit punch in my bed."

"I'm happy to hear that last part," I admitted.

A grin flashed across his face. "Aimee is a beautiful girl. She knows how to have fun, but she isn't the girl for me. Never has been."

That flutter was in my chest again.

He shifted his hands as he tilted his head to the side. "And I know that what's going on in your head is more than just some chick I'd slept with in the past popping up. It's what she said tonight."

I tensed all over again. "Jax—"

He placed his forefinger over my lips, silencing me. Normally, if anyone did that to me, I'd be inclined to bite their finger off, but the subject matter was too intense for that.

"I know," he said quietly. "I know all about the fire."

Air lodged in my throat. I planted one hand in the bed as I leaned back from him, but his hands tightened around my waist. I didn't get very far. I couldn't do this. I could feel the slight grip on my control slipping.

"Mona talked about it every once in a while and Clyde filled in what she didn't go into," he continued in that low, patient voice. "I know how it happened."

My heart started pounding in my chest, and when I spoke, my voice was hoarse. "I don't want to do this."

"I *know*." Jax scooted closer somehow, his pelvis above mine, but his weight was supported by his legs. He was close, too close for this. "The bar was a hit in town. Always busy. Making a ton of money. Your parents decided to build their dream home."

I looked away from his brown eyes, my free hand digging into the comforter. "I don't want to do this," I repeated in a whisper.

He lowered his head, pressing a quick kiss against the center of my left cheek, and my breath hiccupped. "It was the kind of house your parents dreamed of raising a family in, enough room for all of you to grow, especially Kevin and Tommy."

Oh God.

Cold air sliced through my chest, and I shook my head. "I *can't* do this."

Jax didn't let up. "What your parents didn't realize is that they'd hired an electrician who wasn't on the up-and-up. Who cut corners on the job sites so he could pocket more money. His license was under investigation for a bang-up job on the previous house he worked on. What your parents didn't know when they moved you all in and were happy and celebrating, was that the electrician hadn't followed the installation codes on the dimmer switch in the hallway on the second floor—the floor with all the kids' bedrooms."

Dipping my chin, I squeezed my eyes shut. It was a bad idea because I could see that night clearly. To the day I died, I'd be able to see that night, to waking up with my brand-new room, with its pink walls and my name spelled out in block letters attached to the wall, filled with smoke. I'd never forget that the first big breath I dragged in had scorched the very inside of my throat and chest. Panic poured into me as I'd stumbled off the bed and saw the pink paint peeling from the walls, the terror when I opened the bathroom door and the entire world exploded. Smoke had turned yellow and brown—I remembered that—a moment before it all happened. Glass shards had been flung through the air, slicing into my skin. Flames were everywhere, seeming to crawl across the floor and lick over the ceilings and walls. It was like a giant flash. And there had been screams. Horrific screams that no horror movie could even really replicate and some of them had been mine. Some of them had been Kevin's.

"It was so hot. The paint was blistering. There was no air and . . ." I drew in a shaky breath and I didn't realize that I'd spoken out loud until his lips pressed against my temple again.

"I know you were lucky to survive," he said, smoothing his thumbs along the sides of my waist. "Your dad got to you first and he brought you outside. And then he and your Mom tried to get back inside, upstairs again, but it was fully engulfed. They couldn't get back up the stairs . . . it was too late for your brothers."

I twisted again, but Jax held on. The ice in my chest was spreading, becoming a real, tangible pain. "Tommy never woke up." I remembered hearing Mom say that once. That after an autopsy was performed, it showed that he'd died from smoke inhalation. A blessing in disguise, because by the time the fire was put out, his room was nothing but charred cinder and wood. "Kevin . . . he was awake."

Again, with the quiet voice, "I know."

I opened my eyes slowly and my lashes felt damp. "Their coffins," I whispered, squeezing my eyes tight once more and seeing them. "They were so small. You know, smaller than you think they made coffins. And yet, I know they make them even smaller, but God . . . they were so small."

His lips brushed under the corner of my right eye, and I knew—oh God, my chest hurt—I knew he'd caught a tear, and the iciness in my chest, invading my stomach and my soul, eased off a little bit.

"They never had a chance," I said, dragging in another deep breath. "The fire started right outside their rooms, in the ceiling and walls. It spread so quickly."

Jax remained quiet, and a few moments passed before I spoke again. "Our family was awarded a large sum of money once it was discovered that the fire . . . it was due to the faulty wiring. Dad put some in a college fund for me. That's . . . that's the money Mom had drained. And she had a lot of money—hundreds of thousands that she had to have blown through." My fingers eased off the blanket. "Dad left not even a year later. He couldn't deal."

"Fucker," muttered Jax.

My eyes opened wide and I started to defend my dad, but stopped myself. Yeah, he was kind of a fucker. I'd accepted that long ago. The next breath I took was easier. "I've never talked to anyone about this. Not even my friends at home. It's not like I haven't . . . dealt with it, because I have. I was young when all of this happened and I still miss my brothers. It's just so damn sad."

"It is."

Our gazes met, and I felt my heart turn over heavily in my chest. I knew he wasn't done.

"I know this isn't the only thing." He lifted a hand and trailed a finger along the length of my scar. "I know you have other scars."

I couldn't look away. Damn if I didn't want to, but his gaze held me, and his eyes were warm, they were focused.

"And I know you were burned, Calla." At that, my chest clenched with a mixture of embarrassment and relief. "I know you had surgeries and I know those surgeries stopped before they were supposed to."

"Mom . . . she . . ."

"She got caught up in her own shit. She forgot or she couldn't deal," he confirmed. "She never really said why, and I know this doesn't make anything better, but she felt a hell of a lot of guilt over it. That much is obvious."

Yeah, that didn't change anything. It never would. I didn't know if that made me a cold bitch or not, but some things couldn't be easily forgotten. They weren't designed that way.

"I've never . . . no one has ever seen the scars," I said in a voice barely above a whisper. "They're not pretty."

"They're a part of you."

I nodded slowly. My thoughts where awhirl again as my gaze searched out his. He'd known from day one that there were a lot of scars I was hiding. Hell, he'd known before he even laid eyes on me, because of my mom and Clyde. I wasn't sure what to think of them telling someone who had been a virtual stranger to me, but I couldn't muster up the anger over that. I couldn't dredge up any more emotion as I stared at him. "You like me."

His lips twitched. "Not a news flash, honey. I like you, knowing that the scars are a part of you."

"But how?" It wasn't the first time I asked him this.

"I've already told you how." Both hands were back on my waist again, and my breath caught. "I think it's past time for me to just show you."

My brows rose. "Show me?"

"Yeah, show you."

His hands curved under my arms as he lifted me up, and I tightened my hold on my drink. He moved me until I was closer to the headboard, smack dab in the middle of the bed. He reached between us, took my fruit punch, and placed it on the nightstand.

Then he got down to the business of making it real obvious that he was into me.

Twenty-one

$\mathcal{M}$orning sunlight streamed in through the large square window when I blinked open my eyes, and I came awake with a mouth on my neck, trailing tiny, hot kisses down the side of my throat.

Oh wow. My lips curved up at the corners, and then I gasped as his tongue flicked over the sensitive spot just below my ear. My back arched on its own accord when his hand smoothed from where it rested on my stomach, over my shirt to the curve of my hip.

That was a great way to wake up.

Last night was . . . well, it was literally orgasmic, and although we hadn't been asleep that many hours, I woke up feeling like I'd slept for a year. Though I doubted the orgasm he'd given me with his clever hand had anything to do with that. It was the fact that last night, something happened. A bit of the weight lifted off my chest. There wasn't this wall between us.

Was there ever one?

Funny thing was, the wall might have never been there, at least not on his side. He'd known about the fire, about my brothers and the money, the scars and how horrible all of it was. He'd known before he'd even seen me face-to-face. And he didn't care. I didn't fully get it. Probably would never really understand, but when he set out to proving he was into me last night, with all the kissing and the touching, like I had decided before, I was going to stop trying to figure it out.

My shorts were off, lying forgotten somewhere on Jax's bedroom floor, and when his hand drifted below the thin strap of my undies and glided over my bare skin, I bit down on my lower lip. His other hand had made its way down my upper thigh and curled around the back of my knee. He lifted my leg up, forcing my behind into the groove of his lap.

There was definitely more than a flutter between my legs at the feel of him pressing into me from behind. The heaviness was back in my breasts, and with a wet, sensual kiss against my pulse, I was already damp, and it took everything not to immediately start squirming.

Last night, Jax hadn't . . . he hadn't gotten off. After he'd done his thing to me, he'd tucked me to him, my back to his front, and that had been it. I'd wondered then how he could give and not get anything in return, but I'd been too thrown off by everything to question it—and a wee bit blissed out to move—and I hadn't had the courage to change it. Mainly because I had the general idea of what to do to rectify that problem, but I probably needed a learner's curve.

But today was a different day and I was going to grow some lady balls, starting right now. I shifted onto my back, and Jax stared down at me, all sleepy and sexy looking. Before I could say or do anything, his lips were on mine, starting off with a slow and sweet kiss. The slight stubble on his cheek tickled my palm as I skated my hand down his face. He shifted over me, resting one leg between mine, pressing his thigh against the softest part of me, and I could feel his hardness against my lower belly. The feel took my breath.

"Morning," he rumbled against my parted lips.

"Hey."

One side of his lips tipped up.

My heart was starting to speed up for various reasons. For one thing, his mouth was on mine again, and this kiss was much deeper. His tongue was moving against mine and then it was his right hand. It was on the move and I had a feeling it was heading to where it had gone last night. To my breasts. I tensed, like I had before, and I had to force myself not to grab his hand, like I had done before. I didn't this time, because I knew there wasn't a point. When he wanted to touch me, he was going to touch me.

And he touched me again.

His large hand closed over my left breast, and I knew he could feel the scars there, but the caress didn't stumble as he zeroed onto the now-aching tip. Jax was good . . . so good that even through a T-shirt and a tank top, he had my nipple puckered when his thumb and forefinger got going, and sharp tingles arced from my breasts to down south. I gasped into the hot kiss, raising my back, and I wasn't disappointed when he moved to my other breast.

"Fuck, I love that sound you make," he all but growled against my mouth. He kissed me again. "I want to hear it again."

So he made me make that sound again, and I was done with not squirming, but I wanted to touch *him*. I knew I needed to act now, because if I didn't, his hand would be south again, and hell, all bets were off.

Smoothing my hand off the back of his neck, I slid it across the rough skin of his chest, and almost forgot what I was doing when I imagined what our skin would feel like with nothing between us. Not like that was ever going to happen, so I refocused on my path, trailing my hand down his side, then across the flat expanse of his upper stomach.

"What are you up to?' he asked, voice husky.

"Nothing."

Jax lifted up so there was space between our bodies, and I loved the way his abs tightened with the movement. He arched a brow. "Nothing?"

Shaking my head, I bit down on my lip as my fingers skated

around his navel and reached the band on his black boxer briefs. With a deep breath, I slipped my fingers under the band.

He caught my wrist. "You want to touch me?"

Warmth flooded my face and a different kind of heat hit my veins. "Yes." I forced my gaze up, meeting his. "I want to give you . . . what you've given me."

The hunger in his stare sent a shiver of awareness down my spine. "I like that. I want that." Dipping his head, he caught my lower lip in a quick kiss. "I'll make you a deal."

"A deal?"

He trailed his lips across my jaw. "Yeah. A deal. You can touch me." He moved my wrist by mere inches, lowering my hand over the short, crisp hairs. "But you got to take off the shirt."

"My shirt?"

He kissed my temple. "Yes. The shirt. It's got to come off."

My heart pumped as I tensed. Taking off the shirt didn't mean I was getting naked. I had a tank top underneath, but it would show off the scars on my upper chest and it would expose some of my back. But I was also on my back, so it wasn't like he'd see that.

"I want you to touch me," Jax said to me, and I shivered again. "Real bad. You want it, too." His teeth skated over my earlobe. "Just the shirt."

I didn't know if I could do it, but I nodded and then whispered, "Okay."

Jax acted fast. He drew my hand away from him and caught my shirt under the hem in one fist. His other hand slid under my lower back and he lifted me up enough to get the shirt up and then, in a second, it was over my head.

I lay back down, eyes wide and heart racing. His gaze met mine as he dropped the shirt on the floor and then his gaze slowly tracked down my face, over my throat and lower. His stare lingered on my chest, and fear pierced my belly. I moved to cross my arms.

"Don't you dare," he ordered in a gentle way. "There's nothing you need to hide."

My chest squeezed as his hand trailed over my breast. It was then I realized what he was staring at. It wasn't the small visible patch of skin between my breasts or the slice showing above my left breast.

It was something else.

The tips of my breasts were aching and hard, pushing against the thin material of the tank top, and my breath caught in a half laugh, half sob. His gaze flicked back, holding my stare as he lowered his head.

His mouth hit the skin between my breasts first and he kissed me there, then he went to the tip of one breast, also kissing me *there,* through the material, and he sucked deep, causing my back to arch clear off the bed as a riot of sensation rocketed through me.

God, I'd never felt that before.

"You like that?" he asked.

I panted out a breathy "Yes."

He moved to my other breast, and that was awesome. I could barely breathe as his hand got involved, and I almost forgot the purpose behind taking off my shirt, because I had no idea how sensitive I could be there, but then he lifted his head. He got down to his side of the deal, and he was fast about it. Reaching down, he hooked his fingers under the band of his boxers and shimmied it down his hips.

I got my first complete look at him.

Wow.

That was also awesome.

Jax was . . . I stared at him, taking in the thickness and length, and yeah, I really had no words.

"I don't mind you staring at me like that, but this is going to be over before you even touch me if you keep it up."

"Seriously?" I dragged my gaze to his.

He grinned. "Seriously."

"I kind of like that," I admitted.

There was a pause, then he threw his head back and let out a deep laugh. "I bet."

Before I lost my courage, I reached between us and wrapped my hand around him. His laughter faded into a masculine moan and then his hips jerked as I slid my hand up his length.

I didn't have to fumble around and figure out what he liked, because he placed his hand over mine, setting up a rhythm and pressure. He even did this thing with my thumb, where he moved it over his tip, and by the way he kissed me after, going deep, I knew he liked that. So after I made another pass from the root to the tip, I did it again.

"Fuck," he growled, burying his head in my neck; kissing and licking and touching him already had my turned-on body revving into high gear. When he got a hand between our bodies, careful of what I was doing, I spread my legs for him. "God."

His finger moved over the center of my undies and then his fingers were inside. At first contact of his skin against mine, I cried out, and when I said his name, he ground out another "Fuck."

He moved his hand and then he lifted my hips, dragging my panties down my legs. My hand tightened on him as I really started to get breathless. I opened my eyes and tension coiled tight in the pit of my belly.

What I saw was like a blast to the hormones. My hand wrapped around him, and he was swollen, pink, and hard. But beyond that, my undies were down my thighs, almost to my knees, my legs open and his hand between them.

Then he slid a finger inside me, and my body reacted. My hips punched up and my head kicked back.

"Calla, baby, you're so tight," he muttered, and by the heaviness in his voice, I figured this was a good thing. He moved his finger slowly—a lot slower and smoother than what I was doing and then I stopped doing everything, because he picked up pace. "I'm thinking you like this."

"I . . ." I didn't know what to say to that, but I knew I wanted more. I wanted him. The finger was great, but I wanted *more*. I didn't stop to think about where I was taking this. "I want you."

"I know."

My eyes narrowed, and he chuckled as my hand tightened around him. I could feel him pulse against my palm. "I want this," I told him in a thready whisper. "I want this in me."

His hips thrust halfway through what I said, and he made that deep sound again that curled my toes. He dropped his forehead to mine, and the next kiss was sweet and soulful, a different kind of kiss. As that kiss shifted into something far more sensual, he added another finger.

"Oh God," I gasped against his mouth.

"I want nothing more than to be in you. God, I could come just thinking about it." He moved slowly, dragging out the feel. "But this thing of yours has to come off."

His words cleared the haze. "My tank top?"

"Yep, baby, it's got to go." His tongue trailed along the seam of my lips. "You ready for that?"

Okay. Today *was* a different day, but it wasn't *that* different and some things would never change. My shirt might come off, but the tank top was never, *ever* coming off.

"No," I whispered.

"That's what I thought." He kissed the tip of my nose. "But you need to understand something, honey, I'm not going to get in you until we're skin to skin."

My pulse thundered at his words, but the look I gave him said we'd see about that, and he answered with an amused chuckle and another scorching hot, wet kiss. His hand shifted between my legs, putting his thumb right over the most sensitive part of me. It wasn't long before my hips were moving against him, following the pace he set, and then setting my own. He gave me what he could with those two fingers sliding in and out, his thumb pressing on the bundle of nerves.

"That's it." He lowered his mouth to mine, slanting his head and kissing me deeply as the knot built to a point. "Ride my hand."

Any other time, I would probably die of embarrassment hearing those words, and maybe later, I'd care, but right now? I did what he said. I rode his hand as I moved mine over him. Then there was only a subtle warning—a deep flutter—and then the knot whipped out, unraveling inside me, and I cried out as I came. He kept up, prolonging the sensation until my legs went weak.

Then he slowly eased his fingers out of me and then circled his hand around mine. I watched him—I watched us—through heavily hooded eyes. There was something wholly intimate about this, something that nestled in my chest and got lodged there. His body moved beautifully, full of masculine grace. Muscles along his hips flexed and rolled as he thrust against my hand.

His mouth was on mine when he came, and that had to be the most awesome thing out of all of this. Feeling the tremors in his body, the grunt of release that was caught on my tongue, and the way his hips slowed. But the most amazing part was the minutes immediately following.

Jax stayed with me for a few moments, half his weight on me, and the kisses went back to something sweet, a tenderness that meant more, and further lodged that feeling in my chest. When he did get up, he strutted into the bathroom in his naked glory and returned quickly with a damp washcloth. He cleaned up what he left behind and then he slid my undies back up my hips, but he wasn't done there.

Wrapping his hands around my wrists, he forced me up into a sitting position, and it was too late when I realized that this exposed my back and everything he could see that the tank didn't cover.

Panic exploded in my gut and I started to throw myself under the covers, but Jax was quick and the fucker was clever. He slid in behind me, sitting up against the headboard, and then he wrapped his arms around my waist. He tugged me between his spread legs and against his chest—my back completely flush with his chest.

I *knew* he could feel the rougher scars on the back of my shoulder blades, because the tank top was one of those damn razorbacks. And I also *knew* he'd seen them before he pulled me against him. Maybe not a good long look, but he had to have seen them.

Muscles tense, I focused on the window across the room as his arms folded around my waist and he dipped his chin, resting it on my shoulder.

"Did I tell you about the first time I met Clyde?" he said.

Shaking my head, I whispered, "No."

"It was on a Sunday. Met him at the bar. He ended up making me tacos." He paused, chuckling softly in my ear. "Said it was tradition if I was going to be a part of his family."

The next breath I took was sharp as a little more of that drowning weight lifted off me.

It was later in the day and Jax was finishing up with his shower before he took me back to the house so I could get ready for our date.

Our date.

Wow.

It seemed odd to be going on a date, with everything that was happening, but Jax operated on his life-is-short mentality, so I wasn't too surprised by it. And in spite of all the craziness and my hang-ups, I was feeling good about the date—about this morning and about *us*.

Since he was busy, I tried calling Teresa and I was thrilled when she answered on the third ring. "Yo," she chirped into the phone. "I was just thinking about you."

I sat on the edge of Jax's couch. "You were?"

"Yep. I was wondering if you were still bartending, and if so, were you going to become our official drink mixer when you get back to Shepherdstown."

I laughed. "I don't know if you want that. Most of the people up here order straight from the tap, the bottle, or shots, which is a good thing because I'm not that good at mixing drinks."

"I still can't believe you're bartending."

I was sure there were a lot of things that Teresa probably couldn't believe about me. "How's the beach?" I asked.

Teresa's sigh was audible. "It's great. I have an awesome tan, and Jack really loves it here. It's the first time he's been to the beach."

Jack was Jase's little brother, whom he was superclose with.

"And you should see the two of them together out on the sand. Nothing makes your ovaries get all happy than seeing a hot guy with a kid," she explained, and I grinned and then I pictured Jax with a kid, and there was a quiver somewhere down below. "Anyway," she went on. "We're leaving in a couple of days, but I swear, I think I could live at the beach."

I really needed to get my ass to a beach at some point.

"So tell me about things in the great state of Pennsylvania. Is everything cool?"

"Well, yeah, things have been . . . they've been great," I told her, glancing at the stairs. "I've, um . . . I've met a guy."

There was silence.

And more silence.

I frowned. "You there?"

"Yes. Yes! You just caught me off guard. You went from things are good to there's a guy and I was waiting for, you know, more detail." She all but shouted the last word. "Like lots of detail."

With another glance at the stairwell, I told her about Jax and our date tonight. I ended my impromptu confession with "So, yeah, I'm pretty sure he likes me."

"Well, duh. Of course he does. So the place is called Apollo's? Hold on a sec," she said, and then her voice sounded farther away. "Hey, Jase, look up Apollo's outside of Philly. What? Just do it."

Oh my God.

"Back to the liking-you thing. Why would you be surprised that he likes you? Brandon totally liked you, but you—"

"What?" I interrupted her. "He did not."

"Oh, yes, he did. It was cute. You were all quiet when he first started coming around and he was always looking at you, but then you really didn't pay any attention to him. I thought maybe I read you wrong and you weren't into him."

Teresa was smoking crack.

"Do you like him?" she asked suddenly. "Because Jase just looked up Apollo's—and, by the way, Jase says hi."

"Hi," I mumbled back.

"She says hi!" she yelled and then, "He says the place looks pretty classy. Do you like him, Calla?"

I closed my eyes and nodded. "Yeah, I like him. I really do."

"Good. I can't wait to meet him. And to see you. But I really want to meet him." She giggled when I laughed. "I'm happy for you. Seriously."

Sighing, I then admitted something kind of scary. "I'm happy, too."

I got off the phone after making a promise to give her the details, and it was when I tucked my hair back behind my ear, I felt it—the awareness of not being alone.

Oh no.

Biting down on my lower lip, I twisted around and saw Jax standing at the bottom of the stairwell, already dressed for our date. Dark denim jeans and a white button-down. He looked damn good.

He was also grinning a smug little grin. "So you like me? You really do?"

I groaned, cheeks heating. "Shut up."

Jax tipped back his head and laughed. He was lucky he had such a great laugh.

Lip gloss was almost the finishing touch and I was glad I was done getting ready. My tummy was grumbling and I really hoped Jax liked girls with big appetites because I had a feeling I was going to gorge myself on food.

I'd put loose waves in my hair and parted it on the side. I'd skipped on the Dermablend again, opting for the light look with smoky eyes.

The dress I had on, since I had to bring all my clothes with me, was cute and flirty. It was a strappy dark blue sundress that was fitted through the breast and waist. Maybe a little clingy around the hips, too, but then it flowed around, the skirt bouncy and ending just below mid-thigh. I paired it with a pair of sandals with a low heel. The final touch was the baby blue cap-sleeve cardigan that ended just below my breasts and was also fitted.

Checking myself out in the mirror, I had to say that I looked pretty damn good.

I nodded at my reflection like a dork and then marched into the living room. While I'd been getting ready, Jax had puttered around the house and then made his way to the couch, where he was reading his book.

Studying his profile, with his chin dipped and his face masked in concentration, I had to say that he was hot. But when he looked up and saw me he was even hotter.

"I'm ready," I said, and then added, "To go to dinner and eat."

Yep. It was official. I was an uberdork.

His eyes darkened and heated. In a second he was on his feet, and then he was in front of me. One hand curled around the nape of my neck and the other landed on my cheek. His thumb moved along the bottom of my lip and got my stomach doing cartwheels.

"You look beautiful," he said.

And I felt beautiful when he said that. "Thank you. You look beautiful, too."

A dark eyebrow rose.

Ugh.

"You look manly beautiful," I amended, but that sounded even more stupid. "Okay. That was dumb. You look hot."

He chuckled as he moved in, brushing his lips over the curve of my cheekbone. He kissed the scar again, and I tensed, but it was for a different reason than the norm, because his lips had skated to the space below my ear.

"I'm hot and you like me," he murmured. "It's my lucky day."

"Shut up."

Another deep chuckle and then his mouth claimed mine. I liked—no, I loved—the way Jax kissed. It started off slow and then became something entirely different, definitely not slow, and very much deep and hot. Before I knew it, my hands were flat against his chest, sliding up to his shoulders.

"Dinner." He kissed me again, his mouth lingering in the sweetest way. "We're going to be late."

My fingers dug into his shirt as I all but clung to him. I didn't get the chance to respond, because he was kissing me again, in a way I felt devoured.

"Dinner," he repeated, and his lips brushed mine. "I made reservations."

Moving my hands down his chest, I tipped my head back and opened my eyes. "Yeah. Food."

"Steak." His arm tightened around me. "Really good steak."

A grumble came from my stomach, and I broke away as he laughed. "Shut up," I said again.

"It's cute." His hands dropped to my hips, so I didn't get very far.

I rolled my eyes. "More like it, as in my stomach is hungry. Not cute. So if we don't get—"

My words were cut off as something heavy hit the front of the house. Swallowing a startled squeak, I jumped and turned around. "What the hell?"

Jax was already starting toward the door when I heard tires peeling out of the driveway. My heart lodged into my throat as I followed Jax.

"Stay back," he ordered, reaching the door.

I didn't listen.

The muscles in his shoulders tensed as he unlocked the front door and yanked it open.

Slapping my hands over my mouth, I took a step back out of horror. Jax cursed and turned, shielding what waited for us on the front porch, but it was too late. There was no way to un-see the still, ghastly pale body or the small crimson hole smack dab in the middle of its forehead.

Twenty-two

*D*inner at Apollo's was canceled.

A dead body thrown—literally—at the front of the house would do that. And the body was still out there, right where it landed, while the police did whatever forensics they saw fit.

The body had a name, I learned—a name that sent a jolt of fear and dread straight to my very core.

The body belonged to one Ronald R. Miller, also known by the street name Rooster, and rumored to be my mother's boyfriend.

This wasn't good.

Rooster had a bullet in the center of his forehead, and I had heard Reece outside talking to another officer. Rooster's jeans had grass stains on the knees, and it didn't take a huge leap of logic to imagine that he'd been on his knees when that trigger was pulled.

Classic execution style.

Where was Mom? That question played over and over again, because everyone said she'd run off with Rooster.

Who now had a bullet in his head.

I shuddered as I focused my gaze on Jax. He was standing by the window, back tense and his jaw a hard line. He hadn't said much since this all went down. We'd already given our statements, which wasn't much.

Clyde reached over and squeezed my hand. "You doing okay, baby girl?"

I nodded. He'd shown up about an hour after the police. How he'd found out about what happened, I had no idea, but he arrived in his old-ass truck, shouting and bellowing to be let into the house, to see his "baby girl" through this "traumatic" experience that "ain't right" and a whole bunch of things that included curse words. They wouldn't let him come up on the front porch, for obvious reasons, and they hadn't wanted him coming in, but he yelled until he got his way and he came in through the back door, which was off the kitchen.

"How much longer do you think . . . ?" I paused, swallowing against the sudden nausea. "Do you think it will take before they move him?"

"Soon," Clyde said gruffly. "It's gotta be soon."

My gaze shifted to him, and I noticed a fine sheen of sweat glistening on his bald head.

Jax turned from the window and walked over to where I sat next to Clyde. He didn't say anything as he perched on the arm of the couch. A second later, I heard the front door open and Reece walked in with a detective wearing tan dress pants, and a white button-down like Jax's, but paired with a tie that matched his pants.

For some odd reason, I thought about what Roxy had told me about Reece being involved in a shooting. It was the last thing I needed to be thinking about, but I wondered if it bothered him seeing Rooster like . . . like he was. Then again, he probably saw that a lot.

I'd almost forgotten his name—the detective's. He wasn't that much older than us, maybe late twenties or early thirties. He was handsome, very much so, with neatly trimmed brown hair and clear blue eyes.

"We're wrapping up now," he said, his gaze tracking over the three of us. "Right now, we've got some suspects, and we're going to find who did this."

I nodded. "Okay. Um. Thank you?"

His lips twitched. "Now, Officer Anders told me you two have been looking for Miss Fritz."

Officer Anders? I blinked slowly and then I realized he was talking about Reece. My gaze moved to Reece and then to Detective Anders. Wait a sec . . . "Are you two related?"

"Brothers," Jax answered.

"I'm the handsome one," Reece said, grinning.

Detective Anders tilted his head toward what was now obviously his younger brother. "Most definitely not the smart one."

Cop brothers. Hot.

Sigh.

I needed my head checked.

"Anyway," the detective said. "He was telling me you guys have been trying to find your mom and that you had some problems yesterday when you were in the city. I know what's been going on."

Jax's eyes narrowed, and my stomach sank. No matter what, if the police really knew what had been going down, she was in trouble. Lots of trouble.

Reece held his gaze with a look that said sorry, bud, had to. "He knows about Mack. And that lowlife is the first on our suspect list."

"This was obviously a warning to Calla," Jax responded, voice clipped. "But it doesn't make sense. If Mack found Rooster, then how did he not find Mona?"

"Rooster could've decided he wanted out of this mess," Detective Anders said, crossing his arms over his chest. "He could've come back and if what your . . . sources are saying is true, if he came back without the dope or the money equal to what they are holding, he would've gotten a warm welcome."

Yeah, he'd gotten a bullet in the head. Mom didn't have the dope. And she sure as hell didn't have the money.

It had to be Mack, because like Ritchey had said, shit rolled downhill and that shit had rolled all over Mack.

"We're also looking for the man who matches your description that came into the house and took the drugs. We're going to find them," Detective Anders said. "But we need you all to back off. Let us do our jobs. We don't want you around any of these people."

I didn't want to be around any of these people, but I had *days* left before I was supposed to produce my mom. I didn't respond because I really didn't want to listen to them try to talk me out of what needed to be done.

We had a lead.

Ike.

And Jax hadn't mentioned Ike to the police or to Reece as far as I knew. Another officer popped his head into the room, announcing the front porch was cleared, and I breathed a sigh of relief. Jax followed Reece and his older brother out after the convo was wrapped up in here.

Clyde rubbed his hand over his chest. "This is a mess."

I sighed. "I know. Mom . . . do you think she has any idea of what kind of mess she's in?"

Clyde nodded. "I think she does, and I think if she is smart, she's living in Mexico right now."

God, that would suck—her moving far away and me never seeing her again, but if Mom was smart, that's what she should do. There was no way she'd ever be able to come back here. "If she doesn't come back . . . what happens to the bar?" I asked, focusing on the least important thing, because that was better than all the crazy more important stuff. I knew the bar would be left to me if she . . . if she passed on, but I had no idea about the technicalities if she simply disappeared.

"Baby girl, you don't need to worry about that." He lumbered to his feet, his chest moving in deep, heavy breaths. "The bar will be all right."

My brows pinched with concern. "Are you okay?"

"Yeah, I'm doin' fine. You ain't needin' to be worried about me."

I wasn't sure about that, but then Jax returned without the hot cop brothers. He walked straight to where I sat, grabbed my hand, and helped me to my feet. "You want to get out of here?" he asked.

Nodding, I wanted nothing more than to get out of here.

Clyde made his way over to me, and without Jax letting go of my hand, he gave me his bear hug. "I like that you're not staying here. That's good. Real good."

I was reluctant to let him go when he pulled back. "Everything is going to be okay," I told him, because I felt like I needed to say that out loud.

He gave me a toothy smile as his gaze moved to Jax. "Yes, baby girl, it will be."

As Clyde left, I packed up more clothes and personal stuff and then we headed out to Jax's truck. It was hard walking across that porch without picturing the body there.

Once in the cab of the truck, Jax looked at me. "You doing okay?"

I thought about that for a moment. "As okay as I can be."

A slight smile appeared as he reached over, smoothing his thumb along my lower lip. "This shit with Rooster and Mack—with your mom isn't right. It's serious. It's not normal. And it's okay not to be okay with any of this."

"I know," I whispered.

His smile spread on one side of his lips. "Like I said. You're brave."

My chest warmed, and instead of denying that, I smiled a little. "Can we stop on the way to your house and grab something to eat?"

"Anything for you, babe."

I liked the sound of that. A lot.

It was too late to do dinner anywhere, so fast food was on the menu. At this point, I'd probably have eaten horse meat, so I wasn't complaining when he pulled into the burger joint. Not the best steaks in the state, but it would work.

Neither of us really talked on the drive to his townhouse or as we scarfed down our food. It wasn't until we were cleaning up and I was tossing my soda in the trash that I knew we had to talk about this.

Or that I had to talk about this.

"Do you think Mom is okay?" I asked.

Jax was at the table situated by the door that led out to a small deck and postage-stamp-size backyard. He turned to me, chin dipped. "I don't know."

I closed my eyes as a rush of emotion swelled.

"I hate saying that, but I got to be honest with you."

"I appreciate that."

"I know you do," he said, and then I felt him closer and I opened my eyes. He was right in front of me. "If Rooster bounced, then he was probably feeling the heat. That means your mom's got to still be out there."

Because she wasn't lying on the porch alongside Rooster.

"But this isn't good," he finished.

Just like Clyde said. "There's no way she can fix this. Even if they bust Mack for what happened to Rooster, there's this Isaiah. That was a lot of dope and a lot of money. She can't get past this."

"No. She can't."

A ball lodged in the back of my throat. "She really did it this time. I mean, she really did it, Jax. There's no fixing this. There's no making it okay. And she dragged me into this, which has dragged you into this. And I'm so sorry about that. You don't need this. You shouldn't have seen Rooster today."

"Honey," he said softly, cupping my cheeks. He tilted my head back. "None of this is your fault. Know that. There is no need for you to apologize for any of this. You didn't ask for it or bring it on yourself."

What he said was true, but I couldn't help but feel somewhat responsible, because it was my mom after all. Placing my hands on his sides, I did something I hadn't really done before. I leaned into him, resting my cheek against his chest.

"What are we going to do?" And that question was important and it was hard to ask, because I was asking about "us," as in I wasn't expecting to do this on my own. That was a huge step, a scary one.

Jax folded his arms around me. "We still have Ike to talk to. If we can find your mom . . ."

"And what?" I asked. "We can't turn her over. We saw what they did to Rooster."

"I wasn't suggesting turning her over, honey. We get to her first, make sure she understands the kind of shit she's messed up in, and then . . . well, we go from there."

Going from there meant we made sure she understood that the likelihood of her stepping back in Pennsylvania and not getting shot would be slim to none. "But what about Mack?"

"He's not going to get near you." Jax drew back, his eyes meeting mine. "You can trust in that. Neither will Isaiah."

I wanted to believe that. I almost believed that, because he said it in such a way that it came across as if he could control such things.

He dipped his forehead to mine. "Sucks about dinner."

My lips twitched and I said hoarsely, "Yeah, I was really looking forward to that steak."

"There's always tomorrow. Hell, there's always next Sunday."

I closed my eyes, liking the sound of planning that far out. It was only a week, but a week was a lot of time. The next thing just sort of burst out there. "That's the second time I've seen a dead body."

"Babe . . ."

"Not my brothers. Their coffins were closed, and I didn't . . . I didn't see them bringing them out of the house. But I've seen a dead body before." I paused, drawing in a shaky breath. "A bunch of people were partying with Mom. This guy, I guess he overdosed or something, and everyone else was too messed up to realize it. I'd come into the living room and he was lying facedown, not moving or breathing."

Jax's chest rose against mine. "Shit, baby, I don't know what to say. You should've never seen something like that."

"I don't want to see any more dead bodies."

A gap of silence stretched out between us. "It's not something you ever get used to," he admitted. "I saw it a lot in the sandbox—the desert. Sometimes it was insurgents, other times it was innocent civilians caught in the crossfire and . . ."

"And sometimes it was your friends?" I asked quietly.

"Yeah," he replied. "I never forget *any* of their faces."

I bit down on my lip hard. I totally got what he was saying. There were some things that you could never forget.

There was so much going on in my head. Mack. Mom. Dead bodies with bullet wounds in their forehead. Clyde rubbing his chest, obviously worried and stressed over everything. Glorious steak dinners that never happened. Coming back here. Leaving here. The way Jax had held me this morning with my back pressed against his front.

I didn't want to think anymore.

Lifting my gaze, I met his. "I don't want to think."

Jax didn't question or comment on this. There was a flare of something hot and heady in his eyes, and then he dipped his mouth to mine, and he kissed me sweetly—the kind of kiss that went beyond the heavy and sensual ones. It meant something, and I seemed to open up to it, really feeling it, believing in it.

And that was pretty damn spectacular.

When the kiss did run hotter, my mouth opened to his and the moment our tongues touched, his hands dropped to my hips. He pulled me against him, and I could feel him pressing against my belly. I remembered this morning, my hand around him, his powerful body shaking with release. Those memories scorched my skin, but it was nothing compared to the kisses he trailed across my jaw, to my ear and below, over my throat. My head tipped back as my fingers delved into his soft hair.

"You're not going to think," he told me in between those wicked nips. "Not for one fucking second."

"Good," I said.

He chuckled against my throat as his hands slid off my hips and quickly made their way under my dress. I really liked where this was heading, especially when he hooked his fingers under the band of my panties.

They hit the floor in a nanosecond.

"Ready for this?" he asked.

I nodded as I opened my eyes.

He grinned, kissed me quickly, and then gripped my hips. He lifted me right off the floor and placed me on the kitchen counter.

Yep.

My bare ass was on the kitchen counter.

And that was all kinds of inappropriately hot.

Jax ran his hands along the inside of my legs. As he reached my knees, he eased them apart. Air caught in my throat, and instinct demanded that I close my legs, but his thick lashes lifted, and heated eyes locked on to mine.

"Don't close them, baby." His voice was deep and rumbled through me.

I didn't close them.

When he pushed a little farther, I could feel the cool air rushing over me. Warmth crept into my cheeks, turning to a flush that spread down my throat and over my chest. My heart pounded as he dipped his head, kissing me softly as his hands continued up over the top of my thighs. He snagged the hem of my dress the higher his hands traveled. I bit down on my lip as the skirt of my dress ended up tucked around my hips and waist. My hands tightened around the edge of the counter.

"Beautiful," he murmured.

Oh my God. I had no idea what to do or say. I was completely exposed. Like wide open, and his eyes were focused on the lady parts in such an intense way. While I knew that what he was—what we were—about to do wasn't anything abnormal, it was completely awe inspiring and new to me.

Then his hands started moving again, over the inside of my thighs, starting at my knees and slowly, torturously making their way up. "You really are beautiful, Calla. Don't ever doubt that. Hell, there's no way you could doubt that."

My heart grew about five times too big for my chest. My skin tingled with heightened senses as he drew back from me.

"Trust me?" he asked.

Oh goodness, now my heart was about ten times too big. "Yes."

A lopsided grin appeared and then his hands were on my hips. He dragged me across the counter—a counter I'd never look the same at again—until I felt like I would slide right off.

He didn't touch me or fool around. One moment he was grinning at me, and the next, his lower body bent and his mouth was on me. I jerked at the intimate kiss and heat flooded my veins.

What he did was wet and hot and crushing in ways that blew my mind. Jax knew what he was doing. The way he moved his mouth over me, the way he worked his tongue in teasing tastes, building me up until my head kicked back against the cabinets and my hips rose clear off the counter, meeting the strokes of his tongue. The sensations pounding through me were raw and primal and beautiful.

He was doing what I asked. I wasn't thinking about all those terrible things. Nope. My brain had checked out and my body was rocking. I was panting and these tiny noises I didn't even know I was capable of were coming out of me. And then he was going deep, stronger and faster. I thought my fingers would break off from how hard I was clenching the counter.

"Jax," I breathed.

My body was coiling tight as my eyes opened. I couldn't keep them shut anymore. I wanted to see every moment of this. My chin dipped and all I could see was the top of his bronze head between my thighs.

I took a breath. It went nowhere.

The sight of him pushed me over the edge.

I cried out, and he growled against me. Release poured through me, and I was lost as every bone liquefied and the whirl of sensations pulsed and throbbed throughout me.

Jax stayed with me until my spine curved and my breath slowed, then he lifted his body, pressing his mouth to my neck. "I love the sounds you made, honey. Better yet, when you said my name like you did . . . ? Yeah, I really loved that."

My cheek lowered, resting against his. "That . . . that was amazing."

"You're amazing."

Those two words were so simple and sweet that it broke through something deep and muddy in me. It was like the sun breaking through after a month of nothing but dreary rain. But it was more than those two words.

Lifting my head, I let go of the counter and placed my hands on his shoulders. I pushed him back, and he went, only because he seemed caught off guard. I slipped off the counter, feeling my dress settle around my thighs.

It was so much more than those three words.

It was the weeks spent getting to know him. It was the things I shared with him and he shared with me. It was the fact that he saw me, all of me, and beyond the skin, and he knew what existed on me and inside me, and not just the physical.

"Calla?" He tilted his head to the side as he said my name softly.

God, his lips were glistening with *me,* and that was like taking a hit to the chest in the best way. Getting involved with anyone right now with everything so up in the air and just plain crazy wasn't smart. It was dumb.

But it was the right kind of dumb.

As I stared into brown eyes that melted me from the inside out, I tossed my Three F's out of the window as I reached up, caught the edges of the shrug I wore, and slipped it off my shoulders and down my arms. I let it fall to the floor.

His gaze tracked the shrug and then his stare flew back to my face.

I tossed the self-consciousness away as I reached to my side and tugged the zipper of my dress down, and I didn't stop the dress as it loosened all around my body.

A look appeared on his striking face, a tautness that tugged at my heart. "Calla . . ." The way he said my name was different now.

And I let myself admit that I didn't just like him as I caught the thin straps and slid them down my arms. I told myself as the dress gathered around my hips and then with a little shimmy, fell to the floor, that I had fallen for him.

Then I was standing in front of him, in the kitchen, the bright light, in nothing more than my heels, and dear God, I was scared. Fucking terrified out of my mind, and my skin felt numb when I realized that it wasn't because I was practically naked for the first time in my life in front of anyone, but because I was in love with him.

I was *in* love with Jax.

Twenty-three

I was trembling as I stood in front of Jax. Even my fingers were twitching at my sides. I loved him. I was *in* love with him. I had no idea when it happened, but it did, and it was an amazing and terrifying feeling, but damn, it was also so hopeful, because even though I liked guys in the past, even lusted after a few, I had never been in love with one and I hadn't really thought I'd get to know a guy enough to fall in love with him.

But I had.

Jax's eyes were fastened to my face, and it seemed like he read something in my expression because he made a sound in the back of his throat that sent a tremor through my core.

And then he was on me.

His hands clasped my cheeks and he tilted my head back as his mouth landed on mine. The kiss was deep and moving. I could taste him and another salty flavor that I knew belonged to me and that spun my senses. His tongue moved with mine and then flicked over the roof of my mouth before delving deep. Everything I needed to feel was in that kiss.

"Are you sure about this?" he asked.

I took a breath, but it didn't expand my lungs. "I'm standing here naked. I'm sure."

Jax chuckled and the sound danced over my skin. "I'd hope so, but honey, you haven't done this before, and I want to make sure you're a hundred percent with me."

Pressure clamped down on my chest as I nodded. "I'm sure, Jax."

He made that sound again before he kissed me. "I'm so fucking glad to hear that, you have no idea." Then he took my hand and placed it against his chest, above his heart. "You can trust me."

I did trust him.

Holding on to my hand, he drew me out of the kitchen, out of the bright lights, and through the darker living room, then to the stairs. My heart was racing as we went up the stairs and came to a stop in his bedroom, in front of his bed.

He let go of my hand, and I watched him walk to the nightstand. He opened a drawer and fisted what appeared to be a handful of foil wrappers. My brows shot up. Um, how many of them did he need? He grinned when he caught my look and tossed a few onto the bed. Then he faced me.

Eyes locked with mine, he reached down and pulled off his shirt before moving on to the belt he wore. Unhooking that, he flicked the button and then the zipper went down. He shucked off his jeans and the black boxer briefs quickly followed.

And he was as naked as I was.

He was gorgeous. Every inch of him. From the top of his messy bronze hair, across the broad cheekbones and full lips, down the neck, over his chiseled pecs and the tightly roiled stomach. Farther down, he was even more magnificent. The muscles on either side of his hips drew my attention for a moment and then my gaze moved over the fine dusting of hair to where he was the hardest.

Good Lord.

I sucked my lower lip in and felt a pleasant hum in my veins. Jax was so not lacking in that department.

One side of his lips curved up. "Come here."

With my heart pounding in every pulse point, I walked over to where he stood at the side of the bed. He placed his hands on my shoulders and guided me down so I was sitting on the bed. Then he knelt, running his fingers down the outside of my legs, from my thighs to my ankles. Once he reached the strap on my sandals, he nimbly undid them.

"Next time, I want you wearing these shoes," he said, looking up at me through thick lashes. "You got that?"

Oh my. I nodded.

"That's my girl," he murmured, moving on to the other sandal. Once he had that shoe off, his hands made the trip back up my legs as he rose. He didn't stop. Skating over my stomach, the outer curves of my breasts, he eventually reached my cheeks and he stopped there.

His lips were on mine again, moving slowly, tasting and teasing until his tongue ran the seam of my mouth. I opened to him and there was that rush again, the heady warmth. As he kissed me, his hands slipped down to my arms and then under them. He lifted me up, pushing me farther onto the bed as he climbed on, his legs on either side of me.

My breath was stuttered as he guided me onto my back and I was suddenly staring up at him. Nerves exploded in the pit of my stomach. What if I sucked? What if I didn't like it? Not every woman had a great time during sex. I knew that. What if I—

"We can stop at any time you want. Okay?" he said, voice rumbling in a way that made my toes curl. "If it hurts, you let me know. If you're not liking what's happening, you tell me. Okay?"

"Okay," I breathed, forcing myself to relax.

He smiled tightly and then his lips descended on mine. This kiss was different, deeper, more shattering. His mouth worked mine until I was panting for breath, until my hands settled on his shoulders. The nerves eased away as his lips moved away from mine, traveling down my neck and over the straight line of my collarbone with a series of hot little kisses and flicks of his tongue.

God, he knew how to use that mouth of his.

I closed my eyes as his lips moved to my breasts, over the sliced scars, to close over a nipple. My back arched off the bed when he sucked deep and the keening, sudden sound that erupted from me would scorch my ears later. He worried the aching peak as his fingers settled over my other breast. Each pull of his mouth, each tug of his fingers sent a bolt of pleasure throughout my body and straight to my core, where the ball of tension began to build all over again.

He moved his mouth to my other breast and repeated those sensual actions, getting my pulse pounding in several very interesting places. My hips tilted against his restlessly, nudging the hard length of him, and I gasped as a little burst of sensation rocketed through me.

His mouth continued licking, laving, tugging, and teasing as he shifted his body, working a hand between my thighs. I could feel him there, palming me, and my hips reacted out of instinct, pressing against him.

He lifted his head from my breast as he slid a finger inside me. I arched again, sucking in a deep breath as he added another. "That good?" he asked.

"Yeah," I breathed, and then nodded in case he didn't get the point.

His smile turned devilish as he dipped his head, sucking on the tip in tandem with the thrust of his fingers. The dual sensations was like opening lightning in a bottle. A fire started in my blood and my fingers dug into his shoulders. A flutter started deep inside me, pulsing around his fingers. His hand twisted, pressing his palm against the bundle of nerves, and I rocked my hips against his hand shamelessly. The release built quickly and when it broke, I kicked my head back, my cry hoarse as release powered through me for the second time that night.

Jax moved away quickly, reaching for a wrapper on the bed. Tiny little shocks of pleasure were still darting to the ends of my nerves as he rose above me, lining up his hips with me. I felt him there, against my damp flesh, and my eyes shot open.

I was barely breathing as I stared into his eyes.

"You sure?" he asked again, his arms shaking from where he had them braced on either side of my head. "Tell me you are, honey."

"I am."

He closed his eyes briefly before staring down at me. "Thank fucking God. I want you so bad I'm coming out of my fucking skin."

I would've laughed except he shifted his weight onto one arm as he reached between us, guiding himself into me. The first point of pressure stole my breath, and I jerked. He couldn't even have made it in an inch, but I felt myself spreading. There was a burning sensation I wasn't sure I liked or not. I bit down on my bottom lip.

His gaze held on to mine as he moved his hand to my cheek. "Still with me?"

I nodded, because I wasn't sure I could speak. His thumb swept over my bottom lip, drawing it from between my teeth. He moved his hips, a small roll that pushed him in deeper. My thighs clamped on him as the burn spread and increased, tinged in something that wasn't quite painful, but more of a pressure.

His arm beside my head trembled with the control he was exerting. "You're so tight. Damn, Calla, you're killing me."

An apology was on the tip of my tongue, but then his pelvis moved again, and the words came out as a gasp.

He stilled, his hand curving around my jaw. "I need to hear you're ready, honey. I need to hear you say it."

My mouth was dry, but I forced the words out. "I'm ready."

Jax held my gaze for a moment and then he kissed me. My lips were sealed tight at that point, but he worked at them until I opened for him, and as the kiss deepened, he thrust forward, all the way in. The kiss swallowed the cry as a burst of pain radiated out from between my legs, followed by an intense burn. He was in me, not moving, and I knew the very second I was no longer a virgin. Yep. Sure did.

"You okay?" His voice was guttural.

I swallowed. "Yeah."

And that much was true. The pain had faded. The burn was still there. It didn't really feel bad. It just was kind of *there.*

"Well, I'm about to turn it from something okay to something great," he said against my lips, and I wasn't so sure about that.

But as he kissed me again, he started moving, slowly pulling out until he was halfway in and then pushing back in. The fullness of him stretching me was an odd feeling. Again, not painful, but something else, something that every time he pulled out and rocked in, I felt in my entire body.

Jax kept it slow and steady until the burning pressure really wasn't something at all painful, something else entirely different. That burn turned into a low simmer of pleasure that ratcheted up with every pull and push.

Feeling more comfortable with this, I slid my hands down his sides to rest on his hips as I moved my hips with his next thrust.

"Damn," he groaned, and I found out pretty quickly that moving in tandem with him was a good thing, a really, *really* good thing, so I did again and then again, and his next word exhale was harsh against my mouth. "Fuck."

I moved my hips, rolling them at the pace he let me set and that ball of sensation was back, building and building. I moved my legs, wrapping them around his hips, and somehow he got deeper. His kisses turned wild, his tongue thrusting in tune with his hips, and my nails scoured the flesh along his hips.

"More," I heard myself whisper, having no idea where that word came from, but he answered.

He gave more.

Lots more.

His movement picked up and his head dipped into the space between my neck and shoulder. The pressure in my core became everything. Any remnants of pain were long, long gone. Our movements became frantic and whatever rhythm was there was completely lost. He grunted into my ear as my back arched, my hands pulling him down.

"God, Calla, I love the way you feel," he whispered into my ear. "I can feel you tightening. Fucking beautiful."

My breath caught. I was on the edge of something bigger, something beautiful and powerful happening in my body, and he seemed to know because his thrusts turned to his hips grinding against mine. The friction was intense, consuming. I whispered his name as my grip on him tightened. Tension coiled tightly and then it exploded outward, the pleasure forceful and nothing like the times before. It was deeper, more concentrated.

His hips slammed into mine, all pretenses of control gone as he buried his head in my shoulder. He pushed, going deep, and then he stilled for a moment before his hips jerked. My name was a hoarse shot against my skin as he found his own release. I clung to him, moved more than I thought I'd ever be from sex, squeezing my eyes shut as he breathed deeply.

It felt like an eternity before he moved, lifting his head enough to press a kiss against the side of my throat, just below my sluggish pulse. "You okay?"

"Yeah," I whispered. "That was . . ." There were no words for how that felt. None whatsoever.

He rose onto his forearms and dipped his mouth to mine. Still inside me, he kissed me slowly. "That was . . . fucking perfect."

I opened my eyes. "It was. I didn't . . ."

"What?" he asked when I didn't finish.

"I didn't know it could be like that," I admitted, feeling a bit foolish. "I just didn't think it could be like it."

A smug sort of smile appeared on his lips and then he kissed me again before easing out. There was a twinge of discomfort and a weirdness at the feeling of losing the fullness.

My body was boneless as he rolled off the bed and headed into the bathroom. When he returned, he'd gotten rid of the condom and was carrying a damp cloth. As he settled on the bed beside me and gently swiped at the proof of what just went down, I was shocked by the intimacy of the moment. Somehow it seemed more than what we'd just done. My throat was tight as he left to pitch the cloth in the bathroom.

I said nothing as he climbed back into bed with me and tugged the covers up over us. He positioned me so I was facing him and his arm was lying over my waist, our knees curved and pressing against each other. He played with the strands of my hair, twining them around his fingers. The silence stretched out for so long that I began to worry that he hadn't liked it as much as I had, that he wasn't as moved as I was.

"Thank you," he said.

I blinked. "What?"

A funny little smile played out across his lips. "Thank you for trusting me with this."

My mouth gaped.

"It's a big deal." His lashes lifted and his eyes met mine. "What we did. It was your first time. I'm honored."

Was this real?

"So thank you."

Jax closed the distance between us, melding our lips together in what had to have been the sweetest kiss possible, and I realized this was real. Not some orgasm-induced hallucination, and there was truly no wonder why I'd fallen for him.

My fingers dug into Jax's chest as I threw my head back, crying out as I came. His hands palmed my breasts and his hips powered up as

I all but collapsed onto his chest. His arms circled around me as he came, and I focused on breathing, because it was a chore, as I felt his body shuddering around me.

I was sated and made up of nothing but air as one of his hands circled the back of my head, pressing my cheek against his chest. I could feel his heart pounding as fast as mine. Smiling, I closed my eyes.

How he managed to convince me to do it this way—me on top—I had no idea. It probably started with waking up Monday morning with his mouth on my breast, nipping and licking. That had led to him moving inside me, much slower than the night before, if that was possible. And it might have had something to do with the way he got me naked from the waist down Monday night in his kitchen, and we'd re-created what we did the night before, but with his cock and not his tongue.

I'd never, ever look at that kitchen counter the same again.

Or it could've been Tuesday evening, after we'd headed to the campground where Ike was supposed to be hanging out, which turned out to be a total bust. He wasn't there. No one had seen him in days. He was gone, like ashes in a hurricane. That had been disappointing, because I'd been hoping he'd be a good lead, but that disappointment faded in the truck ride back to Jax's place.

Jax could multitask like a beast, driving with one hand on the steering wheel, the other in my pants. And I paid him back for that when we got back to his place, happily on my knees in the living room. There was something incredibly naughty about that.

Maybe it was Tuesday night that helped him convince me to be on top this afternoon, because I was pretty sure after last night, I knew firsthand what "fuck each other's brains out" really meant and felt like.

And it felt *good*.

It could've also been this morning, because he was definitely into morning sex. That was when it took longer for both of us and it turned into an epic sexcapade. But it was when he interrupted me trying to prepare for the shower that I ended up in his bed, with him on his back and me astride him.

I'd been nervous, though. With him being on top, I really wasn't thinking of the condition of my body. He could totally see my entire front, but it had worked out. Very well. Like I think being on top would probably be my new favorite position of all time.

"We need to get ready for work," he said.

"I don't want to move."

He chuckled. "I really don't want you to, but . . ."

I sighed. "Can I just stay here, like this, forever?"

That got another laugh and then he tapped my ass with his palm. Grumbling under my breath, I rolled off him and landed in a pile of bones and mush on the bed beside him. "You can shower first. I'm gonna nap."

He moved onto his side, running his fingers over the curve of my hip. "We can shower together."

I snorted. "We wouldn't shower."

"Why not?" he teased, kissing the tip of my shoulder.

"We'd end up doing it and I'm not sure if I can withstand another orgasm without losing precious brain cells."

He laughed against my skin. "You have a point." Then he moved his head, finding my lips and kissing me. "I won't be long."

"Uh-huh."

Jax took showers longer than any girl I ever knew. I was constantly amazed that there was any hot water left when he got his ass out of there. But whatever. A cold shower might be a good thing at the rate we were going.

So I lay there, drifting in and out of sleep, letting myself go to that warm and fuzzy place where I totally admitted that I was madly, deeply, and maybe dumbly in love with him. But whatever. I didn't care about potential heart-destroying, end-of-the-world heartbreak during post-sex bliss.

When Jax was *finally* out of the shower, it took me a little longer to get ready. I was moving at turtle speed. As I blow-dried my hair boringly straight, because I was beyond the point of putting any effort into it, I wondered how work would be now that we had totally done it. Like multiple times. All over the house. Sex exploding everywhere kind of done it.

I was a wee bit anxious about that as he drove us to Mona's. I was doing everything not to worry about that when I heard my phone ding in my purse. Happy for the distraction, I reached inside and pulled it out, discovering I had an e-mail from the financial aid adviser at Shepherd.

My heartbeat stuttered. "Oh God."

"What?" Jax asked, glancing at me as he hit the main road.

"I have an e-mail from my financial adviser. It has to be about the student loans, if I got my application in on time," I told him.

His gaze moved back to the road. "Well?"

"I'm afraid to read it."

"Want me to read it?" he offered.

I could've hugged and kissed him then. "Yes, but you're driving, and if it's good or bad news I don't want to die in a fifty-car pileup."

He snorted.

Taking a deep breath, I opened the e-mail and waited for the damn message to download. Of course, it took freaking forever and I was close to slamming my head against the dashboard while I waited, but the message finally appeared. I hastily scanned it, looking for key words. When I found the word *congratulations* among other things like loan amounts, I let out an excited squeal and twisted toward Jax so fast I almost choked myself with the seat belt.

His full lips curved into a wide smile. "I'm assuming it's good news."

"Totally! I got approved. It's enough money. The aid is going to go ahead and push my classes through," I told him, practically bouncing in my seat.

He reached over, placing his hand on my knee, and squeezed gently. "That's great news, honey."

It really was. "That's one giant stress off my shoulders. At least I know I'll be able to finish up school. That's huge."

"It is. I'm thrilled for you."

From the tone and the smile on his face, I could tell he really was happy for me, and that made me all warm and fuzzy until I realized that meant I seriously would be leaving in August to go back to school and Jax would be here.

Shit.

How could I have forgotten about that?

Some of my happiness took a nosedive, not a big one, but enough that I was annoyed at myself for letting it do that and frustrated because I suddenly felt like I needed to define exactly what we were and what that would mean when school started back up.

By the time we got inside Mona's, and I was behind the bar, chopping up limes and some fresh green, minty stuff, I managed to find a happy medium between the two. I was going to enjoy what I had now and not worry about what the future held, because there was a lot of stuff still unknown about my future. Like the fact I had to produce my mom before tomorrow night.

And that wasn't looking like it was going to happen.

The fact Jax had kissed me before he disappeared into the office, in front of Nick and Clyde, might've had something to do with not stressing out over a ton of things I had no control over.

"That's my boy," was all Clyde had said before he ambled off into the kitchen.

Grinning, I shook my head as I moved the cutting board aside. All and all, things were good, I supposed. I was no longer a virgin.

I was in love with the guy who took said virginity, and I was pretty sure he liked me. A lot. My financial aid was approved.

And I made it to Wednesday evening without anyone running us over, bodies being dumped on the front lawn, or wearing Dermablend.

A great three days, I decided.

The bar was slow, with just me and Nick behind the bar when a young couple walked in. In the time I'd been here, I knew they weren't regulars as I watched them occupy two empty stools.

They made an adorable couple—she was short, like teeny-tiny Roxy sized, and he was supertall, with messy brown hair. The girl had the prettiest blue eyes, a stark contrast against her darker hair.

"What can I get you two?" I asked.

The girl smoothed a hand over a University of Maryland shirt. "Just a Coke, please."

"And a menu," the guy added, dropping his elbows on the bar top. "And another Coke."

"Coming up." After grabbing their drinks, I handed over a plastic-covered menu for them to share. "The fries are great. So are the chicken wings if you're a fan of Old Bay Seasoning."

The girl's eyes lit up. "I love Old Bay. I think it's a requirement of going to school in Maryland."

University of Maryland wasn't too far from Shepherd. "You guys traveling through?"

He nodded. "Visiting Philly for the day. Syd's never been."

"Have a good time?"

Syd nodded. "He took me to my first Phillies game, but I didn't order anything to eat, so now I'm starving."

The guy scanned the menu. "I think we'll go for an order of fries and wings. Bone in. Sixteen."

I skedaddled off to place the order and when I returned, old man Melvin was at the bar, waiting for me.

Oh no.

I smiled at him even though he looked like he was ready to unload, but my smile faltered as the door opened, and Aimee with two *e*'s rolled in. Her gaze swept the bar, and not finding Jax, she made her way over to the bar farthest from me, in front of an annoyed-looking Nick.

I sat the beer down on a napkin in front of Melvin without him asking, hoping that would somehow fend him off.

It didn't work.

"What's this I hear about Rooster's body being tossed on your doorstep?" he demanded, wrapping his hand around the bottle.

The guy stiffened, and the girl's eyes widened.

"Damn shame what these druggies are doing to this town," Melvin went on, oblivious to the eyes on him. He took a hefty swig of his beer. "This used to be a good town, a good place. Now we have them keeling over dead, bullet wounds to their heads. Freaking shame."

"Kyler," the girl whispered as she talked to him slowly. "Um . . . ?"

He said nothing as his gaze moved to me. Before I could speak, Melvin decided he wasn't done. "Can't say it's a shame about Rooster, though. Who didn't see that messy end coming for him? He was nothing but a lowlife and—"

"Are you wanting wings or fries today?" I asked, hoping to distract him before he sent the poor couple running off into the night screaming bloody murder.

Distracted by my question, he eventually grumbled out an order for wings. As I left to place that order, the couple's wings and fries were ready. When I returned, I was thanking the heavens that Melvin's buddy had showed up and they moved away from the bar.

"Sorry about that," I said, placing the baskets on the counter. "We usually don't have those kinds of problems."

The guy leaned in. "Was there really a body on your porch?"

I winced. "Yeah. Long story."

"Whoa," he murmured, sitting back.

The door swung open again, and I looked up, spying Katie strolling in. I knew the exact moment the girl saw her, because her eyes grew *even* wider. Might have something to do with the fact Katie was wearing a hot pink fishnet dress over what appeared to be a bikini. Or pasties. I didn't want to look long enough to figure it out.

Grinning, she bounced over to where I was at. "Girl, you look good today. Despite the fact you got dead bodies dropping on your head."

Oh. My. God.

"Actually, you look like someone who got recently laid," she continued, and my mouth dropped open. "Yeah, you do. You *so* do."

I was seriously beginning to wonder if she really did have super stripper abilities or something. But I was not discussing this with complete strangers sitting right next to us. "You on break, Katie?"

"Nope. Heading into work. Thought I'd pop over and make sure you weren't rocking in a corner somewhere, whispering to yourself out of trauma or some shit."

"I'm totally okay," I told her. "But thanks for checking on me." And I really meant that.

She started to say something, but then Jax appeared at the end of the hall, coming from the recesses of the office. He glanced over at me and winked. I felt a stupid grin curve on my lips.

"He totally got in your pants," she stage-whispered, and the guy sounded like he choked on a chicken wing.

Jax moseyed off, and before I could even figure out how to handle that statement, Aimee turned to us, displaying an elegant twist of her neck.

"He's so hot, isn't he?" she said, batting big eyes at me. "Jax, that is."

Rolling his eyes, Nick turned away from her and moved to the bottles at the back of the bar.

I opened my mouth, but Katie beat me to it. "Bitch, are you on the crack? Because I'm pretty sure that hot boy named Jax was just all winking at Calla over here and didn't even see you sitting there. Just FYI."

I pressed my lips together so hard I thought they'd split as Aimee's face reddened. She stared at Katie for a moment and then whirled around, flouncing off in the direction of where Jax was grabbing empty glasses and baskets off the table.

I sighed.

Katie turned to me. "I'm gonna yippie-ki-yay that bitch out of this bar one of these days. Mark my words, hand to God, and all that jazz."

Why did I suddenly have visions of Bruce Willis?

Then *she* flounced off in the opposite direction, toward the door.

My gaze drifted to where the young couple sat, their eyes wide and their mouths slightly agape. They looked at me in unison.

"Welcome to Mona's," I said dryly.

Twenty-four

*R*oxy stood behind the bar Saturday night, slim arms folded across her chest and her legs widespread. Her black frame glasses were slid up, resting just under the perfectly messy bun.

Her eyes were narrowed into thin slits and the bitchy jut to her chin was cute. I'd told her that a few minutes before, when I'd hit the bar to get beers for the group of guys in the back, and she hadn't thought that was cute, which made her look more bitchy.

And cuter.

The victim of her death glare was Aimee with two *e*'s. For the fourth night in a row, Aimee was here, sitting at the bar with a friend who sort of looked orange. Roxy had nicknamed the friend Oompa One.

I had to grin because the death glares were for my benefit. Aimee was actually pretty nice to Roxy and even me, but she made it obvious why she was here, and Roxy was so not down with that.

Every time Jax came behind the bar, Aimee monopolized his attention when she could. And like every night before, he must've been ridiculously funny about things, because not a minute passed where Aimee wasn't laughing loudly. Or flipping her hair over her shoulder. Or leaning on the bar, giving Jax and Roxy at times a clear shot at her boobage.

And every so often, like the last four days, Jax would catch my eyes, give me a look, and I wouldn't care about Aimee sitting at the bar, doing everything possible to get some return flirt action.

Then again, I figured Jax could put an end to Aimee's attempt by telling her he wasn't available. I mean, we hadn't given each other labels, but we were together in every way we could be together.

And . . . and I loved him, so whatever. We were together.

He hadn't said those words to me, but I hadn't, either. And I wasn't going to think about that right now or make a big deal out of it. In spite of all the stuff, I was actually kind of happy and it was Saturday with no sign of Mack.

I would not ruin this.

Taking the order of Old Bay chicken wings to Melvin's table, I grinned at the old man as I placed the basket between them. "Here you go. Anything else?"

"We're good." The skin around his eyes settled into deep grooves as he grinned. "As long as you give us another one of those smiles."

I laughed. "You old flirt."

He chuckled as he snatched up a chicken wing. "If I was twenty years younger, you and I would be cuttin' up that floor."

An eyebrow rose. Twenty years? I'd have to go with double that, but what he said made me smile and also made me say, "Whenever you want to dance, you let me know."

I almost couldn't believe I said that, but his dim eyes seemed to glimmer. "I'll do that."

Sending him another one of "those smiles," I turned and started toward another table where their glasses were looking empty, and before I knew, I stole a peek up at the bar.

Roxy was full-out dragon bartender, shaking a cocktail shaker so hard I expected the contents to fly around the bar. My gaze shifted to where Aimee sat and my eyes widened.

What the . . . ?

Aimee was practically sitting *on* the bar and her hands were on Jax's cheeks, *on* his cheeks. She was *cupping* his cheeks. Anger pricked along my skin, but something small and icy and ugly formed in the pit of my stomach, and that small and icy and ugly thing caused my chest to clench in a not pleasant way. Because why—why in the hell—would she be touching him like that and why—why in the holy hell—would Jax be allowing that?

Before I knew it, I was starting toward the bar. I had no idea what I was going to do when I got there, but I was sure it was not going to be pretty and I might regret it later, but screw—

"Hey, girl."

I came to an abrupt halt at the sound of the familiar voice. Disbelief thundered through me. *No way.* So caught off guard, I tore my eyes from Aimee and Jax and spun around. My jaw hit the floor.

Jase Winstead winked.

Jase freaking Winstead was standing here.

Jase—member of the Hot Guy Brigade—was standing in the bar.

"Surprise!" Out popped Teresa from behind him, all tanned and gorgeous.

My gaze moved from Teresa to Jase and then behind them, and I almost fell over dead. They weren't alone. Cameron Hamilton—the president of the Hot Guy Brigade—was with them. So was Avery. He had one arm over her shoulder, tucking her close to his side in the ridiculously adorable way of theirs.

Jase chuckled. "I think we've shocked her into silence."

"Oh my God," I said, blinking a couple of times. "You guys totally did. I had no idea."

"That's why it's a surprise." Teresa glanced over her shoulder at her older brother and his girlfriend. "We decided to come up spur of the minute. I've missed you!"

Then she sprung forward and hugged me. I did miss her and I was happy that they were here, but as I pulled back and Teresa started telling Jase about how she never knew I could use a tap, let alone mix a drink, I realized that they really knew nothing about me. At least nothing that was true.

Holy shit, my house of lying cards was about to bitch-slap me in my face. The only thing I had going for me was that Jax knew about the lies I'd told. He'd probably be conscious enough not to bust me out.

But still, I was a big liar, liar, panties on fire.

My heart rate kicked up. Besides the fact they thought my mom was dead, this could be potentially disastrous if more bodies ended up flung in my direction or if someone said something in front of them. I thought of the adorable couple from Wednesday who'd unwittingly heard all about Rooster's demise.

I suddenly wanted to run through the bar screaming at the top of my lungs.

"So Teresa was telling us there is a guy you've been dating?" Avery asked.

"What?" My mind was elsewhere, still stuck on picturing bodies falling from the ceiling, along with bags of heroin. It would be like raining dead people and dope.

"A guy," Teresa said, loping her arm around Jase's waist. "You said his name was Jax. You guys went out to dinner? He works here? Ring any bells?"

"Oh. Yes." I sounded like an idiot. My hand fluttered to my hair and I brushed it back behind my ear. I noticed that Teresa blinked at the movement. "He's here. He's um . . ." I turned toward the bar.

Oh no.

Roxy had gone from dragon lady to fire-breathing weapon of mass destruction and Jax was still behind the bar. And Aimee with an *i* and two *e*'s wasn't on the bar anymore, but she had her hands *on* his chest, pushing *on* his chest like she was feeling his pecs.

"The guy who's getting a mammogram?" Jase asked.

I swallowed, but my throat was dry as a desert during high noon.

Cam moved forward, bringing Avery along with him. "It's not him, right?"

Oh my God, my friends were here and they wanted to meet Jax and Little Miss Poconos Aimee Grant was currently fondling him.

Teresa was looking around, searching for another guy, but there was only Roxy and she didn't look like a dude, so . . .

As we all stared at the bar, Jax stepped back, out of reach of Aimee, and said something that she laughed at like he was the second coming of Tyler Perry.

"That's Jax," I said in an odd voice.

Jase looked at me, tilted his head to the side, and then glanced back to where Jax was. "Is that so?"

Oh no.

The sound in his voice said he was going to somehow change the fact that the guy was Jax.

I vaguely wondered how weird it would be if I climbed under a table and started rocking.

Jax looked over then and his lips split into a grin when his eyes connected with mine. That grin didn't last very long, because Jase put his hand on my shoulder, and when I looked behind him, Teresa wasn't wrapped around him like a sexy octopus anymore.

His eyes narrowed.

This was all about to go downhill.

Jax started around the bar, which caused Aimee and her friend to wheel around like they were on a turntable, but he prowled past them like they didn't exist.

Which I would've found highly ironic any other day.

He stopped in front of me, but his eyes were on Jase. "Everything okay over here, Calla?"

I couldn't see Jase, but I imagined he had that shit-eating grin on his face. "Yeah, this is Jase." I turned a little. "And this is Teresa. That's Cam and Avery. They're—"

"You're friends from college." Proving that he did listen to me when I rambled, he relaxed as he shoved out a hand toward Jase. "Nice to meet you."

Jase dropped his hand and shook Jax's. "Same here."

Yeah, that didn't sound sincere. And this was awkward. "Um, they came up as a surprise."

"That's cool," he replied, head cocked to the side as he turned to Teresa. "Calla really misses you guys."

"That's because we're awesome," Teresa replied. "And we love Calla. Like for real. All of us. A lot. And we're really protective of her."

Jax stared at her.

Right now, I'd be okay with a dead body landing on my head, and strangely, I wondered who was watching Raphael and Michelangelo, their pet turtles, since Cam and Avery were here.

Cam suddenly stiffened. "What the . . . ?"

I knew who they spotted the second Cam and Jase turned into teenage girls.

"Holy shit," breathed Jase.

"You can say that twice."

Brock was standing a few feet behind Jax, holding a pool stick. It was obvious that Cam and Jase were openly gawking at him, and he played it cool, giving the two guys a chin lift.

"Who's that?" Teresa murmured.

"*Who's that?*" Jase turned wide eyes on her. "I don't think I can be with you anymore."

Her eyes rolled as she smacked his arm. "Whatever."

"You guys want to meet him?" Jax offered, winking at me, and my heart did a little jig, because seriously, he gave good wink.

Jase and Cam effectively forgot the existence of their girlfriends and followed Jax like he was the damn pied piper of UFC fighters.

"Seriously?" Teresa folded her arms. "Who is that?"

"He's a mixed martial arts ninja or something. Fights on TV," I explained. "He trains in Philly."

"Oh." Avery nodded. "Cam's way into those things."

Teresa still looked somewhat unimpressed.

"You guys want to get anything?"

"A soda would be good," Avery said, and that's when I remembered that Teresa wasn't old enough to legally be in here, but at this point, what the hell ever. I walked them over to the bar and then I headed behind it to grab two sodas.

"Friends?" Nick asked.

I nodded.

"Take some time. We got the bar."

"That's not—"

"Take some time, Calla," he repeated solemnly. "It's okay. Roxy and I got the bar."

Smiling at him, I nodded. "Okay. Thanks."

I took the drinks out of the bar and around to where the two girls were huddled behind the occupied stools. Roxy was busying serving up drinks, and I reminded myself I needed to introduce her.

After handing over the drinks, I leaned against the wall, near a framed photo of a guy who looked like he belonged to the Hells Angels. Avery was looking at me strangely and when my eyes caught hers, she smiled tentatively.

"You look really good, Calla."

"Thanks. It's . . . um, it's the makeup." My cheeks heated and I felt like a dork for saying that. "Well, I mean, I'm not wearing that much."

"I like it." She shook her wrist so the silver cuff slid into place.

"You do look great." Teresa bit down on her lip and then she cut right to the point. "Who's the girl?"

I wanted to cry. I wanted to bang my forehead off the bar *and* cry. "She's this girl who he'd hooked up with a while ago."

"A while ago?" Teresa was eyeing Jax as he stood with the guys, facing us. Her tone bled doubt, and I wanted to throw myself in front of a moving truck.

"Yeah," I whispered, taking a deep breath as Jax looked over in my direction. The grin on his face faded. I looked away, focusing on my friends, and I did smile, because I was thrilled that they were here. "Anyway, I'm glad you guys are here. How long are you all staying?"

"We checked into a hotel not too far from here." Avery tucked her hair back behind one shoulder. She was so damn pretty with her red hair and faint freckles. "And we're going to tour the city tomorrow."

"You're off, right?" Teresa asked.

I nodded. "Yeah, I can join you. Should be fun." At least, I hoped I could join them, all things considered.

"Awesome. Avery's never been to Philly before," she explained.

She laughed. "I've pretty much never been anywhere before."

Avery and I . . . yeah, we were kind of kindred souls even though I didn't know her as well as I knew Teresa. I grinned at her. "I've never been half of anywhere, so it's okay."

Her smile spread, reaching her eyes, and she glanced over toward the guys at the exact same moment Cam looked over. His lips curved up.

Damn, they were as cute as a romance book.

I opened my mouth, but then the door opened and Katie strolled in, glimmering like a fairy. The chick shimmered from the top of her blond head, all the way down to her bubble-gum pink toes that peeked through her golden platforms. Her dress was more like a shirt or like an overlong tank top. It clung to her breasts and hips but was loose around the waist and ended mid-thigh. She worked it.

And she even had wings.

Translucent pink wings—not angel wings—but fairy wings strapped to her back, and she also worked them.

Teresa opened her mouth and then snapped it shut, and a laugh bubbled up my throat at the way her eyes crossed.

Katie looked around the bar, eyes narrowing when she spotted Aimee and her friend, but then she looked our way. A wide smile broke out across her pretty face. She trotted our way.

"Girl, I'm on break. You're on break. Obviously!" she chirped. "Our breaks were meant to be."

"Totally," I said, grinning. "Katie, I want you to meet—"

"Your friends from college?" She clasped her hands at her waist demurely.

I had no idea how she guessed these were my friends from college, but I didn't want to ask, because I had a feeling she was going to say it was because she fell off the pole. So, I just let that slide. "Yep. This is Teresa and Avery."

Avery wiggled her fingers somewhat shyly. "Hi."

"Totes-ma-goats, you have gorgeous hair!" Katie reached out, lifting a red lock. "I tried to do red hair once and I ended up looking like a carrot."

Totes-ma-goats? Oh my God. I drew in a sharp breath that ended in an attractive snort.

"And in my line of work, looking like a carrot doesn't get the bills paid," Katie went on as she stopped playing with Avery's hair, turning to Teresa. "And OM Gee, you are stunning. Like I might be considering switching sides."

Ha!

Teresa grinned. "I'll take that as a compliment."

Katie cocked her head to the side. "You'd make a lot of money dancing."

"Oh. I used to dance, actually. So did Avery."

Oh no.

Katie's eyes slid to Avery and then back to Teresa, who was slurping on her soda. "I busted my knee," Teresa added. "But I danced for years."

"I doubt you did the kind of dancing I do. Either of you," Katie explained without an ounce of embarrassment, and I loved her for that. "I work across the street."

Avery's brows pinched, and I knew she was mentally seeing the outside again, and the moment understanding seeped in, her eyes widened. "You . . ."

"Take my clothes off?" Katie laughed. "I flashed my goods from time to time, but it's more classy than your average shoving your vajaja in unsuspecting faces."

I couldn't help it. A laugh burst out of me, but Teresa kept a straight face. "You got to hate it when that happens."

"Or when it's a penis," Katie replied.

My jaw was aching from how hard I had my lips pressed together, and Avery giggled from behind her glass.

"You know, I've always wanted to do that—strip—at least once," Teresa announced thoughtfully, and my eyes almost popped out of my head. "It looks like it would be a lot of fun."

Excitement flooded Katie's face. "I could so help you with that!"

Um. I had a feeling Jase would so not be down for that and neither would her brother. Actually, I wanted to be around when Teresa announced that she wanted to scratch stripping off her bucket list.

Pearl was starting to run around like a madwoman and I was feeling bad about standing around talking. "Guys, I need to help out. I'm sorry, but . . ."

"It's totally okay." Teresa waved her hand, grinning at Katie. "Don't worry. We'll probably be here for a little bit."

"Okay." I hopped forward and kissed her cheek and then Avery's. "Be good."

Teresa giggled as I hugged Katie and then hurried off, hoping that when I came back Teresa wasn't across the street warming up a pole. I skirted around the guys, but I'd made it about three feet when Jax was suddenly by my side. He dropped his arm over my shoulders and steered me down the hall toward the office and stockroom before I could blink an eye.

There, he stopped outside the door and faced me. Head bent down, he spoke in a low voice. "What's wrong?"

"Nothing."

His eyes narrowed. "There's something wrong with you."

There was a lot wrong with me right now, but I really didn't want to get into it with Jax. "I'm fine. I'm probably going to be hanging out with everyone tomorrow since they're going to be in town."

A muscle in his jaw spasmed. "You're not fine. And you're totally bullshitting me."

I folded my arms across my chest. "How so?"

"You were out there, talking to your friends like someone drop-kicked your puppy into oncoming traffic."

"I did not look like someone kicked . . ." My chest rose with a deep breath and then I said screw it and prepared to unload, because what was the point in lying and stewing about it? I met his gaze. "You know what? I'm not okay. And maybe it's because I told Teresa about you."

"You did?" The frustration leaked out of his expression and he started to grin. "Nice."

I was going to hit him. "It isn't nice. Because she told Jase, who in turn told Cam, who then told Avery, who by the way are like the most awesomely adorable couple in coupledom, and they came up here to surprise me, but I also know they all have a hidden agenda, and that's to check *you* out, because I opened my big mouth and told them about that."

His grin spread. "Good friends. I like that."

Actually, I was going to throat-punch him. "Well, I'm so glad you like that, but the first time they see you is when there's *another* girl who has *her* hands all over *you*."

Jax drew back, straightening.

"Yeah. That," I continued. Now that I wasn't bullshitting him, I was on a roll. "They saw you and they saw Aimee before I had a chance to even introduce you guys, and that . . . well, that sucked."

"Babe . . ."

"Don't 'babe' me," I snapped, taking a step back. "I know there aren't any labels between us and we haven't known each other that long and maybe this is something casual to you, but I really wished that the first time my friends met you wasn't when Aimee was giving you a breast exam."

"Something casual?" he repeated, and I wondered if he'd heard anything I'd said. "Is this something casual to you?"

I started to say yes, because . . . well, because I wanted to be a bitch, and that ugly icy feeling was back in my stomach. My feelings were hurt and I was *embarrassed,* and I wanted to play that game, but that's not what I said, because I had no idea how to play that game. "No. This isn't casual for me. Not in the least."

His expression softened as he stepped forward. "Baby, this isn't casual for me, either, and the fact you think it might be blows my mind."

"It does?"

"Honey, every signal, every act and word I've sent in your direction from day one says this isn't casual for me," he said, leaning his hip against the wall. "I know you don't have a lot experience with relationships and that's cool, but I really don't know how else to show you that. And the whole label shit?" he continued as he curved his fingers along my chin. "I think you know what we are."

The thing was, I didn't. I might've had a guess Sunday night when I'd stripped down to my undies and he'd worshipped my body like I was some kind of goddess, and he did so every time since then, but seeing him with Aimee? Yeah, I was inexperienced when it came to relationships, but I wasn't dumb and I wasn't stupid.

And it wasn't like he'd been caught making out with her or that he even knew my friends would be popping by, but there was still the fact that every night he worked, Aimee was here. And every night he worked, Aimee was up his ass. And every night he worked, as far as I could tell if I was being honest with myself and unless she was the densest chick alive, he didn't really do anything to stop her advances.

And he let her touch him.

Repeatedly.

And that wasn't cool.

The back of my eyes stung, because that was that. What was happening wasn't a huge thing, but it was inappropriate. For fuck's sake, I worked right here. And I really didn't know what to say right now, because I wasn't okay with that.

I drew in a deep breath. "Look, I've got to get out on the floor. We're busy."

"And we're not done talking."

"Yeah, we are. For right now, okay? We can talk about this later or whatever." I started to turn around, and his hand slipped off my chin.

"I never thought you'd be the jealous type."

My feet came to a complete stop as I turned back to him and stared. Oh boy, that was the wrong thing to say. "I'm not jealous."

He arched a brow.

I narrowed my eyes on him. "Fine. Maybe I am. Is that so surprising? I mean, I just said this"—I waved my hand between us like I was having a seizure—"isn't casual, so yeah, I'm not going to like seeing a girl get all up on you night after night. Especially a girl you've hooked up with."

Jaw tensed, he inclined his head. "You have nothing to be jealous of, Calla."

A dry laugh burst from me. "Seriously?"

"Yeah, seriously. And the fact of the matter is all you have to do is trust me. Not her. But me. And if you trusted me, then you wouldn't be jealous."

I gaped at him. Part of that made sense. It took two to tango and all that jazz, but seriously?

"And if this is going to work out between us, you're going to have to trust me," he continued, and that—the *if this is going to work out between us*—caused my stomach to drop. "Because your financial aid came through and you're going back to school in August, there's gonna be some miles between us, and all we're going to have is trust. You get what I'm saying?"

I totes-ma-goats got what he was saying. Half of my heart did a little jump and squeal, because he was planning for when I returned to school and that was great, but the other part of my heart was somewhere in my stomach. Trusting him was one thing, but this wasn't okay. I could trust him all I wanted, but that didn't mean I had to be cool with him letting the chicks feel him up and chalking it up to me being jealous.

I needed time to think about this.

He sighed. "Calla . . ."

Shaking my head, I backed away. "I really need to get back on the floor."

When I turned away this time, Jax didn't stop me. I walked back out onto the floor and it took everything in my power not to jump on the back of Aimee's luminous blond head like a rabid spider monkey.

Yeah, I was jealous.

I was also human.

Jase and Cam were over with the girls, and Brock was with them. Katie was nowhere to be seen and I wondered if Teresa was going to be looking into a new profession. I wanted to chat with them, but when I saw Pearl, she looked like the rabid spider money.

Sending Pearl an apologetic look, I started working tables and running orders from the kitchen out to the floor. Before long, my brain was empty with the exception of drink and food orders, and that was perfect. Even though I needed time to think about what had happened, I didn't want to think about it then.

I'd just ran an order of fries smothered in cheese and crab meat—what I planned on gorging myself on during break—to a table along the wall near the door, when I turned to head toward the cluster of round tables circling the pool tables and felt a hand curve around my arm, just above my elbow, and then there was a voice I didn't recognize, right in my ear.

"Cause a scene, and I'm going to light this place up."

Every molecule in my body turned to ice as I froze. The only thing that moved was my pounding heart.

"Good girl," the man said, his hand tightening around my arm. "We're going to walk right out of this bar. Behave and no one gets hurt. Got me?"

My mouth dried, and I jerked as I felt something press into my lower back. A gun? Shock blasted through my system, halting comprehension of what was going on. The man behind me started guiding me toward the door, and I imagined that to anyone around us, we looked like we knew each other. Well, other than what had to be a horrified look on my face, but we were at the door in seconds.

There was a crowd around the bar. Roxy and Nick and Jax were all serving drinks, and there were enough people that I couldn't even see Aimee or my friends as the man reached around me and opened the door.

No one looked over.

No one stopped us.

Twenty-five

*K*idnapped!

I was freaking being kidnapped!

This didn't happen in real life. Maybe in books and in the movies, but not to real people.

But it was happening unless I was having a full-spectrum hallucination. My heart was working into cardiac territory as I was ushered around the side of Mona's, toward the back parking lot, which butted up to trees, empty warehouses, and probably where people went to die.

The hand on my arm was harsh, biting into my skin, and I didn't feel what I suspected had been a gun pressing into my back any longer. My legs were shaking so badly I was surprised I could walk or even stand, but then I saw the dark SUV parked near the Dumpsters, engine running.

The window rolled down on the driver's side and from deep within the dark recesses, a voice boomed. "Hurry the fuck up, Mo."

Oh my God, there were two men, and there was a good chance I was going to end up like Rooster.

Every female in the world was taught to never let a kidnapper take you from whatever location you were originally at. That the risk of fighting back and getting an unexpected hole in your body was far less than allowing yourself to be taken to wherever.

That realization, something I'd learned ages ago, snapped me out of my shock.

I jerked forward, the movement catching my kidnapper off guard. He stumbled, but his grip tightened until I cried out. I twisted back toward him, catching a flash of an unfamiliar face. I opened my mouth to scream louder than I ever screamed in my entire life. I got a small shriek out before the man cursed, yanking on my arm fiercely. My back was suddenly pressed to his front and his hand smacked down on my mouth.

I smelled cigarettes and some kind of antibacterial hand sanitizer, and immediately panic rose as I tried to breathe through my nose, but I realized something important. With one hand on my mouth and his other arm clamped around my waist, that meant he wasn't holding a gun or weapon unless he had a third arm.

So I bit down on his hand, biting down until I felt the skin pop. My stomach roiled, but I kept biting.

"Shit!" Mo exploded, jerking his hand away. I was free for a second and then spun out about a foot from him and twisted around so I was facing him. I saw him raise his hand and that was the only warning I had.

Pain burst along my jaw and mouth, and I stumbled back. Tiny starbursts exploded in my vision as the ache radiated down my neck.

"What the hell?" the guy in the SUV demanded, and then let out a string of curses.

"The bitch bit me!" Mo shouted back. "I'm fucking bleeding."

"You fucking pussy. Jesus. Get her in the car and let's—"

I didn't hear the rest, because my blood pressure was through the roof, drowning out all sound, and I wheeled around and ran.

The flats I was wearing weren't really conducive to booking it, but I ignored the pieces of gravel that dug through the thin soles.

I ran toward the front of the building, letting out an ear-piercing scream that pitched high as I was slammed into from behind. I toppled forward, cracking my knees on the ground.

An arm circled my waist, hauling me up, and this wasn't good. This was bad. So bad. Mo spun around, all but carrying me toward the SUV, which now had the driver's door open.

I struggled like a cat about to be dunked in a bathtub. I was pulling my legs up and moving my arms like windmills while Mo wrestled with me, and my actions slowed him down. The whole time I screamed.

"What the hell?" shouted a voice from behind us.

Hope sprung at the sound of the voice. "Clyde!" I screamed, putting everything into throwing my weight to the side by pushing off the sidewalk with my feet. "Clyde!"

The driver's door slammed shut and the man holding me cursed in my ear, and then he let go, freaking dropped me. Not that I was complaining, but I fell to the ground on my knees and palms.

"Holy crap," I gasped, trying to get control of my breathing as I pushed off my hands and looked up to see Clyde's heavy frame jogging toward me. "Holy *crap*."

My hands shook as I raised them and pushed my hair back from my face. I noticed then that there were more people outside, near the corner of the front of Mona's.

As Clyde reached my side, the SUV tore out of the parking lot, tires spinning and kicking up gravel, pelting the group of people near the front. There was shouting. Someone threw something at the SUV. Glass shattered.

"Calla," Clyde huffed out. "You okay?"

I was pretty sure I was seconds from having a full-blown freak-out, but other than the pain in my jaw and the aches from hitting the ground, I was alive. "I'm all right."

"You sure?" he wheezed, and that sound made me forget about

what just happened. It was the wrong kind of sound—a sound a human shouldn't make.

I settled back on my calves, getting ready to stand. "Are you okay, Clyde?"

His head moved in jerky motions, and I wasn't so sure about that. "I saw you walk . . . outside. I didn't . . . recognize the man. I . . . wasn't sure. With everything that's going on . . ."

Hands were suddenly on my shoulders. Jax was there, kneeling down beside me. His face was pale, strained like it had been the day we were almost run over. "What the hell is going on? People are saying someone tried to grab you."

"Someone did try." My words sounded weird as I stared at Clyde.

Jax's hands tightened on my shoulders. "What in the world were you doing out here?"

"I didn't come out here because I wanted to. The guy was *inside*. He told me that if I caused a scene, he'd light up the place," I said, and my gaze shifted to Clyde. He was looking better. A little pale, but he wasn't wheezing anymore. "I thought he had a gun."

"Jesus. Fuck," muttered Jax. One hand slid around my neck and he tilted my head back. My gaze finally shifted to his, and I sucked in a sharp breath. Fury and concern were etched into his face and then anger won out. "He hit you."

It wasn't a question, and there was no denying it. "I bit him."

"And he hit you? Fuck, baby." Jax dipped his head, pressing his lips to my forehead, and then he pulled back, holding my gaze.

"We need to call the police," Clyde grunted.

Jax's jaw clenched and his eyes never left my face. There was a gleam in his eyes that was scary, a red-hot, explosive anger brimming close to the surface.

"Son, I know what you're thinking," Clyde announced. "But you need to call your boy Reece. This isn't for you to handle."

What? Jax was going to try to handle this? Then it hit me. I kept forgetting that he wasn't like Cam and Jase. Not that there was anything wrong with them, but Jax was different. He was rougher and he'd seen things Cam and Jase couldn't even begin to comprehend. He wasn't them; therefore he could potentially *handle* things.

His hand tightened around my neck as he helped me stand and then he hauled me against his chest, and a shudder worked its way through me. "I'll call Reece."

Over Jax's shoulder, I saw that a lot of people were outside. Half of the bar it seemed like, but most important, my friends. Teresa's mouth was hanging open. Jase and Cam looked pissed, and poor Avery had an expression on her face that said she had no idea what was going on.

Even Brock was outside, and by the look on his face, he appeared ready to put some of his mixed martial ninja awesome arts to use.

But then Teresa stormed forward, her hands clenching at her sides. "What the hell is going on, Calla?"

I squeezed my eyes shut. There was no hiding my background or my troubles from them now.

It was late by the time I found myself standing in Jax's bedroom in his townhouse. I didn't even know what I was doing up there. Wasn't like I was getting ready for bed, because there was a full house downstairs and had been since after Detective Anders and his police crew arrived at Mona's, took my statement, and did all the jazz that was becoming a frighteningly familiar process.

Worse was the fact that the name Mo wasn't one Detective Anders was acquainted with. Obviously, it had to do with Mom, so it wasn't like they had leads, but Mack was in a hidey-hole somewhere and nothing—not a single piece of evidence—led back to the mysterious Isaiah.

Teresa and Jase, and Cam and Avery were downstairs along with Brock. My friends had been all filled in on my drama, partly from me and from being around when Reece had showed up and then his older brother.

Which brought me to the real reason why I was up here. I did know why I was in Jax's bedroom while everyone else was downstairs.

The house of lying cards had collapsed more quickly than I realized it could. Through what was said to Reece and his brother and what I then had to tell them, they now knew that my mom was most likely kicking around and she was embroiled in a ton of nasty crap that had spilled over into my life. The only thing that had not been up for discussion had been the fire, but that was the least of things to know about me at this point.

So, yeah, I knew why I was sitting on the edge of Jax's bed, unable to go downstairs and face my friends. I was going to stay up here, surrounded by the scent of Jax's cologne and the images of all the naughty things we'd done in here, on the bed, the floor . . . the bathroom.

Yep, I was just going to stay up here forever. Sounded like a decent, legit plan. Maybe I could talk Jax into bringing me food at least twice a day. If so, this plan was totally getting better.

"Calla?"

Lifting my head, I twisted toward the open door. My back straightened. Teresa stood in the doorway. She wasn't alone, either. Avery was with her.

"Jax told us we could come up here," Avery explained as Teresa nudged the door farther open with her hip. "So we totally just didn't roam up here."

Figured that Jax had done that. God knows I'd been up here for a while. "Sorry," I said, focusing my attention to my toes. "Time got away from me."

"It's understandable. You've had a crazy night," Avery said softly.

Teresa walked in and plopped down on the bed beside me. "Apparently, you've had a crazy life."

I winced.

Avery sent Teresa a look that pretty much flew right over her head. "You're hiding up here," Teresa said.

My lips twitched, and the movement kind of hurt. When I looked in the mirror earlier, a faint bruise was forming on my jaw, and my lower lip was cut near the right corner. "Is it that obvious?"

She shrugged. "Kind of."

I drew in a deep breath. Since I wasn't going to be able to hide up here, I needed to woman up. Doing so sucked. "I'm sorry, guys. I know I've lied to you all, and I really don't have a good reason for doing so."

Teresa cocked her head to the side as Avery hovered by the edge of the bed, her slim fingers fiddling with the bracelet along her left wrist. "So . . . you're not from around Shepherdstown, are you?"

Mortified, I shook my head. I hadn't felt this way since I was six years old and had thrown bubble gum in the hair of a girl who was about to go onstage before me. I hadn't meant to toss it in the mass of brown curls, but Mom had been standing by the front of the stage and when she'd realized I still had gum in my mouth, she had gotten a crazy stage mom look on her face and I'd panicked.

"I'd been at Shepherd since I was eighteen, and to be honest, it does feel like my only home," I said, glancing at Teresa. She was watching me closely. "I know that doesn't justify lying, but I just . . . I never thought of here as home, at least for a long time."

Teresa nodded slowly. "But what about when you said you went to visit family for break? From what I gathered earlier, you haven't been back here in years."

"I didn't go home." My cheeks heated. "I'd checked into a hotel that time."

Her brows pinched.

Avery's eyes widened with sympathy. "Oh, Calla . . ."

"I know it sounds stupid. I honestly only did it because I wanted to get away for a little bit, and it was really the only option. It was kind of cool, really. And I know what I said about my mom being dead is freaking terrible and you guys probably think I'm a horrible person."

"Actually, no, we don't." Teresa twisted toward me as she straightened out the leg that had been injured first by dancing and then again when her roommate's boyfriend had pushed her, effectively ending Teresa's dreams of dancing professionally for an elite ballet school. "Calla, I don't know all your reasons for not telling us about your mom and your life here, but from what we've learned the last couple of hours, I get why you didn't want to."

"We totally get it," Avery agreed, and I felt a tiny bit of hope flare in my chest.

Teresa nudged my knee with hers. "But I hope you know that whatever your background is or *whatever,* we aren't going to judge you. You can be up front with us."

"Trust us on that," Avery added. "We are the last people to judge you."

My gaze bounced between the two, and they were giving each other a look I didn't fully understand. Then Avery moved to sit on the other side of me. Nervously, she tucked a strand of red hair back behind her ear.

Then she took a deep breath I could hear, looked at Teresa one more time, and then her gaze settled on me. Muscles in my stomach clenched, and I knew she was about to tell me something major. It was written all over her somewhat pale face. "When I was younger, I'd gone to a party that an older guy at school was throwing at his house. He was cute and I flirted with him, but things got out of hand. It really was bad."

Oh God no. Part of me already knew where this was heading, and I reached over, wrapping my hand around hers, and squeezed.

She pressed her lips together, and I could tell what she was about to say was hard—harder than anything I'd ever had to admit to. "He raped me," Avery said quietly, so softly I could barely hear it, but I did, and in response, my chest squeezed. "I did the right thing. At first. I told my parents and I told the police, but his parents and mine were country club buddies, and they offered my parents a whole lot of money if I kept quiet. Plus there had been a picture of me earlier that night sitting in his lap and I had drank. My parents had been more worried about what people would say about me instead of what was done to me, so I agreed. I took the money and it ate at me, Calla. I felt like shit for it."

Tears pricked at my eyes as she pulled her hand free and slowly took off her bracelet. She turned her wrist up, and I sucked in a breath I immediately wished I hadn't. I saw the scar. I knew what it meant.

Avery smiled faintly. "That's not the worst part. Because I didn't press charges, the guy continued doing what he did to me."

"Oh my God," I breathed, wanting to hug her. "Honey, it's not your fault. You didn't make him do those things to you or to anyone else."

"I know." The smile became a little firmer. "I know, but I did carry some responsibility in that. And the reason why I'm telling you this is because I went years without telling anyone what happened to me and when I met Cam, it took a lot for me to open up and tell him the truth. I almost lost him because I didn't." She drew in another breath. "The point? I'm ashamed that I tried to take my own life and that I caved to my parents, but I've gotten to a point—with therapy—that I get why I did those things and they don't make me a bad person or less of a friend to people if I don't open up or whatever."

"No," I whispered, blinking back tears. "You're not a bad person."

Teresa cleared her throat and when she spoke, her voice was thick, and when I looked at her, I tensed up all over again. "When I was in high school, my boyfriend hit me. More than once. A lot of times, actually."

Oh God.

I couldn't believe it. Teresa never came across as someone who would stay in an abusive relationship, but as soon as that thought finished I realized how judgie that was.

"I was young, but that really isn't the greatest excuse for being with a guy who hit me," she said, following my thoughts. "I kept it to myself and I hid it. I made up stories whenever the bruises were visible, but one year, right before Thanksgiving, my mom saw me and there was no hiding what was happening any longer. The thing was, the worst part wasn't that I was in the abusive relationship, but what it did to my brother. He lost it, Calla. He drove over to my boyfriend's house. Cam confronted him and . . . and they got into it. Cam beat him so badly that the guy ended up in the hospital and my brother got arrested."

"Holy crap," I gasped, wide-eyed.

Teresa nodded. "Cam got into a lot of trouble, and I lived with the what-ifs for a long time. What if I didn't stay with him? What if I told someone? Would Cam have ended up almost losing everything? And he did lose a lot. A semester of school. He was off the soccer team, and he also had to deal with the shit he'd done. I carried a lot of guilt because of that. Even to this day, I have regret."

"I'm sure Cam doesn't blame you," I said.

"He doesn't." It was Avery who answered. "He never did."

Teresa's smile was wobbly. "That's because my brother is pretty damn awesome."

I reached over and squeezed her hand, feeling the tears really start to well up in my eyes.

Avery pressed in against my side. "So is Jase. He's also pretty awesome."

A weak laugh bubbled up.

"And he had secrets. Really big and really important ones—secrets I can't elaborate on, because they're his business, but I was in the dark for a long time and when he let me in, I got why he'd kept some things to himself." Emotion poured into Teresa's beautiful face as she went on. "The whole point of this, Calla, is all of us have things we've lied about and things we're ashamed of, and things we wished we talked to someone about a long time before we did."

"But telling someone, fessing up about everything . . ." Avery smiled again when I looked at her. She squeezed my hand back, and I realized that through me, all of us were connected in that moment. "Not to sound completely cliché and cheesy as hell, but it changes everything."

"Especially when you tell your friends," Teresa added softly.

Pressing my lips together, I nodded a couple of times, and I wasn't sure exactly what I was agreeing with. Probably everything, and maybe a half a minute passed before I found whatever it was that had given me the ability to tell Jax that didn't involve tequila.

I told them about Mom—for real. The way she was before and the way she was now and I told them what had caused the change. The fire. I told them about Kevin and Tommy, and my dad, who gave up on all of us. And I told them about the scars, all of them, and I did so weeping like a baby that just had tossed its binky to the floor and no one would pick it up for her. Actually, we all were having a major festival of the sob, but there was something cleansing in opening up and sharing with them after they'd shared private and powerful stories with me. There was also something cleansing in the tears.

By the time I was finished, the three of us had our arms around each other and I finally felt like what Jax had believed—that I was *brave,* because that took a lot for me to tell them. It didn't matter that Jax knew, and these girls understood that it didn't matter how many times you told someone: It might get a little easier, but it is still hard.

And as we held each other, I realized something so important then. It was kind of sad that it took twenty-one years to really realize it, but family wasn't just blood and DNA. Family went way beyond that. Just like with Clyde, even though I wasn't related to Teresa or Avery, they were my family.

And just as important, even with my eyes all puffy and tears streaming down my face, I felt what Jax had said about me, something I'd felt when I'd stripped down for Jax.

I felt brave.

Sniffling, Teresa pulled back and she wiped under her eyes with the sides of her forefingers. "Now that we got all that covered, whose ass do we got to kick to keep you out of your mom's mess?"

Twenty-six

*D*awn was roughly an hour or so away when everyone cleared out of Jax's townhome. Teresa and crew were still planning to tour Philly tomorrow, but as much as I wanted to spend time with them, it wasn't smart and Detective Anders had looked like he'd lose his shit if I did go traipsing through the city.

Which really sucked, because I missed my friends, and there was more than one moment when I wondered if this would be my life now, not doing things because of this threat that really was hanging over my head.

Something had to give. I didn't know what, but I wasn't sure how much longer I could continue like this without losing *my* shit.

However, Jax had come up with a great idea—a late breakfast or early lunch at the townhouse with everyone before they headed into the city and then most likely headed back to West Virginia. So I would get to see them . . . from behind four walls.

It was better than nothing.

I'd just changed into my usual sleepwear when I was finally, after hours, alone with Jax. He stood just inside the bedroom door and his expression was on lockdown, jaw tense and lips pressed into a firm line.

A sudden nervousness rose inside me, mixing with tendrils of unease. With everything that had happened, I hadn't forgotten that we'd kind of gotten into an argument that was unresolved, but it hadn't been on the forefront of my thoughts.

It now raced there, elbowing all the other stuff out of the way. It didn't matter that the stuff with Aimee was no way near as important as everything else.

The intensity carved into Jax's striking face held me immobile as he all but stalked forward, stopping directly in front of me. Our gazes locked, and I swallowed hard as he lifted a hand. Instead of touching my left cheek, something I'd been slowly getting used to, the very tips of his fingers brushed over my lower right jaw and then to the corner of my cut lip.

"Does it hurt?" he asked.

I gave a little shake of my head. "No. Not really."

The hue of his eyes darkened as he dropped his hand. "It shouldn't have happened."

Well, I wasn't going to argue with that.

He thrust his hand through his hair. "I didn't even notice that you'd left. You'd had a gun to your back and I was right there, not that far away, and didn't even notice. I should've known."

"Whoa. Wait a second. This—none of this—is your fault, Jax. You were busy at the bar and I'm glad you didn't see it happening," I told him. "You could've gotten hurt."

Disbelief clouded his expression. "I could've gotten hurt? You got hurt, Calla. The fucker hit you, and you're worried about me?"

"Well, yeah . . . that and an entire bar full of people he'd threatened to shoot." As soon as I said those words I could tell it didn't matter. If anything, it ticked him off more. Moving away, I plopped down on the bed. "I'm okay, Jax. Seriously."

"You had to bite a person. You had your mouth on some fucker's skin and bit down to defend yourself. How in the fuck does that make you okay?"

"When you put it that way? I'm not sure."

His jaw worked as he walked forward and knelt in front of me. "I promised you that you wouldn't get hurt."

"Jax—"

"And you did." His hands curled around the back of my knees and he tugged them apart as he leaned in. He was staring at my arm, and my gaze followed his. There was a bruise there, too. "I'm not okay with that. Fucks with my head—just the thought of what if. I've been down that road before."

I didn't get what he was saying at first, and when I did, I shook my head. "This isn't like with your sister."

Jax said nothing.

"You know that, right? I'm not your responsibility. Not like that," I insisted. "And neither was Jena."

He looked away, jaw clenched.

"Even if you were—"

"Calla," he warned.

I ignored him. "Even if you were home, Jax, there would've been no what-ifs involved."

"Just . . . just drop it."

"No." I was not backing down from this. "She would've overdosed if you were in the room next to her. You being there wouldn't have changed the outcome. One way or another, she would've found a way."

His gaze swung back to mine. "How do you know that?"

"Because I *lived* through it, too." I held his gaze. "There was nothing I could do to alter Mom's path and I tried. I tried a million times. You know deep down it would've been the same with your sister."

Several moments passed, and then a deep sigh shuddered out of him. "I don't know. Calla. That's . . . yeah, that's hard to really accept."

"I know." Oh God, did I ever know, and I also knew there wasn't much I could say to really change whatever guilt Jax harbored. That was something that would take a lot of time, and he'd have to find that in himself.

"I think you need to stay here for a few days," he said after a moment.

My brows pinched. "I'm already staying here, aren't I?"

"That's not what I meant, babe." His fingers brushed over the finger marks above my elbow. "Stay out of the bar until . . . well, until this dies down."

"What?" I pulled my arm away, and his chin lifted, eyes back to mine. "I'm not hiding in this townhouse or anywhere. And it's not because I don't realize what's going on, but I need the money."

His hands curled around the back of my knees again. "Calla . . ."

"I seriously need the money. Over a hundred thousand in debt, Jax. I'm not making a crap ton of money, but I'm making something. I can't afford to chill out in the Jax Relocation Program."

His lips twitched "Jax Relocation Program?"

My eyes narrowed.

He chuckled and some, not all, of the anger eased out of his expression. "I like the sound of this program."

"I'm sure you do," I retorted dryly. "I just . . . I need to be more careful, more aware of my surroundings and stuff. I mean, I'm sure Mo didn't look too harmless in the bar. I need to pay more attention."

"So did I," he agreed firmly.

I started to deny it but figured there was no point. Some of the hardness was still in his face and I remembered the near-murderous fury in his eyes when we'd been at the bar.

As I watched him, something shifted in his eyes. The color was still dark, but it was warmer, hotter. It was late. Or early. Depending on how one looked at it. And there was a lot we needed to talk about, namely Aimee with an *i* and two *e*'s and his "you got to trust me" solution to her feeling him up like he was tenderized meat.

Yeah, we really needed to talk about that.

But as he stared up at me I could tell what he was thinking—I could *feel* what he was thinking. And after almost being kidnapped and after finally opening up to Teresa and Avery, the very last thing I wanted to do at four something in the morning was talk about Aimee, her wandering hands, and how that made me want to turn into a rabid kangaroo and kick her head off her shoulders.

I did need to talk to him. It was serious, and he was right, there would be some miles between us in the fall, and I needed to trust him.

And I did.

Sort of.

My brain sighed, literally sighed.

But then my body did a happy sigh when Jax's hands moved up my thighs, reaching the hem of my shorts. One side of his lips quirked up in that sexy half grin.

Okay.

We could talk later.

Not giving my brain a chance to argue that that was a bad idea and I was tossing girl power or whatever crap to the side for some bow-chick-a-wow, I grabbed the sides of his shirt and tugged up. Wordlessly, Jax backed off and lifted his arms. In no time, he was shirtless and my hands were on his hard, rough chest, and once again I wondered how I'd gone so long without knowing what a man's chest—Jax's chest—felt like under my fingers.

I lowered my head, and Jax went the distance, meeting me before I was even halfway to him, and the kiss was sweet, it was careful and gentle. The tender sweep of his lips reached right down into my chest and squeezed my heart.

God, I was so gone for him.

His hands slid up my sides, catching my shirt and then he had it off me. I was bare from the waist up and the cool air washed over my heated skin as Jax rose, placing his hands on my shoulders. He kissed the corner of my lip softly and then his mouth trailed over the bruised skin of my jaw as he pushed me onto my back. Crisp hairs from his chest teased over my chest as his mouth glided down my throat. My hands settled on his arms, feeling the muscles flex in his biceps as he held himself up.

Then his lips closed over the tip of my breast, and my body sparked alive. My back arched and my mouth opened in a soft whimper.

"You're so sensitive," he said against my breast. "Makes getting you turned on and ready so easy."

He was right. "Sorry?"

Jax chuckled. "Only you would apologize for that." Then he flicked his tongue over the hardened nub, and my fingernails dug into his skin. He shifted his weight to one arm and then his hand got involved with my other breast, and it was Calla happy land, especially when I could feel him hard and pressing against my thigh.

Sensation trilled throughout my veins as his hand left my breast and skated down my belly. His hand flattened just below my belly and then slid under the band of my shorts. I cried out as he sucked deep and hard, as if he could draw me right out of my body.

And I really thought he could.

He nipped at the sensitive flesh and then lifted, rolling completely off me as he sat up and got a hold of my shorts and undies. Off they went and then his clothes were off. He disappeared and came back, a foil package in his hand. Once he was done getting that taken care of and his body was over mine again, he started all over, kissing the corner of my lip gently, moving across my bruised jaw and then down, to my left breast and then my right.

A moan escaped me as my back arched. "Jax . . ."

"Damn." His voice was rough, deep as his hips rolled against mine, and I spread my thighs, welcoming him, wanting him.

When he started to draw away, I knew he meant to slow this

down, to draw this out and drive me out of my mind, but I was having none of that.

"No way," I breathed, panted really. "I want you. Now."

One eyebrow rose. "Patience pays off, babe."

"Screw patience."

He chuckled, but his laugh ended in a groan as I reached between us, wrapping my hand around the base of his cock. "Damn, babe, you really are impatient tonight."

My fingers curled around him as his hips punched again, giving me an eyeful of those sexy muscles on either side of his hips. "Maybe a little."

One of his hands smoothed down my hip, along my thigh, and as he lifted my hip, I guided it right to where I wanted. The tip of him pressed in and everything centered into my core. I moved my hand, circling my arm around his neck

Stronger than me, Jax held back. His grin turned smug.

"Jax," I whispered.

Positioned right there, he slid in maybe an inch as he lowered his mouth until it was mere inches above mine. "You want this?"

"That's a dumb question."

"Oh? Is it?" He smoothed his thumb over my breast, and he caught my nipple between his fingers, and I cried out at the exquisite feeling.

I gasped. "Not fair."

"Not sure how I feel about you saying the question is dumb." Lowering his head, he trailed kisses over the slope of my shoulder as he kept tugging at my nipple until my breasts were heavy and swollen. He nipped at the skin. "Still a dumb question?"

"Yes," I forced out as I wiggled my other leg free. I hooked it around his hip and with both of my legs, I pulled him in as I pushed my hips up.

Air hissed out between his teeth as he sank in, straight to the hilt.

The bite of him filling me was a feeling I could never forget. "Babe," he groaned out. "I think you're hungry for me."

I was.

And he wasn't moving. Nope. The guy had self-control out the wazoo. He was completely still, buried deep, and I was *completely* out of patience. I rocked my hips and we both moaned in unison.

"God, you really do want this like right now." He kissed where my pulse pounded. "You're ready for it."

I felt my cheeks heat as I said, "I am."

Jax dipped his head, running his tongue along the center of my lips until I opened for him. He kissed me deeply, still somehow aware of the cut on my lip, and then he lifted his head. "You with me?"

Remembering him saying that before, our first time, I nodded and whispered, "Yes."

He kissed me again. "Then stay with me."

Before I could question that, he broke the hold of my legs and pulled out. My whimper of protest was lost when he caught my hips and flipped me onto my stomach.

I froze.

My hair had flipped over my shoulder and my back was completely exposed to him, the worst part of me, and he'd seen it before, but this was different, way different. I started to push up, to turn back over, but he gripped my hips and lifted me onto my knees. His front was against my back, and the panic mixed with the thousand other emotions I was feeling.

"Stay with me, baby," he said to the back of my neck.

"Jax—" I lost the ability to speak as he thrust into me from behind.

The feeling of him was different, fuller and tighter. I was on my knees and hands and he was rooted to me. I couldn't breath. The feeling was intense, overwhelming, and powerful.

"You still with me?" he asked.

I was. I couldn't believe it. But I was. I was completely with him.

He smoothed a hand over my shoulder. "Calla?"

"Yes," I breathed out. "I'm with you."

"Good," he murmured.

And then he gave it to me hard.

He moved inside me deep and fast, slowing every couple of thrusts to grind against me, and in this position, from behind me, it was nothing like the other times. A different riot of sensations lit me up. My fingers dug into the comforter as my hips naturally tipped back against him.

"Oh my God," I whispered. I didn't know a lot about sex and every time I'd done it with him, I'd been surprised by it, but I never knew it could feel like *this*.

The rumble of approval from him radiated through me, and he circled an arm around my waist, sealing his body to mine. Then his hand was between my legs, his thumb pressing against the center of me, and it was too much and it was everything. My body shook as sharp pleasure rose so quickly I was dizzy, and I held on as he slammed into me, and my movements became frenzied as I pushed back against him.

Against my neck, he grunted, "It's never been like this. Not with anyone else. Only you."

My breath caught and then I was lost in those words, in how his body moved behind mine, fast and beautiful in its wildness, and soon the room was filled with sounds of our bodies crashing together and our pants and moans. The rhythm between us was lost, as was his iron control, and the tension spiraled tight, and I could feel he was close from the way he spasmed and jerked inside me.

"Never like this," he growled into my ear.

I spun right over the edge then. My body clamped down on him, my arms, my legs, and every part of me as I kicked my head back and cried out. The pressure inside me exploded, whipping through me as he groaned with each powerful thrust. My arms gave out. My cheek hit the bed, and he followed, his weight mind-blowing, and he continued to take me as he wrapped one arm around my leg, sliding it up and hitting every part of me.

The feeling, the sound of him, of our bodies, set me off again, and this time I screamed his name, and then he pushed in deeper than before, his groan heavy and sensual in my ear as he came.

Only then did he slow down, his body seeming to glide on its own as he worked his way through his release, and the aftershocks of my own still surprising me with each sublime jolt.

I don't know how much time passed with him still moving in a sway inside me before he eased out, rolled off me, and left to deal with the condom. I didn't move. I was beyond capable of moving. My muscles were mush. I was where he left me when he returned to bed and I was absolutely no help as he got my body under the covers or when he rolled me onto my side, tucking my body against his.

"You okay?" he asked.

"Mmm-hmm," I murmured sleepily.

There was a pause. "I didn't hurt you?"

"No. It was wonderful."

He kissed the back of my shoulder. "You liked that."

It wasn't a question, not the way he said it, but I murmured again, "Mmm-hmm."

Jax's chuckle brushed the back of my neck as he pulled me back tighter against him so that there was no space between us at all. "You still with me?"

"I'm still with you."

Twenty-seven

$\mathcal{S}$prawled across the bed on my belly, with one arm shoved under the pillow my cheek rested on and the other arm folded next to my side, I slowly came awake to feel a feather-light touch trailing over my hip and down the curve of my behind.

I shifted restlessly, blinked open my eyes, and was immediately blinded by the bright light streaming into the bedroom. Groaning, I closed my eyes and tried to snuggle down. My bones didn't feel like they were attached to any muscles and that somehow was a pleasant sensation. So was the hint of pressure tracing idle designs over my skin.

I'd never slept on my stomach before and I honestly didn't even remember falling asleep. I assumed it was some point after Jax had curved his arms around me and I'd taken my next breath.

My body still felt worked over in the best possible way. So much so that—

Then my eyes popped back open.

All I saw once my vision adjusted to the light was Jax's closet doors, and I figured he was what was responsible for what felt like a figure eight on my right butt cheek unless some random artist had climbed into bed with me.

My back was bare.

Hell, the sheet and covers were somewhere tangled around my upper thighs and I was sure that Jax could see the mess of skin, just like last time when he'd flipped me around and taken me from behind. My back being visible last night had been . . . somewhat okay because I doubted he was really paying attention.

I tensed and let out a shaky breath, preparing to roll away from him, which would give him an eyeful of boobs. And while I wasn't so self-conscious about my front as much as my back around him now, I was sure I had weird lines from his wrinkled sheet embedded in my skin, and that, on top of everything else, would not be sexy. Like I was pretty sure I was in the negative realm of sexy right now.

"Don't."

I stared at the closet, considered pretending I was still asleep, and then dismissed that idea because it was dumb, so I went with *playing* dumb. "Don't what?"

Jax's hand curved over my bare hip. "Don't hide. I know you were getting ready to turn away. Don't."

My eyes fell shut and I forced myself to stay still. After a few seconds, he went back to tracing smiley faces on my ass or whatever the hell he was doing. It felt like his eyes were boring holes into the discolored and rough skin, like peeling back the layers with X-ray vision.

"You have a sweet ass."

Uh.

"I mean, really. Your ass is fucking sweet, babe," he went on, and my lashes lifted and my brows pinched. "You are one of those women just born with a nice ass. No amount of workouts can create this ass."

"That's correct," I said after a few seconds. "I think it was Big Macs and tacos that created that ass."

Jax's deep laugh pulled at the corners of my lips and then I felt his leg moving over mine, followed by his hot and hard length pressed into said sweet ass. "Then don't ever stop eating those Big Macs and tacos."

Immediately, I was wet. Totally. I don't know if it was the feel of him so close to the softest part of me, or the fact he'd just told me to never stop eating Big Macs and tacos. Either way, I was ready.

"I can do that," I said, voice throaty. "Eating Big Macs and tacos."

He dropped a kiss on my shoulder as his knee pushed my thighs apart and his hand slid between his body and mine. "We should be getting up soon."

I might have grunted something to the negative.

His chuckle danced over my shoulder. "It's almost ten. I have no idea when your friends are coming over."

"We have time," I told him when I had no idea if we did or not.

Jax's hand made it between my legs, and my hips jerked as his fingers brushed across the dampness. "Damn, honey, you're fucking insatiable. I love it."

Oh, my heart did a little happy dance at the use of the word *love* even though it probably meant nothing.

His hand disappeared and I expected him to roll off and grab a condom, but he didn't move, and after a few seconds I started to feel those whorls again. Pushing myself up on my elbows, I looked over my shoulder at him.

God, only he could look so freaking, ridiculously sexy after getting only a few hours of sleep, with his hair sticking up everywhere and a rough stubble across his jaw. For a moment, I got kind of lost staring at him and then I realized he was staring at my back. For real. Tension crept into my shoulders, and after what felt like a lifetime, his gaze found mine.

And I said what I needed to say. "I don't like this."

His expression tightened. "Why, baby?"

I knew from the way he'd asked, the question was genuine, and for some reason, that created that damn ball in my throat. My arms slid out and I rested my cheek back on the pillow. "It's ugly," I whispered.

Jax was quiet as he brushed a few strands of my hair back. "Do you know what I see when I see your back?"

"That it kind of looks like the Appalachian Mountains on a map?" I joked, but it fell flat as an iron.

"No, honey." He took a deep breath. "I'm going to be honest, okay? I'm not going to sit here and tell you that what I see right now is easy to look at."

Oh God. My heart dropped and I thought I might hurl.

"But it's not the reasons you think," he continued, and then I felt it, his hand over the worst part of my back, and my entire body seemed to have a reflexive curl, but I couldn't go anywhere, because he was practically lying on me. "When I see your back, what I think about is the pain you had to have experienced. I don't personally know what it feels like, but I had hot shrapnel rip through my skin, and I'm sure that wasn't even a ball's hair worth of what you felt. But when the bomb went off in the desert, I saw soldiers—my friends—catch on fire."

I squeezed my eyes shut, but his words sparked images I didn't want to see but needed to.

"And I know that there is no amount of pain meds that really dulls these kinds of burns and you lived through that. That's what I think about when I see them. And I also think about how these fucking scars shaped your life. How they've beaten you down when you still are one of the most beautiful girls I've ever seen and these scars don't even touch that. They aren't anything compared to your smile or your pretty blue eyes or that sweet ass."

Oh my God.

He wasn't done. "You know what else I see? A physical reminder of how fucking strong you are, Calla, how fucking brave you are.

That's what I see when I look at your back. A map of how brave you are, your strength and your courage."

Oh my God.

Tears pricked at my eyes. That ball of emotion was at my throat again, ready to pour forth and flood the earth.

"And that shit isn't ugly." His voice dropped to a whisper.

I twisted, pushing up on my elbows, and looked over my shoulder at him again. His face blurred. "Jax . . ."

"That shit is beautiful in its own way, but still fucking beautiful."

Some of the tears spilled over, and I knew I was really going to start sobbing, because that was the most perfect thing I'd ever heard, and all I could say was a lame "Thank you."

One side of his lips kicked up.

I wanted to say more and I was so going to cry more, and it was a good thing that his phone started ringing, because I was seconds away from telling him that I loved him and wanted to have his babies. Not have his babies right now, but later, and I figured that might've been too soon to say something like that, but oh God, I did love him.

Jax ignored his phone as he rolled me onto my back. "I think you get it." Leaning onto one arm pressed into the pillow, he brushed away the tears with his other hand. "Finally."

A little kernel of "getting it" was there, and it was small and fragile, but it was there, pitted in my stomach like a little seed that just started to sprout. It needed love and care, but I was starting to get it.

He grinned and said, "Yeah." Then he dipped his head, kissing my left cheek just as his phone started ringing again. He pulled back, shooting a glare in the direction of the nightstand.

"You should get that." My voice was thick.

Jax really didn't look like he wanted to, but with a curse, he shifted off me and snatched his phone. He answered the call with a "What?"

I'd just settled back against the pillow, about to replay his whole speech over again in a slightly obsessive way, when Jax suddenly sat up. "*What?*"

The tone of his voice caused a rush of unease, and I reacted to it. Sitting up, I grabbed the sheet and tugged it to my breasts.

"Yeah, I'm Jackson James. What's going on?" There was a stretch of silence and then he was on his feet, and I was staring at his firm ass. He glanced over his shoulder at me, his jaw hard. "Yes. Thank you. Yep."

"What's going on?" I asked as soon as he lowered the phone.

Jax grabbed his jeans and briefs off the floor. "You got to get up and get dressed, honey."

The tone of his voice brooked no room for argument and I knew something was up, and I did what I was told. I tossed the covers and stood. Jax already had his jeans on when he was suddenly in front of me.

The air left me when I saw the look in his eyes. Oh no. My heart kicked up. "It's Mom, isn't it? They've found her bo—"

"No, honey, it's not your mom." He cupped my cheeks, his eyes searching mine. "It's Clyde. And it's serious. He had a heart attack."

One of the reasons why I wanted to be a nurse was that I hated hospitals. They were a cesspool of unwelcome memories of grief, pain, and desperation, and in a way, becoming a nurse was a way to overcome that hate and that fear. But for even more obvious reasons, I wasn't thinking of my future career and I hated them more so today than I had in a long time, because I was on the verge of having another horrific memory attached to a hospital.

We were in the waiting room outside the intensive care unit and we'd been there for at least a half an hour. We'd checked in, were told that Clyde's doctor would be to see us soon, but no one had come.

That couldn't be good.

The room was empty with the exception of Jax and me, and for that I was grateful, because I was barely holding it together. When Teresa had called because they were five minutes from Jax's house, I'd totally forgotten about them. Once I explained what happened, she immediately said they were coming to Montgomery Hospital, but I'd told them not to and that I'd keep them up to date. First off, I wanted them to enjoy their day in Philly, and second, I would lose it if they were here.

I was going to lose it anyway.

Now I paced the length of the sterile white room with taupe chairs and couches. All I knew was that it was a heart attack and it was bad. Clyde was in surgery. That's it.

"Honey, I think you should sit down," Jax suggested.

"I can't." I passed by the row of chairs. "How much longer do you think it'll be?"

He leaned forward, resting his arms on his thighs. "I don't know. These kinds of things can take a long time."

Nodding absently, I crossed my arms over my chest and kept walking. "I knew something was wrong with him, especially last night. He's been rubbing his chest a lot, looking red in the face or really pale. And he was sweating—"

"Calla, you didn't know. None of us did. You can't blame yourself for this."

He had a point, but I'd seen the way Clyde looked last night when he'd showed up and ran off the kidnapper. I shook my head as anger stole up on me like a shadow in the darkest night. "Damn her," I seethed.

Jax straightened.

I stared at him for a moment and then looked away. "I know a lot of stress has to be on him from the bar and her being gone. Hell, a lot of stress is on you! You've been running the bar for her and for what? Tips and minimum wage?"

A strange look pinched his features as he rubbed a hand along his stubbled jaw.

"I almost got kidnapped last night because of her and Clyde was out there. He doesn't need this kind of stress. Look at what it's done to him?" I stopped, unfolding my arms and squeezing my hands into fists. The anger turned into venom in my blood as I said, "I hate her."

Jax blinked. "Babe . . ."

My breath caught. "I know I shouldn't, but I can't help it. Look at what she's done to everyone. And for what? I know her life has been hard, because I lived it! I was right there with her, Jax! I lived it, too, but I—"

"We probably wouldn't be where we are today. You know that, right?" he said quietly. "She gave us that."

She gave us that.

I clamped my mouth shut, shoulders tight. I stared into his eyes and then I looked away. The burn in my chest ached. And then as quickly as the poisonous bite had entered my veins, it eased away and I whispered, "Yeah, she gave us that."

"You don't hate her."

My eyes closed against the rush of frustrated tears. "I know."

The truth was that sometimes I wanted to hate her, because then I wouldn't care about what was happening to her and what she'd done to her life. I wouldn't worry about what the drugs were doing to her. I wouldn't care if she had a roof over her head or clean clothes on her back. I wouldn't care, and damnit, caring *hurt*.

As raw emotion that had been there long before today, this week, or even this year started to swell inside me, I started pacing again to burn it off. I focused on something else. "Why did they call you?"

"I'm his emergency contact, I guess."

Meaning I wasn't. I wasn't the contact for a man who'd virtually helped raise me. It was stupid to feel guilty about not being Clyde's emergency contact, but I knew that if I'd been around more,

I would've been in the position to be contacted. It terrified me knowing that this could've happened and no one would've notified me.

And it hit me with the force of a speeding semitruck.

I'd been doing this wrong. My life. Completely wrong, because it had been my choices that led to me leaving this town and it had been my choices that had practically ended a relationship with a man who'd been the only good role model in my whole freaking life. I still could've kept in touch. I still could've come around. *Fuck.* Maybe if I had, Mom would've found it harder to wipe me out. Who knew? But I had run at the first chance I got, and I knew Clyde didn't blame me for it, but still. I'd told myself that I hated the bar, but my happiest memories had been there. I lied to myself. A lot.

If I wore a map of courage, bravery, and strength on my back, I sure as hell hadn't behaved that way in a long time. Not since Mom took my money and I met Jax.

My knees went weak, and I had no idea how I didn't plant my ass on the floor. "Oh my God."

Jax glanced at me. "Honey, he's going to be okay."

"If I hadn't come back here this summer and if he still had a heart attack, I wouldn't have known." I stopped in front of him. "Jax, I would've never known, and what if he dies? What if this would've been my last chance to see him?"

His features tensed and then he snagged an arm around my waist and pulled me into his lap. His other hand cupped my cheek. "Honey, if something happened to Clyde I would've gotten in contact with you."

Fresh tears rose. "But how? You didn't know me or really how to find me. You knew of me, but that's different."

That look crossed his face again, but his hand slid around the nape of my neck and he guided my cheek to his chest. "I would've found you, honey, but you're here and that's all that matters."

Snuggling deep, I wrapped my arms around him loosely and did something I hadn't done in years. I prayed, seriously prayed that Clyde would be okay. And I kind of felt like a poser for praying, but I did it.

I stayed there until the door opened and I pulled away, expecting to see the doctor, but it was Reece who walked in, wearing his uniform. He was on duty. I tensed up, and he must've seen the look on my face and immediately reassured me. "I heard about Clyde. Just wanted to check in."

"He's in surgery," I told him. "I don't know anything else."

"Known Clyde for a couple of years," Reece said after he sat in the seat next to us. "He's a strong man. He'll pull through."

I took an unsteady breath and Jax ran his hand up my spine. "Thank you."

Reece didn't say much, but he sat like he planned on staying for a while, and that left me warm and fuzzy. When the door opened again some ten minutes later, I saw Teresa coming through the door, followed by my friends, and my heart clenched.

I stared at them as they made their way over to where we sat. "What are you guys doing here?"

"We had to come," Teresa said, sitting on the other side of us. She reached out and squeezed my arm. "We wanted to make sure you were okay."

Cam and Avery took up the same kind of position across from us, her in his lap and resting her head against his chest. "None of us felt right."

"We wanted to be here with you," Jase tossed in, sitting in the seat beside Teresa.

I opened my mouth, blubbered up some kind of thank-you, and then I turned, burying my face in Jax's throat. His arms tightened around me, and I told myself not to cry, because it was dumb, but I was rocking the overly emotional thing then, and I stayed that way until my eyes felt somewhat dry, and then I thanked them again. I pulled myself together and managed to hold *and* follow the conversation around me.

Over the next couple of hours, Roxy and Nick showed up at different times, staying until they had to get back to the bar. Roxy had steered clear of Reece, but when she left, he'd mysteriously gotten up and walked out, too. I wondered about that. Everyone who worked at the bar showed at some point, and it did good things for my soul to see so many people care about Clyde.

When I whispered that to Jax, he whispered back, "They also care about you."

And he was right. As usual. It was getting kind of annoying.

The door opened again shortly after that and my stomach dropped when I saw that it was the doctor. I started to pull myself free, but Jax tightened his hold on me, and all I was able to do was face the doctor.

"How is he?" I asked, my heart thumping fast.

Dressed in blue scrubs and looking absolutely exhausted, the older woman smoothed a small, delicate hand over the top of her salt-and-pepper hair. "You're family?"

"Yes," I immediately responded. Blood or not, Clyde was family.

Her hazel eyes swept the waiting room. "All of you are family?"

"Yeah, we're all family," Jax responded then, his hand flattening along my stomach. "How is he?"

She walked over to an empty love seat catty-corner to where we sat and clasped her hands between her knees. "He's made it through surgery."

"Oh, thank God," I whispered, slumping back against Jax.

"We're not out of the woods yet," she went on to say, and I knew from my schooling that the next things she said were serious. "He suffered a major heart attack due to several blockages. We put in stents, because we usually . . ."

They usually saw faster recovery in those who had stents versus a bypass. As the doctor continued, two parts of my brain functioned independently of each other—the clinical side and the personal side. But ultimately, Clyde had made it through surgery and although this was a major surgery and I knew things could go horribly wrong from this point, he made it out of surgery and that was huge. Tears of relief built in the back of my eyes.

"He's asleep now and he'll be like that probably for the rest of the day, and right now, we really need to let him rest." The doctor stood, smiling faintly. "If everything pans out tomorrow, at least one of you can visit him if he's up to it."

I came to my feet then, and Jax didn't stop me. "Thank you—thank you so much."

Her faint smile remained. "Now all of you should go home and get some rest. If anything changes between now and tomorrow, we'll let you know. Okay?"

As the doctor left, I turned and Teresa was standing there. She wrapped her arms around me, and I hugged her back. "This is good," she said. "This is really good."

Blinking back the tears, I nodded. "I know. Clyde's strong. He'll pull through." Sniffling, I edged back and smiled at her. Jax was standing beside me, and he took hold of my hand, threading his fingers through mine. He squeezed. "Thank you," I said again, totally choked up as I turned to my friends. "Thank you."

Avery smiled in return, and my eyes dropped to her waist for some reason. I don't really know why, but I saw that they were being their typical most adorable couple in all of coupledom; her smaller hand was in Cam's, their palms pressing together and his fingers curled around hers.

Just like Jax's held mine.

Twenty-eight

It wasn't until Monday afternoon that Clyde was well enough for a short visit. Jax had to stay out in the waiting area while a young nurse led me into his room.

Seeing him lying on the narrow bed, his once big and bulky frame appearing so frail, and covered with tubes and wires, shook me up.

My knees knocked together as he blinked slowly and then I swallowed the raw emotion building in my throat. I sat in the small chair beside his bed. Reaching out, I placed my fingers over his. "Hey there."

A weak, tired smile appeared on his lips. His complexion was terribly pale. "Baby girl . . ."

My breath caught. "How are you feeling?"

"Ready to . . . run a marathon."

I laughed and my smile became wobbly. Several seconds passed as we stared at each other, and I had to swallow hard again. "I want you to get better."

The weak smile fluttered. "On it."

"I want you to get better so that when school starts back up and I come home on the weekends, you'll make me tacos," I told him. "Okay?"

His brows lifted a fraction of an inch and he murmured, "Home?"

Worried that the heart attack had messed with more than his

heart, I nodded. "Yeah, when I come home, I want you . . ." I trailed off as the sharp slice of understanding cut through me.

Home.

I'd called *here* home.

And I hadn't called *here* home in years, because it hadn't felt that way since Mom went downhill and Dad left. My mouth opened wordlessly, but I didn't know what to say. The strangest thing was I had no inclination to correct what I had said, because here . . . here was home again.

Wow.

I had no idea what to do with all that.

That exhausted smile showed off a toothy grin that faded quickly. "Baby girl, I never . . . thought I'd hear . . . that again."

"I . . . I never thought I'd say that again." Damnit. Tears made it to my eyes, and I wondered if this was the summer I went on Prozac. "But it's . . ."

"It's true." He took a deep breath and winced. "It's good, baby girl. It's . . . real good."

I squeezed his fingers gently and leaned forward, whispering, "It is."

And I wasn't lying. It really was. My heart kicked around in my chest as I wiped the back of my other hand across my cheek.

"You feel that?" he asked quietly.

"What?" I croaked out.

"The weight lifting a little . . . off you," he said. "You feel it?"

My lips trembled as I nodded. "Yeah, Uncle Clyde, I feel that."

Another deep breath passed and it took a lot for him to get his hand turned around. He squeezed my fingers back with the pressure of a toddler, and that was hard to see. "Your momma . . . she loved you, baby girl. She still does. You . . . know that, right?"

Smashing my lips together, I nodded. I did know that. In spite of all the terrible stuff she did, I knew she still loved me. She just needed the high more than she needed my love or me. It was just a sad truth about someone addicted to drugs.

His grip relaxed and he closed his eyes. I sat there for a couple more moments. "You need to rest. I'll come back later."

He nodded slowly, but as I started to pull away, his eyes opened and his hand flexed around mine. "That boy . . . he's cared about you for a . . ." He faded out, and I froze, half sitting, half standing. Then he spoke again. "He's a good boy, baby girl. Jackson's always been perfect for you."

"Always been?" I asked.

But there was no answer. Uncle Clyde was out, and his words left me confused. The way he spoke was like Jax had been in my life for a long time and he hadn't. Then again, Clyde was on some pretty damn good painkillers. I stayed for a few more minutes, watching his chest rise and fall, reassuring myself that he was very much alive and that he was going to get better. I pressed a kiss to his cheek and then left the room.

I turned down the hall, passed the busy nurse station, and headed toward the waiting room.

Detective Anders was leaning against the wall, waiting for me. I couldn't stop the tension that crept up over me when I saw him.

"Hey," I said, slowing my step. I glanced at the windows of the waiting room. It was empty.

"Jax ran down a floor to get a drink out of one of the vending machines," Detective Anders explained. "He should be back in a few. I told him I'd wait for you. I'd called your cell and when there was no answer, I called Jax."

"Oh." I folded my arms as I stared up at him, thankful I wasn't thinking about how good-looking he was like last time. *Crap.* Now I was thinking that. The man could work a suit. Looking away, I wanted to kick myself in the teeth. "I left my phone in his truck."

"How's he doing?" he asked.

Taking a deep breath, I refocused. "He was awake for a little while, so I got to talk to him." I hated what I said next. "He's really weak, though, and I know he's in pain, but he'll . . . he'll pull through."

"He's a tough guy. I've got to believe he'll get through this, too."

I nodded, folding my arms against the hospital chill. "Detective Anders—"

"Call me Colton."

Colton? His name was Colton? I'd gone all my life not knowing someone named that, and I thought it fit him, a rugged and sexy name. "Colton, were you just checking on Clyde or . . ."

"A little of that, and I wanted to check in with you and let you know that we're still working hard on everything."

"So there's no bad news?"

A sympathetic look crossed his face. "No, Calla, there's really no news at this point. We haven't been able to locate anyone who matches the description you provided us in criminal records and Mack is still lying low, but that's a good thing. That last part, that is."

I frowned. "How so?"

He looked around, then motioned to the waiting room with a jerk of his chin. "Let's take this in there."

Ruh-roh.

I walked through the door he held open and sat in the first chair. As he unbuttoned his suit jacket, he sat across from me. "We've been putting in a lot of visits to Isaiah. We've got nothing leading back to him, no surprise there, and even though he keeps his hands clean, we know those hands are all over this shit, you follow me?"

Mysterious Isaiah strikes again. "Okay."

"He doesn't like screwups or loose ends. Mack right now is both of those things and he's bringing the heat down on Isaiah, plus Isaiah can't be too happy about the drugs going missing," he explained, eyes fixed on me. "Mack's got it coming from both ends with Isaiah. He's in the same boat as . . ."

"As my mother?"

He didn't break eye contact. "Yes. I hate saying that to you, but yes."

Running my hands over my jeans, I sighed. There was nothing I could say to that. Nothing at all.

"If you hear from your mom, you need to let us know," he continued. "I know that'll be hard, but it's not safe for her. We are literally the lesser of two evils. You get what I'm saying?"

Unsure if I could do that, turn my mom over to the police, I shifted my gaze away. I knew it would be the right thing to do if Mom happened to pop back up and even though I wanted to say I could, it would be different if that situation arose.

Detective Anders stood, and I figured the conversation was over. He stopped at the door, head tilted. "You have a good thing going here, right?"

Thinking that was an odd thing to say, all I did was nod.

"Then take to heart what I said about your mother, Calla. I know she's blood. I know you love her. And I know these things are hard, but don't let her take these good things away from you."

Detective Anders's words lingered with me the rest of the afternoon and into the evening. I tried not to think about it when Jax and I left to grab a late lunch at a small diner in town or as we spent the evening chilling in his living room. It was a lot to deal with—everything—and it was exhausting, both mentally and emotionally.

It was near eight in the evening and I'd just gorged myself on a pack of Twizzlers. On the way back from tossing the package in the trash, I smoothed my hand through my hair even though it probably still looked like a hot mess and then headed around the couch.

From where Jax sat, he leaned forward and settled his hands on my hips as I went to walk past him, to take the seat next to him. Apparently that wasn't happening. "I think I'm going to pull out of Dennis's bachelor party."

God, I'd totally forgotten that was tomorrow night. "Why?"

One shoulder rose as he rubbed his hands up and down my hips. "With everything going on with Clyde and with you, I think the last thing I need to be doing is sitting in a strip club."

"I'm pretty sure with everything that's been going on, you could use the break. Just don't go into any of the private rooms," I joked.

"Thursday nights are kind of busy, hon, and I don't feel—"

"We have the bar and the kitchen handled. And I promise not to get kidnapped or anything crazy."

An eyebrow arched. "You promise?"

"Totes-ma-goats."

He smirked. "I don't think that's something you necessarily have control over."

"If I stay behind the bar, I think I'll be fine. Plus Nick will be there. And you already have him coming in on Thursday to cover you. We'll be fine."

"You sure are fine."

I sighed. "Jax."

With a wicked grin on his lips, he pulled me into his lap and I went to him, straddling his thighs. I liked this. A lot. But he wasn't going to distract me. "Go. Okay. I'll be at the bar and you'll come get me before we close. I'll be fine."

He leaned back against the couch cushion. "But what if I want to take a girl home with me?"

"I don't know about that. The way Katie talks, those girls oil themselves up. You might have a hard time holding on to one of them."

Jax tipped his head back and laughed. "Nice."

Then something occurred to me. "What if Katie's dancing?"

He shook his head. "That will be a bathroom break for me."

"She's really hot."

Hooking his arms around my hips, he spread his legs and I slipped farther onto him. "It's not that. It's just that she's Katie . . . and I don't want to see her like that."

I grinned and hoped that she was dressed as a fairy again. "So you're going?"

One hand slid up the line of my spine, tangled in my hair, and then he tugged my head down to his lips. "I'm going."

"Good."

He nipped at my lower lip. "You're probably the only girl in the world who would just say good to the fact her man is going to a strip club."

My man? I got a little caught up in that phrase so I didn't point out that I thought a lot of girls really didn't care about strip clubs, because then he was kissing me, slow and sweet.

When his mouth left mine, his lips brushed over the curve of my jaw. The bruise from the botched kidnapping had already began to fade, but he placed a kiss there, and my heart did a little dance.

I settled in his arms as he idly flipped through the stations on the TV and it wasn't long before my eyes drifted shut. I was lulled away by the steady sweeping motion of his hand along the line of my spine. It was strange. I never thought I could ever allow someone to touch me there, even if I was wearing clothes, and here I was, comforted by a caress that would've made me cringe not too long ago.

So much had changed.

Once he'd settled on a baseball game, he dropped the remote and his hand ended up in my hair. "Reece called earlier, when you were on the computer doing your school stuff."

My eyes opened, but I didn't move. I was feeling way too lazy for that level of effort. "What did he want?"

"Just keeping us updated on Mack. Reece and Colton really think he's gone to ground, especially since they've been riding Isaiah hard, which won't bode well for Mack, either," he said as he twisted my hair around his fingers.

"Yeah, Detective Anders said something like that yesterday when he talked to me." My hand was on his chest so I started drawing a circle with my finger. "It's just crazy. It's like all of them know that this Isaiah is dirty, but they don't do anything."

"They can't, honey. Isaiah is smart. He cleans up after everything and nothing leads back to him. That's why he's not going to be happy with Mack. He messed up with your mom and Rooster, obviously took Rooster out—"

"Couldn't that have been Isaiah?" I asked.

Jax flipped the mass of hair over my shoulder. "I don't think so. He's cleaner than that. And he's smart. He's not going to drop a body in the daylight on a front porch. He's more of the going for a cement swim type of guy."

I shuddered. "How well do you know Isaiah?"

"As well as I want to and nothing more." His hand flattened along the curve of my behind and stayed there. "He's been in Mona's a few times. I think checking the place out."

"That's kind of creepy."

"He's Isaiah." He patted my behind. "Anyway, if Mack's gone to ground, there's a good chance you're done with this shit."

That's what Detective Anders had said, too, but it really didn't make me feel like I should go traipsing down Main Street or anything. "Have they found Ike?"

"Nope."

"Do you think . . . something happened to him, too?"

"I don't know. The kind of life these people live, it's not odd that they disappear. Could have nothing to do with any of this."

I hoped so. Well, I hoped whoever the Ike guy was, he wasn't missing in a bad way. I didn't know him, never even seen him, but still, a human life was a human life.

"I've been thinking," he said as he gently untangled his fingers from my hair. "When you head back to Shepherd, you're staying in a dorm, right?"

I nodded. "I'm in the Printz apartments this year. Or I had

approval before. I guess I still do, but Printz is a dorm with two- to three-bedroom apartments in them."

"So privacy?"

"Yes. Just like a normal apartment building, but nicer." I laughed.

"This is good, because we're going to need the privacy."

I bit down on my lower lip, but it didn't stop my smile from spreading. "We do?"

"Honey, I don't want to be naked in bed with you with some chick in another bed a couple fucking feet away from us."

"Good point." I giggled.

Actually fucking giggled. I was so dumb.

"If I keep my schedule like it is, I could come down on Sunday and stay with you for a few days." He caught a strand of my hair again and tucked it back. "And maybe when your schoolwork isn't too heavy, you can come up on the weekend."

Lifting my head, I met his gaze.

"Of course, to work, that is."

I laughed at that, and he grinned. "I can do that." His grin turned into a smile and I said, "I think you like me, Jackson James."

He raised a brow. "Wow. Are you finally getting it?"

I pushed my hand at his chest, and he chuckled. "No. I think you *really* like me."

"Like I said, you're finally just getting it?"

"Whatever."

He kissed the corner of my lip. "It's a good thing you have such a sweet ass."

I smacked his pec for that, but then he caught my wrist and lifted my hand to his mouth. He kissed the center of my palm. "Yeah, babe, I *really* like you."

My eyes locked in on his. "I *really* like you, too."

"I know," he murmured lazily.

"Cocky."

"Confident."

"Arrogant," I whispered, and then I kissed him quickly before settling down against his chest again, not wanting him to see that my "really like" went into the "really love" territory.

Conversation faded as he turned his attention to the baseball game, and I relaxed completely, curled up in his arms. I never thought I'd have this with someone, especially someone as wonderful as Jax.

And in a weird way, I had my mom to thank for that.

It wasn't long before I fell asleep like that, and when he was ready for bed, he simply turned off the TV, gathered me closer, and stood.

"I can walk," I mumbled.

His arms tightened. "I got you."

I liked the sound of that and it was way nice, him doing this. As I wrapped an arm around his neck and closed my eyes, I allowed myself to be a total cornball and my insides melted into cornball goo.

In spite of everything, I was lucky. So damn lucky.

He carried me upstairs and then I also liked it when he helped me undress, which ended with me wearing nothing but one of his shirts. I got tucked into bed while he headed back downstairs and locked up. It wasn't long before he was in bed with me, his front pressed to my back, one leg between mine and an arm secured around my waist.

Jax's lips brushed the back of my neck, and before I slipped back into sleepy land, I heard him say for no reason at all, "You're beautiful, babe."

When I woke up, I knew something was different. Jax wasn't behind me, tucked as close as he could get. I rolled into his space, catching the faint scent of his cologne, and blinked until my vision adapted to the darkness.

The green neon light from the clock on the nightstand said it was three in the morning.

Sitting up, I looked around the room. There was no light peeking under the closed bathroom door, but the bedroom door was open.

This was strange to my sleepy brain. I couldn't think of a time where I'd shared his bed that he'd gotten up in the middle of the night. Granted, we hadn't been sharing beds that long.

I sat there for a moment as my mind started to come back on line. I knew that a lot of people who'd seen battle had problems with sleep and Jax had said that when he returned, he had trouble with it. Concern tugged at me, waking me up. Was he having a bad night? Since we hadn't been sleeping together that long, it was possible he had them and I didn't know.

Throwing the cover off, I slipped off the bed. His shirt settled around my thighs as I stepped toward the door left ajar. That's when I heard his voice.

"Not now."

My brows furrowed as I opened the door and walked the short distance to the top of the stairs. From my vantage point, I could see down the whole stairwell and I could see the front door. It was opened, but no one was there.

Then I heard the second voice.

"I know I should've called."

My heart stopped in my chest—stopped like it had hit a brick wall. That was most definitely a female voice. In the house. At three in the morning.

If Jax responded, I didn't hear him, but I heard the girl again. "I was out and I missed you, baby. I've missed you so much."

Oh. My. God.

I reached out, grabbing the wooden ball carved into the top of the banister to steady myself. I had to be dreaming. It was not three in the morning and some girl, who sounded vaguely familiar, was not in Jax's house, telling him how much she missed him and calling him baby. No way.

I heard Jax then, but it was only bits and pieces of what he was saying. " . . . now isn't a good time . . . no time . . . call first, but . . ."

Ice drenched my veins.

From what I could hear, it was pretty obvious. Call before you come over, because there might be someone else here. A second later, my theory was confirmed.

"Is someone here?" The voice rose.

Oh God . . .

Then I heard Jax loud and clear. "Keep your voice down, Aimee."

No wonder the voice sounded familiar to me.

Aimee? Beautiful ex-pageant queen with perfect teeth Aimee, whom he had a history with and who gave him free breast exams at the bar? Maybe a not-too-distant history with?

I think I needed to sit down.

"Is that a purse?" Aimee demanded. "What the fuck, Jax? You do have someone here. Where is she? And does she know that the last time I was in town, we were together? Which, by the way, wasn't like a month ago?"

My stomach dropped to my toes. A month ago? I did a quick calculation of the time from when I came home and now, and really, that didn't add up in a way that made my stomach get back where it belonged.

"Shit, Aimee, it was more than a month ago," Jax said, his voice louder, too. "Look, you know I care about you—"

"Do you?" she fired back.

You know I care about you.

I squeezed my eyes shut. A couple of hours ago, we were in bed, and he'd held me and told me I was beautiful, and a few hours before that he'd told me he *really* liked me, and we were making plans for when I went back to Shepherd, but now Aimee with two *e*'s was in his house and they'd been together a *month* ago, and he *cared* about her. I opened my eyes. They didn't feel dry. The front door was still open.

This was happening. This was really happening.

Something in my chest hurt, like physically hurt, and I let go of the banister and pressed the heel of my palm between my breasts.

Then Aimee was at the bottom of the stairs.

"Holy . . ." She trailed off as her eyes widened. "No. This is *not* happening."

Well, Aimee and I were on the same page for once, because I was thinking the exact same thing.

"You're with her?" Her voice pitched as her head swiveled in the other direction, and I wondered if it could spin right around like the chick from *The Exorcist.* "Seriously? Calla Fritz?"

I flinched.

Son of a bitch, I actually *flinched*.

Because I could totally get the WTF expression she was wearing and the surprise in her tone. I got it. Jax was gorgeous in a way that was almost unreal. He could get girls dropping their panties just by giving them a half smile and a crook of his finger. I had a giant scar down my face and then some. And my mother was a well-known crackhead. I wasn't exactly someone the vast majority of people would picture Jax with. I seriously did get that, because it was human nature to want to pair flawless people with other flawless people.

Jax appeared in my line of vision. Shirtless. All those muscles on display. For some reason that struck me harder. That he was half undressed with Aimee in his house, that there was a level of intimacy between them. Which was a big fucking duh, because they'd been banging each other like a cheap screen door at some point that wasn't *too long ago.*

"You need to leave," Jax said, not looking up at me. "Now."

Aimee ignored that. She raised a slender, golden arm and pointed at me. "You've got to be joking, right? Her? I mean, I know guys like to slum every once in a while but seriously?"

Another direct hit to the chest, but man, that nasty little remark hit me like a spark over a pool of gasoline, and it happened.

I exploded.

Twenty-nine

"*W*hat the fuck?" The words burst out of me like a bottle rocket and I was down the stairs and in Aimee's face before I even knew it. "First off, I don't think anyone in the last ten years used the word *slumming,* but you'd probably know that if you didn't fry your brain fake-baking or overdosing on bleach to get your hair that color." I flicked a strand of her hair, and she took a step back. I advanced, beyond furious. "Yeah, mine's natural. And second, I'm *over* you."

Her skin paled a bit under her tan and then a flush raced across her face and down her neck. "I'm sorry. Is *trash* a better word for you?"

Jax must've snapped out of his stupor and out of the corners of my eyes I could see him moving forward. "That's enough. Aimee, you—"

"Trash?" I cut in, hands balling into fists. Jax was wrong. It so wasn't enough. "Who in the fuck are you calling trash?"

Her gaze raked over me from the top of my bedraggled head, all the way down my bare legs. She sneered. "Could be the whore standing in front of me in nothing but a shirt?"

Jax shot forward, looping an arm around my waist and hauling me out of the way and giving me a shove away from her, and then he was in Aimee's face. "You will fucking apologize. Right now."

"Apologize for what?" she screamed.

His jaw had locked down, muscles tense along his back. "Fucking apologize, Aimee. I'm dead serious."

Aimee must have tasted his anger, because she shrank a little, like a weed choked by a bushel of fucking roses. "Jax," she whispered.

Hearing her whisper his name like that, like she couldn't believe he was defending me over her, sent me off into the stratosphere. I was not going to be placed aside. I stormed forward, coming at Aimee from the other side. "You know what? You don't need to apologize. I don't need your fucking apologies. The fact is you want to be the girl wearing *his* shirt who was sleeping in *his* bed. You reek of jealousy."

She turned a heated glare on me, but my bitch shades were up. "I was the girl, *honey,* and for a hell of a lot longer than you."

Ouch.

Okay. Burn. She got me there. And my anger swirled, mixing with the raw hurt that had sliced deep in my chest. "You know what, Aimee? Call me trash. Whatever. I'm not the girl at the bar every night who's throwing herself at a guy who's with someone else. And I'm not the girl whose idea of making a living is being a 'ring girl.' I'm in college. To be a nurse. You know, doing things with my life. So yeah, if that makes me trash and a whore? Fucking proud of it then."

She laughed harshly. "What? Do you think you're actually special to him?" Before I could answer, she went on. "That you're like his one and only?"

"Aimee," Jax said, voice low.

"Because you're not," she snapped. "His bed is like the Philly train station, especially now."

A pierce hit my chest. I had . . . I had not known that, and as I glanced at Jax, there was nothing on his face that denied it. I exhaled harshly. "Then I guess you are just one of many, too."

Her eyes flashed, and I didn't know if I wounded her or if any of that made a difference to her. "At least I don't have your face, bitch."

Yep. It hadn't made a difference.

My feet moved, and I honestly didn't know what I was going to do, if I was going to introduce her to the epic bitch slap or if I was going to slam my knee into Jax's groin, but he turned to me. Snagging an arm around my waist, he lifted me clear off my feet as he moved and twisted his body so I was facing the wall and he was facing Aimee. I craned my neck to see her.

He had a finger in her face. "Get out."

The white under her tan increased. "But—"

"Get the fuck out, Aimee."

She took a deep breath and her blue eyes turned glassy. Then her face crumbled, and it might've made me the biggest idiot in the world, but there was a teeny, tiny part of me that actually felt bad for her, because I recognized that pain that had broken her face.

I had felt it mere minutes ago.

Then Aimee blinked, sucked her tears right up, and swallowed. "I get it. Whatever this is. I get it."

I wondered what the hell she got.

She smiled then, like he hadn't just told her to get out of his house. "We'll talk later, babe."

And then she flounced out of the house.

What in the fuckity fuck?

Jax all but kicked his door shut and then he turned, settling me on my feet. I started to pull free, but his arm around my waist tightened, and he dragged my back against his chest.

"Let me go," I said, gripping his arm.

"Okay," he murmured in my ear. "I'll admit it. You getting all up in her face like that was hot."

Fury flared and pulsed around the deep, throbbing hurt. "Let me go, Jax."

"Especially with you standing there, all fired up in my shirt? Yeah. Hot as hell," he continued, and my anger overrode the hurting.

One hand dropped from my waist and flattened against my lower belly. He pressed and my bottom tipped back against him, and yeah, I totally got that he really did find that hot. The evidence was right there, and my body, because it was a dumb hooch, reacted. My stomach fluttered and the idiotic area between my thighs throbbed.

And that just pissed me off even more.

"If you don't let me go, I swear to God, Jax," I warned, squeezing his arms with my hands.

He dipped his chin into my shoulder and said, "Is it wrong that I find that hot, too, because I really kind of do."

I lost it and shouted loud enough to wake up the neighbors, "Let me the fuck go!"

Jax's arms dropped like I was a hot potato, and I spun on him, breathing heavy. Our gazes locked, and the amusement in his voice was completely gone from his expression. He stared at me. I stared back. In those moments, I heard what I had when I stood upstairs all over again. I felt what I did when I saw Aimee's expression when she'd seen me standing at the top of the stairs.

Tension formed around his mouth. "Calla . . ."

My feet moved backward. I needed space. I needed time to think about everything that had just happened.

He took a step forward, and I kept moving until my leg bumped into the arm of the couch. He stopped a few feet from me. "I don't know what you're thinking right now, but I'm going to wage a guess here, and say what happened is not what you're thinking."

In my chest, my heart threw itself against my ribs. "It's not?"

"I had no idea she was going to show up tonight. She hasn't been to my house in—"

"A month?" I finished for him. "A whole month?"

The tension around his mouth increased. "It's been more than a month, Calla. I don't know the exact time frame, but she hasn't been here since you came here. You have to believe that. I've practically spent every night with you since you've been here."

"Not every night."

"Every night since she got back into town," he said, and I had to admit, that was true. "You and I aren't together every waking minute, but give me a break on that. It's not like I have all the time in the world to be hooking up with her."

Another good point. "But you were hooking up with her a little over a month ago."

"*Before* you came here, Calla."

Did that matter? I knew it shouldn't. I wasn't even in town and I couldn't be mad over who he hooked up with before we met, but damnit, I was. I was thoroughly pissed and I was jealous. I was woman enough to admit to my irrational anger over that, but there was more.

"For someone you aren't seeing, she was awful angry over the fact that a girl was here, Jax. She showed up in the middle of the night like she had a right to be here."

"Calla—"

"And every night she's been in the bar, hanging all over you and you let her." My hands curled into fists again. "The first time my friends met you she was feeling you up."

Frustration flashed across his face. "We're back to that again?"

"Yes!" I shouted. "We're back to that, *baby*. You know, the whole 'you need to trust me' and basically deal with the fact you have a chick hanging all over you in front of me and my friends."

"I never said you had to deal with it, Calla."

"You didn't?" I laughed harshly. "That's not how I remember the conversation ending."

Jax drew in a breath and a muscle spasmed in his jaw. "Actually, the conversation ended with you walking away. You didn't give me a chance to say anything else or even to explain."

"What's there to explain? She was all over you, multiple times, and you just smiled at her!" My head felt like it was going to explode off my neck. "And I'm just supposed to trust you and be okay with it? Even when you have her showing up in your house at three in the morning like she belongs here and has no idea you're seeing someone?"

"Correction," he growled. "She doesn't care that I'm seeing someone."

Totally caught in my anger, I went on. "And she left here like you two were still going to hook up!"

"Calla—"

"You said you cared about her!" The moment those words left my mouth, I realized how ridiculous they sounded. I turned away, moving into the dining area. I knew he followed without hearing him. "You told her that you cared about her. I heard you. I also heard you tell her this wasn't a good time and that she needed to call first before she came over."

"Wait a minute." His voice got low, got way too calm. "I don't know what you think you heard or what bullshit you're reading into it, but no shit, Calla. She needs to call before she comes by my house and three in the morning isn't a good time."

I whirled back on him, heart racing. "So if she called first and I wasn't here, would it have been a good time then, Jax?"

His shoulders tensed as he drew back. "Are you fucking serious?"

"Are you?" I shot back, fists shaking. "I don't know if you realize this or not, but I'm not the one here who has guys showing up at all hours of the night or giving me free breast exams. And you haven't heard me tell another guy that I cared about them when they were obviously trying to get laid."

Jax looked away as he thrust a hand through his messy hair. "Yeah, I used to think Aimee was an okay chick, you know? I never was serious with her, and to be honest, I never got the feeling she was serious about me. So, yeah, I care about her. Don't want to see any bad shit happen to her. Still don't want to see that, but I'm re-thinking the whole nice-girl thing after tonight." He dropped his hand, gaze back on mine. "Caring about her is not the same thing. Calla. And I'm sorry—"

"Is that why you have so many toothbrushes?" I blurted out.

"What?"

"Toothbrushes," I stated, gesturing behind him, toward the stairs. "You have all these unopened boxes of toothbrushes in your bathroom. Do you have them for the girls you're with? One for me and one for Aimee and whoever else?"

A moment of complete utter silence passed between us as he gaped at me. Like so silent, you could hear a cricket sneeze.

"You really are fucking serious," he said, and that really did nothing to calm me down. "First off, I have so many goddamn tooth-brushes because my mom gets me one for every damn birthday and holiday. She always has. It's a fucking tradition, and I keep them."

Oh.

Well, that sounded kind of believable.

"Second, no girl—not a single fucking girl except you—has ever used one of those toothbrushes. Not even Aimee. When I was with her, when I was with other girls, I fucked them, they fucked me, some might have stayed the night, but they all left in the morning or before then, and they sure as hell didn't use any of my shit. Not even the damn shower."

I really didn't want to hear about him fucking anyone.

"I'm not trying to sound like a dick, and I get the way this looks to you, and I'm sorry—I really am, because this is the last thing you need and to deal with her being here. And I get that you don't have a lot of experience with these things," he went on, and I felt my cheeks heat with color, because what he said was true. I was twenty-one and had absolutely no experience with boys. "So I understand and

I'm trying to be real cool with the fact you don't get the difference between the girls I'd fucked and you."

"I really don't want to hear about the girls you fucked," I said, speaking my earlier thoughts. "But since you brought it up, what about your train station bed?"

Something crossed his face as he drew back, and I didn't know why it looked like hurt, because he was the last person who should be feeling butt sore. "Yeah, okay. I'm not particularly proud of some of the shit I've done in my past—not the drinking and not the sleeping around. Bad decisions, but that shit . . . that shit is so in the past."

Oh my God.

It hit me then—the thing he never told me that he'd done when he'd gotten back to the United States and when he was here, and couldn't get his head to shut down. Alcohol and sex go hand in hand. A bit of guilt wiggled free. "I don't want to hear this."

"You're gonna hear about it, Calla, since it's such a big fucking deal that we're arguing about it in the middle of the night." His voice was still level, but his eyes were so dark, they almost seemed black. "I'm only going to say this once. I've been with enough people that I know the difference between what was going on with them and what's going on with you. You're not one of them. You're not Aimee. You're not even in their ballpark."

Flinching, I stiffened.

"Oh no, no you do not take that like I just insulted you. You're not in their ballpark, because I'm not playing any bullshit games with you. You get me? What I had with them or what I *didn't* isn't anything like what I got going with you. Okay?" He continued before I could answer. "And I wanted to talk to you about what had gone down in the bar when your friends showed up, but you were almost kidnapped and then Clyde had a heart attack, so really, there hasn't been a good time to talk about that shit."

Once again, he made a good point, and I hated that. Like for real.

"But we're going to talk about that now—we're going to finish the conversation you should've let me finish before you walked away from me." He advanced forward, and man, he was pissed. I forced myself not to move. "You were right."

I blinked.

"I should've done more to make sure Aimee got the picture that I wasn't interested and I wasn't into her. Every time she touched me or got up on me, I stepped back. I didn't just stand there and let her. But yeah, I obviously didn't do enough. And I didn't even realize how much I didn't do, because I never expected her to show up here. And not only that, but when I realized how hurt you were and how embarrassed you were, I did feel like shit about that. I *still* feel like shit over that. There wasn't a whole lot of time to tell you that or even show you, but I did." He paused, his dark and intense eyes holding mine. "I never want you to be embarrassed over me or anything I do, but you were, and for that I'm fucking sorry. I really am. And that shit isn't going to happen again."

Some of my anger started to slip away, and I grabbed at it, trying to hold it close, because anger got me through a lot, but what he said was the right thing to say. And he was right. A lot of crap had happened between Saturday and now. So much that I hadn't really even thought about how Aimee had behaved in the bar until she showed up tonight.

"You got anything to say to that?" he asked.

I did. There was a lot I could say. This was the moment that he was giving me to take this whole shitstorm to a rational place, but I didn't say anything, because there was a part of me that was still mad and I still was hurt and I was embarrassed about all of that and more. And I wanted to be a bitch. So I stared back at him in silence.

"Nice," he retorted.

A wave of goose bumps rushed down the back of my neck. I needed to open my mouth. I needed to say something.

Then he moved another step and he was right in front of me. "I'm going to tell you what else, Calla. Like your life hasn't been normal. It hasn't been much of a life."

And that was about when I found the ability to speak. "I have a life!"

"You do? Seriously?" he challenged. "Because I'm pretty sure you've done an awful lot of nothing when it comes to actual living. All you had is your Three F's. What the fuck is that? For real."

Surprise rocked me. "How do you know about them?"

"Tequila, babe. You were quite chatty."

Shit! Of course he'd remember that. And now my embarrassment knew no limit. I'd shared my Three F's, and they were just sad. And damnit, he was right about not really living. But that didn't make it any easier to hear.

"I'm the first guy you've kissed or been with," he said.

"Oh, thanks," I replied snidely, because now I had a firm grip on my anger.

He shook his head. "You aren't getting what I'm saying. That shit isn't something to be ashamed of. All I'm saying is that you haven't let anyone get close and I bet there'd been guys who wanted to and you never saw that. Like I said, you don't have a lot of experience with this."

"Yeah, I think I get that. You've said it enough."

He either wisely ignored that comment or was just generally done with me, because he said, "But there's only going to be so far I'm going to be cool with this shit."

Air leaked out in a slow, low breath as my muscles locked up. "What are you saying?"

"You obviously don't trust me, but that's not even the most messed-up part about this, Calla. You obviously don't think very fucking highly of me if you really think I'd be okay with making plans to hook up with some chick while I had another one in my house, in my bed, wearing my shirt, you also obviously don't know me at all."

This time when I flinched it was for a different reason.

"And that shit burns," he said.

Jax held my gaze while I dragged in deep, pained breaths, and then he turned and walked away. I watched him round the stairs and I heard him head up them. Then I heard a door slam shut.

I don't know how long I stood there before I curled my arms around myself. I squeezed my eyes shut, no longer mad so much as I was confused. How had we gone from me being in the right and him in the wrong, to him being pissed-off at me and shutting me out? I hadn't done anything wrong.

Or had I?

Had I jumped to conclusions? I hadn't heard everything he'd said to Aimee. I'd only heard bits and pieces. And he had apologized for Saturday night. He'd said it would never happen again, but did that make up for what happened? I didn't know. That was the problem. I didn't know.

God knows how long I stood there before I gathered my courage and slowly crept up the stairs. When I reached the landing, I expected to find the bedroom door to be shut, but it was open.

It was the extra bedroom that was closed off. I started to move toward it, to knock on the door, but I stopped short, frozen with indecision. I stood outside the bedroom, hands folded against my chest, but I didn't know what to say if I did knock and he answered. Flecks of red-hot anger still swirled around in me, mixing with the embarrassment and confusion.

My ears strained to hear movement inside the extra bedroom, and I thought I did hear footsteps nearing the door, and I tensed up in expectation of it opening, but after a few moments, I realized it wasn't going to.

Biting down on my lip, I closed my eyes, gave it another couple of moments, and then turned, and because I really didn't know what else to do, I went into the main bedroom and climbed into bed. I scooted over to my spot and waited, watching the clock on the nightstand. Minutes ticked by slowly, and finally I lay down, facing the open door. All of this felt wrong, lying in his bed with him angry at me and me mad at him.

I swallowed, but the knot in my throat went nowhere, and with the next blink of my eyes, my lashes were damp. So were my cheeks. I grabbed the pillow he slept on and tucked it close against my chest as I squeezed me eyes shut. My insides felt so hollow as I lay there, trying to make sense of how everything had gone so wrong and how I was supposed to fix this.

At some point my thoughts rolled into one and I must've fallen asleep and tumbled into a dream where I was in this house following Jax and calling out to him, but I could never seem to get his attention or catch up to him. And when that dream faded, I dreamed I felt his hand on me, skimming over the top of my head, carefully tucking my hair behind my ears. And I felt his lips brushing against my cheek.

It had felt so real that when I woke up, tired and bleary-eyed, I almost thought he'd be in bed beside me. That the spot next to me would not be cold, but it was. I still had his pillow snuggled close to my chest and Jax wasn't there.

I didn't want to get up.

It felt like I hadn't slept more than a few minutes and my eyes ached; my throat and mouth felt too dry. There was an ache in my temples. And I immediately started thinking about what happened between us and with Aimee. In the light of the morning, I could freely admit that Jax had been right. I didn't have a lot of experience with any of this. I didn't know the difference between the different types of relationships, not personally. All I knew was what I'd seen from my friends.

There was so much he'd been right about.

I'd been rightfully upset with him Saturday, but I hadn't given him a chance to explain and he had apologized. And he had no control over Aimee. It wasn't like he'd invited her over.

I squeezed the pillow tight.

Now that the anger had simmered down, I could also admit that I hadn't heard everything he'd said last night, like seriously admit that, and other than not doing enough to deter Aimee's advances, Jax hadn't done anything wrong.

He'd actually stood up for me last night.

He'd apologized and he'd admitted to feeling like shit.

And he'd laid it out to me.

I needed to talk to him without yelling, without overreacting, and I needed to talk to him while listening.

Letting go of the pillow, I climbed out of bed and my bare feet padded over the floors. I went out into the hall. The extra bedroom door was open and he wasn't in there. Turning to the stairs, I headed down them and then through the silent living room and into the kitchen.

He wasn't there, either.

My heart picked up and a sick feeling curdled in my stomach as I turned slowly. Where was he? The townhouse wasn't big enough that I couldn't find him, for crying out loud. My gaze settled on the front windows. I hurried toward them, pulling back the flimsy off-white curtains, and then I peeked through the blinds. The air lodged in my chest as my gaze scanned the parking lot, once and then twice. His truck wasn't there.

It wasn't there.

Jax was gone.

Thirty

$\mathcal{I}$ didn't know what to do or think.

Jax had left and he hadn't said anything. There was no note or text or voice mail on my cell phone. He'd just left the house without waking me and while that didn't seem like a big deal, he'd been really upset.

I sat down on the edge of the couch and I could hear what he said. That he couldn't believe I thought what I did about him and that I didn't know him.

My nails dug into my palms. He'd been really mad, had gone to bed like that or had done whatever he had done in his extra bedroom, and had said some really stupid things. I knew that some words couldn't be unspoken, couldn't be taken back.

Had it gotten to that point?

Was this his way of ending things?

Oh my God.

What if he'd left and wanted me gone before he came back? And here I was, sitting on the couch, still in his shirt, like a dumbass? This was totally possible. He was pissed, because I'd insinuated that he'd been hooking up with Aimee.

I jumped to my feet, hands shaking as I pushed my hair out of my face. Jax was a nice guy. For real. He wouldn't want a scene. Hell, he'd been nice to Aimee up until she called me a name. He'd probably just wanted me gone.

God, he really had defended me and I'd been so . . . dumb.

I darted upstairs, stripped off his shirt, and dropped it on his bed. I quickly changed into mine, pulled my hair into an unbrushed messy bun, and then shoved all my crap into my oversized tote.

As I pulled the zipper closed on the bulging bag, I stopped for a moment and the little voice in the back of my head cautioned me to slow the fuck down, to *think,* because I might be overreacting, but the fear of being here when he returned and him not wanting me here was too much.

I started to leave, but then I wheeled around and I grabbed the shirt of his I'd worn to bed. I don't even know why I did it, but I grabbed it and took it with me as I grabbed my purse and then left his house.

Too much was whirling in my head as I drove, at first not sure where I was going, and then I recognized where my subconscious was leading me.

Mom's house.

I don't even know how I got there, because I didn't remember the drive. The house was silent, warmer than normal because I hadn't been around to turn the air on. I dropped my tote on the couch and then dug out my cell.

There were no calls or texts, and I don't know why I thought there would be. My heart was racing superfast, the insides of my stomach twisting, and I started to call Teresa, because I needed to talk to someone, but she didn't know Jax.

I made a couple of rounds around the couch before I hit Roxy's name on my contacts list. She answered on the third ring.

"Hey," she said, voice throaty with sleep.

I cringed. "I'm sorry. It's early, right? I can call back."

"It's okay." She cleared her throat. "Is everything all right?"

I almost said yes. "No."

"Is it your mom or Clyde?" The sleepiness was gone from her voice.

"No. It's not that. It's . . ." I wetted my lip. "I think Jax and I broke up."

There was a pause and then she shrieked, "What?"

I plopped down on the couch. "I mean, we were together. I guess. We didn't call each other boyfriend or girlfriend. Like we didn't have that talk."

"Girl, I don't think people have that talk. It just sort of happens. You two are totally together."

"He did say he was my man, so yeah, but then last night . . ." I trailed off, feeling sick again. "I don't know. He's gone."

"What do you mean he's gone?"

That sick feeling traveled up my chest. "When I woke up, he was gone and he didn't sleep with me last night."

"Where are you?" she asked suddenly.

"I'm at the house."

"Jax's?"

"No. My mom's house. I just couldn't stay in his place. I don't even know if he wants me there and I didn't want to be there when he came home if that's the case." My hand tightened around the phone. "So I'm . . . I'm at Mom's house."

"Do you think that's a good idea?" she asked, and her voice changed like she was moving around quickly. "With everything going on?"

My heart turned over heavily. Holy crap. "I'm an idiot. I'm like more than just your normal idiot. I'm your uber-idiot. I didn't even think about that." Holy shit, I really hadn't thought about that. I jumped to my feet and then raced to the front door and made sure it was locked. "I'm seriously too stupid to live."

"Okay. You're stressed. Not thinking clearly. Not too stupid to live. Or maybe just a little," she replied, and then her voice sounded farther away. "I got you on speaker. I'm getting dressed. Stay where you are. I'm coming over. Text me the address."

My eyes widened. "You don't have to do that."

"Yes I do. I'm your friend. You're having boy problems and you were almost kiddie-napped a few days ago. This is total friend duty and I'm so coming over. So stay right there, lock your doors, and hide the kids. I'm coming on."

I giggle-snorted. "Did you just quote Antoine Dodson?"

"Maybe." Roxy drew the word out. "I'll be over in like fifteen minutes tops. Okay? I just need to brush my teeth and maybe my hair."

"All right. I'll be here."

I didn't even think twenty minutes passed, which made me wonder where she lived exactly, because I didn't know, and how fast she was driving, but she rolled into the house wearing cutoff jean shorts and an oversized tank top that barely covered her sports bra, and her hair in a messier knot than mine. She looked unbelievably cute, in a way I couldn't hope if I dressed like that.

She was also carrying a white box that she plopped down on the coffee table. "I brought doughnuts. We need fat for this conversation."

I didn't think I could eat without hurling, but it was supersweet of her. She sat on the couch and leaned forward, slipping open the lid and revealing an assortment of goodies. I grabbed some leftover fast-food napkins off the kitchen counter and joined her on the couch.

She'd already demolished half a chocolate-covered doughnut. "Tell me everything."

Exhaling a pent-up breath, I sat beside her and told her every-thing, starting with Aimee, something she was well aware of, and ending with this morning. I even told her about making plans for when I returned to school. When I finished, I surprised myself by picking up a glazed doughnut.

"Okay." She plucked up her fourth doughnut and I wondered

where she'd put the other three. "Let's start with Aimee. The girl does not think any guy will turn her down and I'm pretty sure she has to know he's into you, because everyone knows. Hell. They *see* it."

"See it?"

Roxy grinned around a mouthful of doughnut. "From the minute you showed up, Jax had his eyes on you, literally and figuratively. It's pretty obvious."

Warmth buzzed through me as I mulled that. I liked knowing that people thought that. Then I felt kind of dumb, because it probably wasn't as awesome to other people as it was to me.

"You know I've noticed the way Aimee hangs on Jax," she continued. "I've been perfecting my death glare on her since she hit the bar. Sadly, it isn't working."

I cracked a grin at that as I popped a small bite in my mouth. Her death glare also wasn't working on Reece, either.

"Jax doesn't feed into it. Granted, he could do more to make sure she got the message, but he's not returning the sentiment. Not once. But he's a nice guy." Picking up a napkin, she wiped at her fingers. "It takes a lot to get under his skin. You've seen that. And he's way nice to us females. He was simply raised right."

"He was," I whispered.

"But you also have a right to be pissed with everything."

"I do? Right?"

She nodded.

Thank God, I wasn't completely crazy and a giant screwup.

"I'd cut a bitch if she showed up in the middle of the night at my man's house, if I had a man, but whatever. I'd probably want to cut him, too, and it would take me some time to get over it, but . . ."

I sat back, tucking my knees to my chest. "Here comes the 'I fucked up' part?"

"Yes. And no." Roxy smiled as she twisted toward me. "This is your first relationship and your first fight. Hopefully it's your only relationship, but it's definitely not going to be your last fight. This is probably going to happen a lot of times."

I knew that. I just forgot about that because I was an idiot.

"And you did basically accuse Jax of being an active man-whore while he's been with you, so he's going to be pissed, but he's not going to stop liking you. And if he's does, he isn't worth your time. But that's not how Jax is. He'll cool down and you two will be fine."

Nibbling on my lower lip, I let her words bang around what was going on in my head. Everything she said was reasonable. Hope sparked. "Do you think I should call him?"

"I think you should give him a little time," she suggested. "It's never wrong to let the guy come to you. Right? You both were wrong and you need to remember you weren't the only one who messed up."

"You're right." I sighed, tipping my head back against the couch. "Do you think I should've left this morning?"

"Um . . ." She adjusted her glasses. "Well, if you didn't have all this crazy stuff going on? It probably wouldn't have mattered. Jax probably isn't happy, but he'll see you tonight."

"No. He's going to the party. You and Nick are working tonight, remember?"

"Shit," she groaned, collapsing against the arm of the couch. "I completely forgot."

"Did you make plans, because I'm sure we'll be fine tonight."

Roxy laughed. "I'd need to have a life to have plans, but I was planning on lying out, reading, and eating junk food into the wee hours of the night like any hot, single twenty-two-year-old."

I laughed.

Her smile widened and then our eyes met as she reached over and patted my arm. "Everything's going to be okay."

I smiled back, and even though I'd been on the verge of a complete breakdown this morning, I felt a lot better, like everything really would be okay. "Thank you."

"If not, I'm sure your mom has a little black book around here and she probably knows someone we can hire to kick his ass."

"Oh my God," I said laughing.

She giggled as she curled up against the arm. She was so tiny, she barely took up half a cushion. "We'll call that Plan B."

"What's Plan A?"

"You show up at his place wearing nothing but a sleek black trench coat and when he opens the door, you jump his bones."

Laughing again, I shook my head. "I like Plan A."

"And I bet he would, too."

Wednesday night, I was a bundle of nerves. My stomach was full of them, and I could barely hold down the late lunch I'd grabbed with Roxy after we visited Clyde, which was nothing more than half a chicken salad sandwich.

For a crap ton of girlie reasons, I'd taken my time as I got ready for my shift as Roxy waited for me. I put waves into my hair, expertly applied my eye makeup, and glided on a shade lighter than crimson on my lips. I knew the guys from the bachelor party would probably hit the bar at some point; meaning Jax would be with them.

I hadn't tried getting a hold of Jax until I'd gotten into my own car and Roxy was in hers. I'd sent him a quick text saying that I hoped I'd see him tonight. Then, because I'd been scared like a little girl with a monster in the closet, I'd dropped my phone in my purse and turned the music up. I didn't check to see if he responded until I got to the bar.

No response.

"Not a big deal," I'd told myself as I climbed out and headed in, but my heart was pounding.

There'd been no response at six.

There'd been no response by nine.

And to make everything all the more screwed up, Aimee was

conspicuously absent from the bar. Granted, she could've finally gotten the message, but my heart hadn't slowed down, and I was beginning to think that maybe Roxy had been wrong this morning. Maybe he'd changed his mind.

"You feeling okay?" Roxy asked after I handed over an appletini I wasn't sure I made correctly.

I was feeling totally paranoid. "Yeah."

She watched me carefully. "You haven't heard from him, have you?"

Clamping my jaw shut, I shook my head.

"Calla, I didn't—"

The door opened and my gaze swung toward it sharply and my heart jumped like it had done every time tonight. It wasn't Jax.

Katie strolled in, rocking heels that could double as stilts. She didn't teeter in them. Nope. She sashayed herself over to the bar, tapping a woman on the shoulder. "You're in my seat."

I sighed.

Roxy laughed softly.

The woman must've been accustomed to Katie, because she muttered something under her breath as she exited the seat. Katie dropped down, hitching the sparkly tube top up over her breasts. "Whiskey. Straight up."

My brows rose. "Bad night?"

Her eyes rolled. "June—one of the girls—is trying out a new routine. Belly dancing. The girl can't even grind to hip-hop without sending men running through the door like their wives just showed up."

"Then how does she strip?" Roxy asked.

Even Nick appeared to be listening from where he stood a few feet over, on the other side of the ice well.

"Who knows? She's got great tits and a nice ass. Anyway, I just can't deal with it."

I grinned as I poured her the shot and then slid the glass toward her. Not a drop spilled.

"Aw, look, you're like a real bartender now," Roxy remarked.

Nick snorted.

I shot them both a look and then the door opened. My head swiveled toward it so fast I was surprised I didn't get whiplash. My breath caught and I almost dropped the whiskey bottle.

Reece was the first one in, wearing worn jeans and a button-down shirt, looking fine.

"Damnit," groaned Roxy. "Seriously. I thought for sure that to-night I wouldn't have to deal with looking at him."

I glanced at her.

Katie snorted as she raised her glass. "I'd take several long nights with him." Then she downed the whiskey in one gulp. "Holy guacamole," she gasped.

Damn.

A couple of other guys strolled in. I saw his older brother, and I was surprised to see Colton with them, but it made sense. The husband-to-be was a cop. My heart was really dancing now, because Jax had to be with him.

Katie looked over her shoulder. "See! Even June ran them out!" She threw up her hands.

The door swung closed and the laughing group of men moved to an open table near the pool tables. My heart sank to my stomach.

Jax wasn't with them.

"They were at the club, right?" I heard myself ask.

"Yep. Didn't get out of hand." Katie inspected her nails for a moment and then she looked up, her blue eyes filled with sympathy.

Oh no.

I took a step back, bumping into Sherwood, who, like a damn ghost, had gotten behind the bar and was doing something with the glasses.

Roxy watched me, brows knitted. "Calla . . ."

I seriously doubted that Katie had fallen from the pole and developed super-stripper abilities, but she was staring at me like she knew exactly what I was stressing over.

"Jax was with them," she said.

Not a surprise. I knew he would be.

Roxy moved closer as she scanned the bar. Her gaze caught Nick's and he moved to help a customer.

"Okay," I whispered, and I wasn't sure how she heard me over the noise.

Katie sucked her glossy pink lip in. "The guys were having a good time, but Jax didn't look too happy and then maybe a half an hour before I came over, Aimee showed up."

The worst kind of feeling erupted in my chest.

"It was really different, because Aimee has never stepped foot in the club."

Of course not, because Aimee was there, because Jax was there.

"About ten minutes after she showed up, Jax left." Katie's eyes met mine. "And Aimee left, too, right behind him. I'm not saying they were together. But she was *literally* right behind him."

Oh my God.

"Calla." Roxy touched my arm. "Aimee is like a step up from a stalker. You know Jax didn't ask for her to show up there."

I looked at her, but I wasn't sure I saw her. The hollowness from earlier was back. "He hasn't returned my text I sent him before we came to work. I sent him a text. He hasn't responded."

"Okay. This doesn't mean anything," Roxy said quickly.

Really? Aimee showed up last night. He ran her off, but the conversation was questionable. We got into a huge fight. He didn't sleep with me, was gone when I woke, and he hadn't tried to contact me all day and he didn't respond to me. None of this was looking good.

My throat burned.

Something powerful bled out of me as I stood there, like bleeding out from a well-placed stab wound that was meant to kill you slowly.

"You two are more than friends. You haven't said that to me, but I know," Katie said as she tapped her finger on the side of her head. "I *know*."

"Katie," Roxy sighed.

"I told you that your life was going to change," she went on. "Remember? I told you. I didn't say it would be easy."

I stared at her.

Luckily, a whole crew of people rolled in, rushing the bar, so I didn't get a chance to respond to Katie, and I threw myself into filling orders in a way that bordered on obsessive. I didn't even notice when Katie left.

Roxy tried to talk to me several times, but I avoided her, because I knew she wanted to talk about Jax and I couldn't do that. I couldn't do it.

I made three Long Island iced teas and I smiled. I laughed. I took money. I made tips. And then I made a ton of Jäger bombs for Reece's table since Roxy was suddenly helping Gloria.

He didn't mention Jax.

I didn't, either.

By the time he and the guys left it was almost an hour before we closed for the night, and all I wanted to do was go home and crawl into bed. It probably wasn't the smartest thing to do. At one point during the evening Roxy mentioned I could stay with her, but I needed to be alone. I was willing to take the risk to just be alone, because whatever started bleeding out of me earlier was still doing it.

I glanced at the doors one more time that evening and my lips trembled and the icy pain in my chest filled the hollowness twisting up my insides. I could feel it building inside me. I was going to break and that would be the icing on top of the fucked-up cake.

Whirling toward Roxy and Nick, I took a deep breath. "Will it be okay for me to go ahead and leave?"

Roxy nodded. "Yeah. We got this, but—"

"Okay. Thank you." I rushed over to her, grabbed a quick hug, and then skirted around her and Nick. I snatched up my purse from the office and when I was heading back out, Nick was coming around the bar.

"I can give you a ride," he suggested.

"No," I said quickly, tipping my head to the left. "I have my car. You don't need to do that."

Nick glanced at Roxy, and I took that as my sign to get out before I ended up riding home with one of them, and then I'd also end up crying all over one of them. I hurried out of the bar and the smell of rain was thick in the night air.

I stopped, dug my phone out of my purse, and smacked the button. My screen popped up. No missed calls. No missed texts.

I let out a dry, harsh laugh as I lifted my head, dropping my cell back in my purse. My fingers itched to call him as I stared at the full parking lot across the street. Of course, Jax's truck wouldn't be there, because he'd left mere seconds before Aimee did, and he hadn't showed at Mona's tonight. He hadn't tried to get in touch and he hadn't responded to my call.

I shouldn't have let Jax in.

I shouldn't have fallen for him.

No. That wasn't true.

Wiping under my eyes, I walked across the parking lot. The Wal-Mart down the street was open. I was going to put some of the money I'd been hoarding toward one of the handheld baskets full of junk food and ice cream. Then I was going to go home and eat until I didn't care. Then tomorrow . . . well, I didn't know yet. I was a few feet from my car when I heard my name called.

"Calla?"

My eyes widened and my fingers jerked around the strap of my purse as I spun around, my back to the road, disbelief ringing through me as my gaze darted wildly and landed on the source.

She was standing under the flickering parking lot light. Even in the low light, I could see her washed-out, bottled-blond hair with dark, dark roots, her gaunt face and frame. Clothing was wrinkled. An old T-shirt hung from slim shoulders. Jeans were skintight but billowed out from the knees.

She took a step toward me, and I moved a step back. Her smile was tight and brittle. "Baby . . ."

I couldn't believe it.

Mom was standing right in front of me, looking strung-out and calling me baby. I was literally rooted to where I stood, absolutely dumbfounded. I didn't even know what to say to her, because there were a thousand things I wanted to scream at her, but none of those things came out of my mouth.

"Are you okay?" That was what I said.

She opened her mouth, but whatever she said was cut off by a roaring sound, like an engine gunning it. My head jerked and I looked behind me. A four-door car with tinted windows sped into the parking lot, stopping under the sign. A window rolled down on the driver's side.

Tiny sparks speared into the night.

There was a popping sound.

Mom shouted, and I thought she screamed my name, but there were more popping sounds, like a dozen corks being pulled at once, and more sparks. I dimly realized it was gunfire just as glass exploded all around me. Metal pinged close to me, too close, and my purse slipped out of my fingers as a scream built in my throat.

The sound never left me, because my breath was punched out of me as a strange burn lit up my stomach, sharp and sudden, intense and stealing my breath.

I looked down as I wobbled back, bumping into a Jeep. I thought I heard shouting, but my head was spinning in a funny way. My hands shook as I pressed them against my side. I felt something warm and wet.

"Mom," I croaked as the bones left my legs. I didn't remember falling, but the back of my head hurt, but not as bad as my stomach. I was staring up at the sky, but the stars were moving, like they were raining. "Mom?"

There was no answer.

Thirty-one

$\mathcal{W}$hen I opened my eyes again, I wasn't staring at stars or even a bright light. It was a ceiling, a white drop ceiling with a soft, dim light fixture. The rest was shadowy and as my gaze tracked to the opposite wall, I saw a pale blue curtain. My thoughts were slushy and I felt funny, like I was floating, but I knew I was in a hospital. There was a dull sensation of something in my right hand and as my gaze slowly trekked to where it rested on the bed, I could see an IV.

Definitely a hospital.

Oh yeah, that was right, I'd been *shot*. Actually shot with a gun. Seriously.

God, my luck sucked.

I started to sit up, but the dull ache turned sharper, piercing across my belly, and the air punched out of my lungs at the sudden-ness of it. The walls spun like a bad acid trip.

Movement from the left of my bed stirred the air around me and a gentle hand landed on my shoulder. I blinked the room back into focus as my head was guided back against the surprising stack of pillows.

"Awake for a couple of seconds and you're already trying to sit up."

The heart monitor registered the sudden increase in my heart rate as I turned my head to the left. My beat skipped unsteadily.

Jax was sitting in a chair next to the bed and he looked . . . he looked like crap. Dark smudges bloomed under eyes that were normally the color of warm whiskey. The shadow of stubble along his jaw was thicker than normal.

But he smiled when my eyes met his and he said in a gruff voice that was thick, "There you are."

"I took your shirt."

His brows furrowed together. "What?"

I don't know why I said that. I could tell there were some really sweet drugs rolling through my system right now. So I was going to blame them. "I took your shirt when I left your house, because I wanted a part of you if you decided you didn't want to see me anymore."

He straightened in his chair and his lips parted as he stared at me.

"I feel funny," I admitted. "I think I've been shot."

His expression tensed. "You were shot, honey. In the stomach."

I wetted my dry lips. "That sounds bad." I knew that could be bad, come to think of it. We had, like, an entire week or something dedicated to gunshot wounds in one of my classes.

"You were actually lucky. The doctor said the bullet missed all major vital organs. Clean in and out," he explained, voice low. "There was some internal bleeding."

"Oh. That's definitely bad."

He tilted his head to the side and closed his eyes. "Yeah, hon, that's bad."

Jax sounded so worried, so . . . I don't know, out of it, that I felt the need to reassure him. "It doesn't really hurt."

"I know," he murmured. "They said they were giving you pain meds. I . . . damnit. Calla." He leaned forward, getting so close to my face with his that I caught the faint scent of cologne. "Oh, honey . . ." He shook his head and the darkness in his eyes bordered on a tortured intensity. He placed his hand on my left cheek and I felt the tremor that coursed through it. "I know you probably have questions, but there's something I gotta say, okay?"

"Okay."

"When you woke up yesterday and I was gone, it wasn't what you thought."

The last twenty-four hours started to replay in my head, coming together like a slow-moving picture book.

Yesterday had sucked ass.

"I had to go downtown for a fitting for the wedding and I had to leave early. I should've left a note, but I was still pissed-off about that night before. I left thinking you'd be there when I got back and we'd talk, but Roxy called me."

I frowned up at him. "She . . . she called you?"

"Yeah." His gaze moved over my face and then down, and I swore he was watching my chest move, as if he was reassuring himself that I was breathing. "She called me on the way to your house, because she was worried about your safety. I knew you left, and yeah, I was angry about that. I thought we were on the same page." He coughed out a dry, harsh laugh. "I'd called Reece, letting them know you were at your house. They had a car on you."

I hadn't even noticed that. Granted I wasn't the most observant person *apparently;* so maybe I should rethink that career in nursing.

His thumb smoothed over my jaw as his gaze settled on mine again. "I spent all day yesterday mad at you, at us, at myself."

Well, these were things I really didn't want to hear right now, but I sensed that whatever he needed to say, he had to get it out of him, so I remained quiet as I watched him.

A muscle twitched at the corner of his eye. "All day," he said, shaking his head again. "A whole fucking day wasted on stupid shit and I should know better. I tasted that kind of regret, you know, with my sister. Spending so much time being angry with Jena that when she was gone, I couldn't even begin to tally up all those missed hours I could've spent being there for her."

"Jax," I whispered, my heart squeezing.

He rested his weight on his other arm, careful not to disturb the bed or me, though I wasn't sure how much I'd feel at this point. "The point is, I was angry, but it didn't change how I felt about you or what I want from you. I'm not perfect. Far from it, and I was just being a dick. I could've called you and made sure you understood that. I could've returned your text. I didn't. I thought maybe we both needed some space to cool down so that when we did talk, we could do so. And last night, when I went to the club, Aimee showed up."

Now I remembered that, too, and that sick feeling rose, more muted than before, and for that I was grateful.

"That pissed me off even more. I left. She followed me outside. We had it out in the middle of a fucking parking lot. And I swear, even the messiest breakup with someone I was in an actual relation-ship with was easier than talking to her. She won't be a problem anymore, but damnit, it was more wasted time. After that, I went back to my place. I planned on coming back to the bar to get you before closing. I didn't think you were going to leave early, but I was coming for you. I just never made it."

When he spoke next, the hoarseness to his voice, the very real pain in it, got to me. "I was getting ready to leave. I had my keys in my fucking hand, Calla. I was almost out the door. I was thinking about texting you and my phone rang. It was Colton. I almost didn't answer, because I knew they still could be partying and I wasn't in the mood for the shit, but I did answer. And he told me that he'd just been called by one of the deputies, that there had been a shoot-ing at the bar and someone was injured. That was all he knew, and fuck, babe, my heart . . . it did what it did when I got the call from my parents. It was a sick as fuck feeling, like I wasn't standing but I was. I tried calling you and when you didn't answer, I knew—I just *knew,* because if there had been a shooting at the bar, you would've answered the phone if you could."

"I'm okay," I whispered fervently, because I thought he needed to hear that, but it went largely ignored.

"When I got to the bar I saw your car shot the fuck up and you weren't there. Neither was Roxy . . ." He seemed to gather himself as his hand shook against my cheek. "It was Nick who told me it was you. He'd been outside. Got to me before the police did. All he knew was that you'd been shot and that you hadn't been awake when the paramedics arrived. Calla, I . . . I can't even put into words what I felt in that moment or what I felt getting my ass to this hospital. All I knew was that I fucked up yesterday." His chest rose with a deep breath. "I could've lost you. Fuck, I could've really lost you. And if I didn't get this chance to be talking to you right now and if you were taken from me and I lost the opportunity to spend yesterday with you, being with you, loving you, I'd never forgive myself for that. So you know what, Calla, I'm going to forgo any bullshit right now. And I hope you're with me on this, but even if you aren't, I gotta get it out there and I'm not going to regret saying this to you."

I was starting to breathe heavy, not in a taxing way, but I knew something was coming, and my throat was burning and not because it was dry. So were my eyes. They felt wet, because two words really stood out among all the powerful words he spoke. *Loving you.*

"I gotta tell you that I love you, Calla," he said, and I was surprised the heart monitor didn't catch the fact it felt like my heart had stopped for a moment. "No bullshit. I do. I love the way you think, even if it's annoying as fuck at times and even then it's still cute. I love that there's a shit ton of things you've never gotten to experience and that you're going to get to experience them with me. That I have that honor. I love your strength and everything you've survived. I love your courage and I love that you make shit drinks, but no one cares, because you're so damn nice."

A soft surprised laugh burst from me and my words were wobbly when I spoke. "I do make some shit drinks."

"You do. It's true. I'm pretty sure your Long Island iced teas could kill people, but that's okay." His lips curved up on one side as his gaze held mine steadily. "I love your sense of humor and the fact you never ate grits before. There's so much I love about you that I know I'm *in* love with you. So, honey, you can have all my shirts you want."

My breath caught again, and I opened my mouth, but there were no words at first, because there was so much I wanted to say to him. I wanted to list the things that I loved about him, but all I could say was "I'm in love with you."

Jax drew in a sharp breath as his eyes flared wide, and I realized he didn't think I was going to say that. He was an idiot if so, but he was the idiot I loved, so I said it again, and then he moved, dipping his mouth to mine, and that kiss . . . oh God, I recognized that kiss, because he'd kissed me like this before and it was full of just as much love as it had been every time he'd kissed me like that.

And then, maybe because Jax loved me—was *in* love with me— and I was *in* love with him, or maybe because I'd just been shot and was on some really good meds, I started crying.

Jax murmured something against my lips and then he caught the tears with his thumbs. Because there was no way for him to get in this bed with me, he did the next best thing. He scooted the chair as close as he could and stretched his upper body toward mine, circling an arm around my shoulders as he rested his cheek on the pillow next to mine. Some time passed before the waterworks ceased and I found myself smiling at him. I managed to get my right arm to work and I had my hand on the back of his neck, my fingers slowly threading through his hair as he explained in great detail how he planned on showing me when I got better just how much he loved me, so much detail I was sure my face was as red as a tomato, but boy did I have something to look forward to.

More time passed, enough that I wondered how he got the staff to let him be in my room, but I didn't care. He was here and that was all that mattered. Both of us were getting tired when he said,

"There's some things we need to talk about, but it can wait until you're out of here. Okay?"

At that moment, he'd said everything that I needed so desperately to hear him say, so I could wait to hear whatever else he wanted to tell me. I nodded and my eyelids felt droopy and it was then, after being awake for God knows how long, it hit me.

"Oh God." I started to sit up again, but Jax was there, gently keeping my shoulders down.

"What?" Concern poured into his voice. "What's wrong?"

I grasped his wrist with my right hand. "Mom. Mom was there, Jax. She was in the parking lot. Was she hurt?"

He stared at me a moment and then shook his head as his brows slammed down. "Mona was there?"

"Yes! She was outside waiting for me, but a car pulled up and then someone starting shooting. Was she hit?"

"Okay. You need to calm down." He curled his hand around my cheek again. "This is the first anyone is hearing about your mom, honey. No one knows she was there."

Confused, I stared at him. "Wait. She was there. I talked to her. She called me baby. She was there, Jax."

He didn't say anything.

My mind raced. "She was there when they started shooting, and I heard the car pull away—"

"The police found the car they believed was used abandoned a few miles away from the bar," he explained. "I don't know who it's registered to, but they think it was probably stolen. I'm sure we'll get more info later."

"But . . . but that doesn't make sense."

His eyes met mine and then he kissed my cheek. "Honey, I . . . I'm sorry."

I started to ask him why he was apologizing, but then I knew. I got it. He was apologizing because my mom had showed up at the bar, had seen me and I had seen her, people who were pissed at her had opened fire and I got hit, and . . . and Mom had to have known that.

Blinking slowly, I shook my head. "She had to have known I was hurt."

He smoothed his thumb under my lip, and I felt the disbelief piling up on me. I remembered calling out for her and there being no answer. "She left me there, Jax, in a parking lot, bleeding from a gunshot wound meant for her. She *left* me."

"Honey," he said softly. "I don't know what to say."

Because what the hell did you say to something like that? My own mom had left me bleeding in a parking lot. Good God, did she care at all? My lower lip trembled, and Jax moved back in, his fingers spreading across my cheek as he turned my head toward his.

His lips met mine and he said, "I love you."

I closed my eyes as I nodded slightly. He pressed his forehead against mine, holding me the only way he could until the exhaustion finally caught up with me, washing away all the very good and all the very bad.

Over the next two days while I was kept in the hospital for observation, my room became a very happening place. Detective Anders had been in and out more than once; so had Reece. Roxy and Nick had showed, the former sneaking me in doughnuts that I wasn't allowed to eat yet, but I hadn't the heart to tell her and the latter had been broodier than ever. I felt responsible for that. He'd offered to take me home and maybe if I'd taken him up on that offer, Mom wouldn't have attempted to approach me and I wouldn't be lying in a hospital bed going out of my mind with cabin fever.

The shooting had hit the news, and somehow Cam had heard about it or Teresa had kept calling my cell and Jax had finally answered—I didn't know which or if it was a combo of both, but my friends—God love them—were back in town, having driven up the moment they'd heard I'd been shot. They were staying at a hotel a few blocks from the hospital and they were playing the whole thing cool. Jase had even joked around how I kept summer break interesting for all of them, but I could tell that they were seriously worried, especially when Teresa had said that she wanted me to come home, back to Shepherd as soon as possible. But I also didn't have the heart to tell her that wouldn't solve anything.

Turned out I was in the same hospital as Clyde. He was well enough to be up for short periods and that meant he was in my room, cussing up a storm and usually getting taken back to his room before he had another heart attack.

Throughout all of this Jax rarely left my side. He took time off at the bar, and Nick and Roxy really stepped up to help out. He had some kind of hot guy Jedi mind control over the staff, because he stayed in my room throughout the night and I knew that was a big no-no, but I didn't question it. Those long hours in the middle of the night, when I couldn't sleep and all I wanted to do was get the hell out of there, he was there. We talked about important stuff, like what we'd fought over, and then we talked about stupid things like where to go in case of a zombie apocalypse or what our favorite reality shows were. I admitted that I still watched *Toddlers & Tiaras,* might have a wee crush on *Property Brothers,* and he was a fan of *Kitchen Nightmares* and *Bar Rescue,* and had more than just a wee crush on Robbie Welsh from *Shipping Wars.* When he'd started talking about his favorite football team, I dozed off, and when I woke up some time later, he'd been asleep in what had to have been the most uncomfortable position known to man.

He'd fallen asleep in his chair, but his head had been resting on arms that were folded on the bed beside me. His cheek had been turned to me, and I had hit an exceptional level of creeper, because I didn't know how long I'd lain there and watched the way his lashes fluttered in his sleep or just stared at his face.

It was like that for two nights, and on the morning of day three,

I was being discharged to go home and take it easy. The nurses had given me permission in the morning to wash my hair while Jax made the trip back to the house to grab some clothes for me. Sponge baths weren't cutting it, but the angry little scar on top of the faded scars and the twinge of pain if I turned too quickly or breathed too deeply told me that I needed to be careful.

Even now I couldn't believe I'd been shot.

My friends were still in town and I had no idea how long they planned on staying, but I knew they were going to swing by tomorrow since I'd been ordered to not do crap today, so I guessed they'd turned their second trip into a mini vacation.

As the doctor checked me over, and Jax was back, waiting by the door, the thoughts I'd been avoiding since the first night in the hospital crept into my mind.

Mom.

I closed my eyes as the doctor took my blood pressure.

My own flesh-and-blood mother had left me lying in my blood. That hurt like having a rusty nail driven into your heart. Repeatedly. No matter what excuses she had or how scared she might've been, there was no justification for that, and that was such a hard wake-up call to go through, because I didn't understand until the moment I realized she'd left me that I still fostered a little bit of hope that one day she'd be like she was before the fire, the deaths, and the drugs.

There was no hope now.

I'd done the right thing when I'd spoken to Detective Anders. I told him that I'd seen my mom, and he hadn't looked too happy to hear that and I wasn't too thrilled to even be talking about it.

Right now, I couldn't let myself think about her, because even though getting shot sucked and being forced into debt wasn't too great, either, I was alive and I had a lot to be thankful for.

I glanced over my shoulder at Jax as the doc slipped the pressure cuff off. He winked, and I grinned.

Almost dying really did put things into perspective.

I was cleared to go and we made a pit stop at Clyde's room before heading to Jax's townhome. From what we learned, Clyde would be released by the end of the week, maybe even tomorrow if the tests were positive.

When we got to Jax's townhome, I made it to the couch and plopped down there, tired from a freaking car ride.

"You okay?" Jax knelt in front of me.

I nodded. "Yeah, I'm just tired. Not sleepy."

He didn't look convinced. "Your stomach doesn't hurt?"

I smiled. "Only if I do something stupid."

His eyes searched mine and then he rose, placing one hand on the arm of the couch. He brushed his lips over mine. "You think you can eat something? They said bland food, right? Like chicken noodle soup?"

"That would be nice."

He drew back, his eyes still clouded with worry. He grabbed one of those ultracomfy blankets off the back of the couch and draped it around me. "Stay there."

As he moved away, I clawed my way out of the blanket and grabbed his arm. "Thank you."

An eyebrow rose. "For what?"

"Everything and anything."

His lips twitched and then he swooped down, kissing me once more. "There's nothing you need to thank me for, honey. If anything, it's the other way around."

Confused, I frowned. "How so?"

Before he answered, he eased that frown right off my lips and created a series of shivers low in my belly. "You're sitting here on my couch and there's nothing I could do that will outdo that."

Wow. My chest got all mushy, which was just another reason to be thankful for him. When he left to go fix the soup, I snuggled deep into the blanket and then we ate soup while watching a marathon of

Property Brothers, which made me want to buy an old house and have them renovate it into pure awesomeness. And the fact that they were hot twins might have a little to do it with, too.

It was early in the evening when there was a knock on Jax's door. I was stretched out on the couch, my back to Jax's front, and had almost dozed off. I craned my neck and saw the frown on his full lips.

"Not expecting anyone?" I asked.

He shook his head as he carefully slid his arm out from under my shoulders. "Stay here, okay?"

Nodding, I gingerly sat up after he virtually climbed over me. He stalked around the couch, heading to the door, where he peered through the peephole. "What the fuck?"

Unease exploded in my gut and I jerked to my feet, pulling tender skin. I placed my hand over the wound. "What is it?"

His head cocked to the side as I heard a muffled voice coming from the other side of the door. I had no idea what was being said, but several moments passed and then Jax wheeled around. My jaw dropped open as he went to a hutch in the dining room, opened it, and pulled out a handgun. The unease spiked to a whole new level.

Even though I knew he had a gun and I'd seen it before, it still came as a shock whenever he whipped it out. "Jax . . ."

"It's okay," he said, stopping by where I stood. His free hand wrapped around the back of my neck and he tipped my head back, kissing me quickly. "Just precautionary."

In my book, there was nothing okay about a gun being a precautionary measure, and my heart was pounding as he went back to the door, throwing the lock. My muscles tensed as he opened the door, holding the gun in plain sight.

"I don't give a fuck who you are, make one move I don't like, and you won't be walking out of this house," Jax warned in a low voice as he stepped aside.

There was a beat of silence and then a response in a male voice.

"I'd like to think I'm smart enough not to cause you to use the gun in your hand."

"And I'm smart enough to know that you probably got my place fucking surrounded and if I didn't let you in, you would've found your way in."

What the fuckity fuck was going on?

A deep masculine chuckle resonated. "That may be true, but I'm not here to cause any trouble, Jackson. I'm here to end it."

Those words were like ice being drilled down my spine.

Jax stood there for a moment and then he nodded curtly.

A second passed and then a man walked into the house. Hell, he glided in. Dressed in a deep gray suit that was obviously tailored to fit his narrow hips and broad shoulders, hair shiny black and combed back from a high forehead and cheekbones, he reeked of money and power.

The man stopped just inside, his dark brown eyes settling on me, and I couldn't suppress the shiver that accompanied his acute, sharp stare.

Cursing under his breath, Jax closed the door and faced us. Shoving the gun in the back of his jeans, he sighed. I was rooted to where I stood, breathing shallowly as the man waited until Jax returned to my side and wrapped a careful, protective arm around my waist.

The man drifted forward and stopped a foot from us, extending a hand. "Calla Fritz, it's a pleasure to finally meet you."

My gaze dipped from his handsome face to the hand in front of me. I gave him a weak handshake and immediately dropped his hand. "Hi. Um, and you are?"

He smiled then, flashing perfect straight, white teeth. "Some call me Mr. Vakhrov."

Mr. what the what? I had no idea how to spell that or even repeat what he said.

"But other people know me as Isaiah."

Thirty-two

My eyes widened until they felt like they were going to pop out of my face. Holy crap. This was Isaiah? And he was standing in front of me, in Jax's house? And Jax had let him into said house?

Panic dug its icy fingers into my side as my head swung sharply toward Jax. His arm tightened. "It's fine," Jax reassured me. "Isaiah never does his own dirty work."

My gaze bounced back at him.

Isaiah's smile widened, and that really creeped me the hell out. "There are times I make an exception. Rare, but it does happen."

Uh, that really didn't reassure me one bit.

"May I?" Isaiah jerked his chin at the worn recliner, and when Jax nodded, he sat.

I almost laughed, because he looked so out of place sitting in a chair that had definitely seen better times, wearing a suit that probably cost more than every piece of furniture in the living room. But laughing would've made me sound crazy, and I was feeling pretty crazy. The man that my mom owed potentially millions to and the man who might have something to do with the new hole in my body was sitting across from me.

Jax guided me down on the couch, keeping his arm around me. He got to the point. "What's up, Isaiah."

He tilted his head to the side and the smile was still there, but it never really reached his eyes. The legendary Isaiah was younger than I imagined for a drug and God knows what else overlord. Maybe in his mid-thirties? "First," he said, unbuttoning his suit jacket, and I could feel Jax tense beside me, but Isaiah folded his hands together, "I would like to apologize for Mo."

Mo? Who was . . . ? "The guy who tried to kidnap me?"

"I'm not a fan of the word *kidnap,* my dear."

Really? What did he want me to call it?

"My associate was supposed to bring you to me and not under duress, but I needed to speak with you. Unfortunately, he was a little overeager when it came to his task."

"Overeager?" I repeated dumbly.

"He hit her," Jax said, voice clipped. "I wouldn't call that overeager."

He nodded in agreement. "And that has been dealt with. I abhor violence against innocent women."

My brows crept up my forehead. Innocent women versus . . . ?

"I needed to speak with you about what has been happening. He was just supposed to bring you to me. That was all, and I sincerely apologize for his actions that evening," Isaiah said. "As I've said, that has been taken care of. Just as another problem of yours has been . . . or will be shortly . . . taken care of."

My spine stiffened and I whispered, "Which problem?"

Isaiah watched me for a moment and then sat back, folding one knee over the other as he draped his arm along the recliner. "I have many businesses, Miss Fritz, some you may not know about and others you might speculate on, and I have even more responsibility. Furthermore, I do have an image to maintain and whenever my image is threatened, well, I do take those situations fairly seriously."

I found myself nodding even though I wasn't quite sure where this was heading. I got what he was saying without really saying it. In other words, he had legit businesses and not so legit, as I'd already known.

"A certain associate of mine was responsible for a very large transaction. He outsourced some of that responsibility to people who frankly should not have been trusted," he explained, his dark gaze holding mine. I totally knew who he was talking about—Mack, Rooster, and my mom—and I also knew what that transaction was. "Ultimately, when this transaction fell apart"—again, in other words, crashed and burned in the form of Greasy Guy stealing the heroin—"my associate was the one responsible for it and he was well aware of how much I loathe when things fall apart."

I shivered, knowing I never wanted to be on the end of Isaiah's disappointment.

"Not only has my associate failed in securing the transaction, he has also impacted my image. Not forty-eight hours go by without a member of our esteemed police forces breathing down my neck." That easy, albeit cold smile slipped off his face and his expression became glacial. "And once my associate realized that, he became fairly noncommunicative, and from what I can gather, figured the best way to rectify this situation was by threatening you, an innocent in all of this, and taking measures into his own hands. Apparently, he thought that taking out those to whom he'd outsourced his own responsibility would somehow make me happy. He was wrong."

Oh. Wow.

"So you're telling me you've had nothing to do with Mack messing with Calla or her getting shot a few days ago?" Jax asked.

"Like I said, Jackson, I abhor violence of any kind against innocent women. My associate was desperate. He messed up. He continued messing up, making it very hard for me to continue with my business dealings without interference, and of course, their impact on you, Miss Fritz. I am sincerely grateful to see you sitting here today. I know it could've ended in a much more sad way."

Again, I found myself nodding and wondering if this was all

really happening. I wasn't sure why Isaiah would care what happened to me, and honestly, he probably didn't and it was more a case of not getting dragged into what Mack was doing.

"With that being said," Isaiah continued, smiling in that creeptastic way, "my associate will no longer be a problem."

"What?" I blinked.

Jax's arm slid off my shoulders and his hand ended up around mine. "Are you saying what I think you're saying?"

He inclined his head. "What I'm saying is that he will no longer pose a problem. You will no longer have to worry about anyone showing up at Mona's or at your home or about random drive-bys."

I stared at him.

Jax squeezed my hand.

I totally knew what he was saying, again without really saying it. Mack would no longer be a problem for me and since Isaiah was apparently never a problem in the first place, the fallout from what my mom had done would finally settle around me and for the most part, I'd still be standing.

But I had to know. "Does that mean that Mack—"

"We understand," Jax cut in, squeezing my hand again, and I shot him a look, but he was focused on Isaiah. "Is that everything?"

Isaiah's gaze shifted toward him and a beat passed. "It is."

"Then, I hate to be rude but . . ."

His lips quirked. "I've always liked your bluntness, Jackson."

"I'm assuming that's a good thing."

Isaiah simply smiled as he stood, buttoning his jacket. "I wish you both good luck in the future. I'll see myself out." He strode past the couch, but stopped in front of the door and faced us. "One last thing, Miss Fritz."

My heart thudded against my ribs. "Yes?"

"If you see your mother or hear from her, please let her know that she is not welcome in this county or this state," he said softly. "As I said, I do not like loose ends."

Then he was gone.

"Oh my God," I whispered.

Jax stood swiftly, bent, and kissed my forehead before striding toward the front door. He checked the outside then locked it. Turning to me, he stretched his neck and sighed. "Well then."

I shook my head slowly. "I don't know what to say. He basically just told me everything is going to be okay and then threatened my mom, right? I mean, that is just what happened?"

"Yeah, it is." Jax walked over to me and crouched down so we were eye level. "I was not expecting that."

I coughed out a laugh and then cringed. "Me neither. I mean, wow. That was like something straight out of a mob film. Do you—"

His phone rang from inside his pocket. Straightening, he reached in, looked at the screen, and then cursed before he answered it. "Yeah?"

I watched him turn and walk toward the living room window. "Serious?" He thrust his other hand through his hair and then let his arm drop. "Well, can't say I'm too torn up about that."

My brows knitted. What in the world was going on now? I grabbed the blanket, rolled it into a giant ball, and held it to my chest.

"Okay. Yeah, we need to talk. Tomorrow's good. I got to head back to the bar tomorrow night." He turned to me. "Yeah, Calla is doing good. She'll be fine." Another pause. "All right, talk to you later, man."

Jax hung up, and I waited as patiently as humanly possible as he made his way back over to me. "Well, that was quick. Like really quick."

"What?"

He sat down, got his arms around me, and carefully tucked me into his chest, blanket ball and all. Tilting his chin down, his eyes met mine. "That was Reece. You'll probably end up getting a visit tomorrow morning from his brother."

That familiar burn of anxiety slithered through my veins. "Why?"

His eyes searched mine for a moment. "They just found Mack's body out on a county road. Bullet to the head. Execution-style."

"Holy . . ." I breathed. "Oh my God." He said nothing as he smoothed my hair back from my face, and we were quiet for a long time as that really sank it. I didn't know how to feel. Mack shot at me—had shot me. He'd threatened me. And he probably didn't care if I lived or died as he tried to "fix" things with Isaiah, but still, he was dead now and I didn't think it was right to feel okay with that. So I didn't know how to feel. "That was fast," I said stupidly.

"Yeah."

"So Isaiah really did—"

"Don't finish that." He pressed a finger against my lips for a second. "We don't want to know everything and we don't want to carry it down that road, Calla. It is as simple as that. Plausible deniability, and fuck, you aren't going to have that shit on your conscience. Okay? That's not on us."

I lowered my gaze. "I know it's not on us. Mack's not where he is because of me. It's because of what he did. I just . . . I don't know how to feel about this."

His lips brushed my forehead. "Honey, you don't need to feel anything except a bit of relief. You're safe. And fuck, that's all that matters."

I nodded and then it really sank in. I whispered, "It's over."

His arms tightened around me as he brushed his lips over my cheek. "Yeah, honey, it's over."

I woke up to the most pleasant sensation in the world, so good and so yummy I thought at first I had to be dreaming. But I wasn't. Oh no, this was a dream, but the kind you lived and breathed.

Blinking open my eyes, I bit down on my lower lip as I dipped my chin and looked down the length of my body.

Warm, chocolaty brown eyes, full of playful wickedness, met

mine. "Morning," he grumbled in husky voice that rumbled all over a very, very sensitive spot.

It had to be in the middle of the night or way early in the morning, but it was still dark beyond the window. The light on the nightstand was on and the blankets had been drawn off me and the shirt of his I'd worn to bed—the very one I had stolen days earlier—was pushed up around my waist. The band of my undies was inched down my hips, far enough that there was nothing between his mouth and me.

"Morning," I gasped, and before I could say another word, he swept up over me and kissed me so softly, so tenderly, that a fuzzy little ball formed in my throat. He lifted his head, kissed me again, but this time on the tip of my nose, and then he was moving back down me.

Hooking his fingers under the band of my panties, he tugged them down until they were off and lying somewhere in the great unknown. From between my thighs, he peered up at me through thick lashes. "You promise to behave?"

"Me? You're asking if I promise to behave?"

He sucked his full bottom lip between his teeth and then he said, "You need to stay still, baby. I don't want you messing with your stitches." His gaze dipped to the intimate part of me and then he licked his lips. Holy granola bar, I almost came right there. "I should be waiting until you're a hundred percent, but I'm hungry for you and I couldn't wait."

Tight shivers rolled over me.

He looked up again. "You going to stay still?"

I really couldn't make any promises, but I nodded. His eyes held mine for a moment longer, and then he stretched up and placed a kiss just above my belly button, on the scarred skin.

That didn't even faze me.

Panting, I watched him trail that mouth around my navel until his tongue flicked out, circled, and then slipped in. I gasped again as he continued on, kissing and licking like he was seeking to taste every curve and swell. He took his time on my stomach and by the time he reached the area between my thighs, my head fell back on the pillow.

He touched me first, a soft sweep of his finger and I willed my body to stay still, but there was a slight jerk of my hips that did nothing to my stomach. His finger moved again, circling and then slipping in.

I moaned as I clenched the sheet underneath, but he wasn't done as he slowly moved in and out. My breathing quickened when I felt his mouth against my inner thigh, then his tongue. He was slow—so damn slow that every caress of his lips and flick of his tongue claimed me.

A strangled sound escaped me when his tongue dipped in, replacing his finger, and my hips kicked once more. Before I met Jax, I never thought I'd be into something like that. It just seemed too foreign to me, so intimate, but good God, I'd been wrong. This was amazing. Maybe it was because it was Jax. Maybe all men had a tongue that was literally a mass weapon of assured seduction. Either way, he drew out every gasp, every throaty moan and broken whimper until I was beyond making sounds and breathing in general.

He shifted, tossing an arm over my hips, holding me in place. He seemed to sense that I was close. Tension and heat built in my core, then exploded in a flash, a burst of rioting sensations that frayed every nerve ending with a hot rush of pleasure. Aftershocks of the tight tremors rocked me as he slowed and then lifted his head, kissing my inner thigh and then just below my navel. As he rose, I reached for the band on the old shorts he wore. He sucked in a breath as my fingers brushed the hard ridge of him through the nylon.

"Calla," he warned.

I wetted my lips. "I can return the favor."

"That's not why I did that."

"I know." I rolled carefully onto my uninjured side and found him there, his body braced on one arm. His mouth was so close that I went ahead and kissed it, and was quickly caught up in the taste of him and of me mingled together.

Jax was a kisser. That was something I'd learned right off the bat. He liked doing it, thoroughly enjoyed it, and was damn good at it. And as he got into it, I reached between us again. Sex might be out of the question for the next couple of days, just to be safe, but that didn't mean I couldn't use my hand. Or my mouth.

I tugged on his shorts again, but he caught my wrist and he growled against my lips. "Calla, hon . . ."

"I'm not an invalid, Jax. I want to do this."

He didn't move for what felt like an eternity and then he took my hand and slipped it under the band of his shorts. Well, good to see he was definitely on board.

His body shuddered as my hand wrapped around his thickness and he let go of my wrist, hooking his fingers on his shorts. He got them down his thighs as I kissed his neck.

Easing up, I pushed him down with my other hand and he stared up at me from where he was sprawled on his back. My gaze tracked over him as I slowly moved my hand. God, he was gorgeous. Every stretch of rough skin, every tightly rolled muscle, and every imperfection.

His hips jerked as my thumb smoothed over his tip, and I smiled, remembering him showing me that and how much he liked it.

"God, Calla," he groaned as he reached up, tangling his fingers in the ends of my hair. "You're driving me crazy."

I grinned. "I haven't even done anything."

"Oh, you're doing plenty enough. You're—" His words ended in a deep groan, because I'd slid down and lowered my mouth over him. "Fuck, Calla . . ."

There'd been a slight twinge of discomfort from the sliding part but nothing major and it sure as hell didn't deter me from what I wanted to do for him. My mouth slid over him, and the hand in my hair clamped down on the back of my neck. His thumb moved along the base of my skull as I lifted my head, licking and sucking until his hips were moving in small, barely controlled thrusts. His hand tightened on my neck and I could feel the flutters in his base, the slight pulses. His breathing turned ragged, and as I went as deep as I could, which probably wasn't very much, he let out a hoarse shout.

At the last moment, he dragged me off him and up. The stitches in my side protested only a little. My hand was still around him and I felt his release as his back bowed and his hands tightened on my arms. I watched his muscles flex and roll, the cords stand out in his neck, and the tension flicker across his striking face as his hips slowed and then he settled, breathing heavily.

"Damn, Calla." He pulled me up and laid that mouth on mine, kissing me so deeply I felt the warmth between my thighs and in my veins increasing as he eased me onto my back. The kiss slowed and he rested his forehead against mine. "You're perfect, you know that?"

"No I'm not." I smiled, though, because I liked that he thought that.

"Whatever. If I say it, it's true." I laughed softly as he drew away. "Be right back," he said, and he was only gone for a moment, returning with a damp cloth. He cleaned us both up, and when he finished, he curved his body around mine.

"Sleepy time?" I asked.

His chuckle shook me. "Uh-huh."

I smiled into the darkness. "What time is it anyway?"

"Don't know," he replied, kissing my shoulder. "Don't care."

"So you woke me up in the middle of the night just to . . . ?"

"Damn skippy."

Laughing again, I snuggled into his warmth. "I love you."

His chest rose sharply against my back and then he pressed languid kisses against my throat and cheek. "I love you, too."

"Are you sure you're going to be okay here?" Teresa asked as she pulled back from giving me a hug. "We can hang out. Jase is cool with that."

I glanced over at where Jase was leaning against the wall just inside the townhouse. For the last hour, he'd been eyeing Teresa like he wanted to have *her* for dessert. So I doubted he was cool with that. I smiled at her. "I'm fine. I'm just going to chill out and watch TV the rest of the night and I don't think Jax is going to work an entire shift. I think he said he'd be back around midnight."

"We'll be up late," Jase replied. "So if you need anything, just call."

"I bet you will be," I replied dryly.

Grinning, he pushed off the wall and circled around Teresa's waist from behind. He winked at me as he dipped his head, kissing her temple. "Come on, sweetheart, let's hit the road."

Teresa folded her hands over his arms as he started to walk backward, toward the door. "Don't forget about tomorrow! If you and Jax are up for it, we all can go out to eat before we head back. All right?"

"I won't forget." I followed a rather desperate-looking Jase to the door. They'd been here for hours after Cam and Avery had left to go do whatever adorable couples do on their down time. "It should be fine. You guys have fun."

Jase's grin turned downright wicked. "We will."

Teresa's eyes rolled as he all but dragged her out of the door, but at the last moment she sprang free, ran back to where I stood at the threshold, and hugged me again. "I'm glad everything is going to be okay," she whispered, and then she whirled around on her good leg.

Teresa took off and jumped from the top of the short set of cement steps. Jase, who was at the bottom, cursed as he caught her and staggered back a step. "Jesus, you're going to give me a heart attack."

She giggled as she wrapped her legs around his waist. When he turned to head to their car, she waved at me over his shoulder. I wiggled my fingers back, thinking they were going to give Cam and Avery a run for their money.

I closed the door and made my way back over to the couch. Kind of tired from spending most of the day with my friends and Jax, I yanked the blanket around me and curled up on the end of the couch. It didn't take me long to drift off to sleep and I did so, as cheesy as this sounds, on a cloud of happy thoughts.

Today had been good, great even. It had been normal—my new kind of normal—full of laughs, smiles, conversation, and kisses, lots of sweet kisses and then not so sweet. I could get used to this and I would. It would be hard when I went back to Shepherd, but we'd make it work. That cloud of happiness would keep on being all fluffy and awesome.

I didn't know how long I slept, but I came to, lured out of sleep by the soft sweep of cool fingers along my cheek. Blinking open my eyes, I expected to see Jax beside me, thinking I'd slept longer than I had.

But it wasn't Jax sitting next to me.

Heart leaping into my throat, I sat up so fast I pulled at the tender skin on the side of my stomach and winced. "Oh my God."

Mom was here.

Thirty-three

I stared at her for what had to be a freaking hour before I found my ability to speak. "How did you get in here?" I asked, craning my neck to see if Jax was anywhere, but we appeared to be the only two people in the house. Maybe that wasn't the best question to start with but I was caught off guard, absolutely floored.

She drew away from the couch and stood. That's when I noticed she was wearing the same clothing I'd last seen her in, and when I inhaled deeply, my heart . . . God, it ached like someone had reached inside and wrapped their fist around it. She smelled like someone who hadn't seen the inside of a shower in *days*.

God.

Rubbing her left hand down her right arm, she glanced around. "I let myself in."

"How?"

"The back door. It has one of those old locks. No dead bolts. I picked it."

"You . . . you picked a lock?" When she nodded, I just stared at her. "You know *how* to pick a lock?"

She nodded again as she stopped rubbing her arm. Her hand stayed around the inside of her elbow, though. "Baby, I don't have—"

"You left me." Snapping out of my stupor, I rose to my feet as her gaze swung back to me sharply.

Mom blinked rapidly. "I need to tell—"

"I don't care what you have to tell me." And that was true. As terrible as it was, it was completely true. "I got shot. Did you realize that?"

"Baby—"

"Stop calling me that!" I shrieked, my hands balling tight. "Answer my question, *Mom*. Did you realize I'd been shot?"

Her cracked lips opened, but she didn't speak. Instead she ducked her chin as she started scratching her right arm.

Hurt swelled in my throat like I'd swallowed a bitter pill. I stared at her, *my mother,* and it was like seeing a ghost. "You knew I'd been shot and you left me in the parking lot, bleeding. I was in the hospital for two days. I had internal bleeding. Do you even care?"

Chin jutting up, her watery gaze met mine for a fraction of a second and then her gaze darted away. "I care about you, Calla. I love you. You're my daughter. I just . . . I . . ."

"Love getting high more?" A fissured laugh broke out of me. "Story of my life and your life. Drugs have always been more important."

She didn't say anything at first and then she said what I knew deep down in my heart she would say. "My babies are gone, Calla. Kevin and Tommy, they—"

"They're dead!" I shouted as tears pricked at my eyes. Air rattled in my lungs as everything . . . *everything* came out. "They are dead, Mom. They have been dead for a long time. And you know what else, Dad has been gone for a fucking long time, too. You're not the only person in this whole damn world who lost them. And no amount of shit you put in your body is going to bring them back."

Her legs backpedaled like she could escape what I was saying, but this wasn't the first time I'd said this to her. But I knew it was going to be the last.

And I was on a roll. Years and years of frustration, disappointment, and hurt balled up inside me, exploding over like a shaken bottle. "You stole from me, Mom. Do you even remember that? You drained my account, racked up over a hundred thousand dollars in debt in *my* name, and now I have to take out financial aid to finish school!"

Mom flinched.

"Not only that, but you almost got me killed. Like really dead—dead as in I'm totally fucking dead, Mom." She recoiled again, but it couldn't be like this was the first time this crossed her mind. "Clyde had a heart attack because of the people pissed at you who were messing with me. He almost died."

She moved her mouth, but I didn't hear her.

"My entire life has been turned upside down. Again."

Shaking her head, she looked around Jax's living room as stringy, ratted strands of hair knocked off her gaunt, sallow cheeks. "I thought . . . I thought I could get the money back."

"Yeah, by stealing heroin from Isaiah. Well, that didn't work out, did it?" I was breathing heavy, my heart pounding with fury and a ripe kind of sadness. "You know, he was here. He said you can't even be in this state. Do you know what that means, Mom?"

"I'm leaving," she rasped, her gaze flickering away from me, over the walls. She was as twitchy as a cornered mouse. "I got some friends in New Mexico I'm hooking up with. I wanted to see you before I leave."

She was leaving, like really leaving.

Okay.

Wow. That wigged me out more than I thought it would, which was stupid.

I figured this would have to happen. The only other option was her staying, which equaled certain death, Mack-style. I watched her move in a slow, random circle in front of me, digging at her arm with her dirty nails. I pressed my lips together, cutting off what would've been a sob.

"You're high right now, aren't you?"

She picked up her pace in the little circle she was making. "I'm not high. I just needed something, baby. Things aren't good."

I closed my eyes and drew in a deep breath. So much anger rose inside me, eating away at me like a cancer. And it was a poison that had been inside me, pecking away since I was a little girl. That was nothing new, but as I opened my eyes and watched her scratching her arm as she trekked a path in the floor, I was suddenly too exhausted to hold on to the more razor-sharped edges of the anger. After tonight, I was never going to see my mom again. She would be gone. Over the last couple of years it was like she was dead, but now it would be even more real. Before, I knew she was here or at least in the general vicinity of here, but after tonight, I'd have no idea where she'd be. If she got hurt or something worse happened, there'd be no Jax or Clyde to call me. I'd never know. She would be seriously *gone*.

I sat down, exhaling.

"I'm sorry," she said.

My gaze lifted and she was closer now, still pacing and still scratching at what were most likely track marks. I tensed up. "I know."

She stopped, looking at me like a deer in front of a speeding semi, and then she started walking. Frowning, I twisted around and watched her make her way toward the dining room table I doubted Jax had ever made use of.

There were a couple of sheets of paper.

With trembling hands, Mom swept off the paper and she turned to me. She started forward, stopping a few feet behind the couch. "This is . . . yours."

Brows knitting, I stood and came to her. "What is it?"

She wiped at her sweaty forehead with the back of one emaciated arm. Temperature was set to ice box in his house. "It's your life back."

I stared at her, having no idea what she could've meant by that. Then she extended her arm, holding the papers out to me. Preparing myself for anything, I took them and quickly glanced at them.

Then I really took a real long look at them.

The papers turned out to be only three sheets, and one was longer, folded, and as I unfolded it, my breath caught. "Mom . . ."

"It's yours. The house," she said, and as I glanced up, she was running both hands down the sides of her cheeks. "There was never a loan on it. I never took a loan out against it. I . . . I just left it alone."

I hadn't known that. I assumed there was a loan she was many months behind on and the place would be foreclosed on at any minute. The fact that she hadn't used the house as a source of additional funds blew my mind. I looked down at the papers to make sure the words hadn't changed. Nope. Still a deed. Still signed by Mom and some guy whose name I didn't recognize.

"All you have to do is sign it, but it's done." She moved away from the table and then stopped. "The house is yours. Sell it. You'll get at least a hundred grand for it."

My hands shook and it felt like the floor moved under my feet. I couldn't even process this. The house was mine—if this was legit—the house was mine. I could sell it, make back almost if not all of the money to pay off the debt. My life would be back where it was, but better, shinier, because I had so much more in my life now.

I looked up at her, the ball of emotion back again, but this time the size of a basketball in my chest. "Mom, I don't know what to say."

"Don't thank me. Whatever you do, don't thank me." She swallowed hard. "You and I both know I wouldn't deserve it."

My lower lip trembled. "Mom."

"I love you, baby." She took a step forward, got within arm's distance of me, but then backed away quickly. "I know it doesn't seem like that, but I do love you. I've always loved you. I always will."

I closed my eyes as I inhaled shakily.

"You make me so proud," she whispered.

My body rocked and my eyes shot open. She was standing there, staring at me as she slowly walked backward, away from me, and I knew I could hug her. It would be the last time I saw her in maybe forever. I should hug her. She was my mom and as much as I hated her at times, I loved her. I would always love her.

But she didn't give me the option.

Mom walked away, going to the back door, and I knew this was her way of saying no touching. She was leaving and with my heart firmly lodged in my throat, I watched her open the door—the one she had picked the lock to open.

And then I thought of Mona's.

"Wait," I called out, holding the papers close to my chest. And I knew it wasn't so much my concern for the bar that had me calling out to her. I was delaying the inevitable. "What about Mona's—the bar?"

Her dark brows pinched. "What about it, baby?"

Okay. I doubted she had forgotten about it. "The bar, Mom. What are you doing with that? If you've left me the house, did you sign over the bar, too?" Because that bar only passed to me in case of her death, and I sure as hell didn't want to say or think that.

Mom shook her head. "Baby, I don't own the bar anymore. I haven't in . . . a year or so."

The floor shifted again. "What?"

"I sold it for . . ." She barked out a dry, weak laugh. "That doesn't matter. I sold it and it's in good hands, baby."

The hair on the back of my neck rose and a weird rush of goose bumps raced across my skin. I suddenly thought I should be sitting.

"And you're in the same good hands. I always thought that . . . you and Jackson would be perfect for one another. He's a good boy. Yeah, a really good man. He loves strong and he cares, really cares," she went on as I reached out, bracing myself by putting a hand on the back of the dining room chair. "He's been good for the bar. He'll take care of it like he has been."

I drew in a sharp breath. "Jax owns the bar?"

Mom nodded and her hand tightened on the door handle. "I don't want that kind of life for you. You're going to be a nurse, right? You're going to make a difference in people's lives. Good things. That's your . . . it's your path."

I blinked. Wait. What? "How did you know that?"

She opened her mouth and then her stringy hair bounced around her cheeks again. "I gotta go, baby. Be good. I know you will, but be good and . . . and be happy. You deserve that."

Then she was gone, slipping out the door like a wraith, and I stood there, caught between too many emotions to even move. Mom was gone. She was really gone now, and before she'd left, she'd given me the world.

And she had also rocked a very large part of it straight down to its now-cracked foundations.

I felt like an idiot.

Gathering up the papers Mom had given me, I took them with me to the couch and picked up my phone off the coffee table. I wished I had my car. Since the back window had been shattered and there were a few unnecessary holes in the body of the car during the Pennsylvania version of the O.K. Corral, my car was in the repair shop for the second time around, and I doubted these repairs would be a freebie. None of that mattered right now, though. I just wanted to get out of here. I needed to do something, because my head was spinning and there was pressure building in my chest.

It was almost eleven. Jax should be home soon, and as I eased up my grip on the phone, I considered texting or calling him. Instead, I dropped the phone on the coffee table.

I was so damn unobservant and stupid.

All of it made sense now and I should've known that Mom hadn't had anything to do with the bar anymore. The condition it was in, the way it was running smoothly, and all the legit paperwork in that office screamed that someone else was in control. And Clyde had told me that I didn't need to worry about the bar. Obviously not.

Mom had sold it to Jax and he had never told me. Neither had Clyde, but I wasn't sleeping with Clyde, I wasn't in love with Clyde; therefore Jax's lack of sharing on that minor little detail seemed way more important.

I didn't know what to think. I didn't even understand why he didn't tell me, especially after the first time I was in the office going through papers thinking I had every right to do so when apparently I had no right whatsoever.

Scrubbing my hands down my face, I stared at the deed to my mother's house—now my house, my ticket out of the debt Mom had forced me into. That fixed the major problem looming over my head, the one I never forgot but tried not to dwell on because it would drive me crazy, but now . . . now there was *this*.

Jax had lied to me.

I didn't know what to feel about any of this and I was feeling too much, because Mom was here and she had left for good, and Jax had kept something so big from me. My trust was rocked. It was shattered, barely held together.

If he lied about *this,* if he kept *this* from me, what else had he lied about or kept from me? I didn't think that was an unreasonable question. From past experience I knew that when people kept things from others, there was more hidden in their depths.

Hell, I was a prime example.

My gaze flickered to my phone as I lowered my hands, then I leaned forward, snatched it off the table, and did something that I'd never done in the past.

I kind of felt bad for calling Teresa, because it was way late and I was sure I might have interrupted some one-on-one time with Jase based on his wrinkled clothing and the current tangled state of her hair.

But like a true friend, she answered the call. Not only that, but she and Jase had driven back over to Jax's house and picked me up, taking me back to the suite they were sharing with Cam and Avery.

It was past midnight, the suite door was open, and I was sitting there with them. Curled up in one those uncomfortable as hell floral armchairs, I told them what had just gone down.

Avery looked floored.

Cam, who was sitting behind her on the floor with his arm around her waist, his long legs cradling her body, looked none too happy with the latest revelations—the whole Jax owning the bar I thought would one day be mine part.

Teresa had a thoughtful expression on her face.

Jase was leaning against the headboard of the bed and his face was unreadable, but he was the first to really say something other than "what the fuck" and "holy shit."

"People have their reasons for keeping some things a secret," he said. "I'm not saying that justifies any of it or whatever, but you got to hear him out."

Cam rolled his eyes. "Bud, that's not something you keep a secret."

"Yeah, I know all about things that shouldn't be kept a secret." The look Jase sent Cam had my radar going overboard. There was something in their exchange. "But people have their reasons. He seems like a pretty cool guy and he didn't keep it from her her to just be a dick."

"Jase is right," Teresa said before Cam could respond. "I mean, it isn't cool that he kept this from you. It's important, but there has to be a reason."

I nodded as my gaze dipped to my phone, which rested in my lap. About twenty minutes ago, Jax had called. I hadn't answered, but I texted him back, and all I said was that I was with Teresa. He'd responded, but I hadn't allowed myself to check it. He'd called again, and then I'd turned the ringer off. Not the most mature thing to do, but I still had no idea what to say to him, what to even think.

But Teresa and Jase had a point. We all had our secrets and we all told our lies. I was woman enough to admit that I had told some major lies to my friends and they'd heard me out and they'd forgiven me.

I just needed to get my head on straight. Too much had happened in too little time. I was doubting everything.

"He really cares about you," Avery said, and my gaze moved to her. I wondered if she was a mind reader and a gorgeous redhead. "When you were hurt, he wouldn't leave your side."

"I know," I whispered.

"No," she said. "I mean, when you were out of it, we heard about how he acted from your friend Roxy. He threw a fit when they wouldn't talk to him about your status because he wasn't family."

My heart turned over. "What?"

She nodded. "He almost got kicked out. It was one of his cop friends that finally got him calmed down and talked to the doctors. He really does care about you, Calla, so there's got to be a reason for—"

A knock on the hotel door interrupted her, causing my back to straighten. It was way late, so this was odd. "You guys expecting someone?"

Cam disentangled himself from Avery and rose to his feet. "We're not, but I'm willing to wager a kiss as to who it probably is."

Teresa's eyes widened on me, and my pulse started pounding. I unfurled my legs and gripped the arm of the chair.

Cam peered through the peephole. "Yep. I was right."

Oh wow.

I started to stand, thinking I probably should've answered the phone or whatever, because now I had a sinking suspicion of who it was.

Cam opened the door and stepped aside, revealing who stood in the doorway and that my suspicions were totally correct.

Jax stood there, and the look on his face, the tension in the thin line of his lips and around his dark eyes, told me he knew that I *knew*.

That I knew everything.

He stalked into the room as Cam closed the door, muttering, "Come on in."

Jax ignored him, his gaze fixed on me. "We need to talk."

My heart was pounding as I stood, clenching my cell phone in my hand. "Yeah, we need to talk."

"Am I the only one who is wondering how he knew she was here, in this hotel?" Cam asked as he walked back over to where Avery was.

"There's not too many hotels around the hospital," he replied, still looking at me. "And I have friends who can find shit out for me very quickly."

"Well, that's a little creepy," Cam murmured under his breath as he extended an arm, helping Avery to her feet.

Jax's shoulders were thrown back, tensed. "I know."

I blinked. "Maybe we should—"

"I'm sure they already know, too, because you went to them and didn't come to me, so they're going to hear this, too."

Oh double wow.

Cam and Avery stopped where they stood by their suite door, caught sneaking out of the room. A quick glance at Jase and Teresa told me they were wishing they had popcorn to share.

"Jax, we can go outside."

"I came home and you weren't there," he said, and then he went on. "Considering everything that has been going on, that really fucked with me. Yeah, I know we're all cool, but still a text message or something giving me a heads-up would be appreciated."

"Now. Wait," I said. "I did tell you I was with my friends."

"*After* I came home and I saw those papers on the coffee table," he corrected, eyes flashing almost black. Damnit he had a point, so I kept my mouth shut, and he continued. "You saw your mom. So right off the bat, I know that's got to have fucked with your head and I also see that she left you the house. That's good. I'm happy to see that."

I glanced around the room, feeling my cheeks heat as my friends watched with avid interest, including Cam and Avery.

"But I know that's not why you're sitting in this hotel room instead of in my bed right now."

Oh. My. God. My face went completely red.

Teresa pressed her lips together as her eyes lit up.

Time to nip that direction of conversation in the bud. He wanted to have this out in front of my friends, we were going to have this out. "You own Mona's. You've owned Mona's for over a year, and you never thought you should tell me this?"

His chest rose. "I planned on telling you. I was going to—"

"Is that what you were saying while I was in the hospital, about needing to talk to me about something? You've had time to tell me. Tons of time before that, like when I first showed up and was rummaging through the office!"

Jase's head swung back to Jax, as in, the ball was now in his court.

He didn't respond immediately, which was okay, because now I was gearing up for a whole onslaught of words and questions and maybe a little bit of cursing, but when he spoke, for the second time in one night my entire world was rocked.

"I've known you for over a year," he said, and the tension drained out of his shoulders, as if some kind of weight were lifting off him. "I'm not talking about knowing you through what Clyde or your mom has told me. I knew you. I'd *seen* you before you even knew I existed."

I opened my mouth as confusion poured into me. "What?"

"The first time I saw you was last spring, over a year ago. You were outside of your dorm, walking to class," he said, and I suddenly felt like I needed to sit down. Everyone in the room had faded to the background. It was just him and me. "I was there with your mom. It wasn't the last time. Every couple of months, when Mona would be sober for a day or two, she wanted to see you. So I would drive her down to see you, because I know . . . *I know* what it's like to not get that second chance. You know that. So I'd bring her down. Once you were outside of another building talking to her." He jerked his chin at Teresa. "You were there with another guy. The three of you until Jase showed up."

Oh my goodness, my legs felt weak. My thoughts cycled back and there was a good chance he was talking about Brandon.

"The last time was in the spring. You were sitting on a bench by yourself outside what I think was the library. You were reading. And each time I brought your mother down there, she never followed through. She didn't have the courage to try to make amends for any of the shit she pulled, but she wanted to. It just never panned out, because you always looked so happy." He exhaled slowly. "You always looked so damn happy. Smiling. Laughing. Your mom didn't want to mess with that."

I took a step back, finding it hard to stand still.

"Each trip, she talked about you and it was real, you know? She wasn't high or messed up. It's how I knew about everything. It wasn't Clyde and it wasn't when she was drunk, even though sometimes she would talk about you then, too, but she really talked about you when she was sober. She found out you were majoring in nursing and she wasn't surprised by that. She told me once that you'd grown close to the nurses when you were in the hospital."

I closed my eyes against the unsteady rush. That was true, what Mom had said. I had grown close to the nurses, and now I knew how Mom had known about my major. She'd been to Shepherd, with Jax.

"All those times she came, she came to talk to me?" I asked, and my voice sounded incredibly small.

"Yeah, she did. She recognized her faults and fuckups more than I think anyone gets," he said, and when I opened my eyes, he was still watching me. "She never wanted the bar life for you. She knew that the likelihood of her being around for a while wasn't good. When she knew I'd take the bar off her hands, would make it good, she sold it to me. She didn't want you to even have it as an option."

I really needed to sit down.

He wasn't done. "I didn't tell you about this, because I didn't know how you'd feel knowing your mom had come to see you. You two weren't on great terms, and explaining this makes me come off as a creep, so it wasn't something I was really looking forward to doing, but I was."

"Totally not a creep," whispered an awed Teresa.

His lips twitched for a moment and then he refocused on me. "Each time I saw you, I felt like . . . I felt like I knew you a little bit better. I never talked to you but seeing you always smiling or laughing . . . or being peaceful . . ." He shook his head, and my heart spasmed. "There's something about that . . . it drew me in, Calla. Fuck. I fell for you before you even knew my name."

Oh, holey moley. Tears rushed my eyes and his face blurred.

"And I should've told you about Mona's. I was going to that day in the office, but when you'd said you'd sell it, I didn't think you'd care. And then when I realized that even though you never said it, I knew the bar meant a lot to you." He took a step forward, his progress tracked by everyone in the room. "I didn't know how to break that to you. I've honestly been struggling with the idea of keeping it. The place gave me purpose when I got back home after drifting, but it didn't feel right. Not with you here. Not with me really knowing you."

I swallowed, but the lump was stuck in my throat.

His eyes searched mine. "I love you, Calla. Me owning the bar doesn't change that. If it did, then I don't want a fucking part of it. All I want is you."

Staring back at him, I couldn't get any words out of my mouth. Everything he said whirled around in my head. I was overwhelmed.

"Calla," he whispered.

I shook my head, at a loss for what to say.

"Say something, honey. I don't want to give up on you, but you've got to say something to stop me from walking out that door."

So many things I wanted and needed to say rose in my throat, but nothing came out. It was like having performance anxiety. I was frozen where I stood and it was so quiet in the room I swore everyone could hear my heart pound.

Jax expelled a rough breath as he held my gaze and then he turned and walked away. He walked right out that door, and I stood there, staring at his retreating form, watching the door swing shut.

I didn't say anything.

I seriously stood there.

And I watched him walk away.

Thirty-four

"*O*h God," Avery said, sitting down on the edge of the bed. She stared up at me. "He fell for you before you even knew his name?"

Teresa was also staring at me with wide, watery eyes. "Calla . . ."

I still couldn't breathe, couldn't think of anything to say. I was a statue.

Jase turned his head to me, brows raised. "If I liked guys—you know, swung that way, I'd get naked after that."

I blinked. Um.

"And I'd put a ring on that," Cam added, moving to where Avery sat.

I blinked again. Uh.

Teresa snorted. "I'm in a happy, love-of-my-life relationship, so Jase, take no offense to what I'm about to say, but I'm about to do all those things. My God, girl, that was beautiful. That was real. And that hurt to hear and you just let him walk right out of here."

I did.

I let him walk right out of here.

"Calla," Teresa called softly.

Shaking my head, I looked at her. "What am I doing?"

"I don't know," she said. "But I think you know what you need to be doing."

I did. Oh God, I really did know what I needed to be doing. The bar. The secrets. The whatever. It didn't matter. "I'm so *fucking* dumb," I said.

Cam's brows flew up.

Then I took off, clenching my cell phone like it gave me extra ability to run as if a *T. rex* were chasing after me. I threw open the door without looking back and tore out into the hallway. Of course, Jax wasn't there. I ran down the hall, passing the elevator, and hit the stairwell. They were on the third floor and I'd never run down steps as fast as I did at that moment and not break my neck.

By the time I hit the lobby and ran past a startled-looking hotel clerk, the stitch in my side was spreading across my whole stomach. I barreled through the doors like something straight out of a cheesy Hallmark movie and sucked in oxygen.

"Jax!" I shouted, shooting out from underneath the hotel awning. My eyes scanned the parking lot, not seeing his truck. The place was packed in the front. "Jax!"

There was no answer from the ground or from the stars. I slowed at the edge of the lot, breathing deeply as I turned and jogged down the aisle, my gaze darting over the cars. Had he left? My heart sank as I stopped again, bending over and pressing my hand against my side.

Well, pressing my *cell phone* against my side.

I'd call him. God, I was so dumb. I could've just *called* him. Straightening, I went to tap on the screen when my heart stuttered to a stop.

"Calla."

Wheeling around, I almost dropped my phone when I saw Jax standing several feet away from me. I didn't stop to think about doing anything or turning into another dumbass statue.

My sandals almost flew off my feet as I took off again, running straight toward him and I didn't stop. Nope. I smacked right into his hard body and threw my arms around his shoulders, holding on so tight I could've doubled as a Snuggie.

Jax didn't move for a second and then his arms swept around me as I said, "I love you. Keep Mona's. It's yours. And yeah, you should've told me, but I still love you. I do."

He drew back so I could see his shadowed face. When he didn't say anything, I started rambling. "I'm dumb. Okay? I have this history of doing dumb things, so I just stood there. But in my defense, a lot of crazy shit has happened lately and you just admitted to seeing me way before I even knew you existed. That alone is a lot to process. And you said that you fell for me before you even met me, and now things kind of make sense to me, because I just couldn't figure out how you could be so accepting of me when you just met me, but you—"

He cut off my stream of words with his mouth and there was nothing gentle about this kiss. It was rich and deep, all-consuming, and it wasn't a slow seduction. The kiss seared me, claimed me, and as his tongue swept over mine, I moaned into his mouth.

When he did break the kiss, his lips brushed mine as spoke. "All you needed to say was that you loved me. That was all."

A laugh choked out of me. "I love you, Jackson James. I love you. I love—"

His arms tightened again and his deep growl rumbling out of his chest silenced me. Our gazes locked. "I need to be in you. Now."

My eyes widened.

"No time to go home." Then he took one of my hands and started walking back toward the hotel entrance.

"Jax?"

He looked down at me, his eyes full of hunger. "No time."

Well then. I was all aquiver.

We ended up back in the hotel, standing in front of a wide-eyed hotel clerk. "I need a room," Jax said, smacking down his wallet. "Now."

Maybe tomorrow I might be embarrassed, because the clerk's eyes swept from me to Jax and then to the arm cinched tight around my waist. All the older man did was smile and nod.

We got a room.

On the first floor.

As soon as he kicked the door shut behind us, Jax was on me. His hands spread across my cheeks, tilting my head back, and he kissed me deeply. When we broke apart, I reached for his shirt, but he caught my wrists.

"Before this goes any further, we need to be clear on a few things."

I nodded. "Okay. Name them."

"I'm sorry for not telling you. I've messed up. You deserve to be angry with me."

I heard that. Got it. "You're right, but I've told a worse lie to my friends for a lot longer time. You're not the pot and I'm not the kettle. I wish you did tell me and seriously, I do care about Mona's and you were right, more than I thought, but it's yours, Jax. It's not mine. It's never really been mine, but in a way . . . it still kind of is, because of you. It is."

The hardness in his jaw softened. "You really mean that, because if you—"

"I mean it." I wanted to touch him. Get naked. Show him how much I meant it. "It's yours."

He closed his eyes briefly and then said, "There's just one more thing. I love you, but if you're going to stay with me, you got to be all in. You got to be with me, Calla. When something happens, you don't shut down. You come to me. We talk about it. Okay?"

Pressing my lips together, I nodded. "I'm all in."

"That's—"

"But that doesn't mean I'm not going to do dumb stuff. That I'm always going to know how to react or that I won't need time to digest stuff," I rushed on. "And I do a lot of dumb stuff on a regular basis. Like all the—"

"Hon," he murmured, smiling. "I get that."

I cracked a grin. "We're good?"

Instead of saying we were, he showed me just how good we were.

Our clothes went off in record time. Turned out he had protection in his wallet, to which I raised my brows.

"Never leave home without one," he joked.

I shook my head. "Kiss me already."

We were naked and on the bed, our hands and mouths greedy. He paid extra attention to the new scar and then his head was between my legs, my fingers digging into the silky strands. Right before the tension exploded in my body, he climbed up me, settling between my legs.

"I'll be careful," he said, nipping at my lip.

"I don't want you to be careful."

His mouth kicked up on one corner. "That's one of those dumb things."

"Shut up." I curled my leg around his, bringing him closer.

He chuckled, but then he slid into me and there was nothing to really laugh about. It was as slow and smooth as our first time, him taking extra care and me completely forgetting about my tender side. My back arched and my hips rolled, rocked into his.

One of his hands curled around my breast, fingers working the tingling tip as he supported his weight on the arm braced beside my head. I had both legs around him now, my heels digging into his back, urging him to move faster.

"So impatient." He kissed the corner of my lip and then the other, before deepening the kiss.

And then he moved faster.

His hand left my breast and found mine and he threaded our fingers together as he thrust into me, connecting us in yet another place. He said my name into my ear and it thundered through me. Heat flowed and I was swimming in raw sensations as my chest pressed to his, so close I could feel his pounding heart.

Then he lifted his head, his gaze locking with mine, and the pressure inside me swelled. I tightened all around him.

"That's it," he rasped.

My soft moans rose, joining his grunts as the pace became fever-ish. I moved faster, grinding my hips against his. I was mindless, swept away as I cried out his name and came in tight, sensual waves, and he was right behind me, joining me as he buried his head in my shoulder.

"I think you like me," I said, voice husky and thick, shuddering as a tremor rocked me.

Jax chuckled into my neck and then rolled us so we were both on our sides, facing each other. "You're a dork."

"Yeah." I placed my hand on his cheek. "I am, but you love me."

He curled his fingers around my wrist and brought my hand to his mouth. He kissed the palm. "I do."

I'd kept Jax up half the night, talking and kissing, and making us both wish he'd had more condoms stashed in his wallet. We'd drifted off to sleep a few hours before dawn, and when I felt him kissing my cheek in the morning, it felt like minutes had passed instead of hours.

"It's time to get up, sleepy head," he said. Curling into a ball, I mumbled something about needing more sleep, but he was relent-less, tugging gently on my hair. "We got plans today."

I pried one eye open. And then my other one opened when I real-ized he was dressed and sitting on the bed. "Why are you already in clothes?"

"Because if I didn't get something on me, I'd end up saying fuck being responsible and get inside you with nothing between us."

Well.

He just put that out there like that.

"I need to get on the pill," I told him, closing my eyes again.

Jax laughed loudly. "I think I can totally get behind that, but you need to get your sweet ass up."

"Boo."

"We got plans, hon, and we got to check out, get home, shower, and if you get up now, we'll have enough time to fuck each other's brains out."

My eyes opened again. I liked the sound of that. "What plans do we have?"

"Cool plans. I'm taking off from the bar and you and I are going to do something fun. So get up." He smacked my behind when I didn't move. "Your friends are waiting, too."

"They are?" Like an idiot, I glanced around the room and was grateful to find them not sitting in the hotel room.

"We're going to take care of another one of your firsts."

I rose onto my elbow, gripping the sheet. "My firsts?"

He grinned and his eyes were a warm, beautiful whiskey color. "Yeah, that whole shit ton of stuff you've never experienced? We got to start them today if I have even the slightest hope of scratching some of them off before you head back to Shepherd."

Oh wow, my heart did something like a cartwheel in my chest. He eased my fingers away from the sheet and it slipped to my waist. I was too busy gazing at him to stop it or care that half of my body was hanging out. He swept his thumb over my pebbled nipple, distracted now.

"Which first?" I asked.

He dipped his head, kissing where his thumb had been. "We're going to Hershey Park."

"Hershey Park?"

Lifting his head, he curled that wandering hand behind my neck. "Yeah, honey, it's an amusement park. You've never been. And when I ran into Jase outside, in the lobby, I told him I wanted to take you. They are all on board."

I took a breath and it sounded funny. "You're taking me to an amusement park?"

Grinning, he nodded. "Look at you. You're ready to burst into tears."

"Shut up," I whispered, blinking back those tears. "It's just that—you're amazing, Jax. You really are."

"Nah," he murmured.

"You remembered my list of stupid things." I sat up fully and he followed. I leaned in, pressing my forehead against him. "That makes you amazing."

His other arm came around my waist and he drew me into his lap. I hung on to him, squeezing my eyes shut. A thought occurred to me, something Jax had said once. He'd been right then, too. The circumstances sucked and were crazy, but I did have my mom to thank for this—for Jax. Our relationship turned out to be a very bright silver lining in a sad, dark cloud.

"You still with me?" he asked against my mouth.

My lips curved up in a smile as I worked my fingers into the hair at the nape of his neck. As my heart swelled, tears built in my eyes again, but they didn't fall, and even if they did, they would've been happy tears, because no matter where I was, if I was here or back at Shepherd, I'd be with him. I knew that like I knew I'd taken another breath after the last one faded away. "I'm with you."

Jax grinned as the strong arm around my back tightened. "That's my girl."

Acknowledgments

Writing acknowledgments has never been an easy thing, because I'm pretty sure I'm always forgetting someone, and I think this is like my twenty-seventh or so time writing them. You'd think I'd have it down by now. I don't, but I'm gonna try something a little different this time around and really just start naming people, sort of like roll call.

A big, huge thank to those on the business side of things: Kevan Lyon, Taryn Fagerness, Brandy Rivers, Tessa Woodward, Molly Birckhead, Jessie Edwards, KP Simmon, Caroline Perny, Shawn Nicholls, Pam Spengler-Jaffee, and to the entire team of wonderful people at HarperCollins, William Morrow, and Avon.

Special thanks to Katie (katiebabs!) for letting me name an exotic dancer who slipped off a greased-up pole, hit her head, and developed super stripper powers after her. You're . . . you're welcome?

Another huge thanks to whoever created a tumblr for Theo James eyebrows and coined "he gives good eyebrow," because seriously . . . yeah. Might as well thank him too since I clearly used his physical attributes for inspiration when it came to Jax. That's not creepy, right?

I'd be rocking in the corner somewhere if it wasn't for Laura

Kaye, Sophie Jordan, Tiffany King, Jen Fisher, Vi (VEE!), Damaris Cardinali, Trini Contreras (*I lost my shoe, ba-dub-ba-duh!*), Hannah McBride, Lesa Rodrigues, Stacey Morgan, Dawn Ranson, my husband and family, Tiffany Snow, Valerie Fink, and this is where I know I'm forgetting people.

Last but never least, I want to thank the bloggers/reviewers and readers who will pick up this book. None of this would be possible without you guys. I'd give you all a hug if I could.

Can't get enough?
Turn the page for a sneak peek
at another love story
from J. Lynn . . .

Wait for You

One

There were two things in life that scared the ever-loving crap out of me. Waking up in the middle of the night and discovering a ghost with its transparent face shoved in mine was one of them. Not likely to occur, but still pretty damn freaky to think about. The second thing was walking into a crowded classroom late.

I absolutely loathed being late.

I hated for people to turn and stare, which they always did when you entered a classroom a minute after class started.

That was why I had obsessively plotted the distance between my apartment in University Heights and the designated parking lot for commuter students over the weekend on Google. And I actually drove it twice on Sunday to make sure Google wasn't leading me astray.

One point two miles exactly.

Five minutes in the car.

I even left my apartment fifteen minutes early so I would arrive ten minutes before my 9:10 class began.

What I didn't plan for was the mile-long traffic backup at the stop sign, because God forbid there be an actual light in the historical town, or the fact that there was absolutely no parking left on campus. I had to park at the train station adjacent to the campus, wasting precious time digging out quarters for the meter.

"If you insist on moving halfway across the country, at least stay in one of the dorms. They do have dorms there, don't they?" My mom's voice filtered through my thoughts as I stopped in front of the Robert Byrd Science Building, out of breath from racing up the steepest, most inconvenient hill in history.

Of course I hadn't chosen to stay in a dorm, because I knew at some point my parents would randomly show up, and they would start *judging* and start *talking,* and I'd rather punt-kick myself in the face than subject an innocent bystander to that. Instead, I tapped into my well-earned blood money and leased a two-bedroom apartment next to campus.

Mr. and Mrs. Morgansten had hated that.

And that had made me extremely happy.

But now I was sort of regretting my little act of rebellion, because as I hurried out of the humid heat of a late August morning and into the air-conditioned brick building, it was already eleven minutes past nine and my astronomy class was on the second floor. And why in the hell did I choose astronomy?

Maybe because the idea of sitting through another biology class made me want to hurl? Yep. That was it.

Racing up the wide staircase, I barreled through the double doors and smacked right into a brick wall.

Stumbling backward, I flailed my arms like a cracked-out crossing guard. My overpacked messenger bag slipped, pulling me to one side. My hair flew in front of my face, a sheet of auburn that obscured everything as I teetered dangerously.

Oh dear God, I was going down. There was no stopping it. Visions of broken necks danced in my head. This was going to suck so—

Something strong and hard went around my waist, stopping my free fall. My bag hit the floor, spilling overpriced books and pens across the shiny floor. My pens! My glorious pens rolled everywhere. A second later I was pressed against the wall.

The wall was strangely warm.

The wall chuckled.

"Whoa," a deep voice said. "You okay, sweetheart?"

The wall was *so* not a wall. It was a guy. My heart stopped, and for a frightening second, pressure clamped down on my chest and I couldn't move or think. I was thrown back five years. Stuck. Couldn't move. Air punched from my lungs in a painful rush as tingles spread up the back of my neck. Every muscle locked up.

"Hey . . ." The voice softened, edged with concern. "Are you okay?"

I forced myself to take a deep breath—to just breathe. I needed to breathe. Air in. Air out. I had practiced this over and over for five years. I wasn't fourteen anymore. I wasn't there. I was *here,* halfway across the country.

Two fingers pressed under my chin, forcing my head up. Startling, brilliant blue eyes framed with thick black lashes fixed on mine. A blue so vibrant and electric, and such a stark contrast against the black pupils, I wondered if the color was real.

And then it hit me.

A guy was holding me. A guy had never held me. I didn't count that one time, because that time didn't count for shit, and I was pressed against him, thigh to thigh, my chest to his. Like we were dancing. My senses fried as I inhaled the light scent of cologne. Wow. It smelled good and expensive, like *his* . . .

Anger suddenly rushed through me, a sweet and familiar thing, pushing away the old panic and confusion. I latched on to it desperately and found my voice. "Let. Go. Of. Me."

Blue Eyes immediately dropped his arm. Unprepared for the sudden loss of support, I swayed to the side, catching myself before I tripped over my bag. Breathing like I'd just run a mile, I pushed the thick strands of hair out of my face and finally got a good look at Blue Eyes.

Sweet baby Jesus, Blue Eyes was . . .

He was gorgeous in all the ways that made girls do stupid things. He was tall, a good head or two taller than me, and broad at the shoulders, but tapered at the waist. An athlete's body—like a swimmer's. Wavy black hair toppled over his forehead, brushing matching eyebrows. Broad cheekbones and wide, expressive lips completed the package created for girls to drool over. And with those sapphire-colored eyes, holy moly . . .

Who thought a place named Shepherdstown would be hiding someone who looked like this?

And I ran into him. Literally. Nice. "I'm sorry. I was in a hurry to get to class. I'm late and . . ."

His lips curved up at the corners as he knelt. He started gathering up my stuff, and for a brief moment I felt like crying. I could feel tears building in my throat. I was really late now; no way could I walk into that class late, especially on the first day. Fail.

Dipping down, I let my hair fall forward and shield my face as I started grabbing up my pens. "You don't have to help me."

"It's no problem." He picked up a slip of paper and then glanced up. "Astronomy 101? I'm heading that way, too."

Great. For the whole semester I'd have to see the guy I nearly killed in the hallway. "You're late," I said lamely. "I really am sorry."

With all my books and pens back in my bag, he stood as he handed it back to me. "It's okay." That crooked grin spread, revealing a dimple in his left cheek, but nothing on the right side. "I'm used to having girls throw themselves at me."

I blinked, thinking I hadn't heard the blue-eyed babe right, because surely he hadn't said something as lame as that.

He had, and he wasn't done. "Trying to jump on my back is new, though. Kind of liked it."

Feeling my cheeks burn, I snapped out of it. "I wasn't trying to jump on your back or throw myself at you."

"You weren't?" The lopsided grin remained. "Well, that's a shame. If you were, it would have made this the best first day of class in history."

I didn't know what to say as I clutched the heavy bag to my chest. Guys hadn't flirted with me back at home. Most of them hadn't dared to look in my direction in high school, and the very few who did, well, they hadn't been flirting.

Blue Eyes's gaze dropped to the slip of paper in his hand. "Avery Morgansten?"

My heart jumped. "How do you know my name?"

He cocked his head to the side as the smile inched wider. "It's on your schedule."

"Oh." I pushed the wavy strands of hair back from my hot face. He handed my schedule back, and I took it, slipping it into my bag. A whole lot of awkward descended as I fumbled with my strap.

"My name is Cameron Hamilton," Blue Eyes said. "But everyone calls me Cam."

Cam. I rolled the name around, liking it. "Thank you again, Cam."

He bent over and picked up a black backpack I hadn't noticed. Several locks of dark hair fell over his forehead and as he straightened, he brushed them away. "Well, let's make our grand entrance."

My feet were rooted to the spot where I stood as he turned and strolled the couple of feet to the closed door to room 205. He reached for the handle, looking over his shoulder, waiting.

I couldn't do it. It didn't have anything to do with the fact that I had plowed into what was possibly the sexiest guy on campus. I couldn't walk into the class and have everybody turn and stare. I'd had enough of being the center of attention everywhere I went for the last five years. Sweat broke out and dotted my forehead. My stomach tightened as I took a step back, away from the classroom and Cam.

He turned, brows knitted as a curious expression settled on his striking face. "You're going in the wrong direction, sweetheart."

I'd been going in the wrong direction half my life, it seemed. "I can't."

"Can't what?" He took a step toward me.

And I bolted. I actually spun around and ran like I was in a race for the last cup of coffee in the world. As I made it to those damn double doors, I heard him call out my name, but I kept going.

My face was flaming as I hurried down the stairs. I was out of breath as I burst out of the science building. My legs kept moving until I sat down on a bench outside of the adjacent library. The early-morning sun seemed too bright as I lifted my head and squeezed my eyes shut.

Geez.

What a way to make a first impression in a new city, new school . . . new life. I moved more than a thousand miles to start over, and I had already mucked it up in a matter of minutes.

About the Author

#1 *New York Times* and #1 internationally bestselling author Jennifer L. Armentrout lives in Shepherdstown, West Virginia. All the rumors you've heard about her state aren't true. When she's not hard at work writing, she spends her time reading, watching really bad zombie movies, pretending to write, hanging out with her husband; her Border Jack, Apollo, and Border collie, Artemis; six judgmental alpacas; two rude goats; and five fluffy sheep.

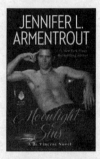
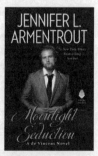
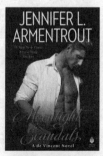